FRACTURED

ALSO BY KARIN SLAUGHTER

Blindsighted

Kisscut

A Faint Cold Fear

Indelible

Like a Charm
(Editor)

Faithless

Triptych

Beyond Reach

KARIN SLAUGHTER

FRACTURED

DELACORTE PRESS

FRACTURED
A Delacorte Press Book / August 2008

Published by
Bantam Dell
A Division of Random House, Inc.
New York, New York

Book design by R. Bull

Library of Congress Cataloging-in-Publication Data
Slaughter, Karin, 1971–
Fractured / Karin Slaughter.
p.   cm.
ISBN 978-0-385-34195-0
1. Daughters—Crimes against—Fiction.   2. Rape—Fiction.
3. Murder—Fiction.   4. Crimes of passion—Fiction.   5. Abused wives—Fiction.
6. Rich people—Fiction.   7. Georgia. Bureau of Investigation—
Employees—Fiction.   8. Atlanta (Ga.)—Fiction.   I. Title.
PS3569.L275F73   2003
813'.544—dc22   2008011047

Printed in the United States of America
Published simultaneously in Canada

www.bantamdell.com

10 9 8 7 6 5 4 3 2 1
BVG

For Irwyn and Nita...
for everything...

PROLOGUE

ABIGAIL CAMPANO SAT in her car parked on the street outside her own house. She was looking up at the mansion they had remodeled almost ten years ago. The house was huge—too much space for three people, especially since one of them, God willing, would be going off to college in less than a year. What would she do with herself once her daughter was busy starting a new life of her own? It would be Abigail and Paul again, just like before Emma was born.

The thought made her stomach clench.

Paul's voice crackled through the car speakers as he came back on the telephone. "Babe, listen—" he began, but her mind was already wandering as she stared up at the house. When had her life gotten so small? When had the most pressing questions of her day turned into concerns about other people, other things: Were Paul's shirts ready at the tailor? Did Emma have volleyball practice tonight? Did the decorator order the new desk for the office? Did somebody remember to let out the dog or was she going to spend the next twenty minutes wiping up two gallons of pee off the kitchen floor?

Abigail swallowed, her throat tightening.

"I don't think you're listening to me," Paul said.

"I'm listening." She turned off the car. There was a click, then

1

through the magic of technology, Paul's voice transferred from the car speakers to the cell phone. Abigail pushed open the door, tossing her keys into her purse. She cradled the phone to her ear as she checked the mailbox. Electric bill, AmEx, Emma's school fees...

Paul paused for a breath and she took that as her cue.

"If she doesn't mean anything to you, why did you give her a car? Why did you take her to a place where you knew my friends might show up?" Abigail said the words as she walked up the driveway, but she didn't feel them deep in her gut like she had the first few times this had happened. Her only question then had been, Why am I not enough?

Now her only question was Why are you such a needy bastard?

"I just needed a break," he told her, another old standard.

She dug her hand into her purse for her keys as she climbed the porch stairs. She had left the club because of him, skipped her weekly massage and lunch with her closest friends because she was mortified that they had all seen Paul out with some bottle-blond twenty-year-old he'd had the gall to take to their favorite restaurant. She didn't know if she would ever be able to show her face there again.

Abigail said, "I'd like a break, too, Paul. How would you like it if I took a break? How would you like it if you were talking to your friends one day and you knew something was going on, and you had to practically beg them to tell you what was wrong before they finally told you that they saw *me* with another man?"

"I'd find out his fucking name and I'd go to his house and I'd kill him."

Why did part of her always feel flattered when he said things like that? As the mother of a teenage girl, she had trained herself to look for the positive aspects of even the most savage remarks, but this was ridiculous. Besides, Paul's knees were so bad that he could barely take the garbage down to the curb on trash day. The biggest shock in all of this should have been that he could still find a twenty-year-old to screw him.

Abigail slid her key into the old metal lock on the front door. The hinges squeaked like in a horror movie.

The door was already open.

"Wait a minute," she said, as if interrupting, though Paul hadn't been talking. "The front door is open."

"What?"

He hadn't been listening to her, either. "I said the front door is already open," she repeated, pushing it open wider.

"Aw, Jesus. School's only been back for three weeks and she's already skipping again?"

"Maybe the cleaners—" She stopped, her foot crunching glass. Abigail looked down, feeling a sharp, cold panic building somewhere at the base of her spine. "There's glass all over the floor. I just stepped in it."

Paul said something she didn't hear.

"Okay," Abigail answered, automatic. She turned around. One of the tall side windows by the front door was broken. Her mind flashed on a hand reaching in, unlatching the bolt, opening the door.

She shook her head. In broad daylight? In this neighborhood? They couldn't have more than three people over at a time without the batty old woman across the street calling to complain about the noise.

"Abby?"

She was in some kind of bubble, her hearing muffled. She told her husband, "I think someone broke in."

Paul barked, "Get out of the house! They could still be there!"

She dropped the mail onto the hall table, catching her reflection in the mirror. She had been playing tennis for the last two hours. Her hair was still damp, stray wisps plastered to the back of her neck where her ponytail was starting to come loose. The house was cool, but she was sweating.

"Abby?" Paul yelled. "Get out right now. I'm calling the police on the other line."

She turned, mouth open to say something—what?—when she saw the bloody footprint on the floor.

"Emma," she whispered, dropping the phone as she bolted up the stairs toward her daughter's bedroom.

She stopped at the top of the stairs, shocked at the broken furniture, the splintered glass on the floor. Her vision tunneled and she saw Emma lying in a bloody heap at the end of the hallway. A man stood over her, a knife in his hand.

For a few seconds, Abigail was too stunned to move, her breath catching, throat closing. The man started toward her. Her eyes couldn't focus on any one thing. They went back and forth between the knife clenched in his bloody fist and her daughter's body on the floor.

"No—"

The man lunged toward her. Without thinking, Abigail stepped back. She tripped, falling down the stairs, hip and shoulder blades thumping the hard wood as she slid headfirst. There was a chorus of pain from her body: elbow hitting the stiles on the railing, anklebone cracking against the wall, a searing burn in her neck as she tried to keep her head from popping against the sharp tread of the stairs. She landed in the foyer, the breath knocked out of her lungs.

The dog. Where was the stupid dog?

Abigail rolled onto her back, wiping blood out of her eyes, feeling broken glass grind into her scalp.

The man was rushing down the stairs, the knife still in his hand. Abigail didn't think. She kicked up as he came off the last tread, lodging the toe of her sneaker somewhere between his asshole and his scrotum. She was far off the mark, but it didn't matter. The man stumbled, cursing as he went down on one knee.

She rolled onto her stomach and scrambled toward the door. He grabbed her leg, yanking her back so hard that a white-hot pain shot up her spine and into her shoulder. She clutched at the glass on the floor, trying to find a piece to hurt him with, but the tiny shards only ripped open the skin of her hand. She started kicking at him, legs flailing wildly behind her as she inched toward the front door.

"Stop it!" he screamed, both his hands clamping down on her ankles. "God dammit, I said *stop*!"

She stopped, trying to catch her breath, trying to think. Her head was still ringing, her mind unable to focus. Two feet ahead, the front door was still open, offering a view down the gentle slope of the walk to her car parked on the street. She twisted around so she could face her attacker. He was on his knees, holding her ankles to keep her from kicking. The knife was beside him on the floor. His eyes were a sinister black—two pieces of granite showing beneath heavy lids. His broad chest rose and fell as he panted for breath. Blood soaked his shirt.

Emma's blood.

Abigail tensed her stomach muscles and lunged up toward him, fingers straight out as her nails stabbed into his eyes.

He slapped the side of her ear with his open palm but she kept at it, digging her thumbs into his eye sockets, feeling them start to give. His hands clamped around her wrists, forcing her fingers away. He was twenty times stronger than her, but Abigail was thinking only of Emma now, that split second when she'd seen her daughter upstairs, the way her body was positioned, her shirt pushed up over her small breasts. She was barely recognizable, her head a bloody red mass. He had taken everything, even her daughter's beautiful face.

"You bastard!" Abigail screamed, feeling like her arms were going to break as he pried her hands away from his eyes. She bit his fingers until teeth met with bone. The man screamed, but still held on. This time when Abigail brought up her knee, it made contact squarely between his legs. The man's bloody eyes went wide and his mouth opened, releasing a huff of sour breath. His grip loosened but still did not release. As he fell onto his back, he pulled Abigail along with him.

Automatically, her hands wrapped around his thick neck. She could feel the cartilage in his throat move, the rings that lined the esophagus bending like soft plastic. His grip went tighter around her wrists but her elbows were locked now, her shoulders in line with her hands as she pressed all of her weight into the man's neck. Lightning bolts of pain shot through her shaking arms and shoulders. Her hands cramped as if thousands of tiny needles stabbed into her nerves. She could feel vibrations through her palms as he tried to speak. Her vision tunneled again. She saw starbursts of red dotting his eyes, his wet lips opening, tongue protruding. She was sitting on him, straddling him, and she became aware of the fact that she could feel the man's hip bones pressing into the meat of her thighs as he arched up, trying to buck her off.

Unbidden, she thought of Paul, the night they had made Emma—how Abigail had known, just known, that they were making a baby. She had straddled her husband like this, wanting to make sure she got every drop of him to make their perfect child.

And Emma *was* perfect...her sweet smile, her open face. The way she trusted everyone she met no matter how many times Paul warned her.

Emma lying upstairs. Dead. Blood pooled around her. Underwear yanked down. Her poor baby. What had she gone through? What humiliation had she suffered at the hands of this man?

Abigail felt a sudden warmness between her legs. The man had urinated on them both. He stared at her—really saw her—then his eyes glassed over. His arms fell to the sides, hands popping against the glass-strewn tile. His body went limp, mouth gaping open.

Abigail sat back on her heels, looking at the lifeless man in front of her.

She had killed him.

DAY ONE

CHAPTER ONE

WILL TRENT STARED out the window of the car as he listened to his boss yell into her cell phone. Not that Amanda Wagner ever really raised her voice, but she had a certain edge to her tone that had caused more than one of her agents to burst into tears and walk off an active investigation—no mean feat considering the majority of her subordinates at the Georgia Bureau of Investigation were men.

"We're at"—she craned her neck, squinting at the street sign—"the Prado and Seventeenth." Amanda paused. "Perhaps you could look up the information on your computer?" She shook her head, obviously not liking what she was hearing.

Will tried, "Maybe we should keep driving around? We might find—"

Amanda covered her eyes with her hand. She whispered into the phone, "How long until the server is back up?" The answer caused her to breathe out a heavy, pronounced sigh.

Will indicated the screen dominating the middle of the wood-lined dashboard. The Lexus had more bells and whistles than a clown's hat. "Don't you have GPS?"

She dropped her hand, considering his question, then began fiddling with some knobs on the dashboard. The screen didn't change, but the air-conditioning whirred higher. Will chuckled, and she cut him off with a nasty look, suggesting, "Maybe while we're waiting for Caroline to find a street map, you can get the owner's manual out of the glove box and read the directions for me."

Will tried the latch, but it was locked. He thought this pretty much summed up his relationship with Amanda Wagner. She often sent him the way of locked doors and expected him to find his way around them. Will liked a good puzzle as much as the next man, but just once, it would have been nice to have Amanda hand him the key.

Or maybe not. Will had never been good at asking for help—especially from someone like Amanda, who seemed to keep a running list in her head of people who owed her favors.

He looked out the window as she berated her secretary for not keeping a street map on her person at all times. Will had been born and raised in Atlanta, but didn't often find himself in Ansley Park. He knew that it was one of the city's oldest and wealthiest neighborhoods, where over a century ago, lawyers, doctors and bankers had built their enviable estates so that future lawyers, doctors and bankers could live as they did—safely cloistered in the middle of one of the most violent metropolitan cities this side of the Mason-Dixon. The only thing that had changed over the years was that the black women pushing white babies in strollers were better compensated these days.

With its twisting turns and roundabouts, Ansley seemed designed to confuse, if not discourage, visitors. Most of the streets were tree-lined, broad avenues with the houses tucked up on hills to better look down on the world. Densely forested parks with walking trails and swing sets were everywhere. Some of the walkways were still the original cobblestone. Though all the homes were architecturally different, there was a certain uniformity to their crisply painted exteriors and professionally landscaped lawns. Will guessed this was because even a fixer-upper started at the one million mark. Unlike his own Poncey-Highland neighborhood, which was less than six miles from here, there were no rainbow-colored houses or methadone clinics in Ansley.

On the street, Will watched a jogger stop to stretch and surreptitiously check out Amanda's Lexus. According to the news this morning, there was a code-red smog alert in effect, advising people not to breathe the outside air unless they absolutely had to. No one seemed to be taking that to heart, even as the temperature inched past the one hundred mark. Will had seen at least five joggers since they'd entered Ansley Park. All were women and all so far had fit the stereotype of the perky, perfect soccer mom with their Pilates-toned bodies and bouncy ponytails.

The Lexus was parked at the bottom of what seemed to be a popular hill, the street behind them lined with tall oaks that cast the pavement into shadow. All of the runners had slowed to look at the car. This wasn't the type of neighborhood where a man and a woman could sit in a parked vehicle for very long without someone calling the police. Of course, this wasn't the kind of neighborhood where teenage girls were brutally raped and murdered in their own homes, either.

He glanced back at Amanda, who was holding the phone to her ear so tightly it looked as if she might snap the plastic in two. She was an attractive woman if you never heard her speak or had to work for her or sit in a car with her for any length of time. She had to be in her early sixties by now. When Will had first started at the GBI over ten years ago, Amanda's hair had been more pepper than salt, but that had changed drastically over the last few months. He didn't know if this was because of something in her personal life or an inability to get an appointment with her hairdresser, but she had lately begun showing her years.

Amanda started pressing buttons on the console again, obviously trying to work the GPS. The radio came on and she quickly turned it off again, but not before Will caught the opening notes of a swing band. She muttered something under her breath and pressed another button, which caused Will's window to slide down. He felt a blast of hot air like someone had opened an oven door. In the side mirror, he saw a jogger at the top of the hill, the leaves on the dogwoods stirring in the breeze.

Amanda gave up on the electronics. "This is ridiculous. We're the top investigatory arm in the state and we can't even find the God damn crime scene."

Will turned around, his seat belt straining against his shoulder as he looked up the hill.

Amanda asked, "What are you doing?"

"That way," he said, pointing behind them. The limbs of the trees overhead were intertwined, casting the street in a dusklike darkness. There was no breeze this time of year, just relentless heat. What he had seen was not rustling leaves but the blue lights of a police cruiser bouncing off the shadows.

Amanda gave another heavy sigh as she put the car into gear and started a U-turn. Without warning, she slammed on the brakes, her arm shooting out in front of Will as if she could stop him from going through the windshield. A large white van blared its horn as it sped by, the driver shaking his fist, mouthing obscenities.

"Channel Five," Will said, recognizing the local news station's logo on the side of the van.

"They're almost as late as we are," Amanda commented, following the news van up the hill. She took a right, coming on a lone police cruiser blocking the next left. A smattering of reporters was already at the scene, representing all the local stations as well as CNN, which had their world headquarters a few miles up the road. A woman strangling the man who had killed her daughter would be big news in any part of the world, but the fact that the daughter was white, that the parents were wealthy and the family was one of the city's most influential gave it an almost giddy, scandalous tinge. Somewhere in New York City, a Lifetime movie executive was drooling into her BlackBerry.

Amanda pulled out her badge and waved it at the cop as she rolled past the blockade. There were more police cruisers up ahead along with a couple of ambulances. The doors were open, the beds empty. Paramedics stood around smoking. The hunter green BMW X5 parked in front of the house seemed out of place among the emergency vehicles, but the gigantic SUV made Will wonder where the coroner's van was. He wouldn't be surprised if the medical examiner had gotten lost, too. Ansley was not a neighborhood well known to someone earning a civil servant's salary.

Amanda put the car into reverse to parallel park between two of the cruisers. The park sensor controls started beeping as she tapped on the gas. "Don't dawdle in there, Will. We're not working this case unless we're taking it over."

Will had heard some variation on this same theme at least twice since they had left city hall. The dead girl's grandfather, Hoyt Bentley, was a billionaire developer who had made his share of enemies over the years. Depending on who you talked to, Bentley was either a scion of the city or a crony from way back, the sort of moneyed crook who made things happen behind the scenes without ever getting his hands dirty. Whichever version of the man's story was true, he had deep enough pockets to buy his share of political friends. Bentley had made one phone call to the governor, who had reached out to the director of the Georgia Bureau of Investigation, who had in turn assigned Amanda the task of looking into the murder.

If the killing had any markings of a professional hit or hinted at something deeper than a simple assault and burglary gone wrong, then Amanda would make a phone call and snatch the case away from the Atlanta Police Department faster than a toddler taking back a favorite toy. If this was just a random, everyday tragedy, then she would probably leave the explanations to Will while she toodled back to city hall in her fancy car.

Amanda put the gear into drive and inched forward. The gap between the beeps got furiously short as she edged closer to the police car. "If Bentley's got someone mad enough to kill his granddaughter, this case goes to a whole new level."

She sounded almost hopeful at the prospect. Will understood her excitement—breaking this kind of case would be yet another feather in Amanda's cap—but Will hoped he never got to the point where he saw the death of a teenage girl as a career stepping-stone. Though he wasn't sure what he should think of the dead man, either. He was a murderer, but he was also a victim. Considering

Georgia's pro–death penalty stance, did it really matter that he had been strangled here in Ansley Park rather than strapped to a gurney and given a lethal injection at Coastal State Prison?

Will opened the door before Amanda put the car into park. The hot air hit him like a punch to the gut, his lungs temporarily straining in his chest. Then the humidity took over, and he wondered if this was what it felt like to have tuberculosis. Still, he put on his suit jacket, covering the paddle holster clipped to the back of his belt. Not for the first time, Will questioned the sanity of wearing a three-piece suit in the middle of August.

Amanda seemed untouched by the heat as she joined Will. A group of uniformed policemen stood clustered at the bottom of the driveway, watching them walk across the street. Recognition dawned in their eyes, and Amanda warned Will, "I don't have to tell you that you're not exactly welcome by the Atlanta Police Department right now."

"No," Will agreed. One of the cops in the circle made a point of spitting on the ground as they passed by. Another one settled on a more subtle raised middle finger. Will plastered a smile on his face and gave the officers a big thumbs-up to let them all know there were no hard feelings.

From her first day in office, Atlanta's mayor had pledged to weed out the corruption that ran unchecked during her predecessor's reign. Over the last few years, she had been working closely with the GBI to open cases against the most blatant offenders. Amanda had graciously volunteered Will to go into the lions' den. Six months ago, he had closed an investigation that had resulted in the firing of six Atlanta police detectives and forced the early retirement of one of the city's highest-ranking officers. The cases were good—the cops were skimming cash off of narcotics busts— but nobody liked a stranger cleaning their house, and Will had not exactly made friends during the course of his investigation.

Amanda had gotten a promotion out of it. Will had been turned into a pariah.

He ignored the hissed "asshole" aimed at his back, trying to focus on the crime at hand as they walked up the curving driveway.

The yard was brimming with all kinds of exotic-looking flowers that Will was hard-pressed to name. The house itself was enormous, stately columns holding up a second-floor balcony, a winding set of granite stairs leading to the front doors. Except for the smattering of surly cops marring the scene, it was an impressive estate.

"Trent," someone called, and he saw Detective Leo Donnelly making his way down the front steps. Leo was a short man, at least a full foot less than Will's six-three. His gait had taken on an almost Columbo-like shuffle since they'd last worked together. The effect was that of an agitated monkey. "What the fuck are you doing here?"

Will indicated the cameras, offering Leo the most believable explanation. Everybody knew the GBI would throw a baby into the Chattahoochee if it meant getting on the nightly news. He told the detective, "This is my boss, Dr. Wagner."

"Hey," Leo said, tossing her a nod before turning back to Will. "How's Angie doing?"

"We're engaged." Will felt Amanda's scrutiny focus on him with a cold intensity. He tried to deflect, indicating the open doorway with a nod of his head. "What've we got here?"

"A shitload of hate for you, my friend." Leo took out a cigarette and lit it. "You better watch your back."

Amanda asked, "Is the mother still inside?"

"First door on the left," Leo answered. "My partner's in there with her."

"Gentlemen, if you'll excuse me." Amanda dismissed Leo the way she might a servant. The look she gave Will wasn't that much more pleasant.

Leo exhaled a line of smoke as he watched her go up the stairs. "Puts a chill on things, don't she? Like fucking dry ice."

Will defended her automatically, in that sort of way that you defend a useless uncle or slutty sister when someone outside of the family attacks them. "Amanda is one of the best cops I've ever worked with."

Leo fine-tuned his appraisal. "Nice ass for a grandma."

Will thought back to the car, the way Amanda's arm had shot out in front of him when she thought they were going to get hit by the news van. It was the most maternal thing he had ever seen her do.

Leo offered, "Bet she's a lot of work in the sack."

Will tried not to shudder as he forced the image from his mind. "How've you been?"

"Prostate's got me leaking like a fucking sieve. Haven't been laid in two months and I got this cough that won't go away." He coughed, as if to prove it, then took another hit off the cigarette. "You?"

Will squared his shoulders. "I can't complain."

"Not with Angie Polaski at home." Leo's suggestive laugh reminded Will of what an asthmatic child molester would sound like if he smoked three packs a day. Angie had worked vice for fifteen years before taking medical leave from the force. Leo was under the impression that she was a whore just because her job had required her to dress like one. Or maybe it was the many different men she'd slept with over the years.

Will offered, "I'll tell her you said hello."

"Do that." Leo stared up at Will, taking a deep pull on the cigarette. "What are you really doing here?"

Will tried to shrug it off, knowing that Leo would be furious if he had his case snatched out from under him. "Bentley's got a lot of connections."

Leo dubiously raised an eyebrow. Despite the rumpled suit and the way his forehead sloped like a caveman's, he had been a cop long enough to recognize when someone hadn't exactly answered a question. "Bentley called you in?"

"The GBI can only involve itself in cases when it's invited by the local police force or government."

Leo snorted a laugh, smoke coming out of his nostrils. "You left out kidnapping."

"And bingo," Will added. The GBI had a task force that investigated bingo parlors in the state. It was the sort of job you got when you pissed off the wrong person. Two years ago, Amanda had exiled Will to the north Georgia mountains, where he had spent his time arresting meth-dealing hillbillies and reflecting on the dangers of disobeying his direct superior. He didn't doubt a bingo transfer was in his future should he ever rile her again.

Will indicated the house. "What happened here?"

"The usual." Leo shrugged. He took a long drag on his cigarette, then stubbed it out on his shoe. "Mom comes home from playing tennis, the door's open." He put the butt in his jacket pocket as he led Will into the house. "She goes upstairs and sees her daughter, dead and diddled." He indicated the curving staircase that swept over their heads. "The killer's still here, sets his sights on the mom—who's fucking hot, by the way—fighting ensues, and, surprise, he's the one that winds up dead."

Will studied the grand entranceway. The doors were a double set, one fixed, one open. The broken side window was a good distance from the knob. Someone would have to have a long arm to reach in and unlock the door.

He asked, "Any pets?"

"There's a three-hundred-year-old yellow Lab. He was in the backyard. Deaf as a freakin' post, according to the mother. Probably slept through the whole thing."

"How old's the girl?"

"Seventeen."

The number echoed in the tiled foyer, where the smell of lavender air freshener and Leo's sweaty, nicotine stench competed alongside the metallic tinge of violent death. At the bottom of the stairs lay the source of the most dominant of all the odors. The man was lying on his back with his hands palms up near his head as if in surrender. A medium-sized kitchen knife with a wooden handle and a jagged edge was a few feet from his hand, lying in a nest of broken glass. His black jeans looked soiled, the skin of his neck bruised red from strangulation. The smattering of a mustache under his nose made his lip look dirty. Acne spotted his sideburns. One of his sneakers had come untied, the laces stiff with dried blood. Incongruously, the killer's T-shirt had a dancing cherry on it, the stem cocked at a jaunty angle. The shirt was dark red, so it was hard to tell if the darker parts were blood, sweat, urine or a combination of all three.

Will followed the dead man's gaze up to the chandelier hovering overhead. The glass made a tinkling noise as it swayed in the artificial breeze from the air-conditioning. White spots of light danced around the foyer, reflecting the sunlight that came in through the palladium window over the doors.

Will asked, "Do you have an ID on him yet?"

"Looks like his wallet's in his back pocket, but he's not going anywhere. I don't want to roll the body until Pete gets here." He meant Pete Hanson, the city medical examiner. "Perp looks pretty young, you know?"

"Yeah," Will agreed, thinking that the killer was probably not old enough to buy alcohol. Amanda had been excited by the prospect of a contract killing. Unless Hoyt Bentley's enemies had a crack team of mercenary frat boys on the payroll, Will doubted there was a connection.

He asked, "Domestic?"

Leo shrugged again, a gesture that was more like a tic. "Looks like it, huh? Boyfriend snaps, kills the girl, panics when the mom comes home and goes after her. Problem is, Campano swears she's never seen him before in her life."

"Campano?" Will echoed, feeling his gut tighten at the name.

"Abigail Campano. That's the mother." Leo studied him. "You know her?"

"No." Will looked down at the body, hoping his voice would not give him away. "I thought the last name was Bentley."

"That's the wife's father. The husband's Paul Campano. He owns a bunch of car dealerships. You heard the commercials, right? 'We never say no at Campano.'"

"Where is he?"

Leo's cell phone started to ring and he slid it off the clip on his belt. "Shouldn't be too much longer. He was on the phone with her when it happened. He's the one who called 9-1-1."

Will cleared his throat so his voice would come back. "Might be interesting to know what he heard."

"You think?" He studied Will closely as he opened his cell phone, answering, "Donnelly."

Leo stepped outside and Will looked around the foyer, taking in the dead body, the broken glass. Obviously, there had been a massive struggle here. Blood streaked the floor, two different sets of tennis shoes leaving smeared waffle prints across the creamy white tile. A frail, antique-looking table had fallen on its side, a glass bowl shattered beside it. There was a busted cell phone that looked as if it had been stepped on. Mail was scattered around like confetti and a woman's handbag was overturned, the contents adding to the mess.

Over by the wall, there was a lamp sitting upright on the floor as if someone had placed it there. The base was cracked and there was a tilt to the shade. Will wondered if someone had turned it right side up or if the lamp, defying all probabilities, had landed upright. He also wondered if anyone had noticed the bloody bare footprint beside the lamp.

His eyes followed the curving line of the polished wooden stairs, seeing two sets of bloody tennis-shoe prints heading down but no other bare footprints. There were scuffs and deep ruts in the walls where shoes and body parts had dug out the plaster, indicating at least one person had fallen. The trip must have been brutal. Abigail Campano had known she was fighting for her life. For his part, the dead kid at the bottom of the stairs was no lightweight. The definition of his muscles was evident under the red T-shirt. He must have been shocked to find himself overpowered even as he pulled his last breath.

In his head, Will sketched a diagram of the house, trying to get his bearings. A long hallway under the stairs led to the back of the house and what looked like the kitchen and family room. There were two rooms off the front entrance, probably originally intended to be parlors to give the men separate space from the women. Pocket doors closed off one room, but the second, which looked to be used as a library, was open. Dark paneling dominated the open parlor. Bookshelves lined the walls and a fireplace with a deep hearth already had wood laid for a fire. The furniture was heavy, probably oak. Two large leather chairs dominated the space. Will assumed the other parlor was the opposite, the walls painted in white or cream and the furnishings less masculine.

Upstairs, there would probably be the usual layout to these old houses: five or six bedrooms connected by a long, T-shaped hallway with what would have originally been servants' stairs leading down to the kitchen in the back. If the other houses in the neighborhood were anything to go by, there would be a carriage house outside that had been converted to a garage with an apartment overhead. Measuring and mapping it all out for the reports would be a lot of work. Will was glad the task wouldn't fall to him.

He was also glad he wouldn't have to explain why the single bloody footprint on the foyer was heading up the stairs instead of running out the front doorway.

Leo came back into the house, obviously annoyed by the phone call. "Like I don't got enough people sticking their heads up my ass with this prostate thing." He indicated the scene. "You solve this one for me yet?"

Will asked, "Who does the green BMW on the street belong to?"

"The mother."

"What about the girl—does she have a car?"

"A black Beemer, if you can believe it, 325 convertible. Parents took it away when her grades started to slide." He pointed to the house across the street. "Nosey neighbor turned her in when she saw the car in the driveway during school hours."

"Did the neighbor see anything today?"

"She's even older than the dog, so don't get your hopes up." He gave a half shrug of his shoulder, allowing, "We've got somebody over there talking to her right now."

"The mother's sure she doesn't recognize the killer?"

"Positive. I had her look at him again when she was more calmed down. Never seen him before in her life."

Will looked back at the dead man. Everything was adding up but nothing made sense. "How'd he get here?"

"No idea. Could've taken the bus and walked from Peachtree Street."

Peachtree, one of the busiest streets in Atlanta, was less than ten minutes away. Buses and trains went back and forth over- and underground bringing thousands of people to the office buildings and shops along the strip. Will had heard of criminals doing more stupid things than timing a brutal murder around a bus schedule, but the explanation didn't feel right. This was Atlanta. Only the desperately poor or ecologically eccentric took public transportation. The man on the floor was a clean-cut white kid wearing what looked like a three-hundred-dollar pair of jeans and a two-hundred-dollar pair of Nikes. Either he had a car or he lived in the neighborhood.

Leo offered, "We've got patrol out looking for a car that don't belong."

"You were the first detective on the scene?"

Leo took his time answering, making sure Will knew that he was doing so as a courtesy. "I was the first cop, period," he finally said. "Nine-one-one came in around twelve-thirty. I was finishing lunch at that sandwich place on Fourteenth. I got here maybe two seconds before the cruiser pulled up. We checked the house, made sure no one else was here, then I told everybody to get the hell out."

Fourteenth Street was less than a five-minute drive from where they stood. It was luck that the first responding officer had been a detective who could secure the scene. "You were the first one to talk to the mother?"

"She was freaked the fuck out, let me tell you. Hands were shaking, couldn't get her words out. Took about ten minutes for her to calm down enough to get the story out."

"So, this looks clean to you? Some kind of domestic violence scene between two teenagers, then the mom comes in and puts a kink in it?"

"Is that what Hoyt Bentley sent you to check out?"

Will skirted the question. "This is a sensitive case, Leo. Bentley

plays golf with the governor. He sits on the board of half the char-
ities in town. Wouldn't you be more surprised if we *weren't* here?"

Leo half shrugged, half nodded. Maybe there was something
bothering him about the scene, too, because he kept talking.
"There's defensive wounds on the mother. You can see signs of the
struggle, what with all the broken shit and the walls being bashed
in. Dead kid's got more of the same, including some bite marks on
his fingers where the mother tried to get his hands off her. The girl
upstairs—he had some time with her. Panties down, bra pushed up.
Blood everywhere."

"Was there a struggle upstairs?"

"Some, but not like down here." He paused before offering,
"You wanna see her?"

Will appreciated the gesture, but Amanda had made it more
than clear that she didn't want him to get involved in this unless it
had the markings of a professional hit. If Will saw something upstairs, no matter how innocuous, he might end up having to testify
about it later in court.

Still she couldn't fault him for being curious. "How was the girl
killed?"

"Hard to tell."

Will glanced behind him at the open front door. The air-
conditioning in the house was on full blast, trying to keep up
with the heat coming in. "Did you already get pictures of everything in here?"

"Upstairs and down," Leo told him. "We'll dust for prints and
the usual shit once the bodies are taken away. By the way, that's
when I'll shut the door, since you seem to have a stick up your ass
about it. I'm trying to keep the tourists down to a minimum here."
He added, "Case like this, there are gonna be some heavy guns on
it."

Will thought that was an understatement. No one had reported
a strange car in the neighborhood. Unless Leo's public transportation theory held up, the kid was most likely a resident of Ansley
Park. Knowing how these things worked, he probably came from a
family of lawyers. Leo would need to do everything exactly by the

book or he'd end up dangling by his short hairs the minute he took the stand.

Will rephrased his earlier question. "How did she die?"

"She's a fucking mess—face like raw hamburger, blood everywhere. I'm surprised the mother even recognized her." Leo paused, obviously seeing Will wanted a more concrete answer. "My guess? He beat her, then stabbed her to death."

Again, Will looked at the dead man on the floor. His palms were covered with dried blood, not what you would expect from a closed fist beating someone repeatedly, or, for that matter, a hand holding a knife. The knees of his black jeans looked dark, too, as if he had knelt in something wet. His T-shirt was bunched up just below his ribs. A fresh bruise spread down into the waist of his pants.

Will asked, "Was the mother injured?"

"Scratches on the back of her arms and hands, like I said before. There's a pretty deep cut on the palm from the glass on the floor." Leo catalogued, "Lots of bruises, busted lip, some blood in her ear. Maybe a sprained ankle. I thought it was broke, but she moved it." He rubbed his mouth, probably wishing there was a cigarette in it. "I called an ambulance, but she said she wasn't leaving until her daughter's removed."

"She say it like that, 'removed'?"

Leo mumbled a curse under his breath as he pulled a spiral-bound notebook out of his pocket. He flipped to the right page and showed it to Will.

Will frowned at the indecipherable scrawl. "Did you fingerprint a chicken?"

Leo turned the notebook back around and read aloud, " 'I will not leave my daughter here. I am not leaving this house until Emma leaves.' "

Will rolled the name around in his head, and the girl started to become a person to him rather than just another anonymous victim. She had been a baby once. Her parents had held her, protected her, given her a name. And now they had lost her.

He asked, "What's the mother saying?"

Leo flipped the notebook closed. "Just the bare facts. I'd bet my left one she was a lawyer before she got knocked up and gave it all up for the good life."

"Why is that?"

"She's being real careful about what she says, how she says it. Lots of 'I felt this' and 'I feared that.' "

Will nodded. A plea of self-defense relied solely on a person's perception that he or she was in imminent danger of death at the time of the attack. Campano was obviously laying the groundwork, but Will didn't know if that was because she was smart or because she was telling the truth. He looked down at the dead man again, the blood-caked palms, the soaked shirt. There was more here than met the eye.

Leo put his hand on Will's shoulder. "Listen, I gotta warn you—"

He stopped as the pocket doors slid open. Amanda stood beside a young woman. Behind them, Will could see another woman sitting on a deep couch. She was wearing a white tennis outfit. What must have been her injured foot was propped up on the coffee table. Her tennis shoes were on the floor underneath.

"Special Agent Trent," Amanda said, sliding the doors closed behind her. "This is Detective Faith Mitchell." Amanda looked Leo up and down like a bad piece of fish, then turned back to the woman. "Special Agent Trent is at your disposal. The GBI is more than happy to offer you any and all help." She raised an eyebrow at Will, letting him know that the opposite was true. Then, maybe because she thought he was stupid, she added, "I need you back in the office within the hour."

The fact that Will had anticipated this very thing happening did not make him any more prepared. His car was parked back at city hall. Donnelly was going to be stuck on the scene until they cleared it and any one of the beat cops outside would love a chance to get Will Trent alone in the back of a squad car.

"Agent Trent?" Faith Mitchell seemed annoyed, which made Will think he'd missed something.

He asked, "I'm sorry?"

"Yeah, you are," she mumbled, and Will could only blink, wondering what he had missed.

Leo didn't seem to find anything unusual about the exchange. He asked the woman, "The mother say anything?"

"The daughter's got a best friend." Like Leo, Faith Mitchell carried a small spiral-bound notebook in her pocket. She paged through it to reference the name. "Kayla Alexander. The mother says we can probably find her at school. Westfield Academy."

Will recognized the expensive private high school on the outskirts of Atlanta. "Why wasn't Emma in school?"

Faith answered Leo, though Will had asked the question. "There've been some truancy issues in the past."

Will was hardly an expert, but he couldn't imagine a teenage girl skipping school without taking her best friend along with her. Unless she was meeting her boyfriend. He looked at the stairs again, wishing that he could go up and examine the scene. "Why wasn't the mom here today?"

Faith said, "She's got some weekly thing at her club. She usually doesn't get back until three."

"So, if someone was watching the house, they'd know that Emma was here alone."

Faith told Leo, "I need some air." She walked out the door and stood at the edge of the porch with her hands on her hips. She was young, probably in her early thirties, of average height, and pretty in the way that thin blond women were naturally thought to be pretty—but there was something that kept her from being attractive. Maybe it was the scowl that had been on her face or the flash of raw hatred in her eyes.

Leo mumbled an apology. "Sorry, man. I was trying to tell you—"

Across the foyer, the pocket doors slid open again. Abigail Campano stood at the entrance, leg bent at an angle so she wouldn't put weight on her hurt ankle. Unlike Faith, there was something radiant about her blond hair and perfect, milky white skin. Even though her eyes were swollen from crying, her lip still bleeding where it had been busted open, the woman was beautiful.

"Ms. Campano," Will began.

"Abigail," she softly interrupted. "You're the agent from the GBI?"

"Yes, ma'am. I'd like to offer my condolences."

She stared at him in confusion, probably because she still hadn't come to terms with her daughter's death.

"Can you tell me a little bit about your daughter?"

The blank stare did not go away.

Will tried, "You told Detective Donnelly that she had been skipping school lately?"

She nodded slowly. "Obviously, she managed to..." Her voice trailed off as she looked at the dead man on the floor. "Kayla got her into skipping last year. She'd never done anything like that before. She was always a good girl. Always trying to do the right thing."

"There were other problems?"

"It all seems so inconsequential." Her lips trembled as she held back her emotions. "She started talking back, doing her own thing. She was trying to be her own person, and we still wanted her to be our little girl."

"Other than Kayla, did Emma have any friends? Boyfriends?"

Abigail shook her head, wrapping her arms around her waist. "She was so shy. She didn't make new friends easily. I don't know how this could have happened."

"Does Kayla have a brother?"

"No, she's an only child." Her voice caught. "Like Emma."

"Do you think you could make a list of the other kids she hung out with?"

"There were acquaintances, but Emma always picked one person to..." Again, her voice trailed off. "She had no one but Kayla, really." There was something to her tone that was so final, so certain about her daughter's aloneness in the world, that Will could not help but feel some of her sadness. He also hoped to God that Leo was making plans to talk to this Kayla. If she was as much an influence in Emma Campano's life as her mother indicated, then she probably knew a lot more about what had happened here today than anyone else did.

Will asked Abigail, "Is there anyone who might have a grudge against you or your husband?"

She kept shaking her head, transfixed by the sight of the dead man lying in her foyer. "It all happened so fast. I keep trying to think what I did...what else I could have..."

"I know you've been asked this before, but are you sure you don't recognize the man?"

Abigail's eyes closed, but he imagined that she could still see her daughter's murderer. "No," she finally answered. "He's a stranger to me."

Suddenly there was a man screaming from the front of the house. "Get the fuck out of my way!"

Will heard scuffling outside, cops yelling for someone to stop, then Paul Campano barreled up the front steps like a man on fire. He rammed Faith Mitchell out of his way as he burst into the house. A uniformed patrolman caught her as she stumbled back, perilously close to the edge of the porch. Neither of them looked happy, but Leo waved his hand, telling them to let it go.

Paul stood in the foyer, fists clenched. Will wondered if this was something genetic—that you were either the type of person who clenched your fists all the time or you weren't.

"Paul..." Abigail whispered, rushing to him.

Even holding his wife, Paul kept his hands fisted.

Faith was obviously still bristling. Her tone was clipped. "Mr. Campano, I'm Detective Mitchell with the Atlanta Police Department. This is Detective Donnelly."

Paul wasn't interested in introductions. He was staring at the dead man over his wife's shoulder. "Is that the fucker who did this?" His voice turned to a growl. "Who is he? What's he doing in my house?"

Faith and Leo exchanged a look that Will would've missed if he hadn't been watching them for his own cues. They were partners; they obviously had a shorthand, and it looked like this time Faith was taking the short straw.

She suggested, "Mr. Campano, let's go out on the porch and talk about this."

"Who the fuck are you?" Paul glared at Will, his beady eyes almost swallowed by the extra weight on his face.

Will shouldn't have been surprised by the question, or even the way it was phrased. The last time Paul Campano had talked to him this way, Will was ten years old and they were both living in the Atlanta Children's Home. A lot had changed since then. Will had gotten taller and his hair had gotten darker. The only thing that changed about Paul was he seemed to have gotten heavier and meaner.

Leo supplied, "Mr. Campano, this is Agent Trent with the GBI."

Will tried to talk Paul down a little, to make him feel like he could help. "Do you know if your daughter had any enemies, Mr. Campano?"

"Emma?" he asked, glaring at Will. "Of course not. She was only seventeen years old."

"How about you?"

"No," he snapped. "No one who would do..." He shook his head, unable to complete the sentence. He looked back at the dead killer. "Who is this bastard? What did Emma ever do to him?"

"Anything you can give us will help. Maybe you and your wife could—"

"She's up there, isn't she?" Paul interrupted, looking up. "My baby's upstairs."

No one answered him, but Leo took a couple of steps toward the stairs to block the way.

Paul said, "I want to see her."

"No," Abigail warned, her voice shaking. "You don't want to see her like that, Paul. You don't want to know."

"I need to see her."

"Listen to your wife, sir," Faith coaxed. "You'll get to see her soon. You just need to let us take care of her right now."

Paul barked at Leo, "Get the fuck out of my way."

"Sir, I don't think—"

Leo took the brunt of his anger. Paul slammed him into the wall as he bolted up the stairs. Will ran up after the man, almost knocking into him as Paul stopped cold at the top of the landing.

He stood frozen, staring at his daughter's lifeless form at the end of the hallway. The girl was at least fifteen feet away, but her presence filled the space as if she were right there beside them. All the fight seemed to drain out of Paul. Like most bullies, he could never sustain any one emotion.

"Your wife was right," Will told him. "You don't want to see her like this."

Paul went quiet, his labored breathing the only audible noise. His hand was to his chest, palm flat as if he was saying the pledge of allegiance. Tears brimmed in his eyes.

He swallowed hard. "There was this glass bowl on the table." His voice had gone flat, lifeless. "We got it in Paris."

"That's nice," Will said, thinking that never in a million years could he imagine Paul in Paris.

"It's a mess up here."

"There are people who can clean it up for you."

He went silent again, and Will followed his gaze, taking in the scene. Leo was right about downstairs being worse than up, but there was something even more sinister and unsettling in the air up here. The same bloody shoe prints were here, crisscrossing the white carpeting up and down the long hall. Streaks of blood slashed across the white walls where either the knife or a fist had arced over the body, repeatedly punching or plunging into the flesh. For some reason, the most troubling part to Will was the single red handprint on the wall directly over the victim's head where her attacker had obviously rested his weight as he raped her.

"Trashcan, right?"

Paul Campano wasn't looking for the garbage. He had called Will "Trashcan" when they were children. The memory put a lump in Will's throat. He had to swallow before he could answer. "Yeah."

"Tell me what happened to my daughter."

Will debated, but only for a moment. He had to turn sideways to get past Paul and go into the hallway. Careful not to disturb anything, he stepped into the crime scene. Emma's body was parallel to the walls, her head facing away from the stairs. As he walked toward her, Will's eyes kept going back to the handprint, the perfect formation of the palm and fingers. His gut roiled as he thought about what the guy had been doing when he left the impression.

Will stopped a few feet from the girl. "She was probably killed here," he told Paul, knowing from the pool of blood soaking into the carpet that the girl had not been moved. He crouched down by the body, resting his hands on his knees so that he wouldn't accidentally touch anything. Emma's shorts were bunched around one ankle, her feet bare. Her underwear and shirt had been yanked out of the way by her attacker. Teeth marks showed dark red against the white of her breasts. Scrapes and bruises trailed up the insides of her thighs, swollen welts showing the damage that had been done. She was thin, with shoulder-length blond hair like her mother and broad shoulders like her dad. There was no telling what she had looked like in life. Her face was beaten so severely that the skull had collapsed on itself, obscuring the eyes, the nose. The only point of reference was the mouth, which gaped open in a toothless, bloody hole.

Will checked on Paul. The man still stood frozen at the top of the stairs. His big, meaty hands were clasped in front of his chest like a nervous old woman waiting for bad news. Will didn't know what exactly he could see, if the distance softened some of the violence or made it worse.

Will told him, "She was beaten. I can see what looks like two knife wounds. One's just below her breast. The other is above her belly button."

"She got it pierced last year." Paul gave a strained laugh. Will looked back at him and Paul took this as a sign to continue. "She and her best friend went to Florida and came back with..." He shook his head. "You think shit like that's funny when you're a kid, but when you're a parent and your daughter comes home with a ring in her belly..." His face crumpled as he fought emotions.

Will turned his attention back to the girl. There was a silver ring looped through the skin of her belly button.

Paul asked, "Was she raped?"

"Probably." He'd said the word too fast. The sound hung in the stagnant air.

"Before or after?" Paul's voice shook. He was more than familiar with the dark deeds men were capable of.

The blood on her abdomen and chest was smeared, indicating someone had lain on top of her after the worst of the beating was over. Still, Will told him, "The coroner will have to answer that. I can't tell."

"Are you lying to me?"

"No," Will answered, trying not to look at the handprint, to let the guilt eat him up inside so that he ended up being the one to tell this man the horrible truth about his daughter's violent, degrading death.

Suddenly he felt Paul behind him.

Will stood, blocking him. "This is a crime scene. You need to—"

Paul's mouth dropped open. He slumped against Will like all the air had left his body. "It's not..." His mouth worked, tears welling into his eyes. "It's not her."

Will tried to turn the man away from the sight of his daughter. "Let's go downstairs. You don't need to see any more of this."

"No," Paul countered, his fingers digging into Will's arm. "I mean it. It's not her." He shook his head back and forth, vehement. "It's not Emma."

"I know this is hard for you."

"Fuck you, with what you know!" Paul pushed himself away from Will. "Has anybody ever told you that your daughter is dead?" He kept shaking his head, staring at the girl. "That's not her."

Will tried to reason with him. "Her navel is pierced like you said."

He shook his head, his words choking in his throat. "It's not—"

"Come on," Will coaxed, pushing him back a few steps, trying to keep him from contaminating the scene any more than he already had.

Paul's words came out in an almost giddy rush. "Her hair, Trash. Emma's got longer hair than that. It goes down to her back almost. And she's got a birthmark on her right arm—Emma does. Look, there's nothing there. There's no birthmark."

Will checked the arm. Except for the blood, the skin was a perfect white.

"Right arm," Paul insisted, annoyed. He pointed to the other arm. "She's got a birthmark." When Will did not respond, he took out his wallet. Receipts and papers fell onto the floor as he dug around inside. "It's weird, shaped like a handprint. The skin's darker there." He found what he was looking for and handed Will a photograph. Emma was much younger in the picture. She was wearing a cheerleading outfit. One arm was cocked to her hip, holding a pom-pom. Paul was right; the birthmark looked as if someone had wrapped his hand around her arm and left a print.

Still, Will said, "Paul, let's not—"

"Abby! It's not her. It's not Emma!" Paul was laughing, elated. "Look at her arm, Trash. There's nothing there. This isn't Emma. It's gotta be Kayla. They look alike. They trade clothes all the time. It's got to be her!"

Abigail ran upstairs, Faith fast behind her.

"Stay back." Will blocked their way, holding out his arms like a crossing guard, physically pushing Paul back. The man was still smiling a fool's grin. All he was thinking was that his daughter wasn't dead. His mind hadn't made the next leap.

"Keep them here," Will told Faith. She nodded, stepping in front of the parents. Carefully, Will walked back toward the dead girl. He crouched down again, studying the shoe prints, the spray on the wall. Crossing the dead girl's body was a fine arc of blood that caught his attention. It went just under her breasts like a finely drawn line. Will hadn't noticed it the first time, but right now, he would have bet his pension that the blood had come from the kid downstairs.

"It's not her," Paul insisted. "It's not Emma."

Faith began, "It's hard sometimes when you lose someone you love. Denial is understandable."

Paul exploded. "Would you listen to me, you stupid bitch? I'm not going through the twelve steps of grief. I *know* what my fucking daughter looks like!"

Leo called, "Everything okay up there?"

"It's under control," Faith said, sounding like the exact opposite was true.

Will looked at the dead girl's bare feet. The soles were clean, seemingly the only part of her body that didn't have some pattern of blood on it.

He stood up, asking Abigail, "Tell me what happened."

She was shaking her head, unable to let herself hope. "Is it Emma? Is that her?"

Will took in the faint streaks of dark red on the skirt of Abigail's white tennis dress, the transfer patterns across her chest. He kept his voice firm, even though his heart was thumping hard enough to press against his ribs. "Tell me exactly what happened from the moment you got here."

"I was in my car—"

"From the stairs," Will interrupted. "You came up the stairs. Did you go to the body? Did you come into this area?"

"I stood here," she said, indicating the floor in front of her.

"What did you see?"

Tears streamed down her cheeks. Her mouth moved, trying to get out words as her eyes scanned the dead body. Finally, she said, "I saw him standing over her. He had a knife in his hand. I felt threatened."

"I know you felt like your life was in danger," Will assured her. "Just tell me what happened next."

Her throat worked. "I panicked. I stepped back and fell down the stairs."

"What did he do?"

"He came after me—came down the stairs."

"Did he have the knife in his hand?" She nodded. "Was it raised?"

She nodded again, then shook her head. "I don't know. No. It was at his side." She tightened her hand to her side to show him. "He was running down the stairs. It was at his side."

"Did he raise the knife when he got to the bottom of the stairs?"

"I kicked him before he got to the bottom. To throw him off balance."

"What happened to the knife?"

"He dropped it when he fell. I— He hit me in the head. I thought he was going to kill me."

Will turned around, looked at the shoe prints again. They were scattered, chaotic. Two people had stepped in the blood, walked back and forth, struggled. "Are you sure you didn't come into the hallway up here at all?"

She nodded her head.

"Listen to me very carefully. You didn't walk around up here? You didn't go to your daughter? You didn't step in any blood?"

"No. I was here. Right here. I stopped at the top of the stairs and he came toward me. I thought he was going to kill me. I thought..." She put her hand to her mouth, unable to continue. Her voice cracked as she asked her husband, "It's not Em?"

Will told Faith, "Keep them both right here," as he headed down the stairs.

Leo was standing in the front doorway, talking to one of the uniformed patrolmen. He asked Will, "What's going on?"

"Don't wait for Pete," he ordered, stepping over the body. "I need an ID on this guy right now." He found Abigail Campano's shoes in the parlor under the coffee table. The tread was a court zigzag, not a waffle pattern. Except for a couple of scuff marks on the toes, there wasn't a trace of blood on them.

In the foyer, Leo was taking a pair of latex gloves from his pocket. "The nosey neighbor across the street says she saw a car parked in the driveway a couple of hours ago. Could be yellow, could be white. Could be four doors, could be two."

Will checked the dead man's sneakers. Waffle pattern, dried blood caked in the tread. He said, "Give me those." Leo handed him the gloves and Will put them on. "You got your pictures, right?"

"Yeah. What's going on?"

Carefully, Will peeled up the dead man's T-shirt. The material was still soaking wet where it had bunched up at the waist, and it left an odd, pinkish hue on the exposed skin.

Leo asked, "You wanna tell me what you're doing?"

There was so much blood that it was hard to see anything. Will gently pressed the abdomen, and a narrow slit opened up in the flesh, black liquid oozing out.

"Shit," Leo hissed. "Did the mother stab him?"

"No." Will saw how it must have happened. The young man kneeling beside the body upstairs, a knife plunged into his chest. He would have pulled out the knife, arterial blood spraying over the dead girl's body. The man would've tried to stand, staggering to get help even as his lung collapsed. That's when Abigail Campano had appeared at the top of the stairs. She saw the man who had killed her daughter. He saw the woman who could possibly save them all.

Leo looked up the stairs, then back at the dead kid, finally understanding. "Shit."

Will snapped off the gloves, trying not to think about all the lost time. He went to the bloody bare footprint, saw that the weight had been on the ball of the foot when it was made. There was a small cluster of blood droplets on the bottom stair—six of them.

Will talked it out for Leo's benefit as much as his own. "Emma was unconscious. The killer carried her over his shoulder." Will narrowed his eyes, putting the pieces together. "He stopped here at the bottom of the stairs to catch his breath. Her head and arms were hanging down his back. The blood drops on the bottom tread are almost perfectly round, which means they fell straight down." Will pointed to the footprint. "He shifted her weight forward. Her foot touched the floor—that's why it's facing up the stairs instead of toward the door. After carrying her down the stairs, he had to readjust the body so that he could carry her out the front door."

Leo tried to cover himself. "The mother's story held up. There was no way I could—"

"It doesn't matter." Will glanced up. Abigail and Paul Campano were staring over the railing, watching, disbelieving. "Does Kayla have a car?"

Abigail spoke hesitantly. "She drives a white Prius."

Will took out his phone and hit the speed dial. He told Leo, "Try to nail down the old lady on the car—show her a photo array if you have to. Check all 9-1-1 calls coming out of the area in the last five hours. Get your guys to recanvass the neighborhood. There were a lot of joggers out earlier who are probably back home by now. I'll notify highway patrol; there's an on-ramp to the interstate less than a mile from here." Will put the phone to his ear just as Amanda picked up. He didn't waste time with pleasantries. "I need a team here. It looks like we've got a kidnapping."

CHAPTER TWO

EMMA CAMPANO'S BEDROOM was almost as big as Will's entire house. He hadn't had his own room as a kid. He hadn't really had his own anything until he turned eighteen and the Atlanta Children's Home gave him a pat on the back and a check from the state. His first apartment was a box, but it was his box. Will could still remember what it felt like to leave his toothbrush and shampoo in the bathroom without having to worry someone else would swipe them—or worse. Even to this day, there was a certain joy he felt from opening the refrigerator and knowing that he could eat anything he wanted.

He wondered if Paul got a similar feeling when he walked through his multimillion-dollar home. Did his chest puff out with pride when he saw the dainty antique chairs and the obviously expensive canvases that hung on the walls? When he locked the front door at night, did he still get that sense of relief that no one had managed to take it all away from him? There was no arguing that the man had made a good life for his family. With the pool out back and the screening room in the basement, you'd never guess he had spent his early years perfecting the role of a juvenile delinquent.

Paul had never been quick, but he was street smart and even as a kid, he knew how to make a dollar. Abigail was obviously the brains in the family. She was right behind Will in figuring out what had really happened that morning in the Campano home. Will had never in his life seen someone so stricken with horror as when the woman realized that she had probably killed an innocent man—worse, an innocent man who might have been trying to help her daughter. She'd become hysterical. A doctor had been called to sedate her.

Typical Paul, he was working the angles before his wife's head hit the pillow. He'd taken out his cell phone and made two calls: one to his attorney and one to his influential father-in-law, Hoyt Bentley. Ten short minutes later, Will's own cell phone had started ringing. Once again, the governor had contacted the director of the Georgia Bureau of Investigation, who had pressed Amanda, and she in turn had pressed Will.

"Don't fuck this up," Amanda had told him in her usual supportive way.

The procedure in kidnapping cases was simple: have a cop with the family at all times and have the family by the phone for the ransom call. Even as the doctor stuck a needle in her arm, Abigail Campano had still refused to leave her home. There was a guest suite in the carriage house. After making sure the apartment was not part of the crime scene, Will had sent the parents there along with Hamish Patel, a GBI hostage negotiator. Paul had bristled about being assigned a babysitter, which meant he either had something to hide or thought he could control the situation without the police getting in his way.

Knowing the way Paul worked, it was probably a little of both. He had been so uncooperative during questioning that Will was actually looking forward to the lawyer showing up so the man could tell his client it was okay to give a straight answer. Or maybe Hamish Patel could work some of his magic. The hostage negotiator had been trained by Amanda Wagner when she'd led the GBI's rapid extraction team. He could pretty much talk the fleas off a dog.

Again following procedure, Will had put out an APB on Kayla

Alexander's white Prius and issued a Levi's Call, Georgia's version of the Amber Alert, for Emma Campano. This meant that all the highway message boards in Atlanta as well as radios and television sets in Georgia would carry some sort of warning asking folks to come forward if they saw the car or the girl. Will had also set up traces on all the family telephones and cell phones, but he doubted there was a ransom call coming any time soon.

His gut told him that whoever had taken Emma Campano didn't want her for money. One look at Kayla Alexander told that story. The young woman had been beaten and raped by a sadist who had probably enjoyed every minute of it. There was only one reason to take a hostage from the scene, and it wasn't for cash. All Will could do at this moment was hope that he found something—anything—that pointed the way to the man before he killed again.

Will stood out in the hallway as he watched the crime-scene tech taking photos of Emma Campano's bedroom. He was trying to get a sense of who she was, but nothing stood out except for the fact that she was a tidy young woman. Neatly folded clothes that were waiting to be put up lined the top of a velvet bench with silk tassels and the books on the shelves were stacked in straight rows. Some sort of floral air freshener gave the room a sickly sweet smell. Outside the window, a small wind chime tinkled from a rare summer wind.

Though Emma's personal mark did not stand out, there was no mistaking the space belonged to a very fortunate teenage girl. The four-poster bed had a bright pink coverlet with purple sheets and heart-shaped pillows. The walls were painted a soothing, light lilac that complemented the geometrically patterned shag rugs on the hardwood floor. There was a flat-panel television mounted over a large fireplace. Two comfortable-looking chairs were by the window. A book was pressed open on the arm of one—a romance from the look of it. Two purses had been thrown onto the other chair. A backpack was on the floor, stuffed with schoolbooks and loose papers. Two pairs of identical flip-flops had been kicked off by the door. One set was a larger size than the other.

That at least explained why the girls were barefoot.

The tech took a couple more photographs, the flash filling the room. He asked Will, "Anything specific you want me to cover?"

"Can you test the fluid on the bed?" The sheets were bunched up in a knot. The dark purple material made signs of sexual activity obvious.

"I need to get the kit out of my truck," the tech said. "You need anything else?"

Will shook his head and the man left. Outside, a heavy door slammed, making the familiar thumping sound that Will always associated with death. He walked to the window and saw Pete Hanson standing behind the coroner's van, hand flat to the back door as he took a moment to pay his respects to the dead bodies inside. Pete had given Will a preliminary rundown, but they wouldn't have hard facts until the autopsies were performed tomorrow morning.

The Atlanta Police Department had moved from a primary to supportive role now that there was a kidnapping involved. Leo Donnelly was probably calling his accountant at the moment, trying to figure out if he could take early retirement. Will had tossed him the task of tracking down Kayla Alexander's parents and telling them that their daughter had been murdered. That seemed punishment enough, though Amanda might have something to say about that.

Will tugged on a pair of latex gloves as he prepared to search Emma's room. He started with the two purses on one of the chairs. Methodically, Will searched each one. He found pens, tampons, candy, loose change at the bottom—exactly what you'd expect to find in any woman's handbag. The leather wallets in each were identical, both with the same designer logo on them, and he assumed the girls had bought them on a shopping trip together. They each had a Visa card with their name on it. Their driver's license photos showed images of two remarkably similar-looking girls: blond haired, blue eyed. Emma Campano had obviously been the prettier of the two, but there was a defiant tilt to Kayla Alexander's chin that made Will think she was the one who'd gotten all the attention.

Not anymore. The news crews were still swarming outside. Will was sure every station had broken into regular programming with the story. Thanks to the endless and annoying commercials, the Campano name was well-known to Atlantans. Will wondered if the family's notoriety would help or hinder the case. He also wondered what was happening to Emma Campano right now. Will looked at her picture again. Maybe he was reading too much into it, but there seemed to be an air of reticence about her, as if she expected the photographer to find fault instead of beauty.

"Adam David Humphrey," Faith Mitchell said. Like Will, she was wearing a pair of latex gloves. Also like Will, she was holding an open wallet and a driver's license in her hands. This one belonged to the dead man downstairs. "He's got an Oregon State license. No car registered in his name in either state. The principal at the girls' school has never heard of him and he was never a student there." She handed Will the plastic ID card. Will squinted his eyes at the tiny letters. "One of the guys back at the station is trying to get in touch with the local sheriff up there. The address makes it hard."

He patted his pockets, looking for his glasses. "Why is that?"

Her tone was almost as condescending as Amanda's. "Rural route?"

"Sorry, I left my reading glasses at the office." A rural route with a box number would not necessarily correspond with a physical address. Unless the Humphreys were well-known in town, this added another hoop to jump through before the dead boy's parents could be informed. Will sat back on his heels, studying the license photo of Adam Humphrey. He was a good-looking kid in a geeky sort of way. His mouth was twisted into a grin and his hair was longer in the photo, but there was no mistaking that Adam Humphrey was the man lying dead downstairs. "He's older than I thought."

"Nineteen is still young."

"What's he doing in Atlanta?" Will answered his own question. "College."

Faith checked through the wallet, calling out what she found. "Six dollars cash, a photograph of an older couple—probably grandparents. Wait a minute." The gloves were too long for her fingers, making it difficult for her to dig around. Will waited patiently until she pulled out a photograph. "Is this Emma?"

He compared the photo against the licenses he had found in the two purses. Emma was happier in the picture from the wallet, her mouth open in laughter. "It's her."

Faith looked at them both, then nodded her agreement. "She looks younger than seventeen."

Will said, "Adam's got a thing for Emma, not Kayla. So why is Kayla dead?"

She put the photo back into the wallet and dropped them both in a plastic evidence bag. "Maybe she got in the way."

Will nodded, though the vicious manner in which the girl had been raped and killed made him think there was more to it than that. "We'll know more when Pete does the autopsy. Do the parents want to see her body?"

"The parents don't even know yet." Will's mouth opened to ask why the hell not, but she talked over him. "The school principal told Leo that the Alexanders are on a three-week vacation in New Zealand and Australia. They left emergency contact numbers for their hotels. Leo called the manager at the Mercure Dunedin. He promised he'd get the parents to call as soon as they get back from sightseeing, whenever that might be. There's an eighteen-hour time difference, so it's already tomorrow morning for them." Faith added, "I sent a cruiser to their house on Paces Ferry. No one was home."

"They couldn't have left their daughter alone for three weeks."

"She was seventeen years old. She was old enough to take care of herself." Her face flushed as she seemed to realize that the exact opposite was true.

"Did Abigail Campano give you anything when you talked to her?"

"It was a different conversation. We both thought her daughter was dead."

Will recalled, "She's the one who told you that Kayla would probably be at school."

"Right. She even said, 'At least Kayla is safe.' "

"Did Leo ask the principal about the girls skipping?"

"She confirmed it's been a problem. Students aren't allowed off campus during lunch, but some of them sneak out and come back in before the bell rings. There's a hole in the security cameras behind the main class building and the kids take advantage of it."

"Send some extra cruisers to the school. Until we know there's no connection, I want to make sure we keep a close eye on the rest of the students. Also, let's try to get a dump on the Alexanders' phone. There has to be an aunt or a family friend who's been checking in on her. Send a uniform to knock on the neighbors' doors. It's coming on suppertime. People should be getting home by now."

She had tucked the wallet under her arm as she wrote down his instructions in her notebook. "Anything else?"

He looked at the book bag, all the papers spilling out of it. "Send someone up here who can work fast to go through all these notes. Tell Leo to talk to the school principal again. I want a list of Kayla and Emma's known acquaintances. If any of the teachers are still at school, tell him to talk to them, see what the girls were like, who they hung out with, then I'll go back at them tomorrow after they've had the night to think about it. The girls were truants, so they might be hanging out with kids from other schools." He stopped, going back to the dead kid downstairs. Finding out who Adam was and what he was doing in Atlanta was the only tangible lead they could follow.

He took out one of his business cards and handed it to her. "Call back that sheriff in Oregon and give him my cell number. Tell him to call me as soon as he gets anything on Adam Humphrey's parents. For now, I want you focused on finding out why Adam was in Atlanta. Track down the college angle first."

She shook her head. "He'd have a college ID on him if he was in school."

"If he came here all the way from Oregon, then it was probably for something specific: law, medicine, art. Start with the big schools first, then move on to the little ones. Emory, Georgia State, Georgia Tech, SCAD, Kennesaw ... There has to be a list online."

She was incredulous. "You want me to call every college and university in the city, track down the registrar who's probably already gone for the day, and ask them to tell me without a warrant whether or not they've got Adam Humphrey on their rolls?"

"I do."

The scowl she had given him before had nothing on her expression now.

Will was fed up with her attitude. "Detective Mitchell, I think your anger is commendable, but the fact that I banged up six of your guys for skimming off of drug dealers doesn't mean a hell of a lot to the parents who lost their kids today or the ones who are waiting to find out whether or not their daughter is still alive, and since the Atlanta Police Department mishandled this case from the get-go, and since the only reason you are still involved in this case is because I need people to do my scut work, I expect you to follow directions no matter how mundane or ludicrous my requests seem to you."

She pressed her lips together, fury burning in her eyes as she tucked the photograph back into the wallet. "I'll bag this as evidence and start calling the schools."

"Thank you."

She made to go, then stopped. "And it was seven."

"What?"

"The cops. It was seven that you banged up, not six."

"I stand corrected" was all Will could think to say. She turned on her heel and left the room.

Will let out a deep breath, wondering how long it was going to take before he kicked Faith Mitchell off this case. Then again, it wasn't like he had the whole police department behind him, so maybe he wasn't in a position to be choosey. Even though Faith seemed to despise him as much as the next cop, she was still following orders. There had to be something said for that.

Will stood in the middle of the room, trying to decide what to do next. He looked down at the rug, the circular patterns that resembled something out of a 1970s James Bond movie. Emma Campano should be his priority right now, but the confrontation with the Atlanta detective still nagged at him. Something rattled loose in his brain and he finally understood.

Seven, Faith Mitchell had said. She was right. Six cops had been fired, but one more had also been affected by the scandal. A police commander named Evelyn Mitchell had been forced to retire. Because Evelyn's daughter was a detective on the force, Faith Mitchell had naturally caught Will's attention. She had a fairly solid record, but her promotion five years ago to detective had raised a few eyebrows. Twenty-eight was a little young for the gold shield, but it was hard to prove that any favoritism had been shown. Nepotism aside, Will hadn't found anything warranting a deeper dig into Faith Mitchell's life, so he had never met the woman in person.

Until now.

"Crap," Will groaned. If there was anyone he'd met today who came by their hate honestly, it was Evelyn Mitchell's daughter. That must have been what Leo had been trying to tell Will when everything started to fall apart—or maybe he'd assumed Will already knew. The investigation had ended several months ago, but Will had worked on at least a dozen more cases since then. Other than being aware of the wall of hate surrounding him at the Campano house, his focus had been on the crime at hand, not the particulars of a case that had been resolved months before.

There was nothing Will could do about it now. He went back to his search, checking the drawers, the cabinets that held the sorts of things you would expect to find in a teenage girl's room. He checked under the bed, then between the mattress and the box spring. There were no secret notes or hidden diaries. All her underclothes were what you would expect, which was to say there was nothing overtly sexy that might indicate Emma Campano was exploring a wilder side of life.

Next, Will went to the closet. From all appearances, the

Campano house was thoroughly modernized. You couldn't get blood from a stone, though, and the closet in Emma Campano's room was as the architect had originally intended, which was to say that it was roughly the size of a coffin. Clothes hung packed so tightly that the rod was sagging. Shoes lined the floor, row after row—so many of them that they were double stacked in places.

Among the Mary Janes and tennis shoes were black knee-high boots and impossibly high heels. Likewise, the light-colored blouses were punctuated by dark black jackets and black shirts with strategically placed rips held together by safety pins. Altogether, they looked like something you'd wear in the military if you were stationed in Hell. Will had worked cases with teenagers before. He guessed Emma was going through some sort of stage that compelled her to dress as a vampire. The pastel sweater sets would indicate her parents were not pleased with the transformation.

Will checked the top shelves, feeling under sweaters, taking down boxes of more clothes and methodically searching through each one. He checked pockets and purses, finding blocks of cedar and sachets of lavender that made him sneeze.

He got down on his hands and knees to search the bottom of the closet. There were several rolled-up posters in the corner, and he opened each one. Marilyn Manson, Ween and Korn—not the sort of groups he would expect a wealthy blond teenager to be listening to. The corners were all ripped, as if someone had torn them down. Will rolled the posters back up then checked Emma's shoes, moving them around, making sure nothing was hidden inside or under them. He found nothing to report home about.

As he turned from the closet, he was struck by the faint smell of ammonia. There was a dog bed beside him, probably meant to serve the ancient Labrador that Leo had mentioned. There were no obvious stains on the yellow bed. Will unzipped the liner, pressing his gloved fingers into the stuffing. This yielded nothing, except for making his gloved hands smell faintly of dog and urine.

Will heard Amanda's voice downstairs as he was zipping up the bed. She was coming up the back stairs and, from the sound of it, she was talking on her cell phone.

He took off the dog-smelling gloves and changed into a fresh pair, then returned to the girls' purses, dumping them out on the floor, searching them again. Emma's cell phone had been located on a charger in the kitchen downstairs. Kayla had her own designer bag and Visa card. She certainly had a cell phone somewhere.

He sat back on his heels, feeling like he was missing something. Will had searched the room in a grid pattern, sectioning each piece, even digging his gloved fingers into the shag carpet under the bed and finding nothing more startling than a piece of Jolly Rancher watermelon candy that crinkled under his touch. He had checked under furniture and felt along the bottom of drawers. He'd flipped all the rugs over.

Nothing.

Where had Emma been while Kayla was being attacked? What had the girl been doing while her best friend was possibly being raped, certainly being beaten and murdered? Was Will looking at this the wrong way? Having often been on the receiving end of Paul's anger at the children's home, Will knew firsthand that the Campano blood ran pretty hot. Did that sort of thing skip a generation, or was it passed down directly? The mother had said that her daughter changed lately, that she had been acting out. Could she have been involved in Kayla's murder? Was Emma not a victim but a participant?

He looked around the room again—the stuffed teddy bears, the stars on the ceiling. Will would certainly not be the first man who had been fooled by the stereotype of an angelic young woman, but the scenario that called for Emma being one of the bad guys didn't feel right.

Suddenly, he realized what was missing. The walls were bare. Emma's room had obviously been professionally decorated, so where was the art, the photographs? He stood up and checked for nail holes where pictures had hung. He found five, as well as scratches where frames had scraped the paint. He also found several pieces of tape that on close inspection revealed torn pieces of the posters from the closet. He could easily imagine Abigail Campano being outraged to find a picture of a breast-augmented, genitalia-neutral Marilyn Manson marring this otherwise perfect girl's room. He could also see a teenage girl taking down all the framed art the decorator had chosen in retaliation.

"Trent? When you have a minute?"

Will stood, following the sound out into the hall.

Charlie Reed, a crime-scene tech who had worked for Amanda almost as long as Will, was at the end of the hallway. Now that the body had been removed, the man was cleared to go about the careful cataloguing of blood and evidence. Dressed in the special white body suit to prevent cross-contamination of the scene, Charlie would spend the next several hours on his hands and knees going over every square inch of the scene. He was a good investigator, but his resemblance to the cop in the Village People tended to put people off. Will made a point of specifically requesting Charlie on all his cases. He understood what it meant to be an outsider, and how sometimes it made you work even harder to prove people wrong.

Charlie pulled down his mask, revealing a finely sculpted handlebar mustache. "This was under the body." He handed Will an evidence bag containing the broken, bloody guts of a cell phone. "There's a shoe print on the plastic that's similar to the print we found downstairs, but not the shoe we found on the second victim. I'd guess our abductor nailed it with his foot, then the girl fell on it."

"Was there a transfer pattern on the body?"

"The plastic cut open the skin on her back. Pete had to peel it off for me."

Through the bag, Will made out the shattered phone. Still, he pressed his thumb on the green button and waited. There was no power to the device.

"Switch out the SIM card in your phone," Charlie suggested.

"Sprint," Will told him, recognizing the silk-screened logo on the back of the silver phone. The phone didn't use a SIM card. The only way to access any information stored on the device would be to have a technician hook it up to a computer and pray. Will said, "It must belong to either the kid downstairs, Kayla or somebody else."

"I'll rush it through the lab once we get prints," Charlie offered, holding out his hand for the phone. "The IMEI has been scratched off."

The IMEI was the serial number that cell phone networks used to identify a particular phone on the grid. "Scratched off on purpose?"

Charlie studied the white sticker near the battery casing. "Looks rubbed off from use to me. It's an older model. There's duct tape residue on the sides. I'd guess it was falling apart long before it was crushed. Not what I'd expect a teenage girl to carry."

"Why is that?"

"It's not pink and it doesn't have Hello Kitty stickers all over it."

He had a point. Emma Campano's phone had a bunch of pink, plastic charms dangling from the case.

Will said, "Tell the lab this has priority over the computer." They had found a MacBook Pro downstairs that belonged to Emma Campano. The girl had enabled FileVault, encryption software so secure that not even Apple could unlock it without the password. Unless Emma had used something simple like the name of the family dog, nothing short of the NSA could break it open.

Charlie said, "I found this over by the table." He held up another plastic bag that contained a brass key. "Yale lock, pretty standard. No usable fingerprints on it."

"Was it wiped down?"

"Just used a lot. There aren't any prints to lift."

"No keychain?"

Charlie shook his head. "If you had it in your pocket and you were wearing baggy pants, it could easily come out during a struggle."

Will looked at the key, thinking that if it had a number or address on it, his job would be so much easier. "Mind if I hold on to this?"

"I've already catalogued it. Just make sure it gets back to evidence."

"Will?" Amanda had been hovering behind him. "I talked to Campano."

He pocketed the key Charlie had found, trying to hide his sense of dread along with it. "And?"

"He wants you off the case," she said, but didn't seem to think that was worth discussing. "He says that they've had some problems with Emma lately. She was a good girl, the perfect child, then she got mixed up with this Kayla Alexander sometime last year and everything went to hell."

"In what way?"

"She started skipping school, her grades started to fall, she started listening to the wrong music and dressing the wrong way."

He told her about what he'd found in Emma's room. "I'm guessing they made her take down the posters."

"Typical teenager stuff," Amanda said. "I wouldn't trust the father so much on where the blame lies. I have yet to meet a parent who admits that his own child is the bad apple." She tapped her watch, her signal that they were wasting time. "Tell me what progress we've made."

Will told her, "The deceased male is Adam Humphrey. He's got an Oregon driver's license."

"He's a student?"

"Detective Mitchell is calling local colleges to see if he's registered. We're still trying to track down Alexander's parents."

"You know the key to breaking this is going to be finding a second person who knows at least one of our victims."

"Yes, ma'am. We're running dumps on all the telephones. We just need a lead to follow."

"GHP is pulling a negative," she said, meaning the Georgia Highway Patrol. "White is a popular color for the Prius, but there aren't that many on the road. Unfortunately, we're heading into rush hour, so it's not going to get easier."

"I've got uniforms pulling video from every ATM and storefront on Peachtree as well as anything in the Ansley Mall area. If the Prius left either way, we might get an image we can work with."

"Let me know if you need more feet on the ground." She rolled her hand, meaning for him to continue.

"The knife doesn't match anything in the kitchen or the carriage house, which points to the killer bringing it with him. It's pretty cheap—wooden handle, fake gold grommets—but it's obviously sharp enough to do some damage. The brand is for commercial use only. It's the kind of thing you'd find at Waffle House or Morrison's. The local supplier says he sells millions of them a year just in the metro area."

Amanda always thought in terms of how she could frame a case for the prosecutor. "Bringing the knife to the crime scene shows intent. Go on."

"There's dried blood on the glass outside the front door. Whoever broke it already had blood on his or her hand—it's on the outside of the pane. I'd guess it would take someone with an arm that was around three feet long to reach in through that window and unlock the front door."

"So, no forced entry—the girls let their attacker into the house. Whoever busted the glass obviously wanted to make it look as if he broke in." Amanda mumbled, "I suppose we have *CSI* to thank for his stupidity."

"Or someone smart enough to make it look stupid."

She raised an eyebrow. "Possibly. Do you think we should be looking at the father more closely?"

"He sells cars and he's a jerk. I'm sure there's a long list of enemies, but this feels deeply personal. Look at Kayla Alexander. Whoever killed her was furious. If you're a hired gun, you go in, take out the target and leave. You don't spend time beating her and you don't use a knife."

"What was your conversation like with Paul Campano?"

"He doesn't seem to know a lot about her life," Will said. Thinking back on the interview, he realized that this fact seemed to be the genesis of Paul's anger. It was as if he had never met his own daughter. "The mother had to be sedated. I'll go back at her first thing tomorrow."

"Do we know if Alexander was raped?"

"Pete isn't sure yet. Bruising would indicate yes, and there's sperm in her vagina, but it's also on the crotch of her panties."

"So, she stood up and put on her underwear at some point after intercourse. Let's see if the sperm comes back to our other victim, if that's what we're calling corpse number two for the moment." Amanda pressed her finger to her lip as she thought this through. "What about the mother? Hysterics, sedation. Pretty dramatic stuff and it conveniently takes her out of the spotlight."

"I think she's genuinely horrified about what's happened and she's scared she's going to be arrested for killing someone in cold blood."

Amanda looked at the dark, congealed pool where the body had lain. "Good defense if you ask me. Let's go back to the father. Maybe he was molesting the daughter."

Will felt his body break out in a sudden cold sweat. "He wouldn't do that."

Amanda studied him. "Do you have a previous relationship with this person that I should know about?"

"What did he say?"

She gave him a sharp smile. "You don't have the luxury of not answering my question."

Will felt his jaw working and made himself stop. "It was a long time ago."

Amanda seemed to realize Charlie was at her feet, picking through carpet fibers with a pair of tweezers. She murmured to Will, "A discussion for another time."

"Yes, ma'am."

Amanda's tone went back to normal. "Charlie, can you walk me through this?"

Charlie finished what he was doing and stood up with a groan, rubbing one of his knees as if he needed to work some life back into it. He pulled down his mask again. "We lucked out with the blood. The female decedent is B-negative, the male decedent is O-negative.

The carpet here"—he indicated the shoe prints—"shows almost exclusively B, indicating the female decedent."

"Charlie." Amanda stopped him. "Just paint me a story. Adam and Kayla. Go."

He allowed a smile at the situation. "This is all supposition, of course, but we might assume Kayla was chased down this hallway, toward the back staircase. The killer caught up with her about here." He indicated a distance of about three feet behind them. "We found a significant patch of hair, part of the scalp still attached, here." He pointed to another spot on the carpet. "From this we might conclude that she was jerked back by her hair and fell onto the floor. Possibly, this is the point at which she was raped—or not. The probability that she died here is very high."

Amanda looked at her watch again. Like Will, she hated the fact that forensics worked in the couched language of "possibly" and "most likely" instead of dead certainty. She asked, "Is this the part where we get past assumptions and down to hard science?"

"Yes, ma'am," Charlie answered. "As I said before, the blood types make it easier. Kayla was beaten and stabbed here. You can see the cast-off pattern on the wall." He indicated slashes of dark blood. "The killer was in a frenzy, probably furious from chasing her or maybe from seeing her with another man—Adam, you could suppose."

Will asked, "How long would the attack have taken?"

Charlie looked at the walls, the stained floor. "Forty to fifty seconds. Maybe a full minute or two if rape occurred."

"Does anything in the pattern suggest that someone tried to stop him?"

Charlie put his hand to his chin, studying the blood. "No, actually. These arcs are fairly perfect. If he'd been interrupted or someone tried to stop his arm from swinging, we would see more variation. This is extremely uniform, almost like a machine going up and down."

Will supplied, "The coroner says Kayla was stabbed at least twenty times, maybe more."

Charlie moved on to the footprints. "There was definitely a lot of activity after she was dead. You can see from the two sets of footprints that two people—one of them with shoes matching Adam's—walked back and forth here."

"Do you see signs that they struggled?"

Charlie shrugged. "It's hard to say because of the carpet. On a smoother surface, I could tell you where the weight of the foot was, if someone was caught off balance or pressing forward to fight with someone else."

Amanda said, "Best guess."

"Well..." Charlie shrugged again. "It seems probable in the greater context of the scene that there was a struggle. What I can definitely tell you is that at some point, Adam was on his knees beside the body. We've got the blood pattern on his jeans as well as the tops of his shoes. I have a theory that he reached out"—Charlie stretched his arm out near the bloody handprint—"and leaned his hand against the wall as he put his ear to Kayla's mouth."

Will stopped him. "Why do you say that?"

"He's got a light spray of B-negative just around here." He indicated his own ear. "There's also that spray of O-negative on Kayla's abdomen, which you pointed out to me earlier. I'd draw the same conclusion as you—he removed the knife from his own chest while he was bending over her. In fact, we found a mixture of both blood types on the weapon."

"Any fingerprints?"

"Just one set. Preliminarily, we'll say they're Adam's, but they'll have to confirm that at the lab. There were also markings on the knife handle that look consistent with someone wearing latex gloves."

Amanda told Will, "Throw wearing surgical gloves in with him bringing the knife to the scene and we've got premeditated murder."

Will didn't point out that they would have to find the killer before they could charge him. "What about the footprint downstairs?"

"That's where it gets interesting," Charlie began. "Type O-positive."

Amanda said, "Different from the two victims."

"Exactly," Charlie confirmed. "We found several spots on the stairs, a couple more up here. My guess is that whoever the blood belongs to was unconscious. As Will and I suggested, she was carried down the stairs. Either the abductor had to stop at the bottom to reposition her or she came to and started to struggle. Somehow, her foot touched the ground at that one spot."

Will told Amanda, "I've asked Charlie to Lumenol the house top to bottom. I'm curious about where Emma Campano was while her friend was being attacked."

"It follows that she was unconscious somewhere."

"Not here," Charlie supplied. "At least, not by what the blood tells us."

Will said, "We've had a lot of mistakes made today. I want to make sure that footprint downstairs belongs to Emma Campano. She's got a ton of shoes in her closet. Maybe you can get a latent?"

"It's a long shot, but I can certainly try."

Amanda asked, "Did you find any sperm in this area?"

"Nothing."

"But Kayla Alexander had sperm on and in her person."

"Yes."

She told him, "I want a rush DNA comparison against both Adam Humphrey and Paul Campano. Check the master bathroom for hair or any tissue you can find that might belong to the father." She looked at Will, as if waiting for him to object. "I want to know who this girl has been having sex with, consensual or otherwise." She didn't wait for a response, turning on her heel after tossing a "Will?" over her shoulder.

He followed her down the back stairs and into the kitchen. Will tried to get ahead of her on the blame game. "Why didn't you tell me Faith Mitchell's mother was part of my investigation?"

She started opening and closing drawers. "I assumed you would use your brilliant detective skills to make a connection between the two last names."

She was right, but Evelyn Mitchell hadn't been a priority for him for a long time. "Mitchell is a common name."

"I'm glad we have that settled." Amanda found what she was

looking for. She held up a kitchen knife, looked at the silver bee on the handle. "Laguiole. Nice."

"Amanda—"

She placed the knife back in the drawer. "Faith will be your partner going forward on this investigation. We've pissed off the Atlanta Police Department enough this year without pulling another major case from them, and I'd rather partner you with a goat than put Leo Donnelly on this."

"I don't want her."

"I don't care," she shot back. "Will, this is a major case I'm handing you. You're thirty-six years old now. You're never going to move up if—"

"We both know this is as far as I'm going to get." He didn't give her room to disagree. "I'm never going to do PowerPoint presentations or stand in front of a chalkboard filling in a timeline."

She pursed her lips, staring at him. He wondered why the disappointment in her eyes bothered him so much. As far as he knew, Amanda didn't have any children or even a family. She wore a wedding ring sometimes, but that seemed to be more for decoration than declaration. For all intents and purposes, she was as much an orphan as he was. Sometimes, he thought that she was like the dysfunctional, passive-aggressive mother he'd never had—a fact which made Will glad that he had grown up in the children's home.

She said, "It's dry erase now. You don't get chalk on your hands."

"Oh, well...sign me up."

She smiled ruefully. "How do you know Paul Campano?"

"I knew him when I was ten years old. We didn't get along."

"Is that why he doesn't want to talk to you?"

"It could be," Will admitted. "But I think my knowing him might also be a way in."

"Hoyt Bentley has posted a fifty-thousand-dollar reward for information leading to his granddaughter's safe return. He wanted to come out of the gate with half a million, but I managed to talk him down."

Will didn't envy her the task. Men like Bentley were used to being able to buy their way out of anything. A more lucrative reward would have backfired in so many ways, including bringing out every fruitcake in the city.

"I bet you they're going to hire their own people to stick their noses into this."

Will recognized a sucker bet when he saw one. Atlanta's wealthy had a bevy of private security forces at their disposal. Hoyt Bentley had enough money to buy every last one of them. "I'm sure Paul and his father-in-law think they can take care of this themselves."

"I hope whoever they hire knows the difference between paying off a CEO's mistress and negotiating a ransom."

Surprised, Will said, "Do you think there will be a ransom demand?"

"I think there will be several—none of them from our kidnapper." She crossed her arms, leaning against the counter. "Tell me what's bothering you."

Will didn't have to think in order to answer her question. "Two teenage girls, at least one teenage boy, alone in a house during the middle of the day. The parents don't know where any of them are. They say their daughter has changed lately, that she's been acting out. Somebody had sex in that bed upstairs. Where were Emma and Adam when Kayla was being butchered? Where was Emma when Adam was stabbed? We have to ask whether or not Emma Campano is a victim or an offender."

Amanda let that sink in, considering the possibilities. "I'm not saying you're wrong," she finally told him. "But there's a big difference between being a rebellious teenager and being a cold-blooded killer. Nothing about the scene points to anything ritualistic. I'm not saying you're wrong to consider the possibility, but let's just treat this as a straight abduction until we find something that points to more nefarious origins."

Will nodded.

"What's your game plan?"

"Charlie's going to be here all night, so anything big forensic-wise should be on your desk first thing in the morning. We've got APD pulling parking tickets in the area for the last week. I've got a two-man unit checking storm drains to see if anything was ditched—another weapon, some clothing, whatever. I want to talk to some folks at the school where these girls went and see if they have any enemies—and spread that out to the Alexanders, too. I think it's sketchy they left their kid alone for three weeks while they're half a world away. Do you have an ETA on the dogs?"

"Barry Fielding was on a training run up in Ellijay when I called," she told him, referring to the director of the GBI canine unit. "He should be here with a team within the next half hour." She returned to something Will had said earlier. "Let's go back two months on those parking tickets in the area. Go ahead and pull 9-1-1 calls, too. There can't be that many, but touching on what you said about the kids being alone here today, if this has been an ongoing thing..." She let Will fill in the blank: Don't stop questioning what Emma Campano's role was in all of this. "What are you going to be doing?"

"I'm going to go to the school myself to get a better idea of who these girls are. Were. I also want to talk to the mother. She was out of it today. Maybe she'll be more helpful tomorrow."

"She's a lot stronger than she looks."

"She strangled a man with her bare hands. I don't think you need to tell me to watch out for her."

Amanda looked around the kitchen, appraising the stainless steel gleaming from every corner, the granite countertops. "This is not going to turn out well, Will."

"You think the girl is already dead?"

"I think if she's lucky she is."

They were both silent. Will couldn't guess what was on Amanda's mind. For his part, he was thinking how ironic it was that Paul had everything they could only dream about when they were kids—family, wealth, security—and yet one violent intervention by fate had managed to sweep it all away. You expected that kind of thing to happen when you were living in an orphanage, kids stacked twelve to a room in a house that was no larger than a shoebox. You didn't expect it living smack-dab in the middle of Mayberry.

Movement outside the kitchen window caught Will's attention. Faith Mitchell looked grim as she walked along the back patio by the pool. She opened one of the French doors, asking, "Am I interrupting?"

Amanda demanded, "What've you got?"

The young woman closed the door and walked into the kitchen, looking almost contrite. "Adam Humphrey was a student at Georgia Tech. He lives in Towers Hall on campus."

Amanda pumped her fist in the air. "This is your break."

Will told Faith, "Call campus security. Have them check the room."

"I did," she answered. "The door was locked, but the room was empty. I've got a number to call when we get on campus. The dean wants to talk to legal before they give us access to the room, but he says that's just a formality."

"Let me know if I need to find a judge." Amanda glanced at her watch. "It's coming on four o'clock now. I'm late for a closed door with the mayor. Call me the minute you have anything."

Will crossed the room to leave. Then he realized that he still didn't have a car. He realized Amanda was still here, leaning against the counter, waiting for him to do exactly what she wanted.

Faith asked, "Do you want me to go wait outside the Alexander house to see if the parents have anyone checking in on Kayla?"

Will thought about Adam Humphrey's dorm room, all the papers and notes that would have to be catalogued, all the drawers and shelves that would have to be searched.

He said, "You're going to come to Tech with me."

Her expression turned from surprised to cautious. "I thought I was only doing scut work."

"You are." Will opened the door she'd just closed. "Let's go."

CHAPTER THREE

THE LITERATURE ON Faith's Mini Cooper claimed that the front seats could easily accommodate a passenger or driver over six feet tall. As with anything, a few extra inches made all the difference, and Faith had to admit that it brought her a small amount of pleasure watching the man who had helped force her mother off the job awkwardly trying to fold his long body into her car. Finally, Will moved the seat back so that it was almost touching the rear window and angled himself in.

"All right?" she asked.

He looked around the cab, his neatly parted, sandy blond hair brushing against the glass sunroof. She thought of a prairie dog poking its head outside its hole.

He gave a small nod. "Let's go."

She let off the clutch as he reached around for the seat belt. For months, even the thought of this man's name could invoke the kind of deeply felt hatred that made Faith feel like she should vomit just to get the taste out of her mouth. Evelyn Mitchell hadn't shared many details of the internal investigation with her daughter, but Faith had seen the toll the relentless questioning had taken. Day by day, her strong, impervious mother had been whittled into an old woman.

Will Trent was a key factor in that transformation.

Being honest, there was plenty of blame to go around. Faith was a cop, and she knew all about the blue code of silence, but she also knew that it was the betrayal of Evelyn's own men—those greedy bastards who thought it was okay to steal so long as it was drug money—that had finally taken all the fight out of her mother. Still, Evelyn had refused to testify against any of her team. That the city had let her keep her pension was a miracle of sorts, but Faith knew that her mother had friends in high places. You didn't become a captain with the Atlanta Police Department by shunning politics. Evelyn was a master at knowing how the game worked.

For her part, Faith had always assumed Will Trent was some kind of bumbling, rat squad jerk-off who loved to put his thumb on good cops and grind them out of the force. She hadn't anticipated that Trent would be the clean-cut, lanky man crammed into the car beside her. Nor had she considered that he might actually know his way around the job. His reading of the crime scene, the way he had been right about Humphrey being a college student—something that Faith, of all people, should have picked up on—had not been the detecting of some Bureau pencil pusher.

Like it or not, she was stuck with him, and somewhere out there was a missing girl, and two sets of parents who were about to get the worst news of their lives. Faith would do everything she could to help solve this case because at the end of the day, that was all that really mattered. Still, she didn't offer to turn up the Mini's air-conditioning, though Will must have been sweating to death in that ridiculous three-piece suit, and she certainly didn't offer him an olive branch by opening up the conversation. As far as she was concerned, he could sit there with his knees around his ears and boil in his own sweat.

Faith signaled as she pulled out onto Peachtree Street and accelerated into the far right lane, only to come to a complete stop behind a dirt-encrusted pickup truck. They were officially caught up in the hurry-up-and-wait game that was Atlanta's afternoon rush-hour traffic, which started around two-thirty and tapered off at eight. Add in all the construction, and this meant that the five-mile trip to Georgia Tech, which was just across the interstate, would take approximately half an hour. Gone were the Starsky and Hutch days of being able to slap a siren on your roof and blow through traffic. This was Will Trent's case, and if he'd wanted to bypass rush hour, he should have commandeered a cruiser to take them to Tech instead of a bright red Mini with a peace sign on the bumper.

As they inched past the High Museum of Art and Atlanta Symphony Hall, Faith's mind kept going back to the crime scene. She had gotten to the Campano house about ten minutes behind Leo. Faith's mother had always said that the hardest scenes to come onto were the ones involving kids. Her advice was to forget your family, focus on the job and cry about it on your own time. Like every piece of good advice her mother had ever given her, Faith had pushed it aside. It wasn't until she'd walked into that house today that she had realized how true her mother's words had been.

Seeing Adam Humphrey's lifeless body, his sneakers the same brand and color as the ones Faith had bought her own son just the weekend before, had been a punch in the gut. She had stood in the foyer, the heat at her back, feeling as if all the air was gone from her lungs.

"Jeremy," Leo had said, invoking her son. He wasn't offering sympathy. He wanted Faith to form some kind of miraculous mother bond with Abigail Campano and make the woman tell them what the hell had happened.

The Mini shook as a bus rumbled by. They were in a long line of traffic, waiting to take a right turn, when she noticed Will was sniffing his hand. Faith stared out the window as if this was some sort of normal human behavior.

He held out his sleeve. "Does this smell like urine to you?"

She inhaled without thinking, the way you smell bad milk if someone holds it under your nose. "Yes."

He bumped his head against the roof as he leaned up to get his cell phone out of his back pocket. He dialed a number, waited a few seconds, then without preamble told the person at the end of the line, "I think there's urine in the back of Emma's closet. I thought it might be from the dog bed, but I'm pretty sure it was fresh." He nodded as if the other person could see him. "I'll hold."

Faith waited silently. Will's hand was on his knee, his fingers playing with the sharp crease in his pants. He was an average-looking man, probably a few years older than her, which would put him in his mid-thirties. Back at the crime scene, she had noticed a faint scar where his upper lip had been split open and stitched back together in a slightly crooked line. Now, with the late-afternoon sun coming in through the glass roof, she could see another scar jagging from his ear down his neck, following the jugular and disappearing into the collar of his shirt. Faith was no forensics expert, but she would have guessed that someone had come at him with a serrated knife.

Will put his hand up to his face, scratching his jaw, and Faith quickly looked back at the road.

"Good," he said into the phone. "Is there a way to compare it to the O-negative at the bottom of the stairs?" He paused, listening. "Thank you. I appreciate the effort."

Will snapped the phone closed and dropped it in his pocket. Faith waited for an explanation, but he seemed content to keep his thoughts to himself. Maybe he just saw her as his personal driver. Maybe he associated her too closely with Leo Donnelly's mistake. She could not fault him for painting her with the same brush. Faith had been at the scene, had stood by chewing the fat with the mother while all the clues at the scene were waiting to be put together. She was Leo's partner, not his underling. Everything he had missed, Faith had missed, too.

Still, curiosity began to nag at her, then anger started to take hold. She was a detective on the Atlanta police force, not a lackey. Because of her mother's rank, rumors had always followed every promotion Faith received, but everyone on the homicide squad had quickly figured out that she was there because she was a damn good cop. Faith had stopped having to prove herself years ago, and she didn't like being left out now.

She tried to keep her tone even, asking, "Are you going to tell me what that was about?"

"Oh." He seemed surprised, as if he had forgotten she was there. "I'm sorry. I'm not used to working with other people." He turned his body as much as he could to face her. "I think Emma was hiding in the closet. She must have urinated on herself. Charlie said most of it was absorbed by the shoes, but it puddled a little on the floor in the back of the closet. I must've transferred it with my gloves when I searched the dog bed and not realized they were wet."

Faith tried to catch up. "They're going to try to match the DNA in the urine to the blood you think came from Emma at the bottom of the step?"

"If she's a secretor, then they can do a surface match in about an hour."

About eighty percent of the population was categorized as secretors, meaning their blood type showed up in body fluids like saliva and semen. If Emma Campano was a secretor, they could easily tell her blood type by testing the urine.

Faith said, "They'll have to confirm it with DNA, but it's a good start."

"Exactly." He seemed to be waiting for more questions, but Faith didn't have any. Finally he turned back around in his seat.

Faith edged up on the clutch as the light changed. They moved about six feet before the light changed back and traffic stopped. She thought about Emma Campano, kidnapped, reeking of her own urine, her last image that of her best friend lying slaughtered on the ground. It made her want to call her son, even if he would be annoyed to hear from his overprotective mother.

Will started to move around again. She realized he was trying to take off his jacket, bumping his head against the windshield and sideswiping the rearview mirror in the process.

She said, "We're going to be at this light for a while. Just get out of the car and take it off."

He put his hand on the door handle, then stopped, giving a forced chuckle. "You're not going to drive away, are you?"

Faith stared at him in response. He moved with some speed as he got out of the car, removed the jacket and returned to his seat just as the light changed.

"That's better," he said, carefully folding the jacket. "Thank you."

"Put it on the backseat."

He did as he was told, and she rolled the car forward another six feet before the light changed again. Faith had never been good at hating anyone face-to-face. Even with some of the criminals she arrested, she found herself understanding, though certainly not condoning, their actions. The man who had come home to find his wife in bed with his brother and killed them both. The woman who shot the husband who had been abusing her for years. People were not that complicated when it came down to it. Everyone had a reason for everything they did, even if that reason was sometimes stupidity.

This line of thought brought her back to Emma Campano, Kayla Alexander and Adam Humphrey. Were they all somehow involved with each other, or were they strangers until today? Adam was a freshman at Georgia Tech. The girls were seniors at an ultra-exclusive private school in a neighboring city about ten miles away. There had to be some kind of connection. There had to be a reason they were all in that house today. There had to be a reason Emma was taken.

Faith let off the clutch, easing up the car. There was a construction flagman in the opposite lane, directing cars to detour. Sweat poured off his body, his orange caution vest sticking to his chest like a piece of wet toilet paper. Like every other major American city, Atlanta's infrastructure was falling apart. It seemed like nothing was ever done until disaster struck. You couldn't leave the house without running into a construction crew. The whole city was a mess.

Despite her earlier vow, Faith turned up the air-conditioning. Just looking at the construction worker made her feel the heat more. She tried to think about cold things like ice cream and beer as she stared blankly at the truck ahead of them—the dirt hanging off the mud flaps, the American flag on the back window.

"Is your brother still overseas?"

Faith was so taken by surprise, all she could say was, "What?"

"Your brother—he's a surgeon, right? In the military?"

She felt violated, though of course Will's investigation into her mother had given him leave to mine her children's lives, as well. He would know that Zeke was in the Air Force, serving at Brandenburg. He would also have had access to Faith's psych evaluations, her school records, her marital history, her child's history—everything.

She was incredulous. "You've got to be kidding me."

"It would be disingenuous of me to pretend I know nothing about you." His tone was completely unreadable, which just annoyed her even more.

"Disingenuous," she echoed, thinking there was a reason this man had been assigned to investigate the narcotics squad. Will Trent didn't act like any cop Faith had ever met. He didn't dress like one, he didn't walk like one and he sure as hell didn't talk like one. It probably meant nothing to him to ruin the lives of men and women who belonged to a family that he could never be a part of.

Up ahead, the light changed, and she popped the clutch, swerving around the truck and turning right from the left-hand lane. Will's hands didn't even move off his knees as she performed this highly illegal maneuver.

She said, "I have been trying to be civil to you, but my brother, my mother—my whole family—is off-limits. You got that?"

He didn't acknowledge her remarks so much as skirt around them. "Do you know your way around Georgia Tech?"

"You know damn well that I do. You subpoenaed my bank records to make sure I could afford the tuition."

The patient way he explained himself set her teeth on edge. "It's been almost four hours since Adam died, more than that since Emma Campano was taken. Ideally, we would go straight to his room instead of waiting for the legal department to okay our access."

"The dean said that was just a formality."

"People tend to change their minds about things after they talk to lawyers."

She certainly couldn't argue with that. "We can't get into the room without a key."

He reached around to his jacket in the backseat and pulled out a plastic evidence bag. She could see a key inside. "Charlie found this in the upstairs hallway. We'll call your contact when we get there, but I see no reason why we shouldn't try the key while we're waiting."

Faith slowed at another red light, wondering what else he had been holding back. It annoyed her that he didn't trust her, but then again, she hadn't really given him a reason to. She allowed, "I know where Towers Hall is."

"Thank you."

Her hands were hurting from clutching the steering wheel too hard. She took a deep breath and let it out slowly. One by one, she released her fingers from the wheel. "I know I sound like a bitch, but my family is off-limits."

"That's a fair request, and you don't sound that way at all."

He stared silently out the window as the car crawled down Tenth Street toward Georgia Tech. Faith turned on the radio and searched for the traffic report. As they crossed over the interstate, she looked down onto I-75, which more closely resembled a parking lot. Over half a million cars used this corridor in and out of the city every day. Emma Campano could have been in any one of them.

The commuters around them followed the on-ramps to 75/85, so that by the time the Mini was on the other side of the bridge, traffic had returned to a more manageable level. Faith exited Tenth Street to Fowler, following familiar roads winding through the campus.

The Georgia Institute of Technology occupied around four hundred acres of prime downtown Atlanta real estate. Georgia residents could attend tuition-free thanks to the lottery-funded HOPE scholarship, but academic requirements barred the way for a large chunk of them. Add to that the financial burden of housing, textbooks and lab fees and even more students dropped to the wayside. If you were lucky, you got a full scholarship to take up the slack. If you weren't, you'd better hope your mother could take out a second mortgage on her house. Tech consistently ranked in the top ten of most college lists and was considered, along with Emory University, to be part of the chain of schools belonging to the Ivy League of the South. You could easily pay your mother back when you graduated.

Faith slowed the car along Techwood Drive for the students who didn't seem to understand the purpose of a crosswalk. A group of young men whooped at the sight of a blonde in a Mini, the combination of hormones and the natural lack of social graces inherent in math and science majors causing several of them to stumble over their own feet. Faith ignored them, scanning the streets for a place to park. Campus parking was a nightmare even at the best of times. Finally, she gave up and pulled the Mini into a handicapped parking space. She flipped down the visor to show her police parking permit, hoping local security chose to honor it.

Will said, "Go ahead and call your contact."

Faith talked to the dean's secretary as Will extricated himself from the car. She ended the call, got out and locked the doors. "Dean Martinez is still talking to legal. We're supposed to wait here. He'll join us as soon as he's off the phone." Faith pointed to a large, four-story brick building. "That's Glenn Hall. Towers is right behind it."

Will nodded for her to lead the way, but Faith's gait was considerably shorter than his and they ended up walking side by side. She had never thought of herself as short, but at five-eight, she felt dwarfed by him.

Classes were still in session, small clusters of students milling around. Though Will was still wearing his vest, his paddle holster and gun were in full view without his jacket. Faith was wearing a short-sleeved cotton shirt and dress pants—sensible considering the hundred-plus temperature, but hardly the best way to conceal the gold shield on her left hip and the gun on her right. The two of them caused quite a stir as they walked toward the quad between Glenn and Towers Hall.

Still, walking through the campus, seeing all those young faces, Faith realized how badly she wanted to work this case. Setting aside that being partnered with Leo Donnelly was not exactly hitching her wagon to a star, Faith could not fathom what it felt like to lose a child. Talking to Abigail Campano had been one of the hardest things she'd ever done in her life. All the mother could remember were the fights they'd had, the horrible things they'd said to each other. The fact that the woman's daughter was missing rather than dead didn't take away any of the horror. Faith wanted to do everything she could to help get Emma back home. Inexplicably, she also felt the need to let Will Trent know that despite today's screwups, she wasn't completely useless.

She started by telling him what little she knew about this part of the Tech campus. "These are both freshman dorms, not coed, about six hundred students between them. They're the closest to the stadium and the loudest. Parking for freshmen is heavily restricted so not many of them have cars, at least not on campus." Her feet sunk into the soft grass, and she looked down to check her footing, saying, "Most classes will be over in half an hour—"

"What are you doing here?"

She recognized the shoes first. They were the same brand and color she'd seen on Adam Humphrey's feet just a few hours ago. Two thin legs stuck out of the top of the sneakers like hairy sticks. His shorts hung around his narrow hips, the top of his boxers showing. He was wearing a torn, faded T-shirt—his Air Force–captain uncle's least favorite—that read "No Blood for Oil."

In retrospect, it seemed likely that she might run into Jeremy, who had been living at Glenn Hall for the last week and a half. Though she knew for a fact that her son was supposed to be in class right now. She had helped him sign up his schedule weeks ago.

She told him as much. "What happened to intro to biomechanics?"

"The professor let us out early," he shot back. "Why are you here?"

Faith glanced at Will Trent, who stood impassively beside her. She supposed one of the few benefits of his investigation into her mother was his lack of shock over a thirty-three-year-old woman having an eighteen-year-old son.

Will said, "One of your classmates has been in an accident."

Jeremy had been raised by two generations of cops. He knew the language. "You mean he's dead?"

Faith didn't lie to her son. "Yes. I need you to keep this between us for a while. His name was Adam Humphrey. Do you know him?"

Jeremy shook his head. "Is he a Goatman?" For reasons unknown, residents of Glenn Hall referred to themselves by this title.

"No," she told him. "He's at Towers."

"Classes just started. Fartley's the only guy I know." Another nickname, this one for his dorm mate. "I can ask around."

"Don't worry about it," she said, fighting the urge to reach up and tuck his hair behind his ear. Since his thirteenth birthday, he had been taller than her. On the few occasions when Jeremy allowed public displays of affection, she had to stand on her toes to kiss his forehead. "I'll come by later."

He shrugged. "Don't, okay? The MILF shit's getting pretty bad."

"Don't say 'shit.' "

"Mom."

She nodded, a tacit understanding. Jeremy ambled away, his brand-new sixty-dollar book bag dragging in the grass. When Faith was sixteen and lugging her one-year-old son around on her hip, she had blushed furiously when people had referred to him as her little brother. At the age of twenty-five, she would bristle angrily when men assumed that her son's age had a direct correlation to her level of wantonness. By thirty, she had become comfortable enough with her past to own up to it. Everyone made mistakes, and the truth was that she loved her son. Life had certainly not been easy, but having him with her made all the gawking and disapproval worthwhile.

Unfortunately, this peace had been quickly shattered when, during freshman orientation last month, Jeremy's new dormmate had taken one look at Faith and said, "Dude, your girlfriend is hot."

Will pointed to the red brick building opposite Glenn Hall. "This is Towers?"

"Yes," she said, leading him across the empty quad. "When I spoke with Martinez, the dean of student relations, he told me that Adam's dormmate is named Harold Nestor, but Nestor hasn't shown up for classes yet. Martinez said there was some sort of family situation—a sick parent, he thought. It's doubtful whether the kid will still attend."

"Does Nestor have a key to the room?"

"No. The kid hasn't even picked up his housing packet yet. As far as Martinez knows, Nestor has never even met Adam."

"Let's confirm that," Will said. "Does anyone else have a key to the room?"

"Campus security has a passkey, I would imagine. They don't really have house masters here—student government runs everything and they haven't had elections yet."

Will tried the front door to the building, but it wouldn't open.

Faith pointed to the large red sign warning students not to let strangers into the dorm. She had forgotten about this part. "You need a security card to get in."

"Right." He pressed his face to the glass, checking the lobby. "Empty."

"Adam didn't have a security card in his wallet." She glanced back at the quad, hoping for a wandering student who could help out, but the field was empty. "I guess we'll have to wait for Martinez and the lawyers after all."

Will had his hands in his pockets as he stared at the many signs on the door. In addition to the red one, there was a blue plaque that had instructions for the handicapped to press the plate on the wall to engage the automatic door as well as a laminated piece of green notebook paper advising students of numbers to call in cases of nonemergencies.

Will stared straight ahead, brow furrowed in concentration, as if he could open the door with his mind.

Faith had given up trying to figure him out since the urine incident. She walked over to the building intercom system, which contained a directory of all the student names. Someone had taped a handwritten note over the buzzers that read, "BROKEN!! DO

NOT TOUCH!!" Out of curiosity, she scanned the names. Humphrey, A. was beside the number 310.

Will stood beside her. She thought he was reading the names until he asked, "What's a MILF?"

She felt herself blush. "That was a private conversation."

"Sorry."

He reached for the directory and she pointed out, "It's broken."

He gave her an awkward half-smile. "I can see that." He pressed the blue handicap plate below the directory. There was a buzz, then an audible click as a lock released and the front door groaned open.

She waited for a well-earned sarcastic comment. All he did was indicate that she should go into the building ahead of him.

The lobby was empty, but the smell of young men was overpowering. Faith didn't know what happened to boys between the ages of fifteen and twenty, but whatever it was made them smell like gym socks and Tiger Balm. How on earth she had never noticed this when she was a teenager herself was one of life's great mysteries.

"Cameras," Will said, pointing them out. "What was the room number again?"

"Three-ten."

He headed for the stairs and Faith followed. The way Will moved made her think he was probably a runner. That would certainly explain why he seemed to have less body fat than a greyhound. Faith quickened her step to follow him, but by the time she reached the top floor, Will was already trying the key in the lock, using the plastic bag to keep his prints off the metal.

He opened the door, but didn't go in. Instead, he walked down the hallway. Three-ten was conveniently located next to the kitchen and across from the bathrooms. Will knocked on the door to 311. He waited, but there was no answer. He went down the hall and tried the next door.

Faith turned her attention to Adam's room, hearing distant

knocks as Will tried each closed door. Like Jeremy's, the room was around fifteen feet by eleven, basically the size of a prison cell. A bed was on either side with desks at their respective ends. There was a wardrobe and closet for each student. Only one bed had sheets, but the other had a pillow on the end opposite the television. It looked as if Adam had been using both sides of the room in the hopes that Harold Nestor would never show up.

Will said, "Nobody seems to be home right now."

She checked her watch. "Give it about twenty minutes. What do you want me to do?"

"My gloves are in my jacket. Do you have an extra pair?"

Faith shook her head. She had long ago gotten out of the habit of carrying a purse on the job and the one pair of gloves she normally kept in her front pocket had been used at the Campano crime scene. "I have a box in my trunk. I can—"

"I'll get it," he said, patting his pockets, a gesture that was quickly becoming familiar. "I left my phone in the pocket, too. I'm batting a thousand today."

She handed him the keys. "I'll make sure no one touches anything."

He sprinted back down the hall toward the stairs.

Faith decided she might as well see what they were up against. She walked over to the first desk, which was overflowing with scraps of paper, used textbooks, mechanical pencils and a small pile of magazines. They were all back issues of *Get Out*, which seemed to specialize in hiking. The other desk held what would be considered college necessities: an LCD television, a PlayStation console, several games and a stack of DVDs with handwritten labels. She recognized the titles of some recent Hollywood blockbusters as well as several that were simply labeled "porn" with stars to indicate, she supposed, their level of pornography.

One of the desk drawers was partially open, and Faith used a pencil from the other desk to pry it the rest of the way. Inside was a *Playboy* magazine, two foil-wrapped condoms and a stack of well-thumbed baseball trading cards. The juxtaposition made Faith sad.

Adam Humphrey would forever be caught in the stages between being a boy and being a man.

She knelt down. Nothing was taped under the Formica desktop or shoved between the drawers. Faith checked the other desk, too. She saw the corners of a plastic bag hanging down. She craned her neck, holding back her hair as she went in for a closer look.

Adam Humphrey probably wasn't the only boy at Tech who had a bag of pot taped under his desk. Hell, he probably wasn't the only boy on this floor who had one.

She stood back up, scanning the room—the Radiohead poster on the wall, the dirty socks and sneakers bunched in the corner, the stack of graphic novels by the bed. His mother must have been feeling indulgent when she let him pick out the black throw rug on the floor and the matching bedspread and sheets.

Faith imagined what it would be like for the Humphreys to pack up their son's meager belongings and take them back to Oregon. Was this all that they would have left of their son? Worse for Faith, who would have to tell them that their child was gone? Will had assigned the Kayla Alexander notification to Leo. Was he going to put Faith in the unenviable position of telling the Humphreys that their son had been murdered?

God, she did not want to do that.

"Who are you?"

Same accusatory tone, different boy. This one stood in the doorway, a hard look on his face. Faith turned toward him, giving him the full benefit of her gun and badge, but his expression did not change.

She asked, "What's your name?"

"None of your fucking business."

"That's a really long name. Were you adopted?"

Obviously, the joke fell flat. "Do you have a warrant?" He rested his left hand on the doorknob. The other one was covered in a cast that stopped just below his elbow. "Does campus security know you broke into his room?"

Strange way to put it, she thought, but told the kid, "I had a key."

"Good for you." He crossed his arms as best he could with the cast. "Now show me a warrant or get the fuck out of my friend's room."

She made herself laugh because she knew it would irritate him. He was a good-looking kid—dark hair, brown eyes, well built and obviously used to getting his way. "Or what?"

Apparently, he hadn't thought that far in advance. His voice wasn't so sure when he said, "I'll call campus security."

"Use the phone in a different room," Faith told him, turning back to the desk. She used the pencil to push through some of the papers, which were filled with mathematical equations and notes from class. She could feel the kid staring at her. Faith persevered. This wasn't exactly the first time she'd had an eighteen-year-old stare at her with burning daggers of hate.

"This is so wrong," he said, more for attention than effect.

Faith sighed, as if she was annoyed that he was still there. "Listen, this isn't about the pot, or the porn or the illegal downloads or whatever else you guys have been up to, so get your head out of your ass, understand that your friend must be in serious trouble if an Atlanta police detective is going through his things and tell me what your name is."

He was quiet, and she felt like she could hear his brain working as he tried to think of a way around answering her question. Finally he relented. "Gabriel Cohen."

"You go by Gabe?"

He shrugged.

"When was the last time you saw Adam?"

"This morning."

"In the hall? At class?"

"Here, maybe eight o'clock this morning." Again, he shrugged. "Tommy, my roommate, he snores. He's kind of an asshole. So I've been sleeping over here to get away from him." His eyes widened, and he seemed to realize that he'd put himself right in the middle of things.

"It's all right," she assured him. "I told you, Gabe, I'm not here because of two ounces of weed and a bootleg of *The Bourne Ultimatum*."

He chewed his lip, staring at her, probably trying to figure out whether or not he could trust her.

For her part, Faith was wondering what was taking Will Trent so long. Though she wasn't sure if his presence would help or hinder the situation.

She asked, "How long have you known Adam?"

"About a week, I guess. I met him on move-in day."

"You seemed pretty eager to take up for him."

She was getting better at reading his shrugs. His main concern had been the illegal bounty—probably the downloads more than the drugs, considering that ripping off movie studios carried a much stiffer penalty.

Faith asked, "Does Adam have a car?"

He shook his head. "His family's pretty weird. They kind of live off the grid. Real eco-minded."

That would explain the rural route. "What about this?" She pointed to the expensive television, the game console.

"They're mine," Gabe admitted. "I didn't want Tommy, my dormmate, fucking with them." He added, "But Adam plays, too. I mean, he likes to be outside and all, but he's a gamer, too."

"Does he have a computer?"

"Somebody swiped it," he responded, and Faith wasn't as surprised as she should have been. Theft was a rampant problem with this generation. Jeremy had had so many scientific calculators stolen from him at school that she had threatened to bolt one to his hand.

She asked, "Where does Adam check his e-mail?"

"I let him use mine. Sometimes he goes to the computer lab."

"What's his major?"

"Same as me. Polymers with a focus on spray adhesives."

That must have impressed the ladies. "Does he have a girlfriend or anyone he hangs out with?"

Gabe's shoulder went up in a slightly defensive manner. "We all just got here, you know? Not much time to hook up."

"Are you from out of state?"

He shook his head. "I went to Grady."

Grady was a magnet school, which meant they drew the top students from other schools in the Atlanta system. "Have you ever met Kayla Alexander or Emma Campano?"

"Are they at Grady?"

"Westfield."

He shook his head. "That's in Decatur, right? I think my girl-friend went there. Julie. She's been kicked out of a lot of schools."

"Why is that?"

He gave a shy half-smile. "We share a distrust for authority."

Faith smiled back. "Does Julie go to Tech?"

He shook his head again. "She went to State a few quarters, then dropped that, too. She tends bar nights in Buckhead."

Buckhead was a wealthy section of Atlanta known for its nightlife. Faith gathered Julie was at least twenty-one if she was al-lowed to serve alcohol. The four-year age difference between her and Emma Campano would have meant the girls would not likely have crossed paths.

Faith asked Gabe, "How'd you hurt your wrist?"

He colored slightly. "Stupid stuff. I slipped and fell on my hand."

"That must've hurt."

He held up the cast, as if he still couldn't believe he'd injured himself. "Like a mofo."

"Which bar does Julie work at?"

He dropped his arm but his guard went back up. "Why?"

Faith guessed he'd been cooperative enough to warrant an ex-planation. "Gabe, I need to tell you what happened to Adam to-day."

There was something like a loud "woof" echoing in the hall-way. Gabe whispered, "Fuck."

Two seconds later, Faith met the reason behind the expletive.

Gabe reluctantly made introductions. "This is Tommy Albertson, my dormmate."

He was as pasty as Gabe was dark, and Faith knew instantly that Gabe's assessment had been right on the money: the kid was an asshole. As if to prove it, Tommy's tongue practically hung out of his mouth as he stared at her. "Yowza. Me likes a woman with a gun."

Gabe hissed, "Shut up, man. Adam's in trouble."

"I was about to tell Gabe..." Faith directed her words to the young man. "Adam was killed this morning."

"Killed?" Tommy rocked onto the balls of his feet as he pointed his fingers at Faith. "Shit, dude, it was him, right? They said it was a Tech student. Fuck me—that was Adam?"

Gabe's confusion was obvious. "He was killed? As in murdered?"

Tommy became even more excited. "Dude, some crazy bitch strangled him to death. To *death*, man. With her bare hands. Seriously, it was all over the news. Where've you been all day, bro?"

Gabe's throat worked. His eyes moistened and his sense of betrayal was profound as he looked at Faith for confirmation. "Is it true?"

She nodded her head once, furious that someone in the department had leaked out that Adam had gone to Tech. "It's more complicated than that, but, yes, Adam is dead."

"How?"

"I can't really talk about details with you, Gabe. I can say that Adam acted heroically, that he was trying to help someone, and then things went very wrong. A girl was kidnapped, and we're looking for her, but we need your help."

His lower lip quivered as he tried to control his emotions.

By contrast, Tommy seemed almost exhilarated. "Are you here to question me?" he asked. "Bring it on. I've got all kinds of information."

Faith asked, "What kind of information?"

"Well, nothing, like, concrete or anything. He was a quiet dude, but you know, there was that intensity underneath. Like...danger."

Faith struggled to remain passive, though she would have loved to take Tommy Albertson to the morgue and ask him what exactly was so exciting about his friend being dead. "Did Adam have a girlfriend? Did he hang around with anyone in particular?"

As with everything else, Tommy found this extremely enter-taining. He clamped his hands on Gabe's shoulders. "Two ques-tions, one answer!"

Gabe squirmed away from him. "Fuck off, asshole. You never even talked to Adam. He hated your guts."

She tried, "Gabe—"

"Fuck you, too." He left the room. A few moments later, she heard a door slam.

Faith narrowed her eyes at Tommy, resisting the urge to tear him down to size. He'd stepped a few feet into the room, and she didn't like the way he was crowding her space. She knew that she would need to establish control or there would be a problem. "Maybe you'd like to answer these questions at the station?"

He showed a toothy grin, coming closer. "My dad's a lawyer, lady. Unless it gets you wet slapping the cuffs on a virile young stud such as myself, no way am I getting into the back of your car."

Faith kept her tone even. "Then I guess we have nothing to talk about."

He smiled smugly, closing the space between them. "Guess so."

"Could you leave now?" When he didn't move, she shouldered him back into the hall. He was taken off guard, or maybe she was madder than she thought, but the push turned into more of a shove, and he landed flat on his ass.

"Jesus," he whined, sitting up. "What is wrong with you?"

She turned the thumb latch on the inside doorknob and pulled the door firmly closed. "Your friend is dead, a girl is missing, and your reaction to all this is to laugh and make jokes about it. What do you think is wrong with me?"

Her words hit their mark, but they didn't have the desired ef-fect. "Why are you such a bitch?"

"Because I have to deal with assholes like you every day."

"Is there a problem here?" A well-dressed Hispanic man was coming up the stairs. He sounded slightly out of breath and a bit concerned that a student was on the floor.

Tommy scrambled to stand. He had the look of a spoiled child who was relishing the prospect of tattling. Faith dealt with it the only way she knew how, admitting, "He got aggressive and I pushed him out of my way."

The man had reached them by now. There was something familiar about his face, and Faith realized he was one of the many nameless administrators she'd seen at Jeremy's freshman orientation the month before.

There was no recognition in his eyes as Victor Martinez looked from Tommy to Faith, then back again. "Mr. Albertson, we have over eighteen thousand students enrolled in this school. It doesn't bode well for you that we are barely out of our first week and I already know your name and student ID number by heart."

"I didn't—"

He turned his attention to Faith. "I'm Dean Martinez," he said, offering his hand. "You're here about Adam Humphries?"

She shook his hand. "Humphrey," she corrected.

"I'm sorry we had to meet under these circumstances." He kept ignoring Tommy, who muttered an insult under his breath before he skulked away. "Maybe you could walk with me? I'm sorry that it seems like I'm not giving this the attention I should, but the first week of school is grueling and I'm between meetings."

"Of course." She caught the scent of his cologne as she followed him toward the stairs. Though it was late in the day, he was clean-shaven and his suit was still neatly pressed. Not counting Will Trent—and why would she?—it had been a long time since Faith had been around a man who paid attention to basic hygiene.

"Here," Victor said, reaching into the breast pocket of his jacket. "This is the master key to his room, his class schedule and his contact details." His hand brushed hers as he gave her the paper, and Faith was so surprised by the sensation it brought that she dropped the paper.

"Whoops," he said, kneeling down to retrieve it. The moment could have been awkward—Victor on one knee in front of her—but he managed to make it look graceful, scooping up the page and standing in one fluid motion.

"Thank you," Faith managed, trying not to sound as stupid as she felt.

"I'm sorry it took so long to clear this through legal, but the university has to cover its ass."

She scanned the paper, a familiar-looking student application with all the pertinent information. "Your candor is refreshing."

He smiled, lightly holding the railing as they walked down the stairs. "Can you tell me a little bit about what's going on? I've heard the news, of course. It's extraordinary."

"It is," she agreed. "I don't know what they're saying, but I really can't comment on an ongoing investigation."

"I understand," he responded. "The police department has an ass, too."

She laughed. "That could be taken two different ways, Dean Martinez."

He stopped on the next landing. "Victor, please."

She stopped, too. "Faith."

"I love the old-fashioned names," he told her, his eyes crinkling as he smiled.

"I'm named after my grandmother."

"Beautiful," he said, and she got the distinct impression he wasn't commenting on the tradition of passing down family names. "Do you mind my asking why you look so familiar to me?"

Despite the circumstances, there had definitely been some sort of flirting banter between them. Faith took a moment to mourn the loss of it before saying, "You probably saw me at freshman orientation. My son is a student here."

He did a terrific impression of a deer staring down an eighteen-wheeler. "Our youngest student is sixteen."

"My son is eighteen."

His throat moved as he swallowed, then came the forced chuckle. "Eighteen."

"Yep." There was nothing to do with the awkward moment but talk over it. "Thank you for the key. I'll make sure it's returned to your office. I'm sure my boss will want to interview some of the students tonight. We'll be as respectful as we can, but I would appreciate your informing campus security so we don't have any problems. You might get some angry phone calls from parents. I'm sure you're used to dealing with that."

"Certainly. I'll be glad to run interference." He started down the stairs. "I really must get to that meeting."

"One more thing?" Faith was only doing her job, but she had to admit it was somewhat rewarding seeing the fear in his eyes as he waited. "Can you tell me why Tommy Albertson is already on your radar?"

"Oh." The dean was obviously relieved it was that easy. "Towers and Glenn have a running rivalry. There are usually some good-natured pranks back and forth, but Mr. Albertson took it a bit far. They're sketchy on the details, but knowing how these things work, I assume water balloons were involved. The floor was wet. People were injured. One boy had to be taken to the hospital."

That would explain the cast on Gabe's arm.

"Thank you." Faith shook his hand again. This time, his eyes didn't crinkle when he smiled, and he let her go down the stairs ahead of him. He seemed to hesitate when they got outside, but once he figured out she was going right, he took a quick left toward the back of the quad.

Faith made her way toward her car, wondering what the hell had happened to Will Trent. She found him leaning over her Mini, his elbows resting on the roof. He had his head in his hands, the phone to his ear. His jacket was draped across the hood.

As Faith drew closer, she could make out what he was saying. "Yes, sir. I'll make sure someone is there to meet you at the airport tomorrow. Just call me back with your flight information." He glanced up, and there was so much pain in his expression that she made herself look away. "Thank you, sir. I'll do everything I can."

She heard the phone snap closed. He cleared his throat. "Sorry, the sheriff called back with a number for the Humphreys. I wanted to get that over with as soon as possible." He cleared his throat. "They're about six hours from a major airport. They're going to drive down tonight and try to get the first flight out tomorrow morning, but it lays over in Salt Lake. Depending on whether or not they get routed through Dallas, it could take them anywhere from seven to twelve hours to get here." He cleared his throat. "I told them to call the airline directly, explain their situation, and see what can be done."

Faith could not imagine what sitting in a car, waiting around at all those airports would feel like. Maddening, she guessed; the most painful day of any parent's life. She chanced a look at Will. His usual passive expression had returned. "Did they have anything?"

He shook his head. "Adam doesn't have a car here. He's been to Atlanta twice. The first time, he flew down with his father for orientation, stayed three days, then flew back. Both parents drove him down two weeks ago to help him settle into the dorm."

"From Oregon?" she asked, surprised. "How many days did that take?"

"The mom said they took a week, but they stopped to see things along the way. Apparently, they're into camping."

"That jibes with the outdoor magazines I found in his room," Faith said, thinking she would just as soon slit her wrists as drive across America. Add Jeremy into the road trip, and they would be looking at a murder/suicide. "So, he's been in Atlanta for fourteen days."

"Right," Will said. "They've never heard of either Kayla Alexander or Emma Campano. As far as they know, Adam wasn't seeing anyone. He had a girlfriend back home, but she moved to New York last year—she's some kind of dancer. It was a mutual split and he's dated off and on since then, but nothing serious. They have no idea why Emma's picture was in his wallet." He rubbed his jaw, his fingers finding the line of the scar. "The mother said that his laptop was stolen last week. They reported it to campus security, but she didn't think it was taken seriously."

Faith figured that was her cue. She told him about Gabe and Tommy, the girlfriend who might have gone to Westfield. As she spoke, she figured she should come clean and told him about shouldering Tommy into the hallway. She also told him about Victor Martinez's comments, though she held back the embarrassing parts for the sake of her own dignity.

Instead of railing her for assault and battery against Albertson, Will asked, "What are there, around fifty bars in Buckhead?"

"At least."

"I guess it's worth a try calling around to see if we can find her," he said. "I hate to say it, but at this point, a girlfriend who might have gone to the same school as Emma and Kayla and who's dating a friend of Adam's is the only lead we've got to follow."

Neither one of them had to vocalize the obvious: every hour that ticked by made it harder to find the killer, and less likely that they would find Emma alive.

He started pressing numbers on his phone. "Someone called while I was talking to the parents," he explained. "Put the incident with Albertson in your report, then put it out of your mind. We've got much bigger problems to deal with right now."

A cream-colored Lexus sedan pulled up while he was listening to his messages. Faith saw Amanda Wagner behind the wheel. She must have been the one who left the message, because Will told Faith, "They found Kayla Alexander's Prius at a copy center on Peachtree. There's blood in the trunk, but no sign of Emma. Security camera's fuzzy, but at least it was working."

He pocketed the phone as he walked toward Amanda's car, rattling off orders for Faith. "Call in a couple of units to help you canvass the dorms. Maybe somebody else knows more about Adam. Search his things, see if there are any more pictures of Emma. Take out anything his parents don't need to see. Go back at that Gabe kid if you think it'll work. If not, give him the night to stew. We can both hit him tomorrow."

She tried to process all of this. "What time do we start?"

"Is seven too early?"

"No."

"Meet me at Westfield Academy. I want to screen the staff."

"Wasn't Leo—"

"He's not on this anymore." Will opened the car door. "I'll see you in the morning."

Faith opened her mouth to ask him what the hell happened to Leo, but Amanda started to pull away before his butt hit the seat. Faith saw that Will's jacket was still on the Mini's hood and waved for them to stop, but Amanda either didn't see her or didn't care. Faith supposed the good news was that she was still on the case. The bad news was that she was definitely still at the scut-work level. She was probably going to be here until three in the morning.

Leo was the first casualty. Faith would be damned if she'd be the second.

She checked Will's jacket and found a handful of latex gloves. She also found something far more curious: a digital voice recorder. Faith turned over the small device in her hand. All the letters had been rubbed off from use. The screen said there were sixteen messages. She guessed the red button was record, so the one beside it would have to be play.

Her cell phone rang and Faith almost dropped the recorder. She recognized Jeremy's number and looked up at the second floor of Glenn Hall. She counted five spaces over and found him standing at his window, watching her.

He said, "Isn't it illegal to go through somebody's pockets like that?"

She put the recorder back in the jacket. "I'm getting really tired of dealing with smart-aleck kids who know their legal rights."

He snorted.

"Answer a question for me: if you didn't have your key card, how would you get into the building?"

"Press the handicap button."

Faith shook her head at the situation. So much for tracking people who'd been in and out of the dorm. "So, do you need pizza money or your laundry done or are you just making sure I don't come up there and embarrass you in front of your friends?"

"I heard about that kid," he said. "It's all over the dorm."

"What are they saying?"

"Not a lot," Jeremy admitted. "Nobody really knew him, you know? He was just some guy you passed in the hall on the way to the toilet."

She heard the sympathy in his voice, and Faith felt a tinge of pride that her son showed such humanity. She had met the alternative and it wasn't pretty.

He asked, "Do you think you'll find that girl?"

"I hope so."

"I can keep my ear to the ground."

"No, you will not," she countered. "You're going to school to learn how to be an engineer, not a cop."

"There's nothing wrong with being a cop."

Faith could think of several things, but she didn't want him to know. "I should go, honey. I'm going to be here late."

He didn't hang up. "If you wanted to do some laundry..."

She smiled. "I'll call you before I leave."

"Hey, Mom?"

"Yeah?"

He was silent, and she wondered if he was going to tell her that he loved her. That was how they trapped you, after all. You walked the floor with them and cleaned up after them and took all the grief and the noise and the swarthy Latin men who looked at you as if you had horns, and then they hooked you back in with those three simple words.

Not this time, though. Jeremy asked, "Who was that guy you were with? He didn't look like a cop."

Her son was right about that. She picked up Will Trent's jacket to lock it back in the car. "Nobody. Just a guy who works for your aunt Amanda."

CHAPTER FOUR

THE COPY RIGHT COPY CENTER was on the street-level floor of an ancient three-story building. It was one of the few structures on Peachtree Street yet to be torn down and replaced by a skyscraper, and the entire building had an air of resignation, as if at any moment it expected to be razed. The high-volume copy machines, made visible through the plate-glass windows by harsh, fluorescent lights, gave the place a dystopic, science fiction feel. *Bladerunner* meets Kinko's.

"Shit," Amanda hissed as the uneven road scraped against the bottom of her car. The asphalt was patched with heavy metal plates that overlapped like thick Band-Aids. Pylons and signs blocked off an entire lane on Peachtree, but the construction workers were long gone.

She sat up, gripping the wheel as the car bounced onto the ramp leading to the parking deck. Amanda pulled up behind a crime-scene van and put the car in park.

"Seven hours," she said. That was how long Emma had been missing.

Will got out of the car, adjusting his vest, wishing that he had his jacket even though the promise of night had done nothing to alleviate the sweltering heat. One of the employees of the Copy

Right had seen the abduction alert on television. He had spotted the car while taking a cigarette break and made the call.

Will followed Amanda down the gently sloping ramp that led to the parking garage behind the building. The space was small by Atlanta standards, maybe fifty feet wide and just as deep. Overhead, the ceiling was low, the concrete beams hanging down less than a foot from the top of Will's head. The second-story ramp was blocked off with concrete barriers that looked as if they had been there a while. A service road ran off the back, and he saw that it was connected to the adjacent buildings. Three cars were in a blocked-off area, he assumed for employee parking. The flood-lights were yellow to help keep mosquitoes at bay. Will put his hand to his face, feeling the scar there, then made himself stop the nervous habit.

There was no gate for the parking lot, no booth with an atten-dant. Whoever owned the lot relied on the honesty of strangers. The honor box by the entrance had numbers corresponding to the spaces. Visitors were expected to fold four single dollar bills into a tight wad and shove them through tiny slits by way of payment. A slim, sharp piece of metal hung on a wire to help people cram in the money.

Amanda's heels clicked across the concrete as they walked toward Kayla Alexander's white Prius. A team had already sur-rounded the car. Cameras flashed, evidence was sifted, plastic bags were filled. The techs were all suited up, sweating from the unre-lenting heat. The humidity made Will feel like he was breathing through a wet piece of cotton.

Amanda looked up, surveying the area. Will followed her gaze. There was one lone security camera up on the wall. The angle was more for catching people going into the building than watching cars parked in the lot.

"What have we got?" Amanda asked.

She spoke softly, but this was her team and they all had been waiting for her to ask the question.

Charlie Reed stepped forward, two plastic evidence bags in his hands. "Rope and duct tape," he explained, indicating each. "We found these in the trunk."

Will took the bag of rope, which appeared to be unused clothesline; there was a plastic tie around the neatly folded line. One side was faintly red where the fibers had wicked up blood. "Was it coiled up like this when you found it?"

Charlie gave him a look that asked if Will really thought he was that stupid. "Just like that," he said. "No fingerprints on either one."

Amanda surmised, "He came prepared."

Will handed back the rope and Charlie continued, "There was a patch of blood in the trunk that matched Emma Campano's blood type. We'll have to check with a doc, but the injury doesn't seem life threatening." He pointed to a semicircle of dark blood in the trunk. Will guessed it was about the same size as a seventeen-year-old girl's head. "Based on the volume of blood, I'd say it was a nasty cut. The head bleeds a lot. Oh—" He directed this toward Will. "We found microscopic sprays of blood in Emma Campano's closet above the urine you found. My guess is she was either kicked or punched in the head, causing the spray. We cut out the Sheetrock, but I'm not sure there's enough to test." He added, "Maybe that's why he didn't need to use the rope and tape. He knocked her out before removing her from the closet."

Amanda apparently already assumed this. "Next."

Charlie walked around the car, pointing to different spots. "The steering wheel, door panels and trunk latch show faint streaks of the same blood we found in the trunk. This is classic glove transfer." He meant the abductor had been wearing latex gloves. "As for the trash, we're assuming it came from the owner."

Will looked inside the car. The keys dangled from the ignition slot just beside what looked like a toggle knob that served as the gearshift. There were go-cups and empty fast-food bags and schoolbooks and papers and melted makeup and sticky spots of spilled soda and other items that indicated Kayla Alexander had been too lazy to find a trashcan, but nothing else that stuck out.

Charlie continued, "We got a positive on body fluids in the seats. Could be blood, urine, sperm, sweat, sputum. The seat material is dark and there's not much, but it's something. I'm going to cut out the patches and see if we can soak something out of them back at the lab."

Will asked him, "The blood on the outside of the car was Emma's only?"

"That's right."

"So he would've changed his gloves from the time he was in the Campano house?"

Charlie considered his answer. "That would make sense. If he was using the same gloves, then Adam and Kayla's blood would also be on the car."

Amanda asked, "Wouldn't it have dried in the heat?"

"Possibly, but the new wet blood would release the dried blood. I would expect to see some cross-contamination."

"How are you sure the blood is Emma's?"

"I'm not, really," Charlie admitted. He found a roll of paper towels and tore off a strip so he could wipe the sweat off his face. "All I can go by is type. The blood we found on the car is O-positive. Emma was the only one in the house that we know of who had that type."

"Not to question your methods," Will began, then did exactly that. "How do you know for sure that it's only type O-positive?"

"Blood types don't get along well," Charlie explained. "If you put O-pos with any type A or B, then you get a violent reaction. It's why they type you at the hospital before they give you a transfusion. It's a simple test—takes only a few minutes."

Amanda piped in. "I thought O-positive was universal?"

"That's O-negative," Charlie told her. "It has to do with antigens. If the blood types aren't compatible, then red blood cells clump together. In the body, this can cause clots that block vessels and bring about death."

Amanda's impatience was clear. "I don't need a science lesson, Charlie, just the facts. What else have you found?"

He looked back at the car, the team collecting evidence and

putting it into bags, the photographer documenting each empty McDonald's cup and candy wrapper. "Not much," he admitted.

"What about the building?"

"The top two floors are empty. We cleared them first thing. I'd guess no one's stepped foot up there in six months, maybe a year. Same with the parking area upstairs. The concrete barricade has been there for a while. My guess is that this place is so old, it wasn't built to handle newer, larger cars so they closed it off to prevent collapse."

Amanda nodded. "Find me if anything else comes up."

She headed toward the building, Will trailing behind her. "Barry didn't find any discarded gloves," she told him, referring to the chief of the canine unit. "This afternoon, the dogs were able to find a trail from the Campano house to the woods at the end of their street, but there were too many scents and they lost the trail." She pointed to an area directly behind the garage. "There's another path back there that goes into those same woods. It would take ten minutes to get to the Campanos from here if you knew what you were doing."

Will remembered what Leo had told him earlier. "The girls were skipping last year until the neighbor across the street told Abigail that Emma's car was in the driveway. They could've started parking here to avoid being told on."

"But Kayla's car was parked in the driveway today," Amanda pointed out.

"Should we recanvass the neighbors, see if they remember anything?"

"You mean for a third time?" She didn't say no, but reminded him, "It's all over the news now. I'm surprised no one has talked themselves into seeing something."

Will knew that was often a problem with eyewitness testimony, especially when the crime involved children. People wanted to help so much that their brains often came up with scenarios that didn't actually happen. "What's the kid's name—the one who called in the Prius?"

"Lionel Petty." She pressed a red button by the door. A few seconds passed, then there was a buzz and click.

Will opened the door for her and followed Amanda down a long hallway that led to the Copy Right. The air-conditioning was a welcome relief from the stagnant heat in the garage. Inside the store, signs hung from the ceiling with cartoon smiling pens writing out helpful directions. The front counter was covered with reams of paper. Machines whirred in the background, swirling out sheets of paper at incredible speeds. Will glanced around, but couldn't see anyone. There was a bell on the counter and he rang it.

A kid poked up his head from behind one of the machines. His hair was a mess, as if he'd just rolled out of bed, though his goatee was neatly trimmed. "Are you the cops?" He walked toward them, and Will saw that he wasn't really a kid. Will would have put him in his late twenties, but he was dressed like a teen and he had the round, open face of a child. Except for the receding hairline, he could have passed for fifteen. He repeated his question. "Are you guys with the cops?"

Will spoke first because he knew from experience that Amanda's style of rattling off questions and demanding quick answers didn't exactly lend itself to eliciting information from strangers. He had to raise his voice to be heard above the machines. "You're Lionel Petty?"

"Yeah," he answered, smiling nervously at Amanda. "Is this going to crack the case?" The slow cadence of his voice had a slight lilt to it, and Will couldn't tell if the man was just that laid-back or had smoked a little too much weed. "I've been watching it on the news all day, and they've been showing the car, like, every five minutes. I couldn't believe when I checked out for a smoke and looked up and there it was. I thought maybe my brain was making it up because what're the odds, right?"

"Petty," a disembodied voice called. Will moved down the counter. He saw the lower half of a body sticking out from a copy machine. "Did you clock out like I told you?"

Petty smiled, and Will saw the crookedest set of teeth he'd ever seen on a man. "So, not to be crass or anything, but is there a reward? 'We can't say no at Campano.' They live in Ansley Park. The family must be loaded."

"No," Amanda answered. She had figured out who was in charge. She asked the kid under the copier, "Where's the tape for the security cameras?"

He crawled out of the machine. There was a splotch of ink on his forehead, but his hair was neatly combed, his face clean-shaven. He was about the same age as Petty, but he lacked the other man's boyish features and stoner charm. He wiped his hands on his pants, leaving a faint trail of ink. "I'm sorry, we've got a ten-thousand-booklet run due first thing in the morning and my machine just jammed up."

Will glanced at the guts of the copier, thinking that its gears and cogs reminded him of a wristwatch.

"I'm Warren Grier," the man offered. "I pulled the tape as soon as your guys got here. You're lucky. We swap out the same two cassettes every day. If you'd shown up tomorrow, it probably would've been recorded over."

Will asked, "Do you have a problem with theft around here?"

"Not really. The construction makes it hard to get in and out of the building. About ninety percent of our clients never see us. We deliver out to them."

"Why the security camera?"

"Mostly to see who's at the door and to keep out the homeless people. We don't keep a lot of cash here, but the junkies don't need a lot, you know? Twenty bucks is a score for them."

"Is it just you and Lionel?"

"There's a girl who works mornings. Monique. She's seven to noon. We use a courier for deliveries. They're in and out all day." He leaned his hand on the counter. "Sandy and Frieda should be in soon. They work the evening shift."

"Who uses the offices upstairs?"

"There used to be some lawyers, but they cleared out maybe a year ago?" He was asking Petty, and the other man nodded confirmation. "They were immigration lawyers. I think they were running some kind of scam."

"Lots of shifty people," Petty provided.

"Here." Warren dug a set of keys out of his pants pocket and handed them to Petty. "Take them to my office. I stopped the tapes when your guys got here. The one on the top is from today. It hasn't been rewound yet, so you can probably find the time frame you need pretty easily." He apologized to Will. "I'm sorry, but I've got to get this machine back up. Just holler if you have any problems and I'll come back and help you."

"Thank you," Will told him. "Can I ask—have you noticed someone using the parking garage a lot lately? Maybe not the Prius, but another car?"

Warren shook his head as he walked back to the machine. "I'm usually chained to the store. The only time I go back through that door is usually when it's time to go home."

Will stopped him before he ducked into the copier. "Have you seen any suspicious characters in the area?"

Warren shrugged. "This is Peachtree Street. It's kind of hard not to."

Petty said, "I keep a lookout, you know?" He motioned for them to follow him to the back of the store. "It's not just like with the car. I called the cops on some homeless people who were crashing in the alley."

Amanda asked, "When was this?"

"Year, maybe two years ago?"

Will waited for her to say something sarcastic, but she held her tongue.

He asked Petty, "Have you ever seen the Prius parked back there before?"

He shook his head.

"What about any other cars?" Will pressed. "Is there one in particular that you've seen back there a lot?"

"Not that I remember, but I'm usually inside to catch the phones."

"What about your cigarette breaks?"

"Stupid, huh?" He blushed slightly. "I quit, like, two years ago, but then I met this girl at the Yacht Club a couple of days ago, and she smokes like freakin' Cruella de Vil. I picked it back up like—" He snapped his fingers.

The Euclid Avenue Yacht Club was a dive in Little Five Points. It was just the kind of place you expected to find a twenty-something-year-old copy store worker with the ambition of a snail.

Will asked, "What about the construction workers outside?"

"They've been there off and on for about six months. At first, they were trying to use the garage during lunch. You know, for shade and all. But Warren got mad because they were leaving all kinds of trash back there—cigarette butts, coffee cups, all kinds of shit. He had a talk with the foreman, all cool about it, just, like, 'show some common courtesy, man. Put litter in its place.' The next day, we get here, and there's fucking steel plates all over the road and they haven't been back since."

"When was this?"

"A week ago? I don't remember. Warren will know."

"Did you have any other trouble with them before this?"

"Nah, they weren't on the job long enough to give a shit. They come and go all the time, usually different crews, different bosses." Petty stopped in front of a closed door. He kept talking as he slipped the key into the lock. "I don't want you to think I'm some kind of greedy bastard asking about a reward."

"Of course not," Will said, glancing around the office. The space was small but well organized, with what must have been thousands of CDs neatly stacked on metal shelves from floor to ceiling. A battered chair sat beside a metal desk, papers stacked on the top. The time clock ticked loudly. A shelf on the opposite wall held a tiny black-and-white television. Hooked up to the front jacks was an array of cables leading to two VCRs.

Petty said, "It's pretty crappy. Warren's right about the tapes being recorded over. I've been working here seven years and he's bought new ones maybe twice."

"What about all these CDs?"

"Customer files, artwork and stuff," he explained, tracing his fingers along the multicolored jewel cases. "Most of the projects are e-mailed now, but sometimes, we get repeats and have to pull them."

Will stared at the television, spotting the top of Charlie's head as he cut a patch of material from the passenger seat of the Prius. Two tapes were beside the set, numbers labeling them one and two. Will checked one of the VCRs, which looked pretty straightforward. The big button was always play. The smaller ones on either side would be rewind and fast-forward.

He told Petty, "I think we've got this."

"I can—"

"Thank you," Amanda said, practically pushing him out the door.

Will went to work, sliding the top tape into the player. The television screen blinked, and the image of the parking garage came up.

Amanda said, "They turned it off two hours ago."

"I can see that," he mumbled, holding down the rewind key, watching the date and time code count backward. Will stopped the tape and hit rewind again, knowing the machine would go faster without having to show the image. The VCR whirred. The clock ticked.

"Try now," Amanda told him.

Will pressed the play button, and the garage flipped back up again. They saw the Prius again, parked in the same space. The time code read 1:24:33.

"Close," she said. Because of her husband's 9-1-1 call, they knew Abigail Campano had arrived at her home sometime around twelve-thirty.

Will kept the VCR in play mode and held down the rewind button with his thumb. The scene was pretty static, just the Prius and the empty garage. The quality of the tape was exactly as you would expect, and Will doubted he would have guessed the car's make from the film alone. Because the camera was angled more toward the door, the parking garage was only captured in a pie-shaped section. Everything on the tape played in reverse, so when the Prius backed out at 12:21:03, that meant that the car had actually arrived at that time. This was good information to have, but what really caught their attention was the second car the Prius had been blocking from the camera's eye.

"What make is that?" Amanda asked.

The grainy film showed the generic front side panel and partial front wheel of a red or blue or black sedan pulling into a parking space. Will could see part of the windshield, the slope of the hood, a side blinker light, but nothing more. Toyota? Ford? Chevy?

He finally admitted, "I can't tell."

"So," Amanda said, "we know that the Prius entered the garage at 12:21. Go back to when the second car first showed up."

Will did as he was told, going back almost an hour, stopping at eleven-fifteen that morning. He pressed play, and the footage slowly played out. The dark-colored car pulled into the space. The image of the driver revealed nothing more than that he was of average build. As he got out of the car, you could see that he had dark hair and wore a dark shirt and jeans. Having the benefit of comparison, Will surmised this was Adam Humphrey. Adam closed the car door, then tossed something—the keys?—across the roof of the car to the passenger, who was out of the camera's eye but for a hand and the upper part of a forearm as the second person caught the keys. The passenger wore no watch. There were no tattoos or other identifying marks. Both driver and passenger left the scene, and Will fast-forwarded the tape until Kayla Alexander's car showed up.

To Will's relief, the events unfolded chronologically now. At exactly 12:21:44, the white Prius parked beside the sedan, blocking the camera's view of the second sedan. The driver got out of the passenger's side door of the Prius, away from the angle of the camera, and opened the trunk. The second sedan's trunk popped open briefly, putting it into the frame. It closed a few seconds later. There was a blur that looked like the top of the abductor's head as he crouched around the sedan, getting in on the passenger's side. There was nothing else on camera after that. They had to assume that the sedan had pulled away.

Will took his hand off the VCR.

Amanda leaned her hip on the desk. "He knew the sedan was here. He knew to change cars because we would be looking for the Prius."

"We've been looking for the wrong car all afternoon."

Amanda said, "Let's have Charlie send the tape to Quantico," meaning the FBI lab in Virginia. "I'm sure they have an expert on front car panels."

Will ejected the tape from the machine. The TV flickered and showed the Prius again. Charlie was on his knees, combing through the driver's-side floorboard. The time stamp read 20:41:52.

Amanda saw it, too. "We've lost another thirty minutes."

◆

AMANDA WAS UNCHARACTERISTICALLY silent when she dropped Will off at city hall. As he walked toward his car, she had only said, "We'll have more information to go on tomorrow." Forensics, she meant. The lab was working overtime to process materials. Amanda knew Will had done everything he could. They both knew that was not enough.

Will drove aimlessly down North Avenue, so caught up in his thoughts that he missed his turn. He lived less than five minutes from City Hall East, but lately, he'd found himself wishing the distance were greater. He had lived alone since he was eighteen years old, and was used to having a lot of time to himself. Coming home to Angie was a big adjustment. Especially on a night like tonight, when Will was so caught up in a case that his head hurt, he craved time alone to just sit and think.

He tried to come up with anything positive that had been achieved today. Kayla Alexander's parents had been reached. Because of the time difference in New Zealand, they would lose a whole day in the air. Still, Leo Donnelly had managed to do one thing right, after all. Well, two, if you counted his sudden medical leave. Will guessed scheduling emergency surgery to have your prostate removed was better than facing Amanda Wagner, though both procedures ran the risk of castration.

Will parked on the street because Angie's Monte Carlo was blocking the driveway. The trashcan was still on the curb, so he dragged it up to the garage. The motion lights came on, blinding him. Will held up his hand to block the light as he unlocked the front door.

"Hey," Angie said. She was lying on the couch in front of the television, wearing a pair of cotton boxer shorts and a tank top. She didn't take her eyes off the set as Will let his gaze travel along her bare leg. He felt the urge to climb onto the couch and go to sleep beside her, or maybe something else. That wasn't how their relationship worked, though. Angie had never been the nurturing type and Will was pathologically incapable of asking for anything he needed. The first time they had met at the children's home, she had smacked him on the side of the head and told him to stop gawking. Will was eight and Angie was eleven. Their relationship hadn't changed much since then.

He dropped his keys onto the table by the door, unwittingly doing a catalogue of the things she had moved or disturbed today while he was gone. Her purse was on the pinball machine, lady crap spilling onto the glass. Her shoes were under the piano bench alongside the pair from yesterday and the day before. The flowers on the deck had been chewed, but Will couldn't really blame her for that. Betty, his dog, had developed a passion for daisies lately. They were all finding their own passive-aggressive ways to act out against the newness of the situation.

He asked, "Are they still running the Levi Alert?"

Angie muted the television and finally turned her attention to him. "Yeah. Any leads?"

He shook his head, taking off his gun and putting it by his keys. "How'd you know it was my case?"

"I made a phone call."

Will wondered why she hadn't just called him directly. He was too tired to pursue it, though. "Anything good on TV?"

"The Man with Three Wives."

"What's it about?"

"Ship building."

Will felt something close to panic as he realized the dog hadn't greeted him at the door. "Did you accidentally lock Betty in the closet again?" Angie wasn't a fan of the Chihuahua, and though Will had only taken in the little thing because no one else would, he felt very protective of her. "Angie?"

She smiled innocently, which ratcheted up his alarm. He still wasn't sure the closet incident had been accidental.

He whistled, calling, "Betty?" Her little bat-head poked out from the kitchen doorway, and he felt a wave of relief as her tiny nails clip-clopped across the hardwood floor. "That wasn't funny," he told Angie, sitting down in the chair.

The day caught up with him quickly. All the muscles in his body felt like they were melting. There was nothing he could do right now, but he felt guilty for being home, sitting in his chair, while the killer was out there. The digital clock on the cable box said 1:33. Will hadn't realized how late it was, and the knowledge brought on something like a slow ache. When Betty jumped into his lap, he could barely move to pet her.

Angie said, "I wish you knew how ridiculous you look with that thing on your knee."

He stared at the coffee table, the fingerprints on the polished wood. There was an empty glass of wine beside an open bag of Doritos. His stomach rumbled at the sight of the chips, but he was too tired to reach down and get one. "You didn't tighten the lid on the garbage last night," he told her. "A dog or something got into it. Trash was all over the yard this morning."

"You should've woken me up."

"It's no big deal." He paused, letting her know that it was. "Aren't you going to ask me about Paul?"

"That soon?" she asked. "I was at least going to give you time to settle."

When Paul had first come to the children's home, Will had idolized him. He was everything Will wasn't: charming, popular, circumcised. It all seemed to come so naturally to him—even Angie. Though honestly, Angie was easy for everybody. Well, everybody at that point but Will. He still didn't know why Paul had hated him so much. It took about a week of tension before the older boy started openly picking on him, then another week before Paul started using his fists.

Will told Angie, "He's still calling me Trashcan."

"You *were* found in a trashcan."

"That was a long time ago."

She shrugged, like it was easy. "Start calling him cocksucker."

"That'd be a little cruel considering what his daughter probably went through." Will amended, "Is still going through."

They both stared silently at the television. A diet pill commercial was on—the befores and afters. It seemed like everybody wanted to change something about their lives. He wished there was a pill he could take that would get Emma back. No matter who her father was, the girl was still just an innocent child. Even Paul didn't deserve to lose his daughter. No one did.

Will glanced at Angie, then back at the TV. "What kind of parents do you think we'd be?"

She nearly choked on her own tongue. "Where the hell did that come from?"

"I dunno." He stroked Betty's head, picking at her ears. "I was just wondering."

Angie's mouth worked as she dealt with the shock. "Wondering what, whether he'd be a drug addict like my mother or a psychopath like your father?"

Will shrugged.

She sat up on the couch. "What would we tell him about how we met? Just give him a copy of *Flowers in the Attic* and hope for the best?"

He shrugged again, tugging at Betty's ears. "Assuming he can read."

Angie didn't laugh. "What are we going to tell him about why we got married? Normal kids ask about that kind of shit all the time, Will. Did you know that?"

"Is there a book about a daddy giving a mommy an ultimatum after she gives him syphilis?"

Will looked up when she did not answer. The corner of Angie's lip curled into a smile. "That's actually the next movie after this one."

"Yeah?"

"Meryl Streep plays the mother."

"Some of her best work has been with syphilis." He felt Angie staring at him and kept his attention on Betty, scratching her head until her back foot started to thump.

Angie smoothly steered the subject back to something easier. "What's Paul's wife look like?"

"Pretty," he said, jerking back his hand as Betty gave him a nip. "Actually, she's beautiful."

"I'd bet you my left one he's cheating on her."

Will shook his head. "She's the whole package. Tall, blond, smart, classy."

Her eyebrow went up, but they both knew Will's type leaned more toward gutter-mouthed brunettes with the self-destructive habit of saying exactly what was on their minds. Natalie Maines in a wig would be a concern. Abigail Campano was nothing more than a curiosity.

"Be that as it may," Angie said, "men don't cheat on their wives because they aren't pretty or smart or sexy enough. They cheat because they want an uncomplicated fuck, or because they're bored, or because their wives don't put up with their bullshit anymore."

Betty jumped onto the floor and shook herself out. "I'll keep that in mind."

"Do that." Angie used her foot to block Betty from getting on the couch. He could easily see her doing the same thing with a toddler. Will stared at Angie's toenails, which were painted a bright red. He couldn't imagine her sitting around with a little girl getting a pedicure. Of course, three months ago, he couldn't imagine Angie ever settling down, either.

When she'd called him to say that he had to go to the free clinic to get tested, he'd been so furious he'd thrown the telephone through a kitchen window. There had been a lot of fighting after that—something Will hated and Angie fed off of. For almost thirty years, they had followed this pattern. Angie would cheat on him, he would send her away, she would come back a few weeks or months later and it would all start over again.

Will was sick of being on that treadmill. He wanted to settle down, to have some semblance of a normal life. There was hardly a long line of women waiting to sign up for the job. Will had so much baggage that he needed a claim check every time he left the house.

Angie knew about his life. She knew about the scar on the back of his head where he'd been whacked with a shovel. She knew how his face had gotten torn up and why he got nervous every time he saw the glow of a cigarette. He loved her—there was no question about that. Maybe he didn't love her with passion, maybe he wasn't really *in love* with her at all, but Will felt safe with her, and sometimes, that was the one thing that mattered the most.

Out of nowhere, she said, "Faith Mitchell's a good cop."

"That was a mighty informative phone call you made today," Will commented, wondering who at the Atlanta Police Department had been so chatty. "I investigated her mother."

"She didn't do it," Angie said, but Will knew her defense was the automatic type that cops used, sort of like a gesundheit when somebody sneezed.

"She's got an eighteen-year-old kid."

"I'm hardly in a position to denigrate teenage slutdom." Angie added, "Be careful around Faith. She's going to figure you out in about ten seconds flat."

Will sighed, feeling it deep in his chest. He stared at the kitchen doorway. The light had been left on. He could see the bread was on the counter, an open jar of Duke's beside it. He had just bought that mayonnaise. Was she that wasteful or was she trying to send him some kind of message?

A shadow crossed over him, and he looked up to see Angie. She got in the chair, straddling him, her arms resting on his shoulders. Will ran his hands along her legs, but she stopped him from going any farther. Angie never gave anything for free, which she proved by saying, "Why did you ask about kids?"

"Just making conversation."

"Pretty strange conversation."

He tried to kiss her, but she pulled away.

"Come on," she prodded. "Tell me why you asked."

He shrugged. "No reason."

"Are you trying to tell me you want kids?"

"I didn't say that."

"What—you want to adopt?"

He stopped her with two simple words. "Do you?"

She sat back, her hands in her lap. He had known her for pretty much his entire life. In all that time, a direct question had never gotten a direct answer, and he knew that wasn't going to change any time soon.

"You remember the Doors?" she asked. She didn't mean the band. When they were growing up, there were certain kids who came and went in the system so many times that it was like the children's home was a revolving door for them. She put her lips close to his ear. "When you're drowning, you don't stop to teach somebody else how to swim."

"Come on." He patted her leg. "I need to take Betty for her walk and I've got an early morning."

Angie had never taken well to being told she couldn't have something. "You can't spare me thirty-two seconds?"

"You leave out a new jar of mayonnaise and you expect foreplay?"

She smiled, taking that as an invitation.

"You know," he began, "you've been living here for two and a half weeks and the only places we've had sex are this chair and that couch."

"You realize that you're probably the only man on earth who would complain about something like that?"

"I bow to your extensive market research."

The corner of her mouth went up, but she wasn't smiling. "It's gonna be like that, huh?"

"Did you call the real estate agent yet?"

"It's on my list," she told him, but they both knew she wasn't going to put her house on the market any time soon.

Will didn't have the strength to continue the conversation. "Angie, come on. Let's not do this."

She put her hands on his shoulders and did something extremely effective with her hips. Will felt like a lab rat as she looked down at him, watching his every move, adjusting the rhythm according to his reaction. He tried to kiss her, but she kept pulling just out of his reach. Her hand went into her shorts, and he felt the back of her fingers pressing against him as she stroked herself. Will's heart started pounding as he watched her eyes close, her tongue dart out between her lips. He nearly lost it when she finally turned her hand around and started using it on him.

"Are you still tired?" she whispered. "You want me to stop?"

Will didn't want to talk. He lifted her up and pushed her back onto the coffee table. His last thought as he thrust into her was at least it wasn't the couch or the chair.

◆

WILL SCOOPED UP Betty and held her to his chest as he started jogging down the street. She pressed her face into his neck, her tongue lolling happily as they left the neighborhood. He didn't slow his pace until he could see the streetlights from Ponce de Leon. Though Betty protested, he put her down on the sidewalk and made her walk the rest of the way to the drugstore.

At two in the morning, the place was surprisingly busy. Will grabbed a basket and headed toward the back of the store, guessing he'd find what he needed near the pharmacy. He walked down two different aisles before he spotted the right section.

Will scanned the boxes, his eyes blurring on the letters. He could make out numbers okay, but had never been able to read well. There was a teacher early on who had suggested dyslexia, but Will had never been diagnosed so there was no telling if he had a real disorder or if he was just painfully stupid—something subsequent teachers agreed was the issue. The only thing he knew for certain was that no matter how hard he tried, printed words worked against him. The letters transposed and skipped around. They lost their meaning by the time they went from his eyes to his brain. They turned backward and sometimes disappeared off the page altogether. He couldn't tell left from right. He couldn't focus on a page of text for more than an hour without getting a blinding headache. On good days, he could read on a second-grade level.

Bad days were unbearable. If he was tired or upset, the words swirled like quicksand.

The year before, Amanda Wagner had found out about his problem. Will wasn't sure how she had found out, but asking her would only open up a conversation he didn't want to have. He used voice recognition software to do his reports. Maybe he relied on the computer spell-check too much. Or maybe Amanda had wondered why he used a digital recorder to take notes instead of the old-fashioned spiral notebook every other cop used. The fact existed that she knew and it made his job that much harder because he was constantly having to prove to her that he wasn't a hindrance.

He still wasn't sure if she had assigned Faith Mitchell to him to help or because Mitchell, of all people, would be looking for something wrong with him. If it got out that Will was functionally illiterate, he would never be able to lead a case again. He would probably lose his job.

He couldn't even think about what he'd do if that happened.

Will put the basket on the floor, rubbing Betty's chin to let her know he hadn't forgotten about her. He looked back at the shelf. Will had thought it would be easier than this, but there were at least ten different brands to choose from. All the boxes were the same except for varying shades of pink or blue. He recognized some of the logos from television commercials, but he hadn't seen the box among the trash strewn across the yard, he had only seen the little stick you pee on. Whatever dog had gotten into the garbage had destroyed the packaging, so this morning, all Will could do was stand in the middle of the driveway holding up what was obviously a home pregnancy test.

There were two lines on it, but what did that mean? Some of the commercials on TV showed smiley faces. Some of them showed pluses. Wouldn't it follow that some would have a minus? Had his eyes blurred and he'd seen two lines instead of a single minus? Or was he so freaked out that he'd read a word as a symbol? Did the test actually say something as simple as "no" and Will couldn't read it?

He would get one of each type, he decided. When the Campano case resolved, he would lock his office door and go through each kit, comparing it to the wand from the trash, until he found the right brand, then he would take however many hours he needed to figure out the directions so he'd know one way or the other what exactly was going on.

Betty had jumped into the basket, so Will loaded the boxes in around her. He carried it against his chest to keep her from spilling out. Betty's tongue lolled again as he headed to the front checkout, her little paws on the edge of the basket so she looked more like a hood ornament. People stared, though Will doubted this was the first time this Midtown store had seen a grown man in a business suit carrying a Chihuahua with a pink leash. On the other hand, he could pretty much guarantee that he was the first one to be carrying a basket full of home pregnancy tests.

More stares came as he waited in line. Will scanned the images on the newspapers. The *Atlanta Journal* had already printed the early edition. As with just about every other paper in the nation this morning, Emma Campano's face was above the fold. Will had plenty of time waiting in line to decipher the bold, block letters over the photograph. MISSING.

He tried to breathe through the tightness in his chest as he thought about all the bad things that people could do to each other. The Doors, the kids who came back from foster care or couldn't make it with their adopted family, told that story. Time and time again, they would be sent out, only to come back with a deadness in their eyes. Abuse, neglect, assault. The only thing harder to look at was the mirror when you came back yourself.

Betty licked his face. The line moved up. The clock over the register said two-fifteen.

Amanda was right. If she was lucky, Emma Campano was dead.

DAY TWO

CHAPTER FIVE

ABIGAIL CAMPANO FELT like her daughter was still alive. Was that possible? Or was she making a connection that wasn't there, like an amputee who still feels a missing arm or leg long after it's gone?

If Emma was dead, it was Abigail's fault. She had taken a life—not just any life, but that of a man who had tried to save her daughter. Adam Humphrey, a stranger to Abigail and Paul, a boy they had never seen or heard of until yesterday, was dead by her own hands. There had to be a price for that. There had to be some sort of justice. If only Abigail could offer herself up to the altar. She would gladly switch places with Emma right now. The torture, the pain, the terror—even the cold embrace of a shallow grave would be better than this constant state of unknowing.

Or would it? What were Kayla's parents thinking right now? Abigail couldn't stand the couple, hated their permissiveness and the mouthy daughter it had produced. Emma was certainly no saint, but she had been different before she met Kayla. She had never failed a class or missed a homework assignment or skipped school. And yet, what would Abigail say to the girl's parents? "Your daughter would still be alive if you had kept her away from mine?"

Or—daughters.

"*Our* daughters would be alive if you had listened to me."

Abigail forced herself to move, to try to get out of bed. Except for going to the bathroom, she had lain here for the last eighteen hours. She felt foolish for having to be sedated—some latter-day Aunt Pittypat who felt the vapors coming on. Everyone was being so careful around her. Abigail had not felt so handled in ages. Even her mother had been gentle on the telephone. Beatrice Bentley had lived in Italy since she'd divorced Abigail's father ten years ago. She was on a plane somewhere over the North Atlantic right now, her beautiful mother rushing to her side.

Adam Humphrey's parents would be coming, too. What awaited them was not a bedside, but a graveside. What would it feel like to bury your child? How would you feel as the coffin lowered into the earth, the earth covered your baby in darkness?

Abigail often wondered what it would have been like to have a son. Granted, she was an outsider, but mothers and sons seemed to have such uncomplicated relationships. Boys were easy to read. With one glance, you could tell whether they were angry or sad or happy. They appreciated simple things, like pizza and video games, and when they fought with their friends, it was never for blood, or worse, for sport. You never heard about boys writing slam notes or spreading rumors about each other at school. A boy never came home crying because someone called him fat. Well, maybe he did, but his mother could make everything better by stroking his head, baking some cookies. He would not sulk for weeks over the slightest perceived insult.

In Abigail's experience, women certainly loved their mothers, but there was always some kind of thing that lived between them. Envy? History? Hate? This *thing*, whatever it was, made girls gravitate toward their fathers. For his part, Hoyt Bentley had relished spoiling his only child. Beatrice, Abigail's mother, had resented the lost attention. Beautiful women did not like competition, even if it was from their own daughters. To Abigail's recollection, she was the only thing her parents ever fought about.

"You've spoiled her rotten," Beatrice would scream at Hoyt, her milk-white complexion seeming to take on the green pallor of envy.

In college, Abigail had met a fellow student named Stewart Bradley who, from all appearances, was just the type of man she was meant to marry. He was of the old money stock that her father approved of, and had enough new money to please her mother in the process. Stewart was smart, easygoing and about as interesting as a jar of pickled beets.

Abigail had been ripe for stealing the day she took her BMW into the dealership for servicing. Paul Campano wore a cheap suit that was too tight in the shoulders. He was loud and unpolished and even days later, just thinking about him would bring on a rush of heat straight between her legs. Three weeks later, she gave up the life of Mrs. Pickled Beets and moved in with Paul Campano, an adopted Jew with Italian parents and a chip on his shoulder the size of Rhode Island.

Beatrice didn't approve, which sealed the deal. Her mother claimed that Paul's lack of money and family name were not the problem. She saw that there was something deep in Paul that would never be satisfied. Even on Abigail's wedding day, Beatrice had told her daughter to be careful, that men were selfish creatures at their core, and there were only a handful of them who managed to overcome that natural inclination. Paul Campano, with his pinky ring and hundred-dollar haircut, was not one of them. Hoyt had for all intents and purposes moved in with his mistress by then, and Abigail had assumed that her mother's warning was the result of her own miserably isolated life.

"Darling," Beatrice had confided, "you cannot fight a man's history."

Undeniably, Abigail and Paul loved each other passionately. He had worshipped her—a role that Abigail, ever the daddy's girl, was more comfortable with than she wanted to admit. Every new milestone, whether it was becoming manager of the dealership, buying his own franchise, then adding another and another, he would run to her for praise. Her approval meant so much to him that it was almost comical.

There came a time, though, when she got sick of being worshipped, and she saw she was not so much on a pedestal as locked in a fairy-tale tower. Paul really meant it when he said that he wasn't good enough for her. His self-deprecating jokes that had seemed so charming in the beginning suddenly weren't so funny. Behind all the bluster and bravado was a need so deep that Abigail wasn't sure she would ever find the bottom.

Paul's adoptive parents were lovely people—Marie and Marty were a rare combination of patience and contentment—but years went by before Marie let it slip that Paul had been twelve when he came to live with them. Abigail had had this image in her mind of a perfect, pink baby being delivered straight into Marie's arms, but the reality of Paul's adoption was more Dickensian than anyone wanted to admit. Abigail had questions, though no one would answer them. Paul would not open up and his parents obviously felt it would be a betrayal to talk about their son, even if the person asking was his own wife.

The affairs started around that time, or maybe they had been going on all along and she'd just then started to notice. It was so much easier to keep your head in the sand, to maintain the status quo while the world crumbled around you. Why was Abigail surprised by his infidelities? She had taken a different route, but the path she was on already showed the familiar footsteps of her own mother.

At first, Abigail had welcomed the expensive gifts Paul brought back from business trips and conferences. Then she had grown to understand that they were payoffs, get-out-of-guilt free cards that he fanned like a croupier. As the years went by, Abigail's smile was not so bright, her bed not so welcoming, when he returned from California or Germany with diamond bracelets and gold watches.

So, Paul had started bringing back gifts for Emma. Their daughter had responded as expected to the lavish gifts. Young girls are built to crave attention, and Emma had stepped into the role of daddy's girl as easily as her mother before her. Paul would give her an iPod or a computer or a car, and she would blissfully throw her arms around his neck while Abigail admonished him about spoiling her.

Abigail's transformation from her self to her mother was that simple. As with any change, there was revelation. She hated seeing Emma so easily swayed by Paul's gifts and unconditional love. He saw her as perfect and she returned the favor in spades. Everything was made so easy for his girl. Paul bought Emma out of every bad mood, every sad day. When she lost her English textbook the second day of school, he bought her a new one, no questions asked. When she misplaced her homework or forgot an assignment, he made excuses for her. Whether it was checking the closet for monsters or getting her sold-out concert tickets or making sure she had the latest style of jeans, Paul was there for her. Why would Abigail begrudge this? Shouldn't a woman be thrilled that her only child was so loved?

No. Sometimes she wanted to grab Emma by the shoulders and shake her, to tell her not to be so reliant on her father, that she needed to learn how to fend for herself. Abigail didn't want her daughter to grow up thinking that the only way to get anything was through a man. Emma was smart and funny and beautiful and she could have everything she wanted so long as she worked for it. Unfortunately, Paul jumping every time Emma snapped her fingers was too alluring. He had built a world for her where everything was perfect and nothing could go wrong.

Until now.

There was a knock on the door. Abigail realized she was still lying in bed, that she had only imagined that she'd managed to sit up. She moved her arms and legs to see if she could feel them.

"Abby?" Paul looked exhausted. He hadn't shaved. His lips were chapped. His eyes were sunken in his head. She had slapped him last night—her hand stinging against his cheek. Until yesterday, Abigail had never raised her hand to another human being in her life. Now, in the course of twenty-four hours, she had killed a teenage boy and slapped her own husband.

Paul had told her that if they hadn't taken away Emma's car, she might be safe now. Maybe men were not so easy, after all.

He said, "No news yet."

She knew this just from looking at him.

"Your mom's flight is gonna be in around three. Okay?"

She swallowed, her throat dry. She had cried so much that she didn't have any tears left. The words came out of her mouth before she knew what she was saying. "Where's my father?"

Paul seemed disappointed that she asked for someone else. "He went out to get some coffee."

She didn't believe him. Her father didn't go out to get coffee. He had people who did those kinds of things for him.

"Babe," Paul said, but there was nothing else. She could feel the need in him, but Abigail was numb. Still, he came into the room, sat by her on the bed. "We'll get through this."

"What if we don't?" she asked, her voice sounding dead in her own ears. "What if we can't get through this, Paul?"

Tears came into his eyes. He had always been an easy crier. Emma had worked him so easily with the car. When they'd told her they were taking it away from her, she had screamed, thrown a tantrum. "I hate you!" she had yelled, first at Abigail, then at Paul. "I hate your guts!" He had stood there with his mouth open long after his little angel had flounced out of the room.

Now, Abigail asked the question that had been on her mind all night. "Paul, tell me. Did you do something...did you make some-body..." Abigail tried to get her thoughts together. Everything was rushing in on her. "Paul, did you piss somebody off? Is that why she was taken?"

He looked as if she had spat on him. "Of course not," he whispered, his voice raspy. "Do you think I would keep that from you? Do you think I'd be sitting on my hands like this if I knew who had taken our baby?"

She felt awful, but deep down she also felt some kind of vindication that she had hurt him so easily.

"That woman I was with...I shouldn't have done it, Abby. I don't know why I did. She didn't mean anything, babe. I just... needed."

He didn't say what he needed. They both knew the answer to that: he needed everything.

She asked, "Tell me the truth. Where's Dad?"

"He's talking to some people."

"We've got half the police department in the house and the rest of them a phone call away. Who's he talking to?"

"Private security. They've handled things for him before."

"Does he know who did this? Is there someone who's trying to get back at him for something?"

Paul shook his head. "I don't know, babe. Your dad doesn't exactly confide in me. I think he's right not to leave this to the GBI."

"That one cop seemed like he knew what he was doing."

"Yeah, well, I wouldn't trust that freak cocksucker as far as I could throw him."

His words were so sharp that she didn't know how to respond.

"I should've never said that to you about the car," he whispered. "It had nothing to do with the car. She just...She didn't listen. You were right. I should've been tougher on her. I should have been her father instead of her friend."

How long had she waited for him to see this? And now, it meant nothing. "It doesn't matter."

"I want her back so bad, Abby. I want another chance to do everything right." His shoulders shook as he cried. "You and Emma are my world. I've built my whole life around both of you. I don't think I could live with myself if something...if something happened."

Abigail sat up, cupping her hands around his face. He leaned into her and she kissed his neck, his cheek, his lips. When he gently pushed her back onto the bed, she didn't protest. There was no passion, no desire except for release. This was simply the only way they had left to console each other.

CHAPTER SIX

AT SIX FORTY-FIVE in the morning, Will parked his car in the teachers' parking lot of Westfield Academy. Rent-a-cops stood sentry in front of the buildings, their short-sleeved uniforms and matching shorts pressed into sharp creases. Well-marked security cars rolled through the campus. Will was glad to find the school on high alert. He knew that Amanda had requested the DeKalb County police send cruisers out to the area every two hours, but he also knew that DeKalb was overburdened and understaffed. The private security team would take up the gap. At the very least, they might help quell some of the sense of panic that was building—which was sure to get worse, judging by the news vans and cameramen setting up across the street.

Will had turned off the television this morning because he couldn't take the hype. The press had even less to go on than the police, but the talking heads were analyzing every scrap of rumor and innuendo they could find. There were "secret sources" and conspiracy theories galore. Girls from the school had been on the national morning shows, their teary-eyed pleas for their dear friend's return somewhat undercut by their perfectly coiffed hair and expertly applied makeup. It took the focus off Emma Campano and put it squarely on the melodrama.

This time yesterday morning, Kayla and Emma had probably been getting ready for school. Maybe Adam Humphrey had slept in because he had a later class. Abigail Campano had been getting ready for her day of tennis and spa treatments. Paul had been on his way to work. None of them had known how little time they had left before their lives were forever changed or—worse—stolen.

Will could still remember the first case he had worked that involved a child. The girl was ten. She had been taken from her home in the middle of the night in a fake abduction staged by her father. The man had used his daughter to his satisfaction, snapped her neck and tossed her down a ravine in the woods behind the family's church. It takes only a few minutes for flies to find a corpse. They start laying their eggs immediately. Twenty-four hours later, the larvae hatch and begin to devour the organs and tissue. The body bloats. The skin turns waxen, almost incandescently blue. The smell is like rotten eggs and battery acid.

This was the state in which Will had found her.

He prayed to God this was not how he would find Emma Campano.

There was laughter from a few teachers as they made their way up the stairs to the main school building. He watched them go through the doors, smiles still on their faces. Will hated schools the way some people hated prison. That was really how Will had thought of school when he was a child: some kind of prison where the wardens could do whatever they liked. Other kids who had parents at least had some kind of buffer, but Will only had the state to look after him, and it wasn't exactly in the state's interest to go after a city's school system.

Will would be the one questioning the teachers today, and he broke out into a cold sweat every time he thought about it. These were educated people—and not educated at the crap correspondence schools where Will had gotten his dubious degrees. They would probably see right through him. For the first time since this all started, he was glad that Faith Mitchell was going to be with him. At least she would be able to deflect some of the attention, and the fact was that Westfield Academy had one dead student and one missing. Maybe the teachers would be too focused on the tragedy to scrutinize Will. At any rate, there were still a lot of questions that needed to be answered.

Because Westfield only offered high school level courses, all of the students were between the ages of fourteen and eighteen. Leo Donnelly had spent most of yesterday talking to most of the student body and come up with the sort of information you would expect from teenagers who've just found out that one classmate was brutally murdered and one was missing: both Kayla and Emma were well-loved, good girls.

If you could go back a week, however, the story might be different. Will wanted to talk to the teachers and find out what their take was on the two girls. He still wasn't getting a clear image of Emma Campano. You didn't turn into a school-skipper overnight. There were generally smaller transgressions that led to bigger ones. No one liked to speak ill of the dead, but in Will's experience, teachers didn't walk on eggshells when there was something that needed to be said.

Will glanced out the window, looking at the buildings. The private school was impressive, the sort of local school with a national reputation that Atlanta was known for. Before the Civil War, only the wealthiest Atlantans could afford to educate their offspring, and most of them sent their children to Europe for the luxury of a well-rounded education. After the war, the money dried up but the desire to educate was still there. Recently impoverished debutantes realized that they actually had marketable skills and started opening up private schools along Ponce de Leon Avenue. People may have bartered tuition with family silver and priceless heirlooms, but pretty soon the classrooms were full. Even after the Atlanta Public School System was established in 1872, wealthy Atlantans preferred to keep their children away from the riffraff.

The Westfield Academy was one of those private schools. It was currently housed in a series of old buildings that dated back to the early 1900s. The original schoolhouse was a clapboard-style structure that resembled a barn more than anything else. Most of the later buildings were red brick and looming. The centerpiece was a marble-sided gothic cathedral that looked as out of place as Will's 1979 Porsche 911 did among the late-model Toyotas and Hondas in the teachers' parking lot.

Will was used to the car standing out. Nine years ago, he had spotted the burned-out shell of the 911 in an abandoned lot on his street. This was back when most of the houses in his neighborhood were of the crack variety and Will had slept with his gun under his pillow in case people knocked on the wrong door. No one had protested when he'd put wheels on the car and rolled it into his garage. He'd even found a homeless man who helped him push it up the hill for ten bucks and a drink from the hose.

By the time the crack houses were torn down and families had started to move in, Will had completely rebuilt the car. On weekends and holidays, he scoured junkyards and body shops looking for the right parts. He taught himself about pistons and cylinders, exhaust manifolds and brake calipers. He learned how to weld and bondo and paint. Without the benefit of anyone's expertise, Will managed to return the car to its original glory. He knew that this was an accomplishment to be proud of, but somewhere in the back of his head, Will couldn't help but think if he'd been able to understand a clutch schematic or an engine diagram, he could have fixed the car in six months instead of six years.

It was the same with the Campano case. Was there something out there—something important—Will couldn't see because he was too stubborn to admit to his own weakness?

Will spread the morning newspaper over the steering wheel, taking another go at the Emma Campano story. Adam Humphrey's and Kayla Alexander's pictures were just below Emma's, all under the headline "ANSLEY PARK TRAGEDY." There was a special pull-out section on the families and the neighborhood along with interviews from people claiming to be close friends. Actual news was sparse, and carefully hidden among the hyperbole. Will had started reading the paper at home, but his head, already aching from lack of sleep, nearly exploded from trying to decipher the tiny print.

Now, Will didn't have a choice in the matter. He had to know what was being said about the case, what details were in the public domain. Routinely, the police held back certain pieces of information that only the killer would know. Because so many Atlanta cops had been on the crime scene, there had been the inevitable leaks. Emma's hiding in the closet. The rope and duct tape in the car. The broken cell phone, crushed under Kayla Alexander's back. Of course, the big story was that the Atlanta Police Department had screwed it all up. The press, an organization known for routinely getting facts wrong, was not so forgiving where the police were concerned.

As Will held his finger under each word, trying to isolate it so he could understand the meaning, he was keenly aware that whoever had taken Emma Campano was probably reading the same story right now. Maybe the killer was getting a charge out of having his crimes on the front page of the *Atlanta Journal*. Maybe he was sweating over each word as much as Will, trying to see if there were any clues he had left behind.

Or maybe the man was so arrogant that he knew there was no way to link him to the crimes. Maybe he was out right now, trolling for his next victim even as Emma Campano's body rotted in a shallow grave.

There was a tap on the glass. Faith Mitchell was standing on the passenger's side of the car. She had his jacket in one hand and a cup of coffee in the other. Will reached over and unlocked the door for her.

"Can you believe that?" She angrily indicated the newspaper.

"What?" he asked, folding up the paper. "I just started reading it."

She shut the car door to keep in the air-conditioning. "A 'highly placed Atlanta police officer' is quoted as saying that we botched the investigation and the GBI had to be called in." She seemed to realize who she was talking to and said, "I know we fucked up, but you don't talk about that sort of thing to the press. It doesn't exactly engender respect from the taxpayers."

"No," he agreed, though he thought it was curious she believed the source was from the APD. Will had actually made it that far into the story and assumed that the source was in the GBI and went by the name of Amanda Wagner.

"It would have been nice if they'd left out how wealthy the parents are, but I suppose you could figure that out from the name. Those car commercials are the most annoying thing on TV right now." She stared at him as if she was waiting for him to say something.

He said, "Yeah, they're pretty annoying. The commercials."

"Whatever." She held up his jacket. "You left this on my car."

He found his digital recorder, relieved to have it back. "These are great," he told Faith, knowing she had probably found it curious. "You wouldn't believe how bad my handwriting is."

She just stared at him again, and he felt the hair on the back of his neck stand up as he tucked the recorder into his pocket. Had she figured it out? If she listened to the recorder, all she would hear was Will's voice cataloguing information about the case so he could later dictate it into his computer and generate a report. Angie had said to watch out for Faith Mitchell. Had he already given himself away?

Faith's lips pressed together in a tight line. "I need to ask you something. You don't have to answer it, but I wish you would."

Will stared straight ahead. He could see teachers going into the main building with large thermoses of coffee and stacks of papers in their hands. "Sure."

"Do you think she's dead?"

His mouth opened, but more from relief than anything else. "Honestly, I don't know." He took his time putting his jacket on the backseat with the newspaper, trying to get some of his composure back. "I take it you didn't find anything earth-shattering last night in the dorm?" He had told her to call him if there were any leads.

She hesitated, as if she had to switch gears, then answered, "Not really. Nothing of interest in Adam's things except the pot, which I think we can agree is not very interesting?" Will nodded, and she continued, "We talked to every student in both halls. No one really knew Adam except for Gabe Cohen and Tommy Albertson, and considering the positive impression I made on both of them, they were reluctant to give any more information. I sent Ivan Sambor to talk to them—you know who he is?" Will shook his head. "Big Polish guy, doesn't take shit from anybody. Frankly, he scares the bejeezus out of me. He got the same story I got: they barely knew Adam, Gabe was crashing at his place because Tommy is an asshole. Even Tommy agreed with this, by the way."

She took out her spiral-bound notebook and flipped through the pages. "Most of the freshmen in Adam's dorm are in the same classes, but we can always go to each class and look for new faces. I reached all of his teachers but one, and all of them said the same thing: first week of class/nobody knows anybody/sorry he's dead/I don't even remember what he looks like. The one I couldn't get in touch with—Jerry Favre—is supposed to call me back today."

She flipped to another page. "Nuts and bolts: The security camera shows Adam leaving the dorm around seven forty-five yesterday morning. He's got an eight-o'clock class; the teacher verified he was there. Adam gave some kind of report the whole period, so there was no sneaking out. The card reader, which doesn't mean jack, by the way—you're not the only genius who figured out the handicap door trick—has him returning to the dorm at ten-eighteen a.m., which jibes with his class ending at ten. We have what's probably the back of his head on the camera. He changed clothes, then left again at exactly ten thirty-two. That's the last we have of him, unless you're holding something back."

Will felt surprise register on his face. "What would I hold back?"

"I don't know, Will. The last time I saw you, you were rushing to the copy center to go over Kayla Alexander's Prius. That's a pretty key piece of evidence, but we've been talking for almost ten minutes about everything but the weather and you haven't told me one damn thing."

"I'm sorry," Will answered, knowing that wasn't much of a

consolation. "You're right. I should have told you. I'm not used to—"

"Working with a partner," she finished, her tone telling him that the excuse was getting old.

He could not blame her for being annoyed. She was working just as hard on this case as he was, and leaving her out was unfair. In as much detail as he could muster, Will told her about the Copy Right's security camera footage, the rope and duct tape Charlie had found. "According to the video, the dark car showed up at the parking garage at exactly eleven-fifteen yesterday morning. Two passengers got out—Adam and a stranger. Kayla Alexander's Prius drove up at twelve twenty-one. We can assume Emma was taken out of the trunk and transferred to the dark car. He was gone a little over a minute later." He summed up, "So, the last time we know Adam's whereabouts is eleven-fifteen a.m. in the parking deck of the Copy Right building."

Faith had been writing the times down in her notebook, but she stopped on this last point, looking up at Will. "Why there?"

"It's cheap, it's convenient to the house. There's no full-time attendant."

Faith provided, "The nosey neighbor told on them last year when they parked in the driveway. Using the garage was a good way to get around her."

"That was my guess," Will agreed. "We're doing background checks on all the Copy Right employees. The two girls came in for the evening shift while we were there—Frieda and Sandy. They really don't go into the garage. It's dark and they don't think it's particularly safe, which is probably true, especially considering the lack of any real security."

"What about the construction workers?"

"Amanda is going to spend today tracking them down. It's not just a matter of calling up the city and asking them for a list. Apparently, the workers just show up in the morning and they're told which fire to put out first. There are all kinds of subcontractors who use subcontractors, and before you know it, you've got day laborers and undocumented workers...it's a mess."

"Has anyone seen the car there before?"

"The parking deck is in the back of the building. Unless the Copy Right people happen to be looking at the security camera, they have no idea who's coming and going, and of course the tape is reused, so we don't have old footage to compare." He turned to face her. "I want to talk about our suspect. I think we need to get a clearer picture in our heads about who he is."

"You mean like a profile? A loner between the ages of twenty-five and thirty-five who lives with his mother?"

Will allowed a smile. "This was well coordinated. He brought the knife, the rope, the duct tape to the house. Someone let him in."

"So, you think this was really a kidnapping and Kayla and Adam got in the way?"

"It feels more personal than that," Will said. "I know I'm contradicting myself, but the scene was sloppy. Whoever killed Kayla wasn't in control. He felt real fury toward her."

"Maybe she said the wrong thing and it got out of hand."

"You have to have a conversation with someone to say the wrong thing."

"What about the second person on the Copy Right tape? Do you think that's the killer? It would make more sense if one of our victims knew him."

"Maybe," Will allowed, but that didn't feel quite right. "Adam left the dorm at ten thirty-two a.m. Somewhere between ten thirty-two and eleven-fifteen, he picked up both a car and a passenger. We've got a gap in the timeline where he's unaccounted for. That's..." Will tried to wrap his brain around the math, but he was too tired and his head was hurting so badly that his stomach ached. "I need more coffee. How many minutes is that?"

"Forty-five," Faith supplied. "We need to know where and how he got the car. No one we spoke with in the dorms last night either let Adam borrow a car or knows where he got access to one. I guess we could look at the security card reader again, cross-reference it with the times Adam was in the dorm?"

"It's something to consider." He nodded at her notebook.

"Let's come up with some questions. Number one, where is Adam's student ID?"

She started writing. "He might've left it in the car."

"What if the killer took it as a souvenir?"

"Or to use it to get into the dorm," she countered. "We need to alert campus security to cancel his card."

"See if there's a way they can leave it active but flag it somehow so we know if someone tries to use it."

"Good point." She kept writing. "Question number two, where did he get the car?"

"Campus is the obvious answer. Check to see if there were any stolen cars. Does Gabe Cohen or Tommy Albertson have a car?"

"Freshmen can't really park on campus, and it's impossible to find a safe place in the city to park, so if they have a vehicle, they tend to leave it at home. That being said, Gabe has a black VW with yellow stripes that his father drives. Albertson has a green Mazda Miata that he left back in Connecticut."

"Neither one of those fits the car on the video."

She stopped writing. "Adam could have a car we don't know about."

"He'd be keeping it from his parents, too. They said he didn't have one." Will thought about something Leo Donnelly had said yesterday. "Maybe he went off campus to get a car. Public transportation is in and out of there all day. Let's put a team on tracking down security cameras from buses. What's the nearest MARTA station?" he asked, referring to the city's bus and train system.

Faith closed her eyes, obviously thinking. "Midtown Station," she finally remembered.

Will stared out the window at the school parking lot. More faculty had shown up, and a few students were straggling in. "It'd take about twenty minutes to drive *here*, though. Then another twenty, twenty-five minutes to the parking garage."

"There's our forty-five minutes. Adam drove here to pick up Emma, then took her to the parking garage."

"The arm in the videotape," he said. "It was pretty small. I suppose it could have been a girl's hand that reached out and caught the keys."

"I've been assuming that Kayla drove Emma from school to the house in her Prius, and that Adam somehow met them there."

"Me, too," Will admitted. "Do you think it's possible Adam drove Emma to the garage, and then they both walked to the house?"

"The killer could've walked from Tech."

"He knew Adam's car was in the garage." Will turned to Faith. "If he knew he was going to take Emma Campano from the scene, he would have to have a place to keep her. Somewhere quiet and isolated—not in the city because the neighbors would hear. Not a dorm room."

"If he didn't dump the body."

"Why take her just to dump her?" Will asked, and the question was one that gave him pause. This was why he had wanted to talk through a profile of the suspect. "The killer came to the house with gloves, rope, tape and a knife. He had a plan. He went there to subdue someone. He left Adam's and Kayla's bodies at the house. If the goal was to kill Emma, he would have killed her there. If the goal was to abduct her, to take her away so that he could spend more time with her, then he accomplished his goal."

"And APD gave him plenty of time to do it," Faith added ruefully.

Will felt a sense of urgency building up at the thought. Less than twenty-four hours had passed since the girl had been taken. If her abductor had removed her from the scene so that he could take his time with her, then maybe Emma Campano was still alive. The question was, how much longer did she have?

He checked his cell phone, noting the time. "I've got to be at the Campanos at nine."

"Do you think they know something?"

"No," he admitted. "But I'm going to have to ask Paul for a DNA sample."

Faith's uneasy expression probably mimicked his own, but

Amanda had told him to do it and Will really didn't have a choice.

He said, "Let's talk to the teachers, get a general sense of the girls. If they think there's anyone else in particular we need to talk to—a student or janitor—I'll leave you to do that. If nothing turns up, then I want you to go sit in on the autopsies. Adam Humphrey's parents will be in later this evening. We need to have some answers for them."

Her expression changed, and Will thought he was getting to know her well enough to see when Faith Mitchell was upset about something. He knew that her son was the same age as Adam Humphrey. Watching the eighteen-year-old being dissected would be horrible for anyone, but a parent would bring a special kind of pain to the experience.

He tried to be gentle, asking, "Do you think you can handle it?"

She riled, taking his question the wrong way. "You know, I got up this morning and I told myself that I was going to work with you and keep up a good attitude, and then you have the nerve to question me—a detective on the God damn homicide squad who steps over dead bodies almost every day of her life—about whether or not I can handle one of the basic requirements of my job." She put her hand on the door latch. "And while we're at it, asshole, where the hell do you get off driving a Porsche and investigating my mother for stealing?"

"I just—"

"Let's just do our jobs, okay?" She threw open the door. "You think you can do me that professional courtesy?"

"Yes, of course, but—" She turned to face him, and Will felt his mouth moving but there were no words coming out. "I apologize," he finally said, not knowing exactly what he was apologizing for, but knowing it couldn't possibly make things worse.

She exhaled slowly, staring at the coffee cup in her hand, obviously trying to decide how to respond.

Will said, "Please don't throw hot coffee at me."

She looked up at him, incredulous, but his request had worked to break the tension. Will took the time to give himself some credit. This wasn't the first time he'd had to extricate himself from a tenuous situation with an angry woman.

Faith shook her head. "You are the strangest man I have ever met in my life."

She got out before he could respond. Will took it as a positive sign that she didn't slam the door.

CHAPTER SEVEN

THE HEAT OUTSIDE was so intense that Faith couldn't finish her coffee. She dropped the cup in the waste can before heading toward the administration building. She had spent more time in schools over the past two days than she had her entire junior year.

"Ma'am," one of the hired security men said, tipping his hat to her.

Faith nodded, feeling sorry for the man. She could still remember what it felt like to wear her full uniform in the Atlanta heat. It was like rolling yourself in honey and then walking into a kiln. Because this was a school zone, no weapons were allowed on campus unless they had a police badge accompanying them. Despite the baton on one side of the man's belt and a can of Mace on the other, he looked about as harmless as a flea. Fortunately, only a cop would notice these things. The rentals were here to give the parents and kids a feeling of safety. In a crazy, mixed-up world where rich white girls could be killed or kidnapped, the show of force was pretty much expected.

At the very least, they were giving something for the press to focus on. Across the street, Faith spotted three photographers adjusting their lenses, going in for the kill. The news had gotten hold of the name of the school sometime last night. Faith hoped the rental cops were capable of forcefully reminding the reporters that the school was on private property.

Faith pressed the buzzer beside the door, looking up at the camera mounted on the wall. The speaker sputtered to life, and an irritated woman's voice said, "Yes?"

"I'm Faith Mitchell with the—"

"First left, down the hallway."

The door buzzed and Faith opened it. There was an awkward shuffling where Will made it clear he wasn't going to let her hold the door for him. Faith finally went in. They stood at the top of a long hallway with branches off to the left and right. Closed doors were probably schoolrooms. She looked up, counting six more security cameras. The place certainly had its bases covered, but the principal had told Leo yesterday there was a gap in coverage behind one of the main classroom buildings. Yesterday morning, Kayla and Emma had apparently taken advantage of it to their own cost.

Will cleared his throat, looking around nervously. Except for the fact that he was wearing yet another three-piece suit in the middle of summer, he had the worried look of an errant student hoping to avoid a trip to the principal's office.

He asked, "Which way did she say?" Even without the woman telling them where to go two seconds ago, he was standing beside a large sign that directed visitors to go to the front office down the hallway.

Faith crossed her arms, recognizing this as a very lame attempt to make her feel useful. "It's all right," she said. "You're a good cop, Will, but you have the social skills of a feral monkey."

He frowned over the description. "Well, I suppose that's fair."

Faith really wasn't the type of person who rolled her eyes, but she felt a pulling at her optic nerve that she hadn't experienced since puberty. "This way," she said, heading down a side hallway. She found the front office behind several stacked cardboard boxes. As a parent, Faith instantly recognized the chocolate bars that schools pawned off onto helpless children and their parents every year. Taking advantage of forced child labor, the administration would send out the kids to sell candy in hopes of raising money for various school improvements. Faith had eaten so many of the bars when Jeremy was growing up that her stomach trembled at the sight of them.

A bank of video monitors showing various scenes around the school was behind the woman at the front desk, but her attention was on the phone system, which was ringing off the hook. She took in Faith and Will with a practiced glance, asking three different callers to please hold before finally directing her words toward Faith. "Mr. Bernard is running late, but everyone else is in the conference room. Back out the door to your left."

Will opened the door and Faith led him down the hallway to the appropriately marked door. She knocked twice, and someone called, "Enter."

Faith had been to her share of parent-teacher conferences, so she shouldn't have been surprised to find all ten of them seated in a half-circle with two empty chairs at the center waiting to be filled. As was befitting a progressive school specializing in the communicative arts, the teachers were a multicultural bunch representing just about every part of the rainbow: Chinese-American, African-American, Muslim-American, and—just to mix things up—Native American. There was one lone Caucasian in the bunch. With her hemp sandals, batik dress and the long, gray ponytail hanging down her back, she radiated white guilt like a cheap space heater.

She held out her hand, offering, "I'm Dr. Olivia McFaden, principal of Westfield."

"Detective Faith Mitchell, Special Agent Will Trent," Faith provided, taking a seat. Will hesitated, and for a moment she thought he looked nervous. Maybe he was having a bad student flashback, or perhaps the tension in the room was getting to him. The security guards outside were meant to make people feel safe, but Faith got the distinct impression that they were doing the exact opposite. Everyone seemed to be on edge, especially the principal.

Still, McFaden went around the room, introducing the teachers, the subjects they taught and which girl was in their classes. As Westfield was a small school, there was a considerable overlap;

most teachers were familiar with both girls. Faith carefully recorded their names in her notebook, easily recognizing the cast of characters: the hip one, the nerdy one, the gay one, the one hanging on by her fingernails as she prayed for retirement.

"Understandably, we're all extremely upset about this tragedy," McFaden said. Faith didn't know why she took such an instant dislike to the woman. Maybe she was having some bad school flashbacks herself. Or maybe it was because of all the faculty in the room, McFaden was the only one who hadn't obviously been crying. Some of the women and one of the men actually had tissues in their hands.

Faith told the teachers, "I'll convey your sympathies to the parents."

Will answered the obvious question. "We can't entirely rule out a connection between what happened yesterday and the school. There's no need to be overly alarmed, but it's a good idea for you all to take precautions. Be alert to your surroundings, make sure you know where students are at all times, report any unexplained absences."

Faith wondered if he could have phrased that any differently to freak them out even more. Glancing around the room, she thought not. Faith stopped, going through the teachers' faces again. She remembered what the front-office secretary had said. "Is someone missing?"

McFaden supplied, "That would be Mr. Bernard. He had a previously scheduled meeting with a parent that couldn't be moved on such short notice. He'll be here shortly." She glanced at her watch. "I'm afraid we're a bit tight for time before the assembly starts."

"Assembly?" Faith gave Will a sharp glance.

He had the sense to look ashamed. "Amanda wants one of us to attend the assembly."

Faith guessed she knew which one was going to draw that short straw. She shot him a look of utter hatred.

McFaden seemed oblivious. "We thought it would be best to call all of the students together and assure them that their safety is our number one priority." Her smile was of the megawatt variety, the kind meant to encourage a reluctant student to accept a fore-gone conclusion. "We really appreciate your help in this matter."

"I'm happy to help out," Faith told the woman, forcing her own smile. She didn't think an assembly was a bad idea, but she was furious that the task fell to her, not least of all because Faith was terrified of public speaking. She could very well imagine what the assembly would be like: myriad teenage girls in various stages of hysteria demanding that their hands be held, their fears be assuaged, and all the while Faith would be trying to keep the tremble out of her voice. This was something more suited to a school counselor than a homicide detective who had thrown up before her oral comps on her detective's exam.

The principal leaned forward, clasping her hands together. "Now, tell me, how can we be of help to you?"

Faith waited for Will to speak, but he just sat ramrod straight in the chair beside her. She took over, asking, "Could you give us an impression of Emma and Kayla—socially, academically?"

Matthew Levy, the math teacher, took the lead. "I spoke to your colleague about this yesterday, but I suppose I need to say it again. The girls didn't really fit into any one social group. I had both Kayla and Emma in my classroom. They tended to keep to themselves."

Faith asked, "Did they have enemies?"

There was a series of exchanged looks. Levy replied, "They were picked on. I know the first question that comes to mind is how we could be aware of that and still let it continue, but you have to understand the dynamics of the school situation."

Faith let them know that she did. "Kids don't tend to report bullies for fear of reprisal. Teachers can't punish activity they don't see."

Levy shook his head. "It's more than that." He paused, as if to gather his thoughts. "I taught Emma for two years. Her aptitude wasn't math, but she was a good student—really, a lovely girl. She worked hard, she didn't make trouble. She was on the fringe of one of our popular groups. She seemed to get along well with other kids."

One of the Asian women, Daniella Park, added, "Until Kayla showed up."

Faith was startled by the teacher's sharp tone of voice. Park seemed unfazed by the fact that the girl had been savagely murdered. "Why is that?"

Park explained, "We see it all the time. Kayla was a bad influence." Confirming nods rippled around the room. "For a long time, Emma was friends with a girl named Sheila Gill. They were very close, but Sheila's father was transferred to Saudi Arabia at the beginning of term last year. He works for one of those soulless multinational oil companies." She dismissed this with a wave of her hand. "Anyway, Emma didn't have anyone else in her group to turn to. There are some girls who gravitate toward one particular person rather than a group, and without Sheila, she didn't have a group. Emma became more introverted, less likely to participate in class. Her grades didn't slip, they actually improved slightly, but you could tell that she was lonely."

"Enter Kayla Alexander," Levy interjected with the same rueful tone of voice as Park. "Smack in the middle of the school year. She's the type who needs an audience, and she knew precisely who to pick."

"Emma Campano," Faith supplied. "Why did Kayla transfer in during the middle of term?"

McFaden chimed in, "She came to us through another school. Kayla was a challenge, but at Westfield, we meet challenges head-on."

Faith deciphered the code. She directed her next question toward Levy, who seemed to have no problem criticizing the dead girl. "Kayla was kicked out of her last school?"

McFaden tried to keep spinning. "I believe she was asked to leave. Her old school was not equipped to meet her special needs." She straightened her shoulders. "Here at Westfield, we pride ourselves on nurturing the special needs of what society labels more difficult children."

For the second time that day, Faith fought the urge to roll her eyes. Jeremy had been on the cusp of the disorder movement: ADD, ADHD, social disorder, personality disorder. It was getting to be so ridiculous, she was surprised there weren't special schools for the boring, average children. "Can you tell us what she was being treated for?"

"ADHD," McFaden supplied. "Kayla has—had, I'm sorry—a very hard time concentrating on her schoolwork. She was more focused on socializing than studying."

That must have made her stick out like a sore thumb from the rest of the teenagers. "What about Emma?"

Park spoke again, none of the earlier sharpness in her tone. "Emma is a wonderful girl."

More nods came, and she could feel the sadness sweeping through the room. Faith wondered what exactly Kayla Alexander had done that made these teachers choose sides against her.

The door opened, and a man wearing a wrinkled sports jacket and holding an armful of papers came into the room. He looked up at the crowd, seemingly surprised they were all there.

"Mr. Bernard," McFaden began, "let me introduce you to Detectives Mitchell and Trent." She turned to Faith and Will. "This is Evan Bernard, English department."

He nodded, blinking behind his wire-rimmed glasses. Bernard was a nice-looking man, probably in his mid-forties. Faith supposed he could easily fit a stereotype with his scruffy beard and generally disheveled appearance, but something about the wariness in his eyes made her think that there was more to him than that.

Bernard said, "I'm sorry I'm late. I had a parent meeting." He pulled a chair up beside McFaden and sat down, a stack of papers in his lap. "Do you have any news?"

Faith realized that he was the first person to ask the question. "No," she said. "We're following all investigative leads. Anything you could tell us about the two girls will help."

Underneath his beard, he bit his bottom lip, and she could tell that he had seen right through her bullshit as easily as Faith had seen through McFaden's.

Will picked this moment to speak up. He directed his words toward Bernard. "We're doing everything we can to find out who killed Kayla and to bring Emma home safely. I know that doesn't sound like much of a comfort, but please know that this case has the full focus of every member of the Atlanta Police Department and every agent with the Georgia Bureau of Investigation."

Bernard nodded, gripping the papers in his lap. "What can I do to help?"

Will didn't answer. Faith gathered she was to take the lead again. "We were just talking about Kayla Alexander's influence over Emma."

"I can't tell you anything about Kayla. I only had Emma, but not for class. I'm the reading tutor at Westfield."

McFaden provided, "Mr. Bernard does one-on-one sessions with our reading-challenged students. Emma is mildly dyslexic."

"I'm sorry to hear that. Can you tell me—"

"How so?" Will interrupted. He leaned forward, elbows on his knees, to look at Bernard.

Bernard sounded puzzled. "I'm not sure I understand the question."

"I mean..." Will seemed at a loss for words. "I don't quite understand what you mean by mild dyslexia."

" 'Mild' isn't really a term that I would use," Bernard countered. "Generally speaking, it's a reading disorder. As with autism, dyslexia has a full spectrum of symptoms. To classify someone as mild would be to put them at the top level, which is more commonly called high functioning. Most of the kids I see tend to be at either one end or the other. There are various symptomatical iterations, but the key identifier is an inability to read, write or spell at grade level."

Will nodded, and Faith saw him put his hand in his jacket pocket. She heard a click, and had to struggle to keep her expression neutral. She'd seen him transfer the digital recorder to that same pocket in the car. While it was perfectly legal in the state of Georgia for a person to secretly record a conversation, it was highly illegal for a cop to do so.

Will asked Bernard, "Would you characterize Emma as slow or…" He seemed hesitant to use the word. "Retarded?"

Bernard appeared as shocked as Faith felt. "Of course not," the man replied. "As a matter of fact, Emma has an exceptionally high IQ. A lot of dyslexics are incredibly gifted."

"Gifted in what ways?"

He rambled off some examples. "Keen observational skills, highly organized, exceptional memory for details, athletically talented, mechanically inclined. I don't doubt Emma will make a fine architect one day. She has an amazing aptitude with building structures. I've taught here at Westfield for twelve years and never seen anyone quite like her."

Will sounded a little skeptical. "But she still had problems."

"I wouldn't call them problems. Challenges, maybe, but all kids have challenges."

"It's still a disease, though."

"A disorder," he corrected.

Will took a breath, and Faith realized that he was getting irritated with the runaround. Still, he pressed, "So, what are some of the problems associated with the disorder?"

The teacher ticked them off. "Deficiencies in math, reading, spelling and comprehension, immaturity, spatial problems, stuttering, poor motor skills, an inability to grasp rhyming meter…It's a mixed bag, really, and every child is different. You might have a math whiz, or you might have someone who can't perform simple addition; hyper-athletic or a total klutz. Emma was lucky enough to be diagnosed early. Dyslexics are very adept at hiding the disorder. Unfortunately, computers make it much easier for them to fool people. Reading is such a fundamental skill, and they tend to be ashamed when they can't grasp the basics. Most dyslexics don't test well unless it's orally, so they tend to do very poorly at school. I don't think I'm alone in saying that some teachers misconstrue this as laziness or behavioral related." Bernard let his words hang in the air, as if they were directed at a specific teacher in the room. "Adding to the problem is that Emma is extremely shy. She doesn't like attention. She's willing to put up with a lot of bullshit in order to fly under the radar. She's certainly had her moments of immaturity, but mostly, she's just a naturally introverted kid who has to try extra hard to fit in."

Will was leaning so far forward he was practically off his chair. "How did her parents react to this information?"

"I've never met the father, but the mother's very proactive."

"Is there a cure for it?"

"As I said before, dyslexia is not a disease, Mr. Trent. It's a wiring problem in the brain. You would just as soon expect a diabetic to spontaneously produce insulin as you would a dyslexic to wake up and suddenly be able to tell you the difference between left and right and over and under."

Finally, Faith thought she understood where Will was going with his questions. She asked, "So, if someone like Emma was being chased, would she be likely to take the wrong route—go up the stairs instead of down, where she could get away?"

"It doesn't work like that. She would probably be more likely than you or I to intuitively know the best route, but if you asked her, 'How did you get out of there?' she wouldn't be able to tell you, 'I hid under the coffee table, then I took a left down the stairway.' She would simply say, 'I ran away.' The most fascinating thing about this disorder is the mind seems to recognize the deficit and create new thinking pathways that result in coping mechanisms that the typical child would not otherwise consider."

Will cleared his throat. "You said that she would be more observant than a normal person."

"We don't really use the word 'normal' around here," Bernard told him. "But, yes. In Emma's case, I would think that she would have better observational skills." He took it a step farther. "You know, in my experience, dyslexics are far more keyed in than most people. We see this with abused children sometimes, where, as a form of self-defense, they've learned to read mood and nuance better than the typical child. They absorb an incredible amount of blame to keep the peace. They are the ultimate survivors."

Faith took some comfort in his words. A glance around the room told her that she wasn't alone in this feeling.

Will stood up. "I'm sorry," he told the group. "I've got another meeting. Detective Mitchell has a few more questions for you." He reached into his pocket, she assumed to turn off the recorder. "Faith, call me when you get to city hall." He meant the morgue. "I want to sit in with you."

"Okay."

He made his excuses and quickly left. Faith glanced at her watch, wondering where he was going. He didn't have to be at the Campanos for another hour.

Faith looked around the room, all the eyes that were on her. She decided to get it over with. "I'm wondering if there was something specific that happened with Kayla Alexander. There doesn't seem to be a lot of sympathy for her considering what happened."

There were some shrugs. Most of them looked at their hands or the floor. Even Daniella Park didn't have a response.

The principal took over. "As I said, Detective Mitchell, Kayla was a challenge."

Bernard let out a heavy sigh, as if he resented having to be the one to clarify. "Kayla liked to cause trouble."

"In what way?"

"The way girls do," he said, though that was hardly an explanation.

"She picked fights?" Faith guessed.

"She spread rumors," Bernard provided. "She got the other girls into a tizzy. I'm sure you remember what it was like to be that age."

Faith had tried her damndest to forget. Being the only pregnant fourteen-year-old in your school was not exactly a walk in the park.

Bernard's tone turned dismissive. "It wasn't that bad."

Matthew Levy agreed. "These spats are always cyclical. They tear into each other one week, then the next week they're best friends and they hate someone else. You see it all the time."

All the women in the room seemed to think otherwise. Park spoke for them. "It was bad," she said. "I'd say that within a month of enrolling, Kayla Alexander had crossed just about everybody here. She split the school in two."

"Was she popular with the boys?"

"And how," Park said. "She used them like toilet paper."

"Was there anyone in particular?"

There was a series of shrugs and head shaking.

"The list is probably endless," Bernard supplied. "But the boys didn't rile up. They knew what they were getting."

Faith addressed Daniella Park. "Earlier, you made it sound like Emma was her only friend."

Park answered, "Kayla was Emma's friend. Emma was all Kayla had left."

The distinction was an important one. "Why did Emma stick by her?"

"Only Emma knows the answer to that, but I would guess that she understood what it meant to be an outsider. The more things turned against Kayla, the closer they seemed to get."

"You said the school was divided in two. What exactly happened?"

Silence filled the room. No one seemed to want to volunteer the information. Faith was about to ask the question again when Paolo Wolf, an economics teacher who had been quiet until this point, said, "Mary Clark would know more about that."

The silence became more pronounced until Evan Bernard mumbled something under his breath.

Faith asked, "I'm sorry, Mr. Bernard, I didn't catch what you said."

His eyes darted around the room, as if to dare anyone to challenge him. "Mary Clark barely knows the time of day."

"Is Mary a student here?"

McFaden, the principal, explained, "Mrs. Clark is one of our English teachers. She had Kayla in her class last year."

Faith didn't bother to ask why the woman wasn't here. She would find out for herself in person. "Can I speak with her?"

McFaden opened her mouth to respond, but the bell rang. The principal waited until the ringing had stopped. "That's the assembly bell," she told Faith. "We should head over to the auditorium."

"I really need to talk to Mary Clark."

There was just a second of equivocation before McFaden gave a bright smile that would rival the world record for fakeness. "I'd be happy to point her out to you."

◆

FAITH WALKED ACROSS the courtyard behind the main school building, following Olivia McFaden and the other teachers to the auditorium. Oddly, they were all in a single line, as were all the students following their respective teachers to the assembly. The building was the most modern looking of all the structures on the Westfield campus, probably built on the backs of hapless parents shilling candy bars, magazine subscriptions and wrapping paper to unsuspecting neighbors and grandparents.

One line of students in particular was getting a bit too rowdy. McFaden's head swiveled around as if it was on a turret, her gaze pinpointing the loudest culprits. The noise quickly drained like water down a sink.

Faith should not have been surprised by the auditorium, which was really more like what you would find housing a small community theater in a wealthy suburb. Rows of plush velvet red seats led to a large stage with state-of-the-art lighting hanging overhead. The barrel-vaulted ceiling was painted in a very convincing homage to the Sistine Chapel. Intricate bas-relief around the stage depicted the gods in various states of excitement. The carpet underfoot was thick enough to make Faith glance down every few steps for fear of falling.

McFaden gave the tour as she walked, students hushing in her wake. "We built the auditorium in 1995 with an eye toward hosting overflow events during the Olympics."

So, the parents had hustled their candy, then the school had charged the state to rent the auditorium.

"Daphne, no gum," McFaden told one of the girls as she passed. She directed her words back to Faith. "Our art director, Mrs. Meyers, suggested the ceiling motif."

Faith glanced up, mumbling, "Nice."

There was more about the building, but Faith tuned out

McFaden's voice as she walked down the steps toward the stage. There was a certain frisson that overtook the auditorium as it began filling with students. Some were crying, some were simply staring at the stage, a look of expectancy in their eyes. A handful were with their parents, which somehow made the situation even more tense. Faith saw more than one child with a mother's arm around his or her shoulders. She could not help but think about Abigail Campano when she saw them, remember the way the mother had so fiercely fought the man she assumed had killed her daughter. The hair on the back of her neck rose, an ancient genetic response to the sense of collective fear that permeated the room.

Doing a quick count with some multiplication, Faith figured that, including the empty balcony, there were around a thousand seats in the auditorium. The bottom level was almost completely full. Most of the Westfield students were young girls. The majority of them were very thin, very well-heeled and very pretty. They ate organic produce and wore organic cotton and drove their BMWs and Minis to Pilates after school. Their parents weren't stopping at McDonald's on the way home to pick up dinner before they went to do their second job on the night shift. These girls probably lived a life very similar to Emma Campano's: shiny iPhones, new cars, beach vacations and big-screen televisions.

Faith caught herself, knowing that the small part of her who had lost so many things when Jeremy came along was acting up. It wasn't these girls' fault that they had been born into wealthy families. They certainly didn't force their parents to buy them things. They were very lucky, and from the looks of them, very frightened. One of their schoolmates had been brutally murdered—more brutally than perhaps any of them would ever know. Another classmate was missing, probably being sadistically used by a monster. Between *CSI* and Thomas Harris, these kids could probably guess what was happening to Emma Campano.

The closer Faith got to the stage, the more she could hear crying. There was nothing more emotional than a teenage girl. Whereas ten minutes ago, she had felt something akin to disdain for them, now Faith could only feel pity.

McFaden took Faith by the arm. "That's Mrs. Clark," she said, pointing to a woman leaning against the far wall. Most of the teachers were standing in the aisle, diligently reprimanding students, keeping the peace in the large crowd, but Mary Clark seemed to be in her own little world. She was young, probably not long out of college, and bordering on beautiful. Her strawberry blond hair hung to her shoulders and freckles dotted her nose. Incongruously, she was dressed in a conservative black jacket, pressed white shirt and matching skirt that hit just below the knee—an outfit much more suitable for a matronly older woman.

McFaden said, "If you could just say a few words to the students?"

Faith felt a surge of panic. She told herself that she was only speaking to a room full of kids, that it didn't matter if she made an ass of herself, but her hands were still shaking by the time they reached the front of the auditorium. The room was efficiently chilled by the air-conditioning, but Faith found herself sweating.

McFaden climbed the steps to the stage. Faith followed her, feeling the same age as the kids she was supposed to be assuring. While McFaden went straight to the podium, Faith stayed in the wings, desperate for any excuse not to have to do this. The lights were bright, so much so that Faith could only see the students sitting in the front row. Their uniforms were probably custom tailored—schoolgirl skirts and matching starched white tops. The boys had fared better with dark pants and white shirts with blue striped ties. It must have been an uphill battle every day to make them tuck in their shirts and keep their ties straightened.

There were six chairs behind the podium. Four of the chairs were filled with teachers, the last with a large hairy man wearing spandex shorts and clutching a wrinkled piece of paper in his obviously sweaty hand. His gut rolled over the waist of his shorts and sitting made it hard for him to breathe; his mouth was open, his lips moving like a fish. Faith studied him, trying to figure out what he was doing, and realized that he was going over the lines from a script in his beefy hand. Faith guessed by the whistle around his neck that he was head coach for the physical education department.

Beside him was Evan Bernard, sitting in the last chair on the left. Daniella Park was in the last chair on the opposite end. Faith noted the distance between the two teachers and guessed from the way they were studiously avoiding each other's gaze that there was some tension between them. She glanced out at Mary Clark, who was still standing in the aisle, and guessed that might be the reason.

McFaden was checking the mic. Hushes went around the room, then the usual feedback through the sound system and the predictable murmur through the crowd. The principal waited for the noise to die down. "We are all aware of the tragedy that struck two of our students and one of their friends yesterday. This is a trying time for all of us, but as a whole, we can—we will—overcome this tragedy and make something good of it. Our shared sense of community, our love for our fellow students, our respect for life and the common good, will help all of us at Westfield persevere." There was a scattering of applause, mostly from the parents. She turned to Faith. "A detective from the Atlanta Police Department is here to take some of your questions. I would remind students to please be respectful to our guest."

McFaden sat down, and Faith felt every eye in the room scrutinize her as she walked across the stage. The podium seemed to get farther away with each step, and by the time she reached it, her hands were sweaty enough to leave marks on the polished wood.

"Thank you," Faith said, her voice sounding thin and girlish as it echoed through the speakers. "I'm Detective Faith Mitchell. I want to assure you that the police are doing everything they can to find Emma, to find out who committed these crimes." She threw in "And the Georgia Bureau of Investigation" too late, realizing that her sentence did not make much sense. She tried again. "As I said, I'm a detective with the Atlanta Police Department. Your principal has my direct phone number. If any of you saw anything, heard anything or have any information that might help the case, then please contact me." Faith realized her lungs were out of air. She tried to take a breath without making it obvious. Briefly, she wondered if this was what it felt like to have a heart attack.

"Ma'am?" someone called.

Faith shielded her eyes against the bright stage lights. She saw that several hands were up. She pointed to the closest girl, concentrating all of her attention on the one person instead of the crowd of onlookers. "Yes?"

The student stood, and then Faith noticed her long blond hair and creamy white skin. The question came to Faith's mind before the girl got it out. "Do you think we should cut our hair?"

Faith swallowed, trying to think of the best way to answer. There were all kinds of urban legends about women with long hair being more likely to be targeted by rapists, but as far as Faith's practical experience had shown, the men who committed these crimes only cared about one thing on a woman's body, and it was not whether or not she had short or long hair. On the other hand, Kayla and Emma looked so much alike that it could certainly point to a trend.

Faith skirted the question. "You don't need to cut your hair, you don't need to change your appearance."

"How about—" someone began, then stopped, remembering protocol and raising her hand.

"Yes?" Faith asked.

The girl stood. She was tall and pretty, her dark hair hanging around her shoulders. There was a slight tremble to her voice when she asked, "Emma and Kayla were both blond. I mean, doesn't that mean that the guy has an MO?"

Faith felt caught out by the question. She thought about Jeremy and the way that he could always tell when she was not being honest with him. "I'm not going to lie to you," she told the girl, then looked up at the group as a whole, her stage fright dissipating, her voice feeling stronger. "Yes, both Emma and Kayla had long blond hair. If it makes you feel more comfortable to wear your hair up for a while, then do it. Don't let yourself believe, though, that this means you are perfectly safe. You still need to take precautions when you're out. You need to make sure your parents know where you are at all times." There were whispers of protest. Faith held up her hands, feeling like a preacher. "I know that sounds trite, but you guys aren't living in the suburbs. You know the basic rules of safety. Don't talk to strangers. Don't go to unfamiliar places alone. Don't go off on your own without letting someone—anyone—know where you are going and when you will be back."

That seemed to mollify them. Most of the hands went down. Faith called on a boy sitting with his mother.

He spoke timidly. "Is there anything we can do for Emma?"

The room went completely silent. The fear started to creep back in. "As I said..." She had to stop to clear her throat. "As I said before, any information you can think of that might help us would be appreciated. Suspicious characters around school. Unusual things Emma or Kayla might have said—or even usual things, something that maybe you are now thinking might be connected to what happened to them. All of that, no matter how trivial it may seem, is very valuable to us." She cleared her throat, wishing she had some water. "As for anything you can personally do, I would ask again that you remember safety. Make sure that your parents know where you are at all times. Make sure that you take basic precautions. The fact is, we have no idea how this connects to your school, or even if it connects at all. I think vigilance is the key word here." She felt slightly idiotic saying the words, thinking she sounded like a bad rip-off of Olivia McFaden, but the nods from both parents and students in the audience made Faith think that she had actually done some good here.

She scanned the crowd. No more hands were up that she could see. With a nod toward the principal, Faith walked back across the stage and took her place in the wings.

"Thank you, Detective Mitchell." McFaden was back at the podium. She told the students, "In a few minutes, Coach Bob is going to do a ten-minute presentation, followed by an instructional film on personal safety."

Faith suppressed a groan, only to hear it echo around the auditorium.

McFaden continued, "After Coach Bob, Dr. Madison, who is, as you know, our school counselor, will have some remarks to make about dealing with tragedy. He will also be taking questions, so please remember, any questions you have should be saved up until Dr. Madison is finished speaking. Now, if we could all just take a moment to quietly reflect on our fellow students—those among us and those who are gone." She waited a few seconds, then, when no one reacted, she said, "Bow your heads, please."

Faith had never been a fan of the moment of silence, especially when it required head bowing. She liked it almost as much as public speaking, which took a close second to eating live cockroaches.

Faith scanned the crowd, looking past the bowed heads to Mary Clark, who was staring blankly at the stage. As quietly as possible, Faith made her way down the stage stairs. She could almost feel Olivia McFaden's disapproval as she sneaked down the side aisle, but Faith wasn't one of the woman's students and, frankly, she had more important things to do than stand in the wings listening to Coach Bob drill students about their safety for the next ten minutes.

Mary Clark stood straighter as she realized Faith was heading her way. If the teacher was surprised to find herself singled out, she didn't show it. As a matter of fact, she seemed relieved when Faith nodded toward the door.

Mary didn't stop in the hallway, but pushed on through the exit before Faith could stop her. She went outside and stood on the concrete pad, hands on her hips as she took deep breaths of fresh air.

She told Faith, "I saw McFaden pointing me out before you started and I was sure she was telling you that she was going to fire me."

Faith thought this was a strange way to open up a conversation, but it seemed like the sort of inappropriate remark she was capable of making herself. "Why would she fire you?"

"My class is too noisy. I'm not strict enough. I don't adhere to the curriculum." Mary Clark gave a forced laugh. "We have very different educational philosophies."

"I need to talk to you about Kayla Alexander."

She looked over her shoulder. "Not Emma?" Her face fell. "Oh, no. Is she—"

"No," Faith assured her. "We haven't found her yet."

Her hands covered her mouth. "I thought..." She wiped away her tears. They both knew what she had thought, and Faith felt like an ass for not being more clear to begin with.

She said, "I'm sorry."

Mary pulled a tissue out of her jacket pocket and blew her nose. "God, I thought I was finished crying."

"Did you know Emma?"

"Not really, but she's a student here. They all feel like they're your responsibility." She blew her nose. "You were terrified up there, weren't you?"

"Yes," Faith admitted, because lying about something so simple would make it harder to lie about bigger things later on. "I hate public speaking."

"I do, too." Mary amended, "Well, not in front of kids—they don't really matter—but in faculty meetings, parent-teacher conferences..." She shook her head. "God, what does any of that matter to you, right? Why don't I say something about the weather?"

Faith leaned against the steel door but thought better of it when her flesh started to blister. "Why weren't you in the meeting this morning?"

She tucked the tissue back into her pocket. "My opinion isn't exactly valued around here."

Teaching was a profession famous for producing burnout. Faith could well imagine the old guard did not appreciate an idealistic young kid coming in to change the world.

Mary Clark said as much. "They all think it's just a matter of time before I run screaming out the door."

"You had Kayla Alexander in your class last year."

The younger woman turned around, arms crossed over her chest, and studied Faith. There was something hostile about the stance.

Faith asked, "Can you tell me what happened?"

Mary was dubious. "They didn't tell you?"

"No."

She gave another laugh. "Typical."

Faith was silent, giving the other woman space.

Mary asked, "Did they tell you that last year, Kayla was so mean to one of the other girls that she ended up leaving school?"

"No."

"Ruth Donner. She transferred to Marist in the middle of last year."

"Daniella Park said that Kayla split the school in two."

"That's a fair statement. There was the Kayla camp and the Ruth camp. It took a while, but pretty soon more and more people went over to Ruth's side. Transferring out was the smartest thing she did, really. It put Kayla center stage, and suddenly, the cracks started to show. I think it's fair to say that by the beginning of the school year, Kayla was universally reviled."

"Except for Emma."

"Except for Emma."

"I'm hardly an expert, but don't girls usually outgrow that kind of behavior in middle school?"

"Usually," the teacher confirmed. "But some of them hang on to it. The really mean ones can't stop circling once they smell blood in the water."

Faith thought the shark analogy was a good one. "Where is Ruth Donner now?"

"College, I suppose. She was a senior."

Finding her would certainly be a priority. "Kayla would have been a junior last year. What was she doing going after a senior?"

"Ruth was the most popular girl in school." She shrugged, as if that explained everything. "Of course, there weren't any ramifications for Kayla. She gets away with everything."

Faith tried to tread carefully. There was something else to this story. Mary Clark was giving off the distinct impression that she felt as if she was being asked questions that Faith already knew the answers to. "I understand that what happened with the other girl was horrible, but this feels very personal for you."

Mary's hostility seemed to ratchet up a notch. "I tried to fail Kayla Alexander last year."

Faith could guess what she meant by "tried." Parents paid a lot of money for their kids to go to Westfield. They expected them to excel in their classes, even if their work did not warrant good grades. "What happened?"

"We don't fail children here at Westfield Academy. I had to tutor the little bitch after school."

The characterization was startling considering the circumstances. "I have to admit, Mrs. Clark, that I find it strange you would talk that way about a seventeen-year-old girl who's been raped and murdered."

"Please, call me Mary."

Faith was at a loss for words.

Mary seemed just as nonplussed. "They really didn't tell you what happened?"

Faith shook her head.

"I almost lost my job over her. I have student loans, two babies at home, my husband's trying to start his own business. I'm twenty-eight years old and the only thing I'm qualified to do is teach."

"Hold up," Faith stopped her. "Tell me what happened."

"Kayla showed up for tutoring, but short of me physically taking her hand and writing her papers for her, there was no way she was going to do the work she needed to do to pass the class." Mary's neck showed a slight blush. "We had an argument. I let my anger get the better part of me." She paused, and Faith was expecting the woman to admit to some sort of physical altercation, but what she said was far more shocking. "The next day, Olivia called me into her office. Kayla was there with her parents. She accused me of making a sexual pass at her."

Faith's surprise must have registered on her face.

"Oh, don't be fooled by the schoolmarm before you," Mary said. "I used to dress a lot better than this—like a human being, almost. I dressed too sexy, according to our illustrious principal. I suppose that's her way of saying I asked for it."

"Back up," Faith said. "I don't understand."

"Kayla Alexander said that I told her she would pass my class if she had sex with me." She was smiling, but there was nothing funny about what was coming out of her mouth. "I suppose I should have been flattered. I was three months out from giving birth to twins. I barely fit into any of my clothes and I couldn't afford new ones because teaching is supposed to be its own reward. I started lactating during the meeting. The parents were screaming at me. Olivia just sat there, letting it all play out like her own personal movie." Angry tears streamed down her cheeks. "I've wanted to be a teacher since I was a little girl. I wanted to help people. Nobody does this for the money and it's certainly not for the respect. I tried to get through to her. I *thought* I was getting through to her. And all she did was turn around and stab me in the back."

"Is this what Daniella Park really meant when she said Kayla had split the school?"

"Danni was one of the few teachers on staff who believed me."

"Why wouldn't they believe you?"

"Kayla is extremely good at manipulating people. Men especially."

Faith remembered Evan Bernard, the easy way he had dismissed Mary Clark. "What happened?"

"There was an investigation. Thank God those stupid cameras are everywhere. She had no proof because it didn't happen, and she's not the brightest bulb to begin with. First she said I propositioned her in my room, then she said it was in the parking lot, then it was behind the school. Her story kept changing every day. In the end, it was my word against hers." She gave a tight grin. "I ran into her in the hallway a few days later. Do you know what she said? 'Can't blame a girl for trying.' "

"Why was she allowed to stay in school?"

Mary did a perfect imitation of Olivia McFaden. "Here at Westfield, we pride ourselves on nurturing the special needs of what society labels more difficult children—at fourteen thousand a year, plus athletic fees, student activity fees and uniforms."

Except for the ending, these were the exact same words the principal had used less than an hour ago. "The parents didn't have a problem with that?"

"Kayla's been kicked out of every other school in town. It was Westfield or the Atlanta Public School System. Trust me, I've met the parents. The Alexanders were much more horrified by the prospect of their precious daughter mixing with the great unwashed than they were about sending her to school with a woman who allegedly tried to molest her."

"I'm so sorry."

"Yeah." Her tone had a bitter clip. "Me, too."

"I have to ask you, Mary, do you know of anyone who would want to kill Kayla?"

"Other than me?" she asked, no humor at the question. "My planning period is at the end of the day," she said, referring to her time off to grade papers and prepare lesson plans. "I had a classroom full of kids from eight o'clock on."

"Anyone else?"

She chewed her lip, really thinking about it. "No," she finally said. "I can't think of anyone who would do something so horrible, even to a monster like Kayla Alexander."

CHAPTER EIGHT

WILL SAT OUTSIDE the Campano house, listening to Evan Bernard's tinny voice coming out of the digital recorder. The sound quality was horrible, and Will had to hold the machine against his ear, the volume at the highest level, to make out the man's words.

It's not a disease, Mr. Trent. It's a wiring problem in the brain.

Will wondered if Paul Campano had been told this information. Had he believed it? Or had he done the same thing to his child as he had to Will?

He put the recorder in his pocket as he got out of the car, knowing this line of thinking contributed nothing toward finding Emma Campano. A cop from the day before was standing in the driveway, hands on his hips. He had obviously been doing a good job, because the scrum of reporters waiting for news from the Campano home were cordoned well across the street. They still shouted questions as Will walked past the cop. The man didn't acknowledge Will, and Will returned the courtesy as he went up the drive.

Charlie Reed's van was parked in front of the carriage house. The back doors were open, showing a mini-lab that had been fitted into the shell of the van. Boxes of plastic evidence bags and examine gloves, various tools, medical-grade vacuums and specimen vials were neatly stacked on the ground by the bumper. Charlie was inside, cataloguing each piece of evidence into a laptop before locking it into a cage that was welded to the floor. If this case ever made it to court, the chain of evidence had to be clearly defined or the forensic part of the prosecution would fall to the wayside.

"Hey," Will said, leaning on the open door. "I'm glad you're here. I've got to ask the father for a DNA sample. Can you do the swab?"

"Are you kidding me?" Charlie asked. "He's going to go apeshit."

"Yeah," Will agreed. "Amanda wants it, though."

"It's funny how she has no qualms about putting our necks on the line."

Will shrugged. You couldn't argue with the truth. "You find anything in the house?"

"Actually, yes." Charlie sounded mildly surprised. "I found a fine powder on the floor in the foyer."

"What kind of powder?"

Charlie traced his finger along a set of plastic vials and plucked one out. "Dirt, I'd guess, but it's not our famous red Georgia clay."

Will took the vial and held it between his thumb and forefinger, thinking he could be holding an ounce of cocaine, except that the grainy powder in this case was a dark gray rather than white. "Where did you find it?"

"Some was embedded in the entrance rug, some at the corner of the stairs."

"That's the only two places?"

"Yep."

"Did you check Adam's shoes and the flip-flops upstairs?"

Charlie picked at his mustache, twirling the end. "If you're asking me whether or not I found the powder in an area that wasn't trampled on by you, Amanda and the Atlanta Police Department—no. It was only in those two spots: on the rug and by the stairs."

Will was afraid that was going to be his answer. Even if the powder led them to a suspect, then the defense could always argue that the evidence should be excluded because the police had contaminated the scene. If Charlie or Will were on the witness stand, both men would have to admit to the likelihood that they could have just as easily brought in the evidence on the soles of their own shoes. Juries liked to be told a story. They wanted to know all the steps the police took between finding the evidence and finding a suspect. Being told that a certain man carried into the crime scene a certain substance on his shoes painted a very pretty picture. The prosecution would be hamstrung if they couldn't mention a key piece of evidence pointed them toward the killer.

Of course, none of that would really matter if Emma Campano was found alive. They were coming up on twenty-four hours since the girl had been taken. Each minute that passed made it less likely she would be found.

Will shook the vial, seeing darker specs in the gray powder. "What do you think it is?"

"That's the million-dollar question." He added, "Literally," not needing to remind Will that analyzing the powder would be a costly test. Unlike Hollywood dream labs, it was very rare for a state laboratory to be equipped with all the cutting-edge computers and microscopes that made it so easy for the heroes to solve crimes in under an hour. They had two choices: send the sample to the FBI and pray they could get to it or shell out the money for a private lab to do the analysis.

Will felt the heat catch up with him, sweat rolling down the back of his neck. "How important do you think this is?"

Charlie shrugged. "I just collects 'em, boss."

Will asked, "Do you have another one of these?"

"Yep, one for each location." He pointed to another vial in the tray. "You've got the sample from the rug, so it's more likely to have cross-contamination." Charlie gave him a curious look. "What are you going to do?"

If he hadn't been to Georgia Tech the day before, Will probably wouldn't have even considered it. "Beg somebody to test it for free."

Charlie advised, "This is a hell of a lot more complicated than letting you have that key yesterday. A key either fits a certain lock or doesn't. With the powder, it's all down to one person's interpretation. We have to document everything. I've got a form you can take with you." He rummaged around in the van and pulled out a yellow sheet of paper. "This is a sign-in sheet. You're going to need a witness every step of the way. First, I need you to sign a release saying you've taken the sample." He found another form, attached it to a clipboard, and offered it to Will. "I've got the other sample if you hit on something. We can always run it through a lab to confirm whatever you find."

Will stared at the form, finding the X and the straight line. His signature was the one thing he could manage without having to think about it, but that wasn't the problem. If there was a geological characteristic to the sample that pointed to a specific location, then that might give them an area to search for Emma Campano.

Will tried to keep his tone even, but he felt a tingling at the base of his spine, like he was walking perilously close to the edge of a steep cliff. "The defense could argue that anybody brought in the powder. If we make an arrest off a lab analysis, and the judge says the analysis can't be used, the killer could walk away free."

Charlie lowered the clipboard. "Yes, that's true."

"But, if we just happen to find the girl..."

He returned to his computer, tapping the keys to wake it up.

Will turned around, checking on the cop at the end of the driveway. The man still had his back turned to them, and he was at least twenty feet away, but still, Will lowered his voice when he asked Charlie, "Have you catalogued this yet?"

"Nope." He scanned the bar code on an evidence bag and tapped some more keys.

Will tightened his hand around the vial, which fit neatly into the palm of his hand. He had never been the kind of cop to bend the rules, but if there was a way to find the girl, how could it be right for him to stand idly by?

Charlie said, "Did you see the Toxic Shocks are battling it out with the Dixie Derby Girls this weekend?"

Will had to repeat the words in his head before he understood their meaning. Charlie was a big fan of women's competitive roller derby. "No, I didn't see that."

"It's going to be a real knockout."

Will hesitated. He checked the cop at the end of the driveway again before putting the sample in his pants pocket. "Thanks, Charlie."

"Don't mention it." He turned to face Will. "Okay?"

Will gave a quick nod. "I'll let you know when you can swab the dad."

Charlie gave a sarcastic, "Great. Thanks."

Will tucked his hand into his pocket, wrapping his fingers around the vial as he walked to the carriage house. He was really sweating now, though the temperature wasn't in the unbearable range yet. There had been times in Will's career when he had walked the tightrope between right and wrong, but he had never done something so blatantly illegal—and desperate. Not that it made a bit of difference, but nothing was breaking on this case. They were a day into it, and there were no witnesses, no suspects and nothing to go on but the gray powder that may or may not lead to anything but Will getting fired from his job.

He had actually stolen evidence from a crime scene. Not only that, but he had implicated Charlie in the process. What gave Will the most trouble was the hypocrisy involved. The disapproving cop standing guard in the Campano driveway suddenly had the moral high ground.

"Will." Hamish Patel was sitting at the top of the steps that led to the apartment over the garage. He held a cigarette between his thumb and forefinger.

Will took his hand out of his pocket as he climbed the stairs. "How's it going?"

"All right, I guess. I've got the computer hooked up to the phone line, but nothing's come in. Mostly, they've been getting calls from family and neighbors. The father's been pretty abrupt with them and no one's called this morning."

"And the family?"

"The mother's been in the bedroom pretty much from the get-go. A doctor came in this morning to check on her, but she refused sedation. Hoyt Bentley was here most of the night, but he left around an hour ago. The father left a few times, too, but mostly he just sat at the bottom of the stairs. He got the morning paper from the end of the driveway before I could stop him."

"What about his parents?"

"I think they're dead."

Will rubbed his jaw. He felt an odd sort of loss at the news. At the home, the older a child got, the less likely he was to be adopted. Paul had been twelve when his foster parents had petitioned the court to make it official. They had all waited for him to be returned like an ugly tie or a broken toaster. When Will himself left at eighteen, they were still waiting.

From nowhere, Hamish said, "I have to say, man, that Abigail Campano is one good-looking woman."

The inappropriate observation wasn't altogether a surprise. Hamish was one of those cops who liked to put on a front, as if the job was just a job.

Still, Will said, "I thought it was against your religion to covet other men's wives."

He flicked ash off his cigarette. "Southern Baptist, baby. Jesus already forgave me." Hamish indicated the pool area, which looked like an oasis in the backyard. "You mind if I take a break while you're in with them? I've been here all night. I could use a change of scenery."

"Go ahead." Will knocked lightly on the door, then let himself in. The main room of the apartment was large, with a full kitchen on one side and the living room on the other. He guessed the bedroom and bathroom were behind the closed doors at the rear of the room. Hamish Patel's laptop was set up on the kitchen table, waiting for the phone to ring. Two sets of headphones were hooked into an old-fashioned tape machine that was the size of a cement block.

Paul was sitting on the couch, his hand on the remote control.

The television was muted but the closed-captioning scrolled across the screen. Will recognized the CNN logo in the corner. The reporter was standing in front of a weather map, her arms waving as she described a storm system moving across the Midwest. The coffee table was littered with newspapers—*USA Today,* the *Atlanta Journal,* printouts of other papers that Paul must have gotten off the Internet. Will could not read the headlines, but all of them showed the same school photographs of Emma, Adam and Kayla.

"Trash," Paul said.

Will didn't know whether or not to correct him. The man's daughter was missing. Was now really the time to dig up old grudges?

"They're fucking idiots," Paul said, waving the remote at the TV. "Two days now, and they're still saying the same damn thing with different graphics."

"You shouldn't watch that," Will told him.

"Why haven't you put us on TV?" he demanded. "That's what they always do on the cop shows. They show the parents so the kidnapper knows that she has a family."

Will was more concerned with getting Emma back than worrying about what cop shows dictated as standard procedure. Besides, the press was there to ravage the Campanos, not to help them. Will was under enough stress from the media without setting up the parents for an on-camera meltdown. The last time Will had seen Abigail Campano, she had been sedated into a fog and could barely open her mouth without sobbing. Paul was a ticking time bomb, waiting for the smallest provocation to set him off. Putting either of them on television would be a disaster, and would invariably cause the press, absent any real information, to start pointing the finger right back at the parents.

Will told him, "We're not talking to the press right now. Anytime you want information, you should come to us."

He snorted a laugh, throwing the remote onto the coffee table. "Yeah, y'all have been real forthcoming."

"What do you think you haven't been told?"

Paul barked a laugh. "Where the fuck my daughter is. Why

nobody noticed they had the wrong fucking body. How the fuck you wasted a whole fucking hour sitting with your thumbs up your asses while my fucking baby was being..." He lost his steam, his eyes filling with tears. His jaw clenched as he stared at the television set.

"I just came from Emma's school," Will said, wishing he had more information. "We've been talking to her teachers, her friends. We spent most of the day yesterday at Georgia Tech, tracking down Adam Humphrey."

"And what did you find out? Jack shit."

"I know you've hired your own people to work on this, Paul."

"That's none of your fucking business."

"It is, because they could get in my way."

"Your way? You think I give a shit about getting in your way?" He pointed to the newspapers on the coffee table. "You know what they're saying? Of course you don't fucking know what they're saying—do you?" He stood up. "They're saying you're incompetent. Your own people are saying that you fucked up the crime scene, that any evidence was lost because you didn't know what the fuck you were doing."

Will couldn't think of a way to explain to him the difference between the Atlanta Police Department and the Georgia Bureau of Investigation without sounding like a condescending twat. He settled on saying, "Paul, I'm in charge of this investigation now. You should know—"

"Know what?" In seconds, he closed the space between the two of them. "You think I'm gonna trust you to find my little girl? I *know* you, Trashcan. Did you forget that?"

Will had flinched when he'd charged, like he was ten years old again, like he wasn't six inches taller and ten times stronger than the asshole in front of him.

Paul shook his head, a look of open disgust on his face. "Just get the fuck out of here and let the grown-ups do their job."

"You don't know a damn thing about me."

Paul pushed the newspaper off the coffee table, finding a sheet of notebook paper. "What does this say, Retard?" He shoved the papers in Will's face. "Can you read this? You asked for a list of Emma's friends. Can you even fucking read it?"

Will tilted up his chin, staring down at Paul. "I need a DNA sample from you to compare with the specimens we took from Kayla Alexander's vagina and the sheets in your daughter's bedroom."

"Motherfucker!" Paul swung wildly, and even though Will had been expecting it, he still lost his balance. Both of them fell back onto the floor. Paul had the superior position, but he was older and slower. Will deflected his strikes, relishing the feel of his fist in Paul's soft gut. He punched him in the kidney, then gave him another jab to the stomach.

The door flew open, popping against the wall. "Will!" Hamish yelled. "Jesus Christ!"

Will literally felt himself come back to his senses. His hearing was first—Hamish's panicked voice, a woman screaming. Pain came next, spreading across the bridge of his nose. He tasted blood in his mouth, smelled Paul's sour breath as the man rolled off Will and onto the floor.

Both men lay on their backs, panting. Will tried to move, feeling something crunch in his back pocket.

No one seemed to notice the phone was ringing until Abigail Campano cried, "It's Kayla! It's Kayla's cell phone calling!"

The woman was holding the telephone in her hand, eyes glued to the caller ID.

Both Will and Paul scrambled to stand. Hamish ran to his computer. He held up a finger, telling Abigail to wait while he pressed the keys. Will slipped on the extra set of headphones as Hamish donned his own pair. He nodded, and Abigail answered the phone, holding the receiver so that Paul could listen in.

"Hello?"

There was static, then a garbled voice that was electronically altered to a menacing monotone. "Is this the mother?"

Abigail's mouth opened, but she wasn't speaking. She stared at Hamish for a cue. He nodded, writing something on a dry erase board in front of him.

"Y-yes," she stuttered. "This is Emma's mother. Is Emma all right? Can I talk to Emma?"

Hamish must have coached her to use her daughter's name as much as she could. It was harder to kill somebody who had a name.

The voice said, "I have your daughter."

Hamish wrote something down, and Abigail nodded as she said, "What do you want? Tell me how to get Emma back."

There was more static. The voice had no inflection, no accent. "I want one million dollars."

"Okay," she agreed. Hamish started furiously writing on the board. "When? Where?" She begged, "Just tell me what you want."

"I will call you tomorrow at ten-thirty a.m. with details."

"No—wait," she cried. "How do I know she's alive? How do I know Emma's alive?"

Will pressed his fingers into the earphones, his ears straining to hear past the static. He heard clicking, but didn't know if that was from Hamish pressing keys on his computer or something else. They all startled in unison as the sound jumped up several levels. "Daddy..." a girl's voice said. Tired, terrified. "Daddy...please help me..."

"Baby!" Paul screamed. "Baby, it's me!"

There was another click, then the line went dead.

"Emma?" Abigail yelled. "Hello?"

Hamish tapped the keys on his computer, working furiously to keep the line engaged. He shook his head at Will. Nothing.

"What do we do now?" Abigail begged, fear pitching her voice up almost as high as her daughter's. "What do we do?"

"We pay the bastard." Paul glared at Will. "I want you out of my house. Take him with you."

Hamish looked startled, but Will shook his head, indicating that the man should stay put. He told Paul, "You can't negotiate with the kidnapper on your own."

"What the fuck do I need you for? You can't even trace the fucking call."

"Paul—" Abigail tried, but he cut her off.

"Get out of my fucking house. Now." When Will did not

move, Paul stepped forward, crowding the space. "Don't think I won't beat your ass again."

"Why do you want me to leave?" Will asked. "So you can call your private security firm and they can tell you what to do?" You didn't have to be able to read to see the answer in Paul's eyes. "The more people you get involved in this, the more people who try to control it, the more likely it's going to be that something bad happens to Emma."

"You think I'm going to trust my daughter's life to you?"

"I think you need to stop for just a minute and realize that I am the only person you've got who knows how to keep her safe right now."

"Then I'm fucked, ain't I?" Paul's lips drew into a sneer. "You stupid piece of shit. Get the fuck out of my house."

"Please," Abigail murmured.

Paul persisted, "Get out of my God damn house."

"It's my house, too," Abigail countered, her voice stronger. "I want them to stay."

Paul told her, "You don't know—"

"I know that they're the police, Paul. They know what they're doing. They deal with this kind of thing all the..." Her voice started to tremble again. She clutched her hands in front of her, nervously gripping the phone that had just brought her daughter's voice back to her life. "He said he'll call back tomorrow. We need their help. We need them to tell us what to do when he calls."

Paul shook his head. "Stay out of this, Abby."

"She's my daughter, too!"

"Just let me take care of this," he pleaded, though it was obvious his wife's mind was already made up. "I can handle this."

"The same way you handle everything else?"

The room went silent. Even the fan on Hamish's computer stopped spinning.

Abigail did not seem concerned that she had an audience. "Where were you, Paul? How did you handle it when Emma started hanging around Kayla?"

"That's not—"

"You said she was just acting out, that she was just being a teenager. To leave her alone. Look where leaving her alone got her. She sure as hell is alone now."

Paul was wholly unconvincing when he mumbled, "She was just being a kid."

"She was?" Abigail repeated. "You're still spouting that same parental wisdom? 'Just let her figure things out on her own,' you said. 'Just let her sow some wild oats.' Just like you did at that age. Only, look at you now—you're just a pathetic, needy bastard who can't even keep his daughter safe."

"I know you're upset," Paul said, sounding like the reasonable one. "Let's just talk about this later."

"That's exactly what you told me," she insisted. "Time and time again, you said we'd just talk about it later. Emma skipped school? We'll talk about it later. Emma's failing English? Talk about it later. Later, later, later. It's later!" She threw the phone across the room, smashing it into pieces against the wall. "It's later, Paul. Do you want to talk about it now? Do you want to tell me how I'm overreacting, how *I'm* the crazy one, *I'm* the overprotective one, how I just need to calm down and let kids be kids?" Her voice caught. "Are you calm, Paul? Are you calm while you're thinking about what that man, that animal, is doing to our daughter?"

All of the color drained from Paul's face. "Don't say that."

"You know what he's doing to her," she hissed. "You always said she was your beautiful girl. Do you think you're the only man who thinks that? Do you think you're the only man who can't control himself around hot young blondes?"

Paul glanced at Will nervously, telling him, "Get out."

"Don't," Abigail told Will. "I want you to hear this. I want you to know how my loving and devoted husband screws every twenty-year-old who crosses his path." She indicated her face, her body. "It's the car salesman in him. Every time one model gets out of date, he trades up to the newer one."

"Abigail, this isn't the time."

"When is the time?" she demanded. "When is it time for you to fucking grow up and admit that you were *wrong*?" Her fury heightened with each word. "I trusted you! I trusted you to keep us safe. I looked the other way because I knew that at the end of the day, you would always come back home to me."

"I did. I do." He was trying to soothe her, but Will could see it only made her angrier. "Abby—"

"Don't say my name!" she screamed, throwing her fists into the air. "Don't speak to me. Don't look at me. Don't say a God damn word to me until my daughter is home."

She ran toward the front door, slamming it behind her. Will heard her footsteps as she ran down the steps. When he looked out the window, he could see her on her knees in the grass, bending over at the waist as she keened.

"Get out," Paul said. His chest was heaving up and down as if the wind had been knocked out of him. "Please—just for now. Both of you. Just please get out."

CHAPTER NINE

FAITH STOOD OUTSIDE the morgue, her finger pressed into one ear to block out the noise as she talked to Ruth Donner on her cell phone. Tracking down Kayla Alexander's former nemesis had been somewhat easier than speaking in front of a group of terrified teenagers. In retrospect, Olivia McFaden's relieving her of the podium had been somewhat reminiscent of Travis and Old Yeller in the woodshed.

Still, Faith had managed to persuade Olivia McFaden to put her in touch with Ruth Donner's mother. The woman had given Faith an earful about Kayla Alexander, then volunteered her daughter's cell phone number. Ruth was a student at Colorado State. She was studying early childhood education. She wanted to be a schoolteacher.

"I couldn't believe it was Kayla," Ruth said. "It's been all over the news here."

"Anything you could think of would help," Faith said, raising her voice over the whir of a bone saw. She went up the stairs to the next landing, but she could still hear the motor. "Have you seen her since you left school?"

"No. Truthfully, I haven't had much contact with anybody since I left."

Faith tried, "Can you think of anyone who might want to hurt her?"

"Well, I mean..." Her voice trailed off. "Not to be cruel about it, but she wasn't very well liked."

Faith bit back the "no shit" that wanted to come, asking instead, "Did you know her friend Emma?"

"Not really. I saw her with Kayla, but she never said anything to me." She remembered, "Well, sometimes she would stare at me, but you know how it is. If your best friend hates somebody, then you have to hate them, too." She seemed to realize how childish that sounded. "God, it was all so desperate when I was in the middle of it, but now I look back and wonder why the heck any of it mattered, you know?"

"Yeah," Faith agreed, feeling in her gut that this was a dead end. She had checked flight manifests going in and out of Atlanta for the last week. Ruth Donner's name had not shown up on any airline manifests. "You have my number. Will you call me if you remember anything?"

"Of course," Ruth agreed. "Will you let me know if you find her?"

"Yes," Faith promised, though updating Ruth Donner wasn't high on her list of priorities. "Thank you."

Faith ended the call and tucked her phone into her pants pocket. She went back down the stairs, the scent of burned bone wafting up to meet her. Despite her earlier bravado with Will Trent, she hated being in the morgue. The dead bodies didn't bother her so much as the atmosphere, the industrial processing of death. The cold marble tile that wrapped floor to ceiling to deflect stains. The drains on the floor every three feet so that blood and matter could be washed away. The stainless steel gurneys with their big rubber wheels and plastic mattresses.

Summer was the medical examiner's peak period, a particularly brutal time of year. Often, you would find ten or twelve bodies stacked in the freezer. They lay there like pieces of meat waiting to be butchered for clues. The very thought brought an almost unbearable sadness.

Pete Hanson was holding up a pile of bloody, wet intestines when Faith walked in. He smiled brightly, giving her his usual greeting. "The prettiest detective in the building!"

She willed her stomach not to heave as he dropped the intestines onto a large scale. Despite being underground, the room was always disgustingly warm in the summer months, the compressor on the freezer pushing heat into the confined space faster than the air-conditioning could keep up with it.

"This one was full as a tick," Pete mumbled, writing down the number from the scale.

Faith had never met a coroner who wasn't eccentric in one way or another, but Pete Hanson was a special kind of freaky. She understood why he'd been divorced three times. The perplexing question was how he had found three women out there in the world who had agreed to marry him in the first place.

He motioned her over. "I take it there are no breaks if you're gracing me with your presence?"

"Nothing yet," she told him, glancing around the morgue. Snoopy, an elderly black man who had assisted Pete for as long as Faith had worked homicide, but whose real name she had still never learned, gave her a nod as he rolled Adam Humphrey's face back along his skull, pressing the skin into the crevices. His bony fingers worked meticulously, and Faith was reminded of the time her mother had made her a Halloween costume, her firm hands smoothing pieces of material onto the Butterick pattern.

Faith made herself look away, thinking that between this and the heat, there was no way she was going to leave this room without tasting something awful in the back of her throat. "What about you?"

"Same bad luck, I'm afraid." He took off his gloves and put on a fresh pair. "Snoopy's covering it up, but I found a pretty bad smack to the right side of Humphrey's head."

"Fatal?"

"No, more of a glancing blow. The scalp remained intact, but it would've made him see stars."

He walked over to a large soup pan with a ladle sticking out of it. She had arrived at the worst part of the autopsy. Stomach contents. The smell was vicious, the sort of scent that ate into the lining of your nose and back of your mouth, so that the next day you woke up thinking you had a sore throat.

"Now, this," Pete said, using a long set of tweezers to hold up what looked like a large crystal of salt. "This is obviously gristle, common to most fast-food hamburgers."

"Obviously," Faith echoed, trying not to be sick.

"Think of that the next time you go to McDonald's."

Faith was fairly certain she was never going to eat again.

"I would guess the young man had some type of fast food at least thirty minutes prior to death. The girl had French fries but seems to have passed on the burger."

She said, "We didn't find any fast-food bags in the trashcans or the house."

"Then perhaps they ate on the run. Worst possible thing for digestion, by the way. There's a reason why there is an obesity epidemic in this country."

Faith wondered if the man had looked in a mirror lately. His gut was so large and round that he looked pregnant under the billows of his surgical gown.

Pete asked, "How's Will doing?"

"Trent?" she asked. "I didn't realize you knew him."

He took off his gloves, motioning for Faith to follow him. "Excellent detective. It must be a nice change working with someone who is, shall we say, more cerebral than your usual bunch."

"Hm," she said, unwilling to pay Will a compliment, even though Pete was right. There were only three women in Atlanta Homicide Division. There had been four when Faith first got there, but Claire Dunkel, a thirty-year veteran, had taken retirement the first week Faith had been on the squad. Her parting advice was, "Wear a skirt every once in a while or you'll start to grow testicles."

Maybe that's why Faith was having such a hard time gelling with Will Trent. For all his faults, he actually seemed to respect her.

He hadn't once drawn a ludicrous connection between Faith's hair color and her mental abilities, nor had he scratched himself repeatedly or spat on the floor—all things Leo Donnelly usually did before his second cup of coffee.

Pete untied his surgical gown, revealing a shirt that was of the loud Hawaiian variety. Faith was glad to see that he was wearing shorts. Beneath the gown, the sight of his hairless legs, bare but for the black socks he'd pulled up to his knees, had been alarming.

"Horrible situation with your mother," Pete said. Faith watched him punch the soap dispenser and lather up his hands. "It's one of those cases where 'just doing my job' seems like a lame excuse, isn't it?"

"Yes," she agreed.

"Though I've been in this building for many years, and I've seen a lot of things happening that shouldn't. I certainly wouldn't volunteer any information, but if someone asked me directly, I would feel compelled to tell them the truth." He smiled at her over his shoulder. "I suppose that would make me what you guys call a 'rat.' "

She shrugged.

"Will is a good man who had to do a dirty job. I can relate to that." He pulled a handful of paper towels off the stack and dried his hands as he walked to his office.

"Sit," Pete said, indicating a chair by his desk.

Faith sat on the stack of papers in the chair, knowing Pete didn't expect her to move them. "What do you have so far?"

"Nothing of consequence, I'm afraid." He retrieved a paper bag from the small refrigerator in the corner. Faith concentrated on finding a clean page in her notebook as he took out a sandwich. "The girl was stabbed at least twenty-seven times. I would assume from angle and trajectory that the wounds match the kitchen knife you found at the crime scene. The killer was most likely on his knees, superior to the body, when he attacked her."

Faith wrote furiously, knowing he would not pause to let her catch up.

"There was bruising around her thighs and some tearing in the vaginal canal. I found traces of cornstarch, which indicates a condom was used, but we can assume from the sperm that the condom tore, as often happens with rough sex. Also, I noted some faint bite marks around the breasts. I would say this was more consistent with consensual sex, though that's really just speculation on my part."

He unwrapped his sandwich and took a bite, chewing with his mouth open as he continued. "You can certainly leave those kinds of marks by raping a woman, but then again, if you were feeling a little eager and the woman was willing, you could make an argument that the marks were left not by rape, but during a particularly ardent session of lovemaking. I wouldn't be surprised if, after a couple of bottles of tequila and some dancing, the current Mrs. Hanson happily exhibited the same sort of trauma."

She tried not to shudder. "The bite marks, too?"

There was a loud snap as Pete clamped his dentures together, and Faith wrote nonsense words in her notebook, praying he would stop. "So, you're saying that the girl wasn't raped."

"And as I told Agent Trent at the crime scene, there was semen in the crotch of the panties, indicating that after having sex, she put on her underwear and stood up. Now, unless the perpetrator raped her, made her dress and stand up, then chased her down the hall and killed her, then pulled down her panties again, then I would say that she was not raped. At least not during the attack."

Faith noted this word for word in her notebook.

Pete took another bite of his sandwich. "Now, as for cause of death, I would say there are three likely candidates: blunt-force trauma, the pierced jugular and just plain old shock. The nature of the attack was intense. There would have been a cascade effect with the body. There comes a time when the brain and the heart and the organs just throw up their hands and say, 'You know what? We can't take this anymore.' "

Faith dutifully recorded his words. "Which one is your money on?"

He chewed thoughtfully, then laughed. "Well, an armchair coroner might go for the jugular!"

Faith managed a chuckle, though she had no idea why she was encouraging him.

"The jugular was sliced. I would say that, in and of itself, the cut was fatal, but it would've taken time—say, three to four minutes. My official report will reflect the more likely culprit: massive shock."

"Do you think she was conscious during the attack?"

"If the parents ask you that question, I would tell them unequivocally that she was instantly rendered unconscious and felt absolutely no pain." He took a bag of potato chips out of the paper sack, leaning back in his chair as he opened them. "Now, the boy, not so much."

"What's your best guess?"

"It jibes with Will's theory. I can't believe how well he reads a crime scene." Pete popped a potato chip into his mouth, seemingly lost in thoughts of Will Trent's expertise.

"Pete?"

"Sorry," he said, offering her a potato chip. Faith shook her head, and he went on. "I haven't culled all my notes, but I think I have a clear picture." He sat up in the chair and drank from the Dunkin' Donuts cup on his desk. "Physically, he presents pretty straightforward. I already told you about the head wound. The stab to the chest alone was enough to kill him. I would imagine it was through pure adrenaline that he managed to put up the struggle he did. The knife punctured his right lung—easy math, we're looking for a left-handed killer—bypassing the bronchial trunk. We can assume the victim removed the knife, which exacerbated the negative airflow. The lung is vacuum sealed, you see, and a puncture deflates it much as a balloon being pierced by a pin."

Faith had dealt with a victim who'd died of a collapsed lung before. "So, unless he managed to get help, he only had a few minutes."

"Well, here's the funny thing: he would've been panicked, his breathing would have been shallow. When a lung collapses, it's like a self-fulfilling prophecy. You gulp for air, and the more you breathe, the worse it gets. I'd say that the panic bought him some extra time."

"What's the cause of death?"

"Manual strangulation."

Faith wrote down the words, underlining them. "So, Abigail Campano actually did kill him."

"Exactly." Pete picked up his sandwich again. "She killed him right before he died."

◆

THE INTERIOR OF the morgue had spotty cell reception at best. Faith used this as an excuse to leave Pete to finish his lunch by himself. She dialed Will Trent's number as she walked toward the parking garage for some air. Faith needed to tell him about Mary Clark and Ruth Donner. She also wanted to talk about Kayla Alexander some more. The picture she was getting of the girl was not a pretty one.

Will's phone rang several times before she was sent to voice mail.

"Hi, Will—" Call-waiting beeped and she checked the screen, reading the words "Cohen, G." Faith put the phone back to her ear, not recognizing the name. "I'm just leaving the morgue and—" Her phone beeped again and Faith finally realized who was calling. "Call me," she said, then switched the line over. "Hello?"

"It's Gabe." His voice sounded far away, though she guessed he was still at Tech.

"What can I do for you?"

He was silent, and she waited him out. Finally, he told her, "I lied to you."

Faith stopped walking. "About what?"

His voice was so low she had to strain to hear him. "I thought she was younger."

"Who?"

"I've got..." His words trailed off. "I need to show you something Adam had. I should've shown you before, but I..."

She started to jog, heading toward the Mini. "What do you have of Adam's?"

"I have to show you. I can't tell you on the phone."

Faith knew that was bullshit, but she also knew that Gabe Cohen was ready to talk. She would dance like a monkey if it got the truth out of him. "Where are you?"

"The dorm."

"I can be there in fifteen minutes," she said, unlocking the door.

"You're coming?" He sounded surprised.

"Yes," she said, switching the phone to her other ear as she put the key in the ignition. "Do you want me to stay on the phone with you while I drive over?"

"I'm okay," he said. "I just...I've got to show you this."

She glanced over her shoulder and swerved the Mini out of the space so sharply that it squealed up on two wheels. "I'll be right there, okay? Just stay right where you are."

"Okay."

Faith had never driven so fast in her life. Part of her wondered if Gabe was just stringing her along, but there was always the slim chance that he had something important to tell her. She called Will Trent's cell phone again, leaving another message, telling him to meet her at the dorm. Her heart raced as she blew through red lights, nearly causing a bus to slam into another car, heading into oncoming traffic to whip around construction crews. On campus, she didn't bother to look for legal spaces, again parking the Mini in the handicapped section. She flipped down the visor and jumped out of the car. By the time she reached Towers Hall, she was panting from exertion.

Faith bent over at the waist, trying to catch her breath. She opened her mouth, taking in big gulps of air, cursing herself for not being in better shape. She let a minute pass, then hit the handicapped plate and headed up the stairs, taking them two at a time. There was the distant thump of music, but the building felt empty. It was the middle of the day; most kids were in class. She trotted past Adam's room, expecting Gabe to be in his own dorm, but the door to 310 was cracked open.

Faith pushed the door the rest of the way open, noting that the police tape sealing off the room had been cut. Adam's things had been boxed up. The mattress was bare, the television and game set gone. Black fingerprint powder was smeared all around the room where they had dusted for prints.

Gabe sat on the bare floor, his back to one of the beds, his book bag beside him. His elbows were on his knees, his head pressed against the cast on his arm. His shoulders shook. Still, Faith could not forget the angry man who had threatened to call security on her yesterday. Was that the real Gabriel Cohen, or was this crying child closer to his real self? Either way, he had something to tell her. If Faith had to play along with his game to get the information, then that was how it was going to be.

She rapped her knuckles lightly on the open door. "Gabe?"

He looked up at her with swollen, red eyes. Fresh tears rolled down his cheeks. "Adam told me she was young," he sobbed. "I thought, like, fourteen or something. Not seventeen. The news said that she was seventeen."

Faith used his book bag to prop open the door before sitting beside him on the floor. "Tell me from the beginning," she said, trying to keep her voice calm. Here was proof that Adam had talked to Gabe about Emma.

"I'm sorry," he cried. His lip trembled, and he put his head down, hiding his face from her. "I should have told you."

She should have felt sorry for the kid, but all Faith could think was that Emma Campano was somewhere crying, too—but there was no one there to comfort her.

"I'm sorry," he repeated. "I'm so sorry."

Faith asked him, "What did you want to tell me?"

His body shook as he struggled with his emotions. "He met her online. He was on this video Web site."

Faith felt her heart stop mid-beat. "What sort of Web site?"

"LD." Faith had known the answer before he opened his mouth. Learning disabilities. Will Trent's instincts had been right yet again.

Gabe told her, "Adam went online with her all the time, like, for a year."

"You said it was a video site?" she asked, wondering what else the kid had been hiding.

"Yeah," Gabe answered. "A lot of them weren't really good at writing."

"What learning disorder did Adam have?"

"Behavioral stuff. He was homeschooled. He didn't fit in." Gabe glanced up at her. "You don't think that's why he was killed, do you?"

Faith wasn't sure about anything at this point, but she assured him, "No. Of course not."

"She seemed younger than she was, you know?"

Faith made sure she understood. "That's why you didn't tell me that you knew Adam was seeing Emma? You thought she was underage and you didn't want to get him into trouble?"

He nodded. "I think he had a car, too."

Faith felt her jaw clench. "What kind? What model?"

He took his time answering—for effect or from genuine emotion, she could not tell. "It was an old beater. Some graduate student was transferring to Ireland and he posted it on the board."

"Do you remember the student's name?"

"Farokh? Something like that."

"Do you know what the car looked like?"

"I only saw it once. It was this shitty color blue. It didn't even have air-conditioning."

Adam would have had thirty days to register the car with the state, which might explain why they hadn't pulled up anything on the state's system. If they could get a description, then they could put it on the wire and have every cop in the city looking for it. "Can you remember anything else about it? Did it have a bumper sticker or a cracked windshield or—"

He turned petulant. "I told you I only saw it once."

Faith could practically feel the irritation in her voice, like an itch at the back of her throat. She took a deep breath before asking, "Why didn't you tell me about the car before?"

He shrugged again. "I told my girlfriend, Julie, and she said... she said that if Emma's dead, it's my fault for not telling you. She said she never wants to see me again."

Faith guessed that *that* was what was really bothering him.

There was nothing more self-involved than a teenager. She asked, "Did you ever meet Emma in person?"

He shook his head.

"How about her friend Kayla Alexander—blond girl, very pretty?"

"I'd never even heard of her until I turned on the news." Gabe asked, "Do you think I did a bad thing?"

"Of course not," Faith assured him, hoping she managed to keep the sarcasm out of her voice. "Do you know the Web site Adam and Emma used?"

He shook his head. "He had it on his laptop, but then his laptop got stolen."

"How did it get stolen?"

Gabe sat up, wiping his eyes with his fist. "He left it out at the library when he went to pee, and when he came back, it was gone."

Faith was hardly surprised. Adam might as well have put a "take me" sign on it. "Did you ever see what name he used on the site? Did he use his e-mail address?"

"I don't think so." He used the bottom of his shirt to wipe his nose. "If you put in your e-mail address, then you get all kinds of trolls for spam and shit."

She had assumed as much. Compounding the problem, there were probably nine billion Web sites for people with learning disabilities, and those were just the American ones. She reminded him, "When you called me, you said you had something to show me. Something that belonged to Adam."

Guilt flashed in his eyes, and she realized that the other stuff—the Web site, the car, the fear about Emma's age—was just preamble to the information that had really compelled him to call her.

Faith struggled to keep the urgency out of her tone. "Whatever it is that you have, I need to see it."

He took his sweet time relenting, making a show of leaning up on his heels so he could dig his hand into the front pocket of his jeans. Slowly, he pulled out several pieces of folded white paper. He explained, "These were slipped under Adam's door last week."

As he unfolded the three pages, all she could think was that between the creases, smudges and dog-eared corners, the paper had been handled many, many times.

"Here," Gabe said. "That's all of them."

Faith stared in shock at the three notes he'd spread out on the floor between them. Each page had a single line of bold, block text running horizontally across it. Each line heightened her sense of foreboding.

SHE BE LONGS TO ME!!!
RAPIST!!!
LEV HER ALONG!!!

At first, Faith didn't trust herself to speak. Someone had tried to warn Adam Humphrey away from Emma Campano. Someone had been watching them together, knew their habits. The notes were more proof that this was not a spur-of-the-moment abduction. The killer had known some if not all of the participants.

Gabe had his own concerns. "Are you mad at me?"

Faith could not answer him. Instead, she gave him back her own question. "Did anyone else touch these besides you and Adam?"

He shook his head.

"What order did they come in—do you remember?"

He switched around the last two sheets before she could stop him. "Like that."

"Don't touch them again, okay?" He nodded. "When did the first one come?"

"Monday last week."

"What did Adam say when he got it?"

Gabe was no longer being emotional about his answers. He seemed almost relieved to be telling her. "First, we were like, you know, it was funny, because everything is spelled wrong."

"And when the second one came?"

"It came the next day. We were kind of freaked out. I thought Tommy was doing it."

The asshole dormmate. "Was he?"

"No. Because I was with Tommy the day Adam got the third note. That was when his computer was stolen, and I was like, 'What the fuck? Is somebody stalking you or what?' " Gabe glanced at her, probably looking for confirmation on his theory. Faith gave him none, and he continued, "Adam was pretty freaked out. He said he was going to get a gun."

Faith's instincts told her that Gabe was not blowing smoke. She made her tone deadly serious. "Did he?"

Gabe looked back at the notes.

"Gabe?"

"He was thinking about it."

"Where would he get a gun?" she asked, though the answer was obvious. Tech was an urban campus. You could walk ten blocks in any direction and find meth, coke, prostitutes and firearms in any combination on any street corner.

"Gabe?" she prompted. "Where would Adam get a gun?"

Again, he remained silent.

"Stop screwing around," she warned him. "This is not a game."

"It was just talk," he insisted, but he still wouldn't look her in the eye.

Faith no longer tried to hide her impatience. She indicated the notes. "Did you report these to campus security?"

His chin started to quiver. Tears brimmed in his eyes. "We should've, right? That's what you're saying. It's my fault, because Adam wanted to, and I told him not to, that he'd get in trouble because of Emma." He put his head in his hands, shoulders shaking again. She saw how thin he was, how his ribs pressed into the thin T-shirt he wore. Watching him, listening to him cry, Faith realized that she had read Gabe Cohen completely wrong. This was no act on his part. He was genuinely upset, and she had been too focused on the case to notice.

His voice cracked. "It's all my fault. That's what Julie said. It's all my fault, and I know you think that, too."

Faith sat there, not knowing what to do. The truth was, she was mad at him, but also at herself. If Faith had been better at her job, she would have spotted this yesterday. The time lost was down to her. Gabe had probably had these notes in his pocket when he challenged her less than twenty-four hours ago. Blaming him for her own failure would not get them any closer to finding Emma Campano, and right now, that was all that mattered.

She sat back on her heels, trying to figure out what to do. Faith could not tell how fragile the young man was right now. Was he just another teenager caught up in his emotions or was he playing up the situation for her attention?

"Gabe," she began, "I need you to be honest with me."

"I *am* being honest."

Faith took a moment, trying to find the best way to phrase her next question. "Is there something else you're not telling me?"

He looked up at her. There was suddenly such sadness in his eyes that she had to force herself not to look away. "I can't do anything right."

His life had been turned upside down over the last couple of days, but she knew he was talking about more than that. She told him, "I'm sure that's not true."

"Adam was my only friend, and he's dead—probably because of me."

"I promise you that's not true."

He looked away, staring at the bare mattress across from him. "I don't fit in here. Everybody's smarter than me. Everybody's already picking fraternities and hanging out. Even Tommy."

Faith was not stupid enough to offer Jeremy as his new best friend. She told Gabe, "It's hard to adjust to a new school. You'll figure it out eventually."

"I really don't think I will," he said, sounding so sure of himself that Faith could almost hear an alarm going off in her head. She had been so concerned about the information Gabe had withheld that she had lost sight of the fact that he was just a teenager who had been thrown into a very bad situation.

"Gabe," Faith began, "what's going on with you?"

"I just need to get some rest."

She knew then that he wasn't talking about sleep. He had not called her to help Adam, he had called to help himself—and her response had been to push him around like a suspect she was interrogating. She made her voice softer. "What are you thinking about doing?"

"I don't know," he answered, but he still would not make eye contact with her. "Sometimes, I just think that the world would be a better place if I was just...gone. You know?"

"Have you tried anything before?" She glanced at his wrists. There were scratch marks that she hadn't noticed before, thin red streaks where the skin had been broken but not punctured. "Maybe tried to hurt yourself?"

"I just want to get away from here. I want to go..."

"Home?" she suggested.

He shook his head. "There's nothing there for me. My mom died of cancer six years ago. My dad and me..." He shook his head.

Faith told him, "I want to help you, Gabe, but you need to be honest with me."

He picked at a tear in his jeans. She saw that his fingernails were chewed to the quick. The cuticles were ragged and torn.

"Did Adam buy a gun?"

He kept picking at his jeans. He shrugged his shoulders, and she still did not know whether to believe him.

She suggested, "Why don't I call your father?"

His eyes widened. "No. Don't do that. Please."

"I can't just leave you alone, Gabe."

His eyes filled with tears again. His lips trembled. There was such desperation in his manner that she felt like he had reached into her chest and grabbed her heart with his fist. She could have kicked herself for letting it get to this point.

She repeated, "I'm not going to leave you alone."

"I'll be okay."

Faith felt caught in an untenable position. Gabe was obviously a troubled young man, but he could not be her problem right now. She needed to get the threatening notes to the lab to see if there were any usable fingerprints on them. There was a student in

Ireland who had sold his car to Adam—a car that had probably been used to transport Emma Campano from the Copy Right. There were two sets of parents who would identify their dead children tonight. There was a mother and a father on the other side of Atlanta waiting to find out whether or not their daughter was still alive.

Faith took out her cell phone and scrolled through her recent calls.

Gabe asked, "Are you going to arrest me?"

"No." Faith pressed the send button on the phone. "I'm going to get you some help, and then I have to go do my job." She didn't add that she was going to search every item in his room, including the computer he'd let Adam borrow, before she left campus.

Gabe sat back against the bed, an air of resignation about him. He stared at the mattress opposite. Faith resisted the impulse to reach out and tuck a stray strand of hair behind his ear. Pimples dotted his chin. She could see stubble on his cheek where he had missed a spot shaving. He was still just a child—a child who was very lost and needed help.

Victor Martinez's secretary answered on the second ring. "Student Services."

"This is Detective Mitchell," she told the woman. "I need to speak to the dean immediately."

CHAPTER TEN

WILL STOOD BEHIND Gail and Simon Humphrey as they waited in front of the viewing window. The setup was the sort that was always shown on television and in movies: a simple curtain hung on the other side of the glass. Will would press a button, and the drape would be slowly drawn back, revealing the cleaned-up victim. The sheet would be tucked up to the chin in order to cover the baseball stitches holding together the Y-incision. Cue the mother slumping against her husband.

But the camera couldn't capture everything. The pungent smell of the morgue. The distant whine of the giant freezers where they stored the bodies. The way the floor seemed to suck at the soles of your shoes as you walked toward that window. The heaviness of your arm as you reached out to push that button.

The curtain pulled back. Both parents stood, silent, probably numb. Simon was the first to move. He reached out and pressed his hand against the glass. Will wondered if he was remembering what it felt like to hold his son's hand. Was that the sort of thing fathers did? At the park, out in public, fathers and sons were always playing ball or tossing Frisbees, the only contact between them a rustle of the hair or a punch on the arm. This seemed to be how dads taught their boys to be men, but there had to be a point, maybe early on, when they were able to hold their hands. One tiny one engulfed by one big one. Adam would have needed help crossing the street. In a crowd, you wouldn't want him to wander off.

Yes, Will decided. Simon Humphrey had held his son's hands.

Gail turned to Will. She wasn't crying, but he sensed a familiar reserve, a kindred spirit. She would be at the hotel later tonight, maybe in the shower or sitting on the bed while her husband went for a walk, and then she would allow this moment to crash over her. She would be back in front of that window, looking at her dead son. She would collapse. She would feel her spirit leaving her body and know it might never return.

For now, she said, "Thank you, Agent Trent," and shook his hand.

He led them down the hallway, asking them about the hotel where they would stay, giving them advice on where to have supper. He was aware of how foolish the small talk sounded, but Will also knew that the distraction would help them make it through the building, to give them the strength they needed to leave their child in this cold, dark place.

They had rented a car at the airport, and Will went with them as far as the garage. Through the glass panel in the door, he watched Gail Humphrey stumble. Her husband caught her arm and she shrugged him off. He tried again and she slapped at him, yelling, until he wrapped his arms around her to make her stop.

Will turned away, feeling like an intruder. He took the stairs up the six flights to his office. At half past eight, everyone but the skeleton crew had already gone home for the day. The lights were out, but he would have known his way even without the faint glow of the emergency exit signs. Will had a corner office, which would have been impressive if it hadn't been this particular corner. Between the Home Depot across the street and the old Ford Factory next door that had been turned into apartment buildings, there wasn't much to look at. Sometimes, he convinced himself that the abandoned railroad tracks with their weeds and discarded hypodermic needles offered something of a parklike view, but daydreaming only worked during the day.

Will turned on his desk lamp and sat down. He hated nighttime on days like this, where there was nothing he could do but catch up on paperwork while he waited for other people to bring him information. There was an expert in Tennessee who specialized in detecting fingerprints on paper. Paper was tricky and you only got a couple of tries developing prints before the process ruined the evidence. The man was driving down first thing in the morning to look at the notes. The recording of the ransom call was being hand-delivered to the University of Georgia's audiology lab, but the professor had warned them it would take many hours to isolate the sounds. Charlie was working late at the lab trying to process all the evidence they had collected. Tips from the hotline were being followed up on, cops sifting through the pranksters and nutjobs, trying to find a viable lead.

Will had paperwork to do on all of this, but instead of turning to his computer, he sat back in his chair and stared at his blurred reflection in the dark window. They were coming up on thirty-six hours since Abigail Campano had come home to find her life turned upside down. Two people were still dead. One girl was still missing. And, still, not a single suspect was in sight.

He didn't understand the ransom demand. Will was no rookie. He had worked kidnapping cases before. He had worked abduction cases. There were basic tenets to both. Kidnappers wanted money. Abductors wanted sex. He could not reconcile the brutal way in which Kayla Alexander had been killed with the phone call this morning demanding one million dollars. It just did not add up.

Then there was the fight between Abigail and Paul Campano. Angie had been right: Paul was cheating on his wife. Apparently, he liked young blondes, but did that include his own daughter, and possibly Kayla Alexander? Amanda had told Will to get the man's DNA. Maybe she was right, too. Add in Faith, who had managed to get Gabriel Cohen to talk, and that just left Will as the odd man out—literally—because he was the only one who brought absolutely nothing to this case.

Will turned back to his desk, knowing that overthinking the problem would not bring him any closer to a solution. His cell phone was laid out on his desk in two pieces. During his fight with Paul, the clamshell had snapped off and the screen had cracked. Will held the lid in place and taped it back onto the phone with several pieces of Scotch tape. The phone still worked. When he'd left the Campano house, he had been able to hold it together in order to check his voice mail. Faith Mitchell's messages had gotten progressively more important, her voice going up in excitement as she told him about the threatening notes Gabe Cohen had kept from them.

Will still wasn't sure she had made the right decision about keeping the kid out of the system, but he had to trust her instincts.

At least they had more information on the car now. A computer search of graduate students working at the Georgia Tech Research Institute in Ireland had revealed the name Farokh Pansing. After a few phone calls, they had located a cell phone number and woken the man up from what sounded like a very deep sleep. The physics major had given Will a loving description of the blue 1981 Chevy Impala he had left behind. No air-conditioning. No seat belts. The driver's door stuck when it rained. The engine leaked like a sieve. The undercarriage was so rusted out that, from the backseat, you could watch the road pass under your shoes. Because of its age, the state of Georgia considered the car a classic and it was therefore exempt from any emissions requirements. Farokh had sold the ancient car to Adam Humphrey for four hundred dollars. The state had no record of Adam ever applying for insurance or a tag.

They had issued a new alert on the Impala, but the warning only pertained to the state of Georgia. Emma Campano could easily be in Alabama or Tennessee or the Carolinas. Given the almost two days that had passed since her abduction, she could well be in Mexico or Canada.

Will's computer gave a chug like a train, indicating that the system was running. Will had been out of the office for two days. He needed to check his e-mail and file his daily reports. He put on the headphones and adjusted the microphone, preparing to dictate the report. After opening up a blank Word document, he pressed the start key, but found himself at a loss for words. He stopped the recorder and sat back in his chair. When he reached up to rub his eyes, he gasped from the pain.

Paul hadn't broken his nose, but he'd managed to whack it hard enough to move the cartilage. With the ransom recording to analyze and the threatening notes to rush to the lab, Will hadn't had time to look at himself in the mirror until about ten minutes before the Humphreys had shown up to identify their son. Will's nose had been broken several times in the past. It was already crooked enough. With the bruises, he looked like a bar brawler, which did not exactly engender trust in the Humphreys. The father had accepted his mumbled excuse about a rough football game the weekend before, but the mother had looked at him as if he had a giant "liar" sticker pinned to his head.

Will tapped the space bar on his computer and used the mouse to click on the e-mail icon. He slipped the headphones on and listened to his e-mails. The first three were spam, the second was from Pete Hanson, telling him the basic information Faith had already relayed about the autopsies of Adam Humphrey and Kayla Alexander.

The third e-mail was from Amanda Wagner. She had called a press conference for six-thirty the next morning. Will guessed she had been following the news as closely as he had. Absent anything else to cover, the reporters had started targeting the parents, picking apart their lives, slowly pointing the finger back at the victims. The press would be in for a disappointment if they thought they'd be able to talk to the Campanos tomorrow. Amanda was a master at controlling the press. She would parade out Paul and Abigail for the cameras, but she would do all the talking. Will couldn't think how she would manage to put a muzzle on Paul, but he'd seen her pull too many rabbits out of her hat in the past to worry about logistics.

Amanda's e-mail ended curtly. "You are to be in my office directly after the press conference," the computer read. Will gathered she had heard about Paul Campano bashing his face in.

Will pressed play again, listening to Amanda's terse message as if he could divine some nuance. The program allowed you to assign different voices to people. Pete sounded like Mickey Mouse. Amanda was Darth Vader. Sitting alone in his dark office, the sound gave Will an involuntary shudder.

Then it gave him an idea.

He opened up Pete's e-mail again and selected a different voice to read the text. He went through each option, listening to the nuances. Will realized he was doing this the wrong way. He opened a new e-mail and clicked in the text area, then took out his digital recorder and selected the file that had the kidnapper's voice on it.

He held the player up to the microphone and let it dictate the text:

"Is this the mother?"

Then Abigail, stuttering, *"Y-yes... This is Emma's mother. Is Emma all right? Can I talk to Emma?"*

"I have your daughter."

"What do you want? Tell me how to get Emma back."

"I want one million dollars."

"Okay... When? Where? Just tell me what you want."

"I will call you tomorrow at ten-thirty a.m. with details."

"No—wait! How do I—"

Will cut off the recording, excitement taking hold. Playing back each line, he isolated the kidnapper's sentences and deleted Abigail's. Next, he went through each voice option, searching for one that sounded similar to the kidnapper's.

The last one in line was the one he used for Amanda Wagner. His finger hovered over the mouse. He clicked the button. The headphones sent out a foreboding, deep voice.

"Is this the mother?"

Will looked up, sensing he was not alone. Faith Mitchell stood in the doorway.

He jumped up, yanking off the headphones as if he had something to be guilty about. "I thought you were going home."

She walked into his office and sat down. The desk lamp cast her in a harsh light. She looked older than her thirty-three years. "What are you doing?"

"The audiotape of the ransom demand," he began, then figured he could just as easily show her. He picked up his digital recorder and pressed play. "This is the audio." Will kept his thumb on the button, listening along with Faith to the kidnapper's phone call this morning, Abigail Campano's terrified responses. He stopped it at the same place as before. "Now this is something I just did in my computer. It's got one of those speaking options for lazy people where it reads stuff to you." He moved the mouse over to the start button, saying, "I didn't even remember I had it on here. I guess it's some ADA thing." He pulled out the headphone jack so the speakers would play. "Ready?"

She nodded.

He pressed play, and the kidnapper's words came out of the computer speakers in the Darth Vader voice.

"Is this the mother?"

"Jesus Christ," she murmured. "It's almost exactly the same."

"I think he must have written the sentences and prerecorded them coming out of the computer speakers."

"That's why the sentence construction's so simple. There aren't any contractions."

Will looked at the computer screen as he repeated them back from memory. "I have your daughter. I want one million dollars. I will call you this time tomorrow with details."

He picked up the phone and called Hamish Patel, who was driving the tape up to the University of Georgia in Athens.

Hamish sounded as excited as Will felt. He told Will, "If you manage to keep your job, you might actually break this case."

Will made excuses. He didn't want to think about what Amanda had in store for him tomorrow morning, but he imagined she was concocting a special kind of hell for the agent who had gotten into a fight with the father of a kidnapping victim. The GBI was planning another sex sting at the Atlanta airport. Will might be stuck in a bathroom stall on the B Concourse, waiting for a married father of three to tap his foot and ask for a blow job.

He rang off with Hamish and told Faith, "They're going to

check into it. These guys deal with computers and audio enhancement all of the time. I'm sure they would've figured it out in ten seconds."

"Saves them ten seconds, then," she pointed out. "I can't help but think where we'd be if I'd been able to get Gabe to talk yesterday."

"He wasn't ready," Will told her, though there was no way of knowing whether or not that was true. "Maybe if you'd pushed him yesterday, he would have gone over the edge without telling us anything."

"What do you think about the notes?"

"Someone—probably the kidnapper—was trying to warn or threaten Adam."

" 'She belongs to me,' " Faith quoted. "That's a pretty definitive statement."

"It supports the kidnapper knowing Emma, at least."

"What about the way they were written?"

Will nodded, as if he knew what she was talking about. "That's a good point. What do you think about it?"

She tapped her finger to her mouth as she considered it. "Either the person who wrote them is dyslexic or they're trying to make it seem like they are."

Will felt the glimmer of pride from a few moments ago disappear like a flash of lightning. The notes were misspelled. He had missed an important clue because of his own stupidity. What else had he missed? What other evidence had gone by the wayside because Will couldn't wrap his head around them?

Faith asked, "Will?"

He shook his head, not trusting himself to speak. He would have to call Amanda, tell her what he had missed. She had a way of finding out these things on her own. He didn't know how to handle it other than to confess and wait for the ax to fall.

"Go ahead and say it," Faith told him. "It's not like I haven't been wondering."

He clasped his hands under the desk. "Wondering what?"

"Whether or not Emma's involved in this."

Will looked down at his hands. He had to swallow past the lump in his throat. "It's possible," he admitted. He tried to refocus his attention, using a roundabout question to find out how Faith had arrived at Emma Campano being involved. "Kayla certainly knew how to inspire hate in people, but it's a huge leap, don't you think?"

"Kayla was such an awful person, and from the sound of it, Emma was one step up from her lapdog. She might have snapped."

"You think a seventeen-year-old girl is capable of doing all this—killing people, staging her own kidnapping?"

"That's the question, isn't it?" Faith leaned her elbows on his desk. "I hate to say this, but considering what Mary Clark said about her, if Emma was dead and Kayla was missing, I would have no problem believing Kayla was in on it."

"Did Clark's alibi for yesterday check out?"

"She was in class all day." Faith continued, "Ruth Donner, the girl who was archenemies with Kayla last year, was out of the state. There aren't any other girls in particular at the school who were Kayla's sworn enemies. I mean, not any one who stands out from the crowd."

"What about Gabe Cohen?"

She pressed her lips together, not answering for a moment. "There's no evidence that links him to either of the girls." She added, "I think he's told us everything he knows."

"What about the gun?"

"He mentioned it for a reason, but I checked his book bag and his dorm top to bottom. If Adam bought a gun, he didn't give it to Gabe. Maybe he kept it in his car."

"Which means our abductor probably has it," Will pointed out. "Where was Gabe yesterday when this was all going down?"

"In a class, but it was in one of those huge lecture halls. He didn't have to sign in, the teacher doesn't take attendance. It's a shaky alibi." She paused. "Listen, if you think I made a bad call, we can go pick him up right now. Maybe sitting in a jail cell will jog his memory."

Will did not relish the prospect of sweating an eighteen-year-old kid based on a hunch, especially considering Gabe Cohen's suicidal ideation. He listed the points in Gabe's favor. "He doesn't have a car on campus. He doesn't have a place to hide Emma. We have no connection between him and either girl. No motive, no opportunity, no means."

"I think he's troubled," she said. "But I don't think he's capable of this sort of thing." Faith laughed. "Of course, if I was good at spotting the ones who had murder in their hearts, I'd be running the world."

It was a sentiment Will had often thought himself. "What's the school doing with him?"

"Victor says it's a delicate situation," she said. "They're really caught in the middle."

"How so?"

"Do you remember the dozen or so suicides at MIT back in the nineties?"

Will nodded. The stories of parents suing the university had made national news.

"The schools have a legal obligation—*in loco parentis*," she cited, the phrase that basically said the school acted as parents to the students while they were enrolled. "Victor's going to recommend to the father that Gabe be committed for psychiatric evaluation."

Will couldn't help but notice that she kept using the dean's name. "Have him committed?" he asked. "That seems kind of drastic."

"They have to be careful. Even if Gabe's just blowing smoke, they have to take him seriously. I doubt Tech will allow him back in without a doctor's assurance that he's okay." She shrugged. "Even then, they'll probably make him check in with counselors every day."

Will liked the idea of Gabe Cohen being on psychiatric lockdown instead of left out in the world to his own devices. At least this way, he knew how to get his hands on the kid if he wanted to.

He said, "Let's go back to the murders."

"All right."

"Kayla was killed by someone who hated her. I can't believe the killer would take that much time with her otherwise. All those stab wounds, pulling down the underwear, pushing up the shirt. Classic debasement and overkill. You don't punch somebody's face off unless you know who they are and despise them for it." He suggested, "Maybe you're right. Maybe Emma snapped."

"She would have to kill her best friend—beat her, stab her, possibly rape her with something that, according to Pete, had a condom on it—*then* hit Adam over the head and stab him, *then* create this hoax for her parents to fall for." She added, "And that still doesn't explain the sperm found in Kayla Alexander's vagina."

"Or maybe Emma just stood by while it was all happening." He reminded her, "Charlie says there were four people in that house."

"True," Faith conceded. "But I have to put this in there somewhere: for a girl like Emma Campano, living where she lives, having the father and grandfather that she has, a million dollars isn't a lot of money."

Will hadn't considered that, but she was right. Ten million would be more on par with Paul's lifestyle. Then again, one million would be a lot easier to hide.

He said, "Bernard, Emma's teacher, said that she was highly organized. This took a lot of planning."

Faith shook her head. "I don't understand kids anymore. I really don't." She stared out the window at the apartments next door. "I hope I did the right thing with Gabe."

Will gave her one of Amanda's more solid pieces of advice. "You can only make decisions with the information you have at the time."

She was still looking out the window. "I've never been up to this floor before."

"We try to keep out the hoi polloi."

She smiled weakly. "How did it go with the Humphreys?"

"As bad as you would expect."

Faith chewed her lip, still staring out the window. "When I first saw Adam yesterday, all I could do was think about my son.

Maybe that's why I missed so many things. We lost hours when we could have been looking for her."

It was the most personal thing she had ever shared. Will had said so many wrong things to her lately that he knew better than to try to comfort her.

"I feel like we should be doing something," she said, her frustration obvious.

He told her the same things he had been telling himself. "It's a waiting game now. We're waiting on Charlie to process the evidence. We're waiting on the fingerprint guy. We're waiting on—"

"Everything," she said. "I'm half tempted to follow up nutjobs from the tip line."

"That wouldn't be the most productive use of your time."

Faith sighed in response. She looked bone-tired. Will imagined that getting some sleep was probably the only productive thing they could do tonight. Being fresh tomorrow morning when some of the evidence came in was key.

Will told her as much. "We'll have more to go on tomorrow morning." He checked the time. It was almost nine o'clock. "They're going to turn off the air-conditioning to the top floors in ten minutes. You should go home and try to get some sleep."

"Empty house," she told him. "Jeremy is enjoying his independence a little too much. I thought at least he'd miss me a little."

"I guess children can be stubborn sometimes."

"I bet you were a real handful for your mother."

Will shrugged. He supposed that was true enough. You didn't stick a baby in a trashcan because he was easy. "Maybe I could..." Will hesitated, but decided he might as well. "Would you like to go get a drink or something?"

She startled. "Oh, my God."

He realized two seconds too late that he'd put his foot in his mouth again. "I have a girlfriend. I mean, a fiancée. We're engaged." The details rushed out. "Angie Polaski. She used to work vice. I've known her since I was eight."

She seemed even more startled. "Eight?"

Will realized he should close his mouth and think about what he was saying before he let it out. "It sounds more romantic than it actually is." He paused. "I just...you said you didn't want to go to an empty house. I was just trying to...I don't know." He laughed nervously. "I guess my feral monkey is acting up again."

She was nice about it. "We've both had a long day."

"I don't even drink." Will stood as Faith did. He put his hand in his pocket and felt something unfamiliar mixed in with the change. He pulled out the vial with the gray powder in it, surprised the plastic hadn't broken during his scuffle with Paul.

"Will?"

He realized that his initial impression of the vial was probably hers, that he was holding an ounce of cocaine. "It's dirt," he told her. "Or some kind of powder. I found it at the Campano house."

"You found it?" she asked, taking the vial from him. "Since when do you work collection?"

"Since, uh..." Will held out his hand for the sample. "You really shouldn't be touching that."

"Why not?"

"It's not evidence."

"It's sealed." She showed him the unbroken strip of tape with Charlie's initials on it.

Will didn't have an answer for her.

Faith was instantly suspicious. "What's going on here?"

"I stole it from the Campano crime scene. Charlie turned his back and I swiped it before he could catalogue it into the system."

She narrowed her eyes. "Is that recorder on?"

He took the player off his desk, opened the back and shook out the batteries. "The powder was found in the foyer. It's ripe for a cross-contamination argument. We were all in and out of the area. It could have been brought in by one of us. Hell, for all I know, it was, but—"

"But?"

"But maybe not. It doesn't match any of the soil around the house. It wasn't on Adam's shoes or the girls' shoes. It could have been brought in by the killer."

"That sounds like information you got from the person who collected the evidence."

"Charlie has no idea that I'm doing this."

She obviously did not believe him, but Faith did not press the point. "Hypothetically, what would I do with it?"

"Maybe reach out to someone at Tech?"

She vehemently shook her head. "I'm not getting my son involved in—"

"No, of course not," he interrupted. "I thought maybe you could talk to Victor Martinez?"

"Victor?" she echoed. "I barely know the man."

"You knew him well enough to call him about Gabe Cohen."

"That's different," she insisted. "He's head of student services. Taking care of Gabe Cohen is his job."

Will tried, "He wouldn't think the request was odd coming from you. If I called him out of the blue, there would be all kinds of formalities, red tape. We need to keep this quiet, Faith. If that powder leads us to an area we can search, and we find the man who did this..."

"Then the chain of evidence would be compromised and the arrest might get thrown out." She gave a heavy sigh. "I need to think about this, Will."

He had to make sure she understood the implications. "I'm asking you to break the law. You realize that?"

"It runs in the family, right?"

He could see her words were angrier than she'd intended, but he also knew that she had been struggling over the last day and a half to make the best of their marriage of convenience.

Will told her, "I don't want you to do something you can't live with, Faith. Just make sure you get the sample back to me if you decide against it."

She wrapped her hand around the vial and held it to her chest. "I'm going to go now."

"Are you—"

She kept the vial in her hand. "What are we doing tomorrow?"

"I've got a meeting first thing with Amanda. I'll meet you back here around eight o'clock. Gordon Chew, the fingerprint expert, is driving down from Chattanooga to see if he can find any latents on our notes." He glanced around the office, his parklike view. "If I'm not here by eight-fifteen, check the men's toilets at the airport."

CHAPTER ELEVEN

FAITH SAT AT her kitchen table. Except for the night-light on the stove, the room was bathed in darkness. She'd gotten out a bottle of wine, a glass, the cork-screw, but they all sat unused on the table in front of her. All those years, she had wanted nothing more than to have Jeremy old enough to move out of the house so she could have some semblance of a life. Now that he was gone, she felt like she had a gaping hole in her chest where her heart used to be.

Drinking wouldn't help. She always got maudlin with wine. Faith reached for the wineglass to put it away, but ended up knock-ing it over instead. She grabbed for it, but the rim bounced off the edge of the table, then shattered on the tile floor. Faith knelt down, picking up the sharp shards of the broken wineglass. She thought about turning on the lights the second before a sliver cut into her skin.

"Dammit," she muttered, putting her finger in her mouth. She walked over to the sink, let cold water pour over the wound. She turned on the light above the sink, watching the blood pool and wash away, pool and wash away.

Her vision blurred as tears welled into her eyes. She felt foolish at the melodrama, but no one was around to ask her why she was crying over what amounted to a nasty paper cut, so Faith let the tears come. Besides, she had plenty to cry about. Tomorrow morning would mark the third day since Emma had been taken.

What was Abigail Campano going to do when she woke up tomorrow? Would sleep bring some kind of amnesia, so that at first light, she would have to remember all over again that her baby was gone? What would she do then? Was she going to think about all the breakfasts she had made, all the soccer practices and school dances and homework she had helped with? Or would her thoughts move to the future rather than the past: graduation, weddings, grandchildren?

Faith took a tissue and wiped her eyes. She realized how faulty her thinking had been. No mother could sleep when her child was in danger. Faith had spent many sleepless nights of her own, and she'd known exactly where Jeremy was—or where he was supposed to be. She had worried about car accidents and underage drinking and, God forbid, some little girl he was seeing who might be just as stupid as Faith had been at that age. It was bad enough to have a son fifteen years her junior, but a grandchild who was a mere sixteen years younger than that would have been crushing.

Faith laughed out loud at the thought, tossing the tissue into the trashcan. She should call her mother and commiserate, or at the very least apologize for the millionth time, but the person Faith really wanted right now was her father.

Bill Mitchell had died of a stroke seven years ago. The whole ordeal had been mercifully quick. He had clutched his arm and fallen down on the kitchen floor one morning, then died peacefully at the hospital two nights later. Faith's brother had flown in from Germany. Jeremy had taken off the day from school. Bill Mitchell had always been a considerate man, and even in death he managed to be mindful of the needs of his family. They were all in the room with him when he passed. They'd all had time to say good-bye. Faith did not think a day went by when she didn't think of her father—his kindness, his stability, his love.

In many ways, Bill Mitchell had handled his teenage daughter's pregnancy better than his wife. He had adored Jeremy, had relished the role of grandfather. It wasn't until much later that Faith found out the real reason Bill had stopped attending his weekly Bible study meetings and quit the bowling team. At the time, he'd said he wanted to be with his family more, to do some projects around the house. Now Faith knew that they had asked him to leave because of her. Faith's sin had rubbed off on him. Her father, a man so devout that he had once considered the ministry as a vocation, had never stepped foot in a church again, not even for Jeremy's baptism.

Faith wrapped a paper towel around her finger to catch the remaining trickles of blood. She turned on the lights and got the broom and dustpan from the pantry. She swept up the glass, then got out the stick vacuum to get the smaller pieces. She hadn't been home in two days, so the kitchen was messier than she usually kept it. Faith ran the vacuum over the tiles, angling the bristles into corners.

She rinsed off the dishes in the sink and put them in the dishwasher. She scoured the sink and put the dish towels in the washing machine along with a load of clothes that she found in her bathroom hamper. She was cleaning out the dryer lint trap when she remembered the uncomfortable moment with Will Trent, when just for a moment, she had thought he was asking her out on a date.

Angie Polaski. For the first time since she'd met him, Faith felt sorry for the man. Talk about sloppy seconds. Was there such a thing as sloppy thousandths? Polaski's conquests were legend in the squad room. There were even jokes to rookies about how they had to pass through those legs to become one of the finest cops in the city.

Will had to know about the rumors—or maybe he was just one of those people who couldn't translate the skills they showed on the job to their personal lives. Standing in his office doorway tonight, watching him work on his computer, Faith had been struck by his sense of isolation. Will had literally jumped out of his chair when he'd seen her. With the bruises around his eyes, he'd looked like a startled raccoon.

That was another thing. How was he going to keep his job after getting into a fistfight with Paul Campano? Talk about police gossip. Hamish Patel gossiped like a woman. Faith had gotten a phone call from one of her fellow homicide detectives before she'd even left Georgia Tech.

Will didn't seem to be worried about his job. Amanda was tough, but she could also be very fair. Or maybe tolerance was the new buzzword at the GBI now. Faith had called Will an asshole and a monkey in the space of two days and he still had not thrown her off the case. He had just given her a vial of gray powder and asked her to break the law.

Her cell phone started ringing, and Faith ran to the kitchen like an anxious schoolgirl, expecting to hear Jeremy's voice.

She said, "Let me guess, you need pizza?"

"Faith?" She felt herself frowning, trying to place the voice. "It's Victor Martinez."

"Oh," was all she could manage.

He said, "Were you expecting someone else?"

"I thought you'd be my son."

"How is Jeremy doing?"

Faith didn't recall having told him Jeremy's name, but she said, "He's fine."

"I met him this afternoon. He's in Glenn Hall. Fine young man."

"I'm sorry," she began. "Why were you talking to him?"

"I've spoken with all the students who lived near Adam Humphrey. I wanted to check on them, make sure they knew they had someone to turn to."

"More ass covering?"

"Have I made myself seem that callous?"

Faith stumbled through an apology. "It's been a long day for me."

"Me, too."

She closed her eyes, thinking about the way Victor Martinez's eyes crinkled when he smiled—the real smile, not the "oh-shit-you've-got-a-son-at-my-school" smile.

"Faith?"

"I'm here."

"There's an Italian restaurant on Highland. Do you know the one I'm talking about?"

"Uh..." Faith shook her head, as if she needed to clear her ears. "Yes."

"I know it's late, but would you meet me there for dinner? Or maybe just a drink?"

Faith was sure she had misunderstood him. She actually stuttered. "S-sure. Okay."

"Ten minutes."

"All right."

"I'll see you then."

Faith held the phone in her hand until the recorded message beseeched her to hang up. She dropped the phone and rushed around the house like a madwoman, looking for a clean pair of jeans, then deciding on a skirt, then realizing the skirt was not only too tight but had a guacamole stain from the last time she had eaten out with a man—if you counted Jeremy as a man. She settled on a strapless sundress and headed for the front door, only to turn around and change when she caught her reflection in the mirror, the pasty skin under her arm rolling up over the dress like the top of a Starbucks sour cream blueberry muffin.

Victor was sitting at the bar when she finally made it to the restaurant. He had a half-empty glass of what looked like scotch in front of him. His tie was pulled down, his jacket on the back of his chair. The hands on the clock over the bar were coming up on eleven. Yet again, Faith found herself wondering if this was even a date. Maybe he had just asked her out as a friend, or someone who was a peer, so they could talk about Gabriel Cohen. Maybe he just didn't like to drink alone.

He stood up when he saw her, a tired, lazy smile on his lips. If this wasn't a date, then Faith was the biggest fool on the planet; her knees went weak at the sight of him.

Victor rubbed his hand along her arm and she fought the urge to purr. He said, "I thought you'd changed your mind."

"Just my clothes," she admitted. "Four times."

He took in her outfit, which was a variation on the same work clothes he'd seen her in since they'd met yesterday. "You look very...professional."

Faith sat down, feeling exhaustion overcome desire. She was a bit old to be acting like a heartsick schoolgirl. The last time that'd happened, she'd ended up pregnant and alone. "Believe me, considering what I found in my closet, it could have been a lot worse."

He pulled his bar stool close to hers and sat. "I like it without the gun and the badge."

She felt naked without them, actually, but she chose not to share the information.

"What'll you have to drink?"

Faith looked at the bottles of liquor stacked behind the bar. She knew she should have chosen something ladylike—a wine spritzer or a cosmopolitan, but she couldn't bring herself to do it. "Gin and tonic."

Victor motioned over the bartender and placed the order.

Faith asked, "What happened with Gabe?"

Victor turned toward her. She could see that the sparkle in his eyes was not as intense. "Are you asking in an official capacity?"

"Yes, I am."

He rolled his palm along the outside of his glass of scotch. "Honesty isn't really a problem with you, is it?"

"No," Faith admitted. She had yet to meet a man who considered this an asset.

Victor said, "Can I ask you—when you called me today, you said you didn't want to put Gabe into the system. What did you mean by that?"

She was silent as the bartender put a large gin and tonic in front of her. Faith allowed herself a sip before telling Victor, "I think the easiest way to sum it up is to say that the police are known for using sledgehammers to drive in thumbtacks. The department has a procedure for everything. With Gabe—I would've placed him in protective custody, either called an ambulance or taken him to Grady hospital myself. I would tell them what he told me: He admitted to trying to kill himself before. He admitted to me that he was thinking about doing it again. Suicide is the eighth-leading cause of death among young men. We take that very seriously."

His eyes had not left hers the entire time she'd talked. Faith could not remember the last time a man had kept eye contact with her, really listened to what she had to say. Well—unless she was reading them their rights, but that was hardly flattering.

Victor said, "So, you take him to the hospital. What happens next?"

"He would have a twenty-four-hour observation period, then if he freaked out and refused treatment, which in this case would be completely understandable, he would have a right to go before a judge and petition for his release. Depending on how he presented, whether the judge thought he was being reasonable or not, whether the doctor who evaluated him actually had time to show up in court, he would be released or sent back for a more extensive evaluation. Either way, his name would go into a computer. His personal life would forever be recorded on a national database. That's assuming he wasn't under arrest for something."

"I thought the public university system was convoluted," Victor said.

"Why don't you tell me about that?" she suggested. "Trust me, office politics are much more interesting than police procedure."

He draped his arm over the back of her bar stool. She could feel the heat from his body through her thin cotton blouse. "Humor me," he said, or at least that's what Faith heard. Her hearing had faded out as soon as he'd touched her—maybe it was the angels playing harps or the exploding fireworks. Maybe her drink was too strong or her heart was too lonely. With some effort, she made herself lean forward, taking a healthy swig from her glass.

Victor stroked her back with his thumb, either a playful, flirting gesture or a nudge to keep her talking. "What would an arrest entail?"

She took a deep breath before listing it out, "Handcuffing him, driving him to the station, fingerprinting, photos, taking away his belt, his shoestrings, his personal belongings, putting him in a cell with the dregs of society." She leaned her chin in her hand, thinking about Gabe Cohen being locked up with the drunks and the dealers. "That late in the day, he would probably spend the night in jail, then be taken over to the courthouse in the morning, where he would wait three or four hours for his bail hearing, then he would have to wait to be processed out, then wait some more for his trial." Faith took a heftier sip of her drink, then leaned back into his arm. "And from then on, every time he got a speeding ticket or an employer did a background check or even if a crime happened in his neighborhood and his name came up, he would be subjected to the kind of scrutiny that would make a proctologist blush."

Victor put his thumb to work again, and again she didn't know if it was blanket encouragement or a more intimate gesture. "You did him a favor today."

"I don't know," she admitted. "It seems like I just pawned him off on you."

"I'm glad you did. We had a student last year who overdosed on oxycodone. She lived off campus. No one found her for a while."

Faith could all too easily imagine what the scene had looked like. "In my experience, the ones who talk about it don't usually do it. The quiet ones, the ones who just close in on themselves, are the ones you have to worry about."

"Gabe wasn't being quiet."

"No, but maybe he was getting there." She took another drink so she wouldn't fidget with her hands. "You never know."

Victor told her, "Gabe's father took him to a private hospital."

"Good."

He loosened his tie some more. "What else happened today? How is your case going?"

"I've already dominated the conversation too much," she realized, feeling slightly embarrassed. "Tell me about your day."

"My days are tedious, trust me. I solve squabbles between students, I rubber-stamp requests for kids to build lofts in their dorms, take endless meetings on the same, and if I'm lucky enough, I get to deal with spoiled little jerks like Tommy Albertson."

"How fascinating. Tell me more."

He smiled at her teasing, but asked a serious question. "Do you think you'll be able to find that girl?"

"I think that..." She felt the darkness come back, the deepening pull of the abyss. "I think I like me better when I'm not wearing my badge, too."

"Fair enough," he said. "Tell me about Jeremy."

Faith wondered if that was really what this date was about—idle curiosity. "We're just another Reagan-era statistic."

"That sounds like a stock answer."

"It is," she conceded. There wasn't really a way to describe what had happened. In the course of a month, she had gone from singing Duran Duran songs into a hairbrush in front of her bathroom mirror to worrying about hemorrhoids and gestational diabetes.

Victor gently pressed, "Tell me how it was."

"I don't know. It was how you would think. Horrible. I kept it from my parents as long as I could and then it was too late to do anything about it."

"Are your parents religious?"

She gathered he was asking about abortion. "Very," she answered. "But they're also realists. My mom in particular wanted me to go to college, to have a family when I was ready, to have choices in my life. My dad had some qualms, but he would've supported any decision I made. Basically, they both left it up to me."

"So what happened?"

Faith gave him the truth. "It was too late for a legal abortion, but there was always adoption. I hate to admit it, but I was selfish and rebellious. I didn't think about how hard it would be or how it would impact everyone in my family. Everything my parents told me to do, I did the exact opposite, damn the consequences." She laughed, saying, "Which might explain how I got pregnant in the first place."

He was staring at her again with the same intensity that had sent a jolt through her the first time they had met. "You're beautiful when you laugh."

She blushed, which was just as well because her first inclination had been to throw herself at his feet. The effect he had on her was both exciting and humiliating, mostly because she had no idea how he felt in turn. Was he asking all of these questions out of idle curiosity? Or was he really interested in something deeper? She was far too inexperienced to figure this out on her own, and much too old to be bothering.

Faith had actually brought her purse with her, a concession to femininity when her earlier dressing debacle had ended with her wearing her extremely unsexy but moderately clean work outfit. She dug around in the bag to give herself something to do other than stare like a lost puppy into the fathomless, deep black of his beautiful eyes.

Kleenex, her wallet, her badge, an extra pair of hose, a pack of gum. She had no idea what she was supposed to be looking for as she rummaged around in the bag. The back of her hand brushed against what she thought was one of those annoying little perfume samples they give you at the mall, but turned out to be the plastic vial of gray powder that Will Trent had given her. She had thrown it into the bag at the last minute, not really thinking about it. Now, she felt nauseated as she held the vial in her hand, considered the implications behind the theft.

Victor asked, "Is something wrong?"

She forced out the question before logic had time to stop her. "Does Tech have someone who specializes in . . ." She didn't know what to call it. "Dirt?"

He chuckled. "We're ranked the seventh-best public university in the country. We've got a whole dirt department."

"I need to ask you a favor," she began, but didn't know where to go from there.

"Anything you want."

She realized that this was her last chance to change her mind, that she could always make up an excuse, change the subject, and be the kind of straight-arrow cop that her mother had taught her to be.

Faith was a mother too, though. How would she feel if some

cop out there was playing it so close to the rulebook that Jeremy's life was lost?

Victor motioned over the bartender. "Maybe another drink will help loosen your lips."

Faith put her hand over her glass, surprised that it was empty. "I'm driving."

He took her hand away, holding on to it. She could feel his other hand wrap around her waist. There was no mistaking his meaning now. "Tell me your favor." He stroked her fingers, and she felt the warmth of his skin, the firm caress of his thumb. "I'll make sure you get home safe."

DAY THREE

CHAPTER TWELVE

ABIGAIL SAT ON the couch as she watched her mother fuss around the room, straightening pillows, opening curtains. Beatrice had flown fourteen grueling hours to get here, but her makeup was neatly applied and her hair was tightly swept into a bun. When Abigail was growing up, her mother's unflappability had annoyed her to no end. She'd spent years trying to shock her with tight jeans and garish makeup and inappropriate boyfriends. Now she could only be grateful for the normalness the older woman brought to the situation. Emma may have been missing for three days and Abigail may have killed a man, but the bed would still be made and fresh hand towels would still be put out in the bathroom.

"You need to eat," Beatrice told her. "You want to be strong when Emma comes home."

Abigail shook her head, not wanting to think about food. Her mother had been speaking in these sorts of declarative statements since she'd arrived yesterday afternoon. Emma was the fulcrum to everything, whether it was coaxing Abigail to get out of bed or making her comb her hair for the press conference.

Beatrice addressed Hamish. "Young man, would you like something to eat?"

"No, thank you, ma'am." He kept his head down, checking his computer equipment again. Bless his heart, the man was terrified of Beatrice and her desire to put everything in order. From the moment she started straightening, Hamish had stationed himself in the kitchen, hovering over his equipment for fear she would touch something. When the other technician came to relieve him for the night, Hamish had told the man to go away. Abigail wanted to think his actions were out of concern for his computer equipment rather than any indication that the situation had escalated.

She shuddered, the mechanical voice on the phone coming back to her.

Is this the mother?

The ransom call had changed everything. The whispers between Paul and her father had increased. They had talked about the money, the logistics of putting their hands on the cash, as if the kidnapper had asked for billions instead of one million. Abigail knew for a fact that they had at least a million and a half in their money market account. Barring that, her father could have the sum couriered to his doorstep with just a phone call. Something was going on—something that they didn't want to tell Abigail about. She was at turns furious and relieved that they weren't involving her.

"Now," Beatrice said, sitting on the opposite side of the couch. She was on the edge of the cushion, her knees pressed together, legs slanted to the side. Abigail could not remember ever seeing her mother slump against anything. She seemed to have a spine made of titanium. "We need to talk about what you are doing to yourself."

Abigail glanced back at Hamish, who was studying something on his computer screen. "Do we need to have this conversation now, Mother?"

"Yes, we do."

She wanted to roll her eyes. She wanted to flounce. How easily she fell back into that rebellious pattern when Abigail could plainly see that all her mother was doing was trying to help her. Why was it so much easier with her father? Why was it that Hoyt had persuaded her to eat a piece of cheese toast and change into a fresh set of clothes? Why was it so much easier to cry on his shoulder than to take comfort from her mother?

Beatrice took her hand. "You're crying again."

"Am I allowed to do that?" Abigail stared at the stack of newspapers on the coffee table, the printouts from the *Washington Post* and the *Seattle Intelligencer*. Paul had downloaded every story he could find, scouring the reports for some detail that he was certain the police were withholding from them. He was paranoid about everything, quizzing Abigail about crime-scene details the press had made up, conjecture they'd put out as real news. Three years ago, Adam Humphrey had been cautioned for driving without proof of insurance. Did that point to a darker side the police weren't talking about? Kayla had been kicked out of her last school for smoking on campus. Did that mean she was doing harder drugs? Did her drug dealer bring this insanity into their lives? Was there some thug out there who was pumping Emma full of dope right now?

Making matters worse, Paul's temper was more uncontrollable than ever. Abigail had pressed him for details about the fight with Will Trent yesterday and he had gotten so angry with her that she'd left the room rather than hear his tirade. She wanted to say that she didn't even know him anymore, but that wasn't true. This was exactly the Paul she had always known was there. Tragedy just brought out the finer points, and, frankly, their privileged lives had made character flaws easier to overlook.

They were used to living in eight thousand square feet of space—plenty of room to get away from each other. The carriage house, with its cozy kitchen/living room and single bedroom, was too small for them now. They were tripping over each other, constantly in each other's way. Abigail thought that she was just as much a prisoner of this space as Emma was—wherever that may be.

What she really wanted to do was grab him, punch him, do something to punish him for letting this terrible thing happen to Emma. Paul had broken their silent deal and she was furious with him for his transgression. He could fuck around with his women and spoil their daughter to within an inch of her life, but at the end of the day, the only thing Abigail wanted from him, the only thing she expected from him, was to keep their family safe.

And he had failed miserably. Everything had gone so horribly wrong.

Beatrice stroked Abigail's hand. "You need to be strong."

"I killed someone, Mother." She knew she wasn't supposed to talk about it in front of Hamish, but the words flowed. "I strangled him with my bare hands. Adam Humphrey was the only person here who tried to help Emma, the only person who could tell us what really happened, and I killed him."

"Shh," she hushed, stroking Abigail's hand. "You can't change that now."

"I can feel remorse," she said. "I can feel anger, and helplessness and fury." She gulped for air, her emotions overwhelming her. How could they expect her to go on camera today, to expose herself to the world? They weren't even going to let her speak, a fact that had made Paul furious but had secretly relieved Abigail.

The thought of opening her mouth, begging some unseen stranger for the return of her child, made Abigail feel physically ill. What if she said the wrong thing? What if she answered a question the wrong way? What if she came across as cold? What if she came across as hard? What if she sounded too harsh or too needy or too pathetic?

The irony was that it was other women—other mothers—she was worried about. The ones who so easily passed judgment on their own sex, as if sharing certain biological characteristics made them experts on the subject. Abigail knew this mind-set because she had shared it back when she had the luxury of her safe and perfect life. She had read the stories about Madeleine McCann and JonBenet Ramsey, following every detail of the cases, judging the mothers just as harshly as everyone else had. She had seen Susan Smith pleading to the media and read about Diane Downs's despicable violence against her own children. It had been so easy to pass judgment on these women—these mothers—to sit back on the couch, sip her coffee, and pronounce them too cold or too hard or too guilty, simply because she had caught five seconds of their faces on the news or in *People* magazine. And now, in the ultimate karmic payback of all time, Abigail would be the one on the cameras. She would be the one in the magazines. Her friends and neighbors, worst of all, complete strangers, would be sitting on their own couches making snap judgments about Abigail's actions.

Beatrice said, "It's all right."

"It's not all right." Abigail stood up from the couch, snatching her hand away from her mother. "I'm sick of everyone walking around on eggshells. Somebody needs to mourn Adam. Somebody needs to acknowledge that I fucked everything up!"

Beatrice was silent, and Abigail turned around to look at her mother. The harsh light did her skin no favors, picking out every crevice, every wrinkle that the makeup could not hide. Her mother had had work done—a lift of the brow, a sharpening of the chin— but the effect was not drastic, more a softening of time's ravages so that she looked young for her age rather than like a silicon-lipped, plastic figurine.

She spoke quietly, authoritatively. "You did fuck up, Abby. You misread the situation and you killed that boy." Her mother didn't like to use such language, and it showed on her face. Still, she continued, "You thought he was attacking you, but he was asking you for help."

"He was only eighteen years old."

"I know."

"Emma may have loved him. He had her picture in his wallet. He might have been her boyfriend." She thought about what that meant—holding hands, their first kiss, awkward fumbling and touching. Had her daughter made love with Adam Humphrey? Had she experienced the pleasure of a man holding her, caressing her? Was that first love the memory she would have, or would Emma only recall her abductor hurting her, raping her?

This time yesterday, the only thing Abigail had thought about was Emma's death. Now she was finding herself wondering what would happen if Emma lived. Abigail was no fool. She knew that money was not the only reason a grown man would steal a seventeen-year-old girl from her family. If they got her back—if Emma was returned—who would that child be? Who would that stranger be in the place of their daughter?

And how would Paul deal with it? How could he ever look at his little angel again without thinking about what had been done to her, how she had been used? After yesterday's fight, Paul hadn't even been able to look at Abigail. How could he face their daughter?

She spoke the words that had been choking her since they had realized Emma was not dead, but taken. "Whoever has her...he'll hurt her. He's probably hurting her right now."

Beatrice gave a curt nod. "Probably."

"Paul won't—"

"Paul will handle it, just like you."

She doubted that. Paul liked for things to be perfect, and if they couldn't be perfect, then he liked the appearance of perfection. Everyone would know what had happened to Emma. Everyone would know every single detail of her damaged life. And who could blame them for their bloodlust, their curiosity? Even now, the smallest part of Abigail's brain that remembered details from movies of the week and sensational magazine cover stories threw out the names of abducted and returned children: Elizabeth Smart, Shawn Hornbeck, Steven Stayner...what had become of them? What had their families done to cope?

Abigail asked, "Who will she be, Mama? If we get her back, who will Emma be?"

Beatrice's hand was steady as she tilted up Abigail's chin. "She will be your daughter, and you will be her mother, and you'll make everything fine for her, because that is what mothers do. You hear me?"

Abigail had never seen her mother cry, and that wasn't about to change now. What she saw in her eyes was Beatrice's strength, her calm in the storm. For just a moment, the certainty in her voice, the sureness of her words, brought something like peace to Abigail for the first time since this waking nightmare had started.

She said, "Yes, Mama."

"Good girl," Beatrice answered, patting her cheek before she walked toward the kitchen. She rummaged through the cabinets, saying, "I told your father you'd have some soup before he got back. You don't want to disappoint your daddy now, do you?"

CHAPTER THIRTEEN

WILL HAD ALWAYS been a good sleeper. He supposed it came from sharing a room with a handful of strangers for the first eighteen years of his life. You learned to sleep through the coughs and the cries, the passing of wind and the one-handed lullabies every teenage boy practiced from a very young age.

Last night, the house had been quiet except for Betty's soft snores and Angie's occasional groans. Sleep, on the other hand, had been an impossibility. Will's brain would not shut down. Lying in bed, staring at the ceiling, his mind had shuttled through what little evidence they had on the case until the sun had come up and Will had finally forced himself out of bed. He'd done his usual routine—taken Betty for a stroll, then taken himself for a run. Even as he jogged, the predawn heat pressing out every drop of moisture in his body, all he could do was think about Emma Campano. Was she being held somewhere in the air-conditioning or was she exposed to hundred-plus temperatures? How long could she survive on her own? What was her abductor doing to her?

It did not bear thinking about, but as Will stood on the loading dock behind City Hall East, waiting for Emma's parents to show up, all he could think was that for the first time in his life, he was no longer envious of Paul Campano.

Will wondered how Amanda had broken it to the man that he was not to open his mouth during the press conference. Paul would not have taken the order lightly. He was used to bossing people around, controlling the situation with his anger—or the threat of it. Even when he didn't speak, Paul managed to convey his displeasure. Will knew that the kidnapper would be watching the parents for any indication that he should just kill the girl and move on. Keeping a lid on Paul would be an uphill battle. He was glad it wasn't his job.

Amanda had obviously not been pleased that the press had basically forced her into calling a conference. She had scheduled it at a time when most reporters were sleeping off the night before. They weren't as savage at six-thirty in the morning as they were at eight or nine, and, as usual, she liked exploiting the advantage. In a fit of compassion, Will had not bothered Faith with the early call. He thought it best to let her sleep in. He didn't know her well, but he guessed the detective had spent her night tossing and turning over the case just like he had. Maybe the extra two hours would help clear her mind this morning. At least one of them would know what they were doing.

A black BMW 750 pulled up to the loading dock. Of course, Paul had refused to let a cruiser bring him in. Amanda had told the Campanos to meet Will on the North Avenue side of the building because a couple of photographers were already milling around the front steps of City Hall East. The back was restricted to police vehicles and various support vehicles, so the vultures couldn't get in without risking arrest.

Paul got out of the car first, his hand smoothing back the flap of hair that covered the top of his balding head. He was wearing a dark suit with a white shirt and blue tie—nothing flashy. Amanda would have coached them not to appear too wealthy or too well dressed; not for fear of the kidnapper, but because the press would be scrutinizing every inch of the parents to find a vulnerability that could be exploited for their lead paragraph.

Abigail opened her car door just as Paul reached for the handle. Her long, shapely legs were bare, her shoes modestly heeled. She was wearing a dark blue skirt and an off-white cotton blouse of the sort Faith Mitchell seemed to favor. The overall look was understated, reserved. Except for the ninety-thousand-dollar car, she could be any soccer mom within a five-mile radius.

Yesterday's fight was obviously still fresh for the couple, or maybe there had been some new ones in between. There was a distance between them. Even as they walked up the stairs to the loading dock, Paul did not offer his arm, nor did his wife reach to take it.

"Agent Trent," Abigail said. Her voice was thin, her gaze almost lifeless. He wondered if she was still medicated. The woman seemed to have trouble standing upright.

Paul, on the other hand, was almost bouncing on his toes. "I want to talk to your boss."

"You'll see her in a minute," Will said, opening the door to the building. They walked down the narrow hallway to the private elevator that serviced the police station. Will could not help but put his hand at Abigail's back as she walked. There was something so fragile about her. The fact that Paul was oblivious to this was not surprising, but Will was taken aback by the renewed anger he felt at the man. His wife was falling apart in front of him and all Paul could think to do was demand to talk to the person in charge.

Will kept his pace slow so that Abigail would not have to struggle to keep up. Paul bounded ahead of them toward the elevator, as if he knew where to go.

Will kept his voice low, telling the woman, "This won't take long."

She looked at him, her red-rimmed eyes filling with tears. "I don't know what to do."

"We'll get you back home as soon—"

"I've got a statement to make," Paul told Will, his loud voice an intrusion in the small space. "You're not going to stop me."

Will tried to temper his anger, but the other man's smug certainty was grating. "What exactly do you want to say?"

"I'm going to offer a bonus."

Will felt sucker punched—again. "A bonus for what?"

"I'm going to tell the kidnapper we'll double the ransom money if Emma isn't harmed."

"That's not how these things—"

"Let me talk to your boss," he interrupted, pressing the call button for the elevator just as the doors opened. "I don't have time to fuck with you."

A crowd of cops filled the ancient elevator. They all recognized the Campanos and gave them a wide berth, vacating the car as quickly as possible.

Paul got on. Will pressed his hand to Abigail's back, gently persuading her to move. He entered his code on the grimy keypad, then pressed the button for the third floor. There was a rumbling somewhere in the bowels of the building, then the doors creaked closed and the car jerked as it slowly started upward.

Among other things, Will had discussed the press conference with Amanda last night. The Campanos were not going to talk to the media because Abigail was too vulnerable and Paul was too volatile. Once they opened their mouths, the press would attack. Even the most innocuous statement could be spun into a damning indictment.

Will told Paul as much now. "This isn't like what you see on television. We don't need you to make a statement. We just need you to be there to remind the kidnappers that Emma has parents who love her."

"Fuck you," Paul barked back, his fists clenching. "You can't stop me from talking to the press."

Will's nose still ached from yesterday. He wondered if he was about to get punched again and how much it would bleed. "I can stop you talking at this particular press conference."

"We'll see what your boss says," Paul told him, crossing his arms. Maybe he wasn't ready to get hit again, either. "I told you yesterday, I'm not fucking around. This guy wants money and we'll give it to him. Whatever he wants. I'm not going to let my baby get hurt."

"It's too late," Abigail said. Her voice was barely more than a whisper, but she still managed to be heard. She told her husband, "Don't you know that the worst has already happened?"

Paul looked as if he'd been sucker punched. "Don't say that."

"The only reason he's giving her back is because he's finished with her."

Paul jabbed his finger in her face. "Don't you talk like that, God dammit!"

"It's true," she said, unfazed by the sudden flash of fury. "You know it's true, Paul. You know he's used her every way—"

"Stop it!" he screamed, grabbing her by the arms, shaking her. "You shut up, do you hear me? Just shut up!"

The doors slid open, the bell dinging to indicate they had reached the third floor. A tall man with steel gray hair and bronzed skin stood in front of the open doors. He looked like something out of *Garden & Gun,* and his face was familiar to Will from the newspaper reports: Hoyt Bentley, Emma Campano's wealthy grandfather. Amanda was beside the man. If she was surprised to find Paul Campano threatening his wife, she didn't show it. She took in Will, her eyes traveling over his bruised face. Her eyebrow lifted, and he instantly understood that they would be having a conversation about how he'd gotten his face punched at a more convenient time.

Hoyt spoke like a man used to being obeyed. "Let go of her, Paul."

"Not until she says it's not true," Paul insisted, as if this was some kind of pissing contest he knew he could win by bullying his wife.

Abigail had obviously dealt with this before. Even in her grief, a hint of sarcasm crept into her tone. "Okay, Paul. It's not true. Emma's fine. I'm sure whoever took her hasn't hurt her or abused her or—"

"Enough," Amanda said. "This is why you're not talking to the press—both of you." She held out her hand, stopping the elevator doors from closing. She directed her words to Paul. "Unless you want your wife to take questions about killing Adam Humphrey?

Or perhaps you'd like to talk about your extramarital affairs?" She gave one of her icy smiles. "This is how it's going to work: you're both going to sit there on the dais and let the cameras roll. I am going to read from a prepared statement, while the press takes photographs, then you are both going to go home and wait for the second call from the kidnapper. Is that clear?"

Paul dropped his hands, fists tight. "Emma's okay," he told his wife, unable to let her have the last word. "This is a ransom, not a kidnapping. Kidnappers don't hurt the victims. They just want money."

Will glanced at Amanda, guessing she was thinking the same thing that he was, which was that Paul's words pretty much confirmed he had hired an outside expert to advise him—and possibly more. The offer of extra money was a calculated risk, but men who were paid by the hour tended to be good at coming up with a scattershot of ideas that justified their large paychecks.

Hoyt spoke in a deep, resonant voice that perfectly matched his zillion-dollar suit and handmade loafers. "The only thing we're going to do by waving around more money is convince the kidnapper that he should hold out for more."

Paul shook his head. His lips were moving, no words coming out. It was as if his anger had a stranglehold on him. For Will's part, he was surprised to find that Paul wasn't more cowed by the father-in-law. He sensed a camaraderie between Hoyt and Amanda that Paul seemed to be missing. They had already decided how to approach this, the best way to get things done. Will was not surprised that the two would see eye-to-eye. In her own way, Amanda Wagner was a captain of her own industry. Hoyt Bentley would appreciate that.

Amanda suggested, "Why don't we talk about this?" She indicated the long hallway before them, the skanky set of windows overlooking the railroad trellis.

Paul looked back and forth between his father-in-law and Amanda. He nodded once, then walked down the hallway with them. No one talked until they were far away enough not to be heard.

Will tried not to feel completely emasculated as he watched them—the child who wasn't allowed to sit at the adult table. As if to put a fine point on it, he noticed that he was standing right by the women's restroom. Will made himself look away, leaning his shoulder against the wall. Before he turned, he noticed that Paul's opening tactic was the usual one—he jabbed his finger in Amanda's face. Even from twenty feet away, Will could feel the tension his bluster created. There were just some people in the world who had to be the center of attention at all times. Paul was king of them.

Abigail said, "He's not all bad."

Will raised his eyebrows, his nose throbbing from the gesture. He realized he should stop feeling sorry for himself and take the opportunity to talk to Abigail Campano, whom he'd yet to find alone.

"I said some horrible things to him yesterday. Today. This morning." She gave a faint smile. "In the bathroom. In the driveway. In the car."

"You're under a lot of pressure."

"I've never been the type of person to strike out," she said, though, to Will, yesterday's performance in the carriage house had seemed pretty natural. "I think maybe I used to be. Maybe some time ago. It's all coming back to me now."

She wasn't making much sense, but Will preferred talking to her rather than straining to hear the exchange between the adults. "You just need to do what you can do to hold on. The press conference won't take long, and Amanda will handle everything."

"Why am I here?" Her question was so straightforward that Will found himself unable to answer her. She continued, "I'm not going to make a plea. You're not going to let me beg for the safe return of my daughter. Why is that?"

He did not tell her that if a sadist had her child, watching Abigail's pain might inspire him to get more creative with his victim. Even without that, Abigail proved every time she opened her mouth that she was unpredictable.

He told the woman a softer version of the truth. "It's easier if you let Amanda do all the talking."

"So they won't ask me about killing Adam?"

"Among other things."

"Aren't they going to wonder why I'm not at home waiting for the second phone call?"

He gathered she was speaking more for herself than the members of the press. "This is a very tense time—not just for us, but for whoever has Emma. We need the press to tone down the rhetoric. We don't need them running with some wild story, making up clues and chasing down crazy theories while we're trying to negotiate for Emma's return."

She slowly nodded her head. "What will it be like in there? In front of all those cameras?"

Excruciating, Will thought, but said, "I'll be standing in the back of the room. Just look at me, okay?" She nodded, and he continued, "There will be a lot of cameras flashing, lots of people asking questions. Just stare at me and try to ignore them. I'm kind of easy to pick out of a crowd."

She didn't laugh at the joke. He noticed that she was holding her purse against her stomach. It was small, what he thought was called a clutch. Will had seen her closet, a spectacularly furnished room that was larger than his kitchen. There were evening gowns and designer labels and slinky high heels, but nothing in her wardrobe had appeared understated. He wondered if she had bought the outfit for the occasion, or borrowed it from a friend.

As if she could read his mind, she asked, "Do I fit the part of the bereaved killer?"

Will had heard the news call her as much this morning. The reporters were having a field day with the savage-mother-protecting-her-daughter angle. The irony was too rich to pass up. "You shouldn't watch television. At least until this is over."

She opened her purse. He saw a tube of lipstick, a set of keys, and a bundle of photographs that she rested her fingers on but did not take out. Instead, she pulled a tissue from the bottom and used it to wipe her nose. "How can I not watch? How can I not soak up every horrible thing that comes out of their mouths?"

Will did not know how he was expected to answer, so he said nothing.

One of Paul's ubiquitous "fuck you"s came from down the hallway. Whatever Amanda said was more of a murmur, but the tone sent out a chill that could be felt even from this distance.

Abigail said, "I like your boss."

"I'm glad."

"She wrote my statement for me."

Will knew this already. Amanda wouldn't have trusted the mother to prepare a plea for the return of her child. The semantics were too important. One wrong word could send the wrong message, then they would suddenly find themselves going from working a kidnapping to working a murder case.

"She doesn't lie to me," Abigail said. "Are you going to lie to me?"

"About what?"

"Are they going to ask me questions about Adam?"

"If they're any good at their jobs—yes. They'll try. But keep in mind, you're not here to answer questions. The reporters know the ground rules. That doesn't mean they'll necessarily follow them, but *you* have to. Don't let them bait you. Don't let them force you into a situation where you have to explain yourself, or where you say something that might later be used against you."

"I killed him. In every sense of the word, I murdered him."

"You probably shouldn't say that to a cop."

"I used to be a lawyer," she said. "I know how this works."

"How?"

"It all depends on how things go from now on, doesn't it? Whether or not you charge me. If Emma comes back in one piece, or if she's..." Abigail sniffed, wiping her nose again. "If the newspapers are with me, if they paint me as some kind of cold-blooded killer, if the parents push for prosecution...so many ifs."

Will assured her, "I'm not going to charge you with anything."

Abigail indicated Amanda. "She might."

Will admitted to himself that the woman had a point. "It's not my place to advise you, but you're not going to do yourself any favors talking like this."

"He was just a child. He had his whole life in front of him." She pressed her lips together, taking a moment to gather her thoughts. "Think of all the things I took from him—from his parents. There's nothing for them now. Just eighteen years, then nothing."

Will wasn't sure what he would be saying in her place, but he found himself wondering if Abigail was focusing so much on Adam Humphrey because the alternative—focusing on the fate of her own daughter—was too much to bear.

She asked, "What should I say when the reporters ask me about Adam?"

"Nothing," he told her. "We told them from the start that they're only supposed to direct their questions to Amanda. They won't do that, of course, but you don't have to talk to them."

"What if I want to?"

"What would you say?" Will asked. "Because if it's the things you just told me, I can tell you right now that they'll have you nailed to a cross by nightfall." He added, "If you want to punish yourself for what happened to Adam Humphrey, then take some pills or try experimenting with heroin. You'll be much better off than throwing yourself onto the mercy of the press."

"You *are* honest."

"I guess I am," Will admitted. "Save yourself for Emma. If you can't be strong for yourself, then be strong for her."

"I'm so sick of people telling me to be strong."

Will wondered what else could be said—be weak? Fall on the floor? Rend your clothes? Wail? All of these things seemed like obvious reactions that a normal person might have, but they certainly wouldn't play well for the cameras.

Abigail said, "I'm not usually this melodramatic. I'm afraid I might..." She shook her head. "What if he sees me on television and thinks that Emma deserves it? What if I do something wrong or don't look grieved enough, or look too grieved, or—"

"You can't keep playing this game in your head."

"Game?" she asked. "I want this all to be a game. I want to wake up tomorrow morning and yell at Emma to get ready for school. I want to scream at my husband for screwing around on me. I want to play tennis with my friends and throw dinner parties

and decorate my house and ignore my husband's affairs and..."
Her composure had held up longer than he'd thought it would.
Slowly, she started to shatter. It started in her mouth—a slight
tremble of her bottom lip that spread up her face like a tic. "I want
to change places with her. He can do whatever he wants to me.
Fuck me, sodomize me, beat me, burn me. I don't care." The tears
came pouring now. "She's just a baby. She can't take it. She won't
survive..."

Even as he took her hand, Will felt the awkwardness of the gesture. He did not know this woman and certainly was in no position
to comfort her. "Emma's alive," Will reminded her. "That's what
you need to hold on to. Your daughter is alive."

Impossibly, the moment turned more awkward. Gently, she
slipped her hand from his. She ran her fingers under her eyes in that
magical way women do to keep their eyeliner from smudging.
Unexpectedly she asked, "How do you know my husband?"

"We met a long time ago."

"Were you one of the boys who bullied him?"

Will felt his mouth open, but could not find any words to answer.

"My husband doesn't talk much about his childhood."

Will could've told her some stories. Instead he said, "That's
probably a good thing."

Abigail looked at him—really looked at him—for the first time
since they'd met. He could feel her eyes scanning the scars on his
face, the thin, pink line where his lip had been split so badly that
there wasn't enough good skin left to sew it back together straight.

Her gaze was so intimate that it was almost like a touch.

They both looked away uncomfortably. Will checked his watch
to make sure the battery was working. Abigail rummaged around
in her purse.

Footsteps clicked against the tiles as Hoyt, Amanda and Paul
made their way back up the hallway. Paul looked positively de-
feated, and Will wished that he had paid more attention to the exchange. Paul silently took his wife's hand and placed it on his arm.

Amanda said, "Thank you," to Hoyt, shaking his hand. He kissed his daughter on the cheek, gave Paul a clap on the shoulder, then headed toward the exit. Will guessed the millionaire's work here was done.

Amanda took both of Abigail's hands in hers. The naturalness of the gesture was surprising, but women—even Amanda—could get away with that sort of thing. "Chin up," she said. "Don't let them see you break."

Will chewed his lower lip, knowing that Amanda was hoping for the exact opposite. The grieving-mother card could never be played enough times in situations like this. Paul was simply an accessory. Knowing how these things worked, Will guessed that half the people following the story assumed that the father was the root of all this evil. If Abigail came across as too strong, then they would toss her onto the list of suspects, as well. Then, of course, there was the only opinion that mattered—that of the person who was holding Emma Campano. If the abductor thought that the parents were unworthy, then he might have second thoughts about returning their child.

"This way," Amanda said, indicating the opposite end of the hallway. She opened the door to the pressroom and lights flashed like a strobe, blinding them all for several seconds.

Will stood at the edge of the door, making sure the cameras followed Amanda and the Campanos to the impromptu stage at the end of the narrow room. He didn't want his picture in the paper. He didn't want to answer their stupid questions. He just wanted the kidnapper to see Abigail Campano, her sunken eyes and chapped lips, her thin shoulders. He wanted the man who had taken Emma Campano to see what he had done to her mother.

The reporters shuffled around as Amanda took her sweet time adjusting the microphone, unfolding the prepared statement. There were about fifty reporters in all, most of them men, all of them giving off a slightly desperate smell in the cramped room. The air-conditioning wasn't doing much to help matters, and hot air was blasting through a broken window like heat from a flame. Not much news had leaked out on the case, mostly because no one on Amanda's team was stupid enough to open their mouths. This had left the press to their own devices, and from what Will had heard on the radio this morning, they had started to report on what other stations were reporting.

Without preamble, Amanda read from the statement. "The reward for any information leading to the safe return of Emma Campano has been increased to one hundred thousand dollars." She gave the particulars—the toll-free number, the assurance that the call would be completely anonymous. "As you already know, Emma Eleanor Campano is a seventeen-year-old girl who attends a private school outside of the city. Emma was abducted from her home three days ago between the hours of eleven a.m. and twelve noon. At approximately ten-thirty yesterday morning, a call was made from a man claiming to be Emma's kidnapper. A ransom demand was made. We are awaiting details and will brief you at this same time tomorrow morning. I will now read from a statement written by Abigail Campano, Emma Campano's mother."

The cameras flashed like mad, and Will could see Abigail Campano looking for him in the back of the room. He stood up straighter, his height giving him a natural advantage. She finally found him, and he could read the terror in her eyes.

Maybe Will had spent too much time with Amanda lately. He was glad to see the terror, glad that the cameras would pick up this woman's fear. You could read every second of the last three days in the mother's expression—the sleepless nights, the arguments with her husband, the absolute horror of what had happened.

Amanda read, " 'To the man who has Emma: please know that we—her father and I—love Emma and cherish her, and will do whatever you want in order to have our daughter returned to us. Emma is only seventeen years old. She likes ice cream and watching reruns of *Friends* with us on family night. Her father and I are not interested in vengeance or punishment. We just want Emma returned.' " Amanda looked up over her glasses. " 'Please return our Emma to us.' " She folded the paper. "I'll take a few questions."

A local reporter shouted, "Abby, what did it feel like to kill—"

"Rules, please," Amanda cut him off. "Remember to direct all your questions to me."

The reporter didn't give up. "Are you going to press charges against Abigail Campano for the murder of Adam Humphrey?"

"We have no plans to pursue charges at this time."

Abigail stared blankly at Will, as if unworried about the equivocation. Beside her, Paul seemed to be struggling to hold his tongue.

Another local reporter asked, "What leads do you have at the moment? Are there any suspects?"

"Obviously, we're full speed ahead on this investigation. I can't tell you about particulars."

And yet another question came. "You've posted police around Westfield Academy. Are you worried this is the work of a serial killer?"

The serial killer angle was a hot topic of debate on the talk shows. The Hiker Murders back in January were still fresh on everyone's mind.

Amanda told them, "This has absolutely none of the markings of a serial case at this time."

Will felt a bead of sweat roll down his back. The flashes seemed to be making the room hotter. He opened the door to let in some fresh air.

"When do you think an arrest will be made?" someone in the front asked.

Amanda artfully dodged, "As soon as we are certain we have our bad guy."

"What other lines of investigation are you following?"

"We're pursuing any and all leads."

"Which are?"

Amanda smiled. "I can't go into particulars at this time."

Will caught Abigail's eye again. He could see that she was swaying and did not know if it was the heat or the circumstances. Her face had turned completely white. She looked like she might faint.

Will tilted up his chin, which was enough to get Amanda's attention. She did not need to look at Abigail to know what was worrying him. Instead of calling the meeting to a close, she asked, "Any more questions?"

A man in the back wearing a blazer that screamed New York and a sneer that screamed Yankee even louder, asked, "Don't you agree that valuable time was lost due to the incompetence of the Atlanta Police Department?"

Amanda's eyes found the man, and she gave him one of her special smiles. "At this point in time, we're more focused on finding Emma Campano than we are on pointing fingers."

"But wouldn't—"

Amanda cut him off. "You've had your turn. Give the others a chance."

Will heard some of the more seasoned local reporters snicker. For his part, Will was more interested in Abigail Campano. She was searching in her purse again, her head down. She was leaning too far forward in the chair. For just a moment, it seemed like she might fall to the floor, but Paul caught her at the last moment, putting his arm around her, shoring her up. He whispered something in her ear and Abigail numbly nodded her head. She looked up at the people crowding in on her, the crush of humanity seeking to drain every emotion from her face. Her mouth opened for air. The camera flashes blinked wildly. Will could almost hear the reporters trying to come up with adjectives for the captions: devastated, crushed, mournful, broken. Amanda's plan had worked beautifully. Abigail had swayed them all without even saying a word.

More questions were allowed, each asking for details that Amanda skillfully sidestepped. Some were valid—they pressed again on what clues had been found, what progress had been made. Some were meant to be inflammatory, like the man who asked again whether or not this was the work of a sadistic serial killer who was "targeting affluent young girls."

Amanda gave them nothing, rapping her knuckles on the podium like a judge ending a court session, then leading the Campanos off the stage.

Another barrage of photographs were taken as Amanda followed the parents back toward the exit. Abigail could barely walk on her own. She leaned into Paul like a crutch. The reporters kept their distance, not crowding the group. If Will didn't know any better, he would have sworn they were being respectful.

Outside, Amanda made all the right noises. She took Abigail's hand, saying, "You did perfectly."

Abigail nodded, obviously not trusting herself to speak. The ordeal had taken the last bit of strength out of her.

Amanda said, "The second call from the kidnapper is in three hours. I'll be with you at the house."

Paul said, "Thank you."

Amanda shook Paul's hand. She gave Will a sharp look. "My office. Ten minutes."

He nodded, and she walked off toward the stairs.

For the first time since this had all started, Paul seemed concerned about his wife. "Are you okay?"

"I just got a little too warm," she murmured, hand covering her stomach.

Will offered, "There's a bathroom down here."

She didn't look at him. Still leaning on her husband, she made her way to the ladies' room. Outside the door, she put her hand to his face, then his chest. "I'm okay."

"You sure?"

She pressed her fingertips to his mouth, then went into the bathroom. Paul stood outside, facing the closed door as if he could still see her.

Will found himself feeling something like jealousy, coupled with confusion. How could someone like Abigail love Paul? How could she have a child with this man? He'd never been attractive, but Paul had let himself go over the years. He'd put on more than a few pounds. His hairline was receding. This, coupled with his roving eye, did not exactly make him a catch. What did she see in him that was attractive?

And why was it that even after almost thirty years had passed, Will was still comparing himself to the bastard?

Paul let out a long sigh. He walked a few feet away, then turned on his heel and walked back, as if keeping sentry. Will put his hands in his pockets and leaned against the wall, wondering why he kept ending up outside the ladies' room.

Paul stopped. He indicated his own face, asking, "Does it hurt?"

Their fight the day before was the last thing on Will's mind, though the bruise that spanned the bridge of Will's nose and ran under his eyes was reminiscent of an Egyptian Pharaoh. Instead of answering the man, Will looked down at the ground, noting that his shoes were badly scuffed.

"Here." Paul held out the stack of photographs that Will had spotted in Abigail's purse. All of them, he knew, would show Emma in various stages of happiness. "My wife wanted you to have these." He did not look at the photos. "She wanted you to know what Emma looks like."

Will took the photos, but did not look at them, either. The girl's face was already seared into his mind. He did not need more visual cues.

Paul lowered his voice. "You hit back a lot harder than you used to."

Will tried not to take that as a compliment.

"Anyway," Paul said, but nothing else followed.

Will could not stop himself. "You're a dumb bastard to cheat on her."

"I know."

"She's too good for you."

"I can't look at her." He kept his tone low, mindful his wife was on the other side of the door. "You heard her yesterday. I know she blames me."

Will felt his radar come on. "Is there something you're not telling me?"

"No," Paul told him. "Believe me, I wish there was. I wish there was some guy out there I pissed off, or somebody I fucked over, who I could point to. I'd beat the shit out of the fucker."

"What about this girl you're seeing?"

"She's a *woman*," Paul said, putting emphasis on the word. "It's a casual thing. She works at the dealership. She was there when I was talking to Abby—when all of this started."

"Is she married?"

"No."

"Does she have a jealous ex-boyfriend?"

Paul shook his head. "She lives with her parents. She knows I'm married. She was just looking for some fun. Trust me, she's had fun like this before. Lots of times before."

"I'm still going to need to talk to her."

"I'll write down—" He stopped himself. "Give me your business card. I'll tell her to call you as soon as I get home."

Will took out his wallet and fished around for a card. "You won't listen to me, so listen to your father-in-law. Let us handle this. We know what we're doing. *I* know what I'm doing."

Paul looked at Will's business card, his eyes moving back and forth over the words. His voice was barely more than a whisper when he spoke. "You and me—we lived that life. We knew that there was always a bad guy around the corner. With Em, I thought it would be different. You saw my house, man. I'm a fucking millionaire. I've got more money than I know what to do with." He stopped, his emotions catching up with him, tears flooding into his eyes. "I'd give it all up if I could have my little girl back."

Will was uncomfortable being in the position to assure the man that everything was going to be okay, not least of all because they both knew better.

"Fuck me," Paul whispered, sniffing, wiping his eyes. "I'm like a fucking girl here."

Will looked back at his shoes. He'd paid seventy-five dollars for them a year ago. Maybe he should get some new ones. He looked at Paul's shoes. They gleamed as if they'd been freshly polished. He probably had people who did that. At night, he put his shoes in the closet all scuffed, and then in the morning they were perfect again. Or maybe he just bought new ones when the old ones got marked up. How many hand-me-down shoes had they both suffered through at the children's home? Pinched toes, blistered heels. If Will had Paul's money, he'd have a new pair of shoes for every day of his life.

Paul let out another stream of breath, oblivious to Will's observations. "I've been letting myself think about all the bad things he could be doing to her."

Will nodded. Paul would know firsthand the nasty things men could think to do to children. Will had seen the scars, the bruises. He had heard Paul screaming in the middle of the night.

"You're the only one I can talk to about this kind of shit."

"Abigail doesn't know?"

"She's still with me, isn't she?"

Will could hear the shame in the man's tone. It was a familiar sound to his ears. He looked back up at Paul. "Why did you hate me so much when we were kids?"

"I dunno, Trash, it was a long time ago."

"I mean it, Paul. I want to know."

Paul shook his head, and Will thought that was the only answer he was going to get until the man said, "You had it down, Trash. You knew how to do the time."

"What do you mean?"

"You just accepted it. Being there, trapped at the home for the rest of your life. Not ever having anybody." He stared at Will as if he still could not believe it. "You were content."

Will thought about all the visiting days, all the times he combed his hair and changed into his best clothes and prayed that some couple would see him coloring pictures or playing on the swing and think, "That's him. That's the boy we want for our son." No one did. No one ever did. That wasn't contentment, that was resignation.

He told Paul, "It wasn't like that at all."

"That's how you made it seem. Like you didn't need anybody. Like you could handle everything. Like you were fine with whatever they gave you."

"It was the exact opposite."

"Maybe it was," Paul admitted. "You know, when you're a kid, you see things differently."

Will heard the words come out of his mouth before he could stop himself. "I'm going to get Emma back for you."

Paul nodded, obviously not trusting himself to speak.

"You're going to have to be strong for her. That's what you need to be thinking about: how you can help her." Will added, "She's got you, Paul. That's the difference. Whatever she's going through right now, she's got you waiting at the end of it to help her."

"I wish I could be strong," he said. "I feel so fucking weak right now."

"You're not weak. You were the meanest bastard in a house full of bastards."

"No, buddy." He seemed resigned as he patted Will on the shoulder. "I was just the most scared."

Behind the door, the sink turned on, water flooding out of the faucet. The paper towel dispenser screeched as the crank turned, then the door opened. Abigail's makeup had been fixed, her lipstick reapplied.

"Okay," Paul said, more to himself. He reached out his hand and she took it, nothing awkward in the gesture. Will led them down the hall and pressed the call button. Abigail had her head on Paul's shoulder, her eyes closed as if she was willing herself to get through this. When the doors slid open, Will reached in and pressed his code into the keypad. Emma's parents got on.

Paul gave him a stiff nod—not a thank-you, but an acknowledgment that Will was there.

Abigail didn't give Will a second glance as the doors closed.

Will looked down at the photographs in his hand. Emma Campano smiled back at him in a toothy grin. He thumbed through the pictures. In some, she was with her parents. Others showed her with Kayla Alexander. Younger shots showed Emma with a group of girls in the school choir, another group on a skiing trip. She seemed even more vulnerable with a group than when she was alone, as if she could feel her separateness, her outsider status, as keenly as the prick of a pin. He saw in her eyes the trepidation of a kindred spirit.

Will tucked the photos into his pocket and headed toward the stairs.

✦

AMANDA'S CORNER OFFICE was on the opposite side of the building from Will's and a lifetime away from the squalor in which he toiled. Ahead was the ubiquitous view of the Home Depot parking lot. Up the street, the city loomed—skyscrapers, regal old buildings and in the mist-covered distance, the greenery of Piedmont Park.

Her desk was not the requisitioned metal type whose sharp corners had taken out more than one poor civil servant's kneecap. Polished wood gleamed from under her leather blotter with its pink phone messages Caroline had left her. Her in and out trays were always empty. Will had never seen a speck of dust in the place.

Pictures of Amanda with various dignitaries hung alongside newspaper articles touting her triumphs. The walls were painted a soothing gray. The ceiling was made of crisp white squares rather than the dingy, water-stained tiles that were the hallmark of every other office in the building. She had an LCD TV and her own coffee bar. The air really was better up here.

"Get you anything?" Caroline, Amanda's secretary, asked. She was the only woman who worked on Amanda's team. Will supposed this was because Amanda had come up during the age of tokenism, when there was only one spot for a woman at the top. Or maybe it was because Amanda knew that men were easier for her to control.

"No, thank you," he said. "Did Amanda tell you we're—"

"Expecting a phone call?" she interrupted.

"Thanks."

She smiled and returned to her desk outside the office.

Will had called Evan Bernard, Emma's reading teacher, first thing this morning. The man had agreed to look at the threatening notes that Adam Humphrey had been sent. As Faith had suggested, Will was hoping the teacher could give his opinion as to whether or not they were looking at the work of a dyslexic. A cruiser had been dispatched to show him copies of the letters. Bernard was supposed to call as soon as he got them.

Will checked the time on his splintered cell phone, wondering where Amanda was. The numbers didn't glow as brightly. Sometimes it rang when someone called, sometimes it flashed silently. Earlier, it had started vibrating for no apparent reason, and he had to take out the battery to get it to stop. He was worried about the phone, which was three years old and about three million models out of date. A new one would require him to learn a whole new set of directions. He would have to change over all the numbers and program in the functions. There went his vacation. Or maybe not. You needed a job to take a vacation.

"Looks like we're getting good feedback from the press," Amanda said, breezing into her office. "Paul Campano denied getting into a scuffle with you. He said it was an accident, that you fell."

Will had stood when she entered the room and he was so shocked that he forgot to sit back down.

"Hamish Patel and his big mouth say otherwise." Amanda eyed him as she fanned through the notes on her desk. "I'm going to guess from your appearance that Campano took a swing at you?"

Will sat down. "Yeah."

"And I gather from the black eyes and swollen nose that you valiantly suffered his blows?"

Will tried, "If that's what Hamish says."

"Care to tell me why he took the swing in the first place?"

Will told her a favorable version of the truth. "The last thing I said to him before he hit me was that we needed a DNA sample."

"That puts it nicely back on me."

He asked, "Did Paul give the sample?"

"Yes, actually. So, either he's extremely arrogant or he's innocent."

Will would've bet on both, but he still could not believe that Paul had covered for him. He hadn't even hinted at the favor less than half an hour ago. Maybe this was the man's way of paying him back for being such a jerk all those years ago. Or maybe he was still the same old Paul who liked to settle his scores when the adults weren't watching.

"What about his affairs?"

"I called the dealership as soon as I got back to my office. If she doesn't get back to me by noon, I'll send a squad car to pick her up." Will had to add, "My gut tells me Paul doesn't have anything to do with this. Maybe if it was just a simple kidnapping—but it's not."

"We'll know soon enough," Amanda said. "I've fast tracked the comparison between Paul Campano and the DNA we found on Kayla Alexander. Beckey Keiper at the lab is going to call you as soon as the results are in."

"I sent a cruiser over to Emma's school," Will said, barely able to get past his shock. "Bernard should be calling us any minute."

"It's extremely ironic that our resident dyslexic can't tell us, isn't it?"

Will tried not to squirm in his chair. He had called his boss at home only one other time in the last ten years, and that was to tell her that a colleague had been killed. Last night, she had been even icier to him when he'd explained that he had been unable to see anything unusual about the notes someone, probably the killer, had slipped under Adam Humphrey's dorm room door.

He cleared his throat. "If you want my resignation—"

"When you leave this job it'll be with my foot up your ass, not slinking out the door like a wounded kitten." She sat back in her chair. "God dammit, Will."

"I'm sorry."

"Sorry doesn't cut it right now." She twisted the screw tighter. "Those letters are the first pieces of real evidence we have. 'Leave her alone.' 'She belongs to me.' Those are direct threats from our killer to one of our victims. If this is the work of someone with some kind of handicap—that's our blood in the water, Will. We should have been circling this information as soon as we got it."

"I'm aware of that."

"Where would we be right now in this case if you had followed up on the spelling yesterday afternoon instead of first thing this morning?" She didn't let him answer. "We're going on three days here. Three days. I don't have to tell you what that means."

"What else do you want me to say?"

For once, she seemed to be at a loss for words. The condition was fleeting. "We're burning daylight. When is this teacher supposed to call?"

"The cruiser should be there any minute."

"What time is Gordon Chew supposed to be here?"

She meant the fingerprint expert from Tennessee. "Around eight-thirty. He was going to drive down first thing this morning."

"He drove down last night," she said, but didn't elaborate. "What do we have?"

"A lot of nothing," Will told her. "Charlie found fibers and footprints at the Ansley Park house, but we need someone or something to match them to before we can use them." The gray dirt Charlie had found also came to mind, but he kept that information to himself, hoping against hope that something came of it. He cleared his throat before continuing. "The ransom call yesterday came from Kayla Alexander's phone. It bounced off a cell tower that covers most of north Atlanta on up to Kennesaw Mountain."

"We can try to triangulate the second call today, but I'm sure he watches enough television to know it takes time." She paused, thinking. "I didn't peg this for a kidnapping."

"Neither did I," Will said. "I'm still not sure I do."

"There was proof of life."

"I know."

"Both parents confirm that it was their daughter's voice on the phone. Are you still thinking that Emma Campano might be involved in this?"

"Something isn't sitting right," Will told her. "The scene was too sloppy."

"Charlie says that based on the blood and shoe-print evidence he believes that only four people were in the house during the time of the crime."

"I know."

Amanda added another point that he had yet to consider. "If you've got a thing for young girls, you don't leave one dead at the scene. You take them both with you."

"Kayla was a fighter. Maybe she wouldn't go peacefully."

Amanda held up her hands. "We can talk in circles like this all morning and it won't get us anywhere. I heard the proof of life from the call yesterday. The girl sounded terrified. Not movie terrified, not fake, this-is-how-I-think-I-should-sound-when-I'm-trying-to-sound-terrified terrified. She was making the sorts of noises you only make when you know that you are about to die."

Will let her words sink in. Amanda was right. They had both heard true fear before—more times than either of them cared to remember. Emma Campano had not been acting. There was an ungodly tremble to her voice, a harsh rasp to her breathing. You couldn't make that up. Absolute terror was a secret language you only learned by experience.

Will asked, "Was there any background noise on Emma's part of the tape?"

"They say it'll be noon at the soonest before they have anything substantive. Preliminarily, there's traffic noise, a dog barking. The girl was in an enclosed area when her part of the recording was made."

"So he drove her somewhere, took her out of the car, then made the recording."

"That tells us that the ransom demand wasn't an afterthought. We've seen how these guys work before. They get heated up, they take the girl, they rape her, they kill her, and *then* they make their plan. This was thought out from the beginning. Before he stepped foot in that house, he bought rope and duct tape. He found a knife. He had a place picked out where he knew he could take her."

"If I were a more optimistic person, I would say that proves she's still alive."

"That was yesterday," Amanda reminded him. "We'll know about today in a little over two and a half hours."

"Was the lab able to tell anything about the kidnapper's voice?"

"You were right about him taping it off a computer and playing it back over the phone." She read from one of the notes, " 'The VoiceOver utility is a standard feature found in Apple Macintosh's universal access software. The voice selected by the caller is called Bahh.' " She looked up from the note. "So that narrows our suspect pool down to several million smug Apple computer owners."

"Kayla Alexander's parents should be—"

"They're back," she interrupted. "And you're not to go within a hundred miles of them without an attorney."

"Why?"

"They're filing lawsuits against Westfield Academy, the Campanos and the Atlanta Police Department. I'm sure as soon as they realize we're on the case, they'll slap us with one, too."

"On what grounds?"

"The school couldn't keep the girl from leaving, the Campanos couldn't keep the girl from dying and the police department couldn't find their asses if you drew them a map."

Caroline called from her office, "Evan Bernard is on line three."

Will told Amanda, "Please let me handle this."

"Are you trying to redeem yourself?"

"I'm trying not to piss off the man who's trying to help us."

"Don't be ridiculous." She pressed the speakerphone button. "Mr. Bernard, this is Amanda Wagner, I'm the deputy director of the special criminal apprehension team. I've got agent Will Trent here with me. Thank you so much for helping us this morning."

"No problem," he answered. "The policeman you sent came with his lights and siren blaring right up to the front door." He gave a forced chuckle. "I have to admit, it was a little disconcerting."

Amanda smiled her grandmotherly smile. "Consider it incentive to keep your nose clean."

Will shook his head at the silence on the other end of the line. He took over the call, asking, "Mr. Bernard, can you give us your impression of the letters?"

"I have to admit, I find them curious."

"Can you explain why?"

"The first one, which I would read as 'she belongs to me,' just doesn't ring true. I told you yesterday that each dyslexic is different, and perhaps you'd be better off talking to a linguist for regional dialect and such, but in my opinion, you're dealing with a phonetic speller, not a dyslexic."

Will asked, "How can you be sure?"

"Well, I'm not." He made a thinking noise. "All I can speak from is my own experience. With a dyslexic, I would expect the letters to be mixed up, not just misspelled or run together. Transposition is the most notable characteristic. For instance, Emma continually transposed the 'e' and 'l' in help, spelling it 'h-l-e-p.' "

Amanda did nothing to hide her impatience. "What about the other ones?"

"The second one, 'rapist,' is correct, of course, but the third one, the 'lev her along' for 'leave her alone'—and again, let me qualify this by saying that each person is different—but the 'along' seems odd. Typically, you would not expect to find the 'g' there. It's what I would call a heavy letter, meaning it has a definitive sound within a word. You often see it used for 'j' or a 'j' used in its place, but you never see it just thrown in for no reason." He made the thinking noise again. "But then the 'lev' gives me pause."

Will was having a hard time following all the spelling, but he still asked, "Why is that?"

"Because, generally, that's a dyslexic spelling. It's the word in its purest form. No run-on, no 'g' thrown in for effect. I would assume that spell-check added it there."

"So, what's your opinion? Is someone trying to appear dyslexic or do they really have the disorder?"

"Well..." The man hesitated. "I'm not a doctor. I'm a reading teacher. But if you were to put a gun to my head, I'd say that you are looking at the work of an adult, probably of average intelligence, who simply never learned basic reading skills."

Will looked up at Amanda and found her staring back at him. They were both unused to getting straight answers. Just to clarify, Will asked, "You don't think this person has some sort of reading disability?"

"You asked for my honest opinion and I gave it to you. I would say that the person who wrote these letters never learned how to properly read or spell. At best, they're on a second- or third-grade level."

Amanda was obviously skeptical. "How is that possible?"

"I saw it more when I taught in the public school system, but it happens. Kids with all kinds of reading problems can slip through the cracks. You try to help them, but there's nothing you can really do. That's one of the reasons I moved to Westfield."

In the background, they heard the class bell ring.

Bernard said, "I'm sorry, but I need to get to class. I can get someone to cover if you—"

"That's okay," Will told him. "Thank you for your time. If you could give those notes back to the patrolman who gave them to you?"

"Of course. Please call me if anything else comes up. I wish I could have been more help to you."

"You were very helpful," Will told him. "I would appreciate if you kept this conversation to yourself. We don't want to do anything to jeopardize Emma's situation."

"Of course not. I think our students are damaged enough by this tragedy as it is."

"Thank you very much, Mr. Bernard."

Amanda ended the call. "Did you follow any of that?"

"Yes," Will said. "Our letter writer is an adult of average intelligence who happens to be a functional illiterate."

"You don't know how refreshing I find it for an expert to give me their honest opinion."

Caroline came into the office with a file folder in her hand. "Background checks on the Copy Right employees, and Gordon Chew called to say he's running half an hour late."

Amanda did not bother to thank the woman. She opened the file and skimmed the pages, giving Will the highlights. "Everyone's clean except for Lionel Edward Petty, who has a drug conviction. During a traffic stop, they found two ounces of pot in his glove compartment."

"Was he hit with intent to distribute?" Will asked. Though it was discretionary, one ounce of marijuana would generally buy you a misdemeanor. Two ounces could be construed as drug trafficking.

Amanda told him, "He ratted out his dealer and they knocked it down to a fine and time served."

"Faith found some pot taped under Adam Humphrey's desk," Will said. "It's a tenuous connection, but the Copy Right is close to Tech. If he really was dealing, then he could easily walk to campus during his lunch hour."

"I'm sure there are dealers living right on campus who have that business all wrapped up." She closed the file folder. "I'm getting the runaround from the contractors who had construction crews outside the copy center. My gut says they were using illegals. Maybe we should go back and see if anyone in the store talked to the workers. There's a Hispanic girl who works the morning shift." She referenced one of the pages in the folder. "Maria Contreras. Maybe she had some contact with them. Maybe I'm racial profiling. Check the other girls, too. They may have flirted with the men." She started to hand the sheet to Will, then thought better of it.

He held out his hand. "I can give it to Faith."

She put the paper on the desk and slid it over, making her point loud and clear. "You need a partner, Will."

"You know I don't work well with others."

"You seem to be working fine with Faith Mitchell."

"Because she knows there's an end to it."

"Ah," she said. "There it is. The famous Trent self-esteem."

He bristled. "What does that mean?"

"I'm not your mama, Will, but it's time to grow a pair and stop feeling sorry for yourself because you have a disability."

He did not ask why she kept throwing his dyslexia back in his face if she thought his problem was so inconsequential. Amanda had built her career around knowing people's weak points and exploiting the hell out of them.

She leaned forward, making sure she had his attention. "You see cases as puzzles and whatever it is that's so different in your brain makes it possible for you to solve them the way no one else can." She paused, letting that sink in. "I trusted you with this case because I knew that you could handle it. I don't need a crisis of confidence from you right now. I need you to go out there and work with Faith and do your job the best way you know how."

"Amanda—"

"And while I'm at it, you could probably do a hell of a lot better than Angie Polaski."

"That's out of line."

"Probably, but consider yourself put on notice. When this case is over, I'm going to ask Faith to join the team."

"She's APD. She'll lose her benefits and pension and—"

"I'll worry about the details. You worry about finding a way to tell Faith about your little problem, Special Agent Trent. She's going to figure it out on her own eventually and she'll be furious at you for hiding it." She added, "And I'm not too pleased myself about having to babysit you on this phone call when I could be off doing something that actually moves this case forward instead."

He opened his mouth to respond, but she talked over him.

"No more," she commanded. Will stood up because she did. "Speaking of pissing away time, I've got to go talk to our lawyers about the Alexanders, then I'm heading over to Ansley to wait with the Campanos for the ten-thirty ransom call." Her heels clicked across the floor as she crossed the room. "Wait for Gordon Chew to see what he comes up with on the threatening notes, then canvass the Copy Right again to see if they remember anything about those construction workers. We'll reconvene outside the Campano house." She paused in the doorway, repeating, "*Outside* the house, Will. I have no idea why Paul Campano covered your ass over the little contretemps you two had, but don't think for a moment you've got me fooled."

CHAPTER FOURTEEN

FAITH COVERED HER mouth as she yawned hard enough to pop her jaw. She was almost punch-drunk with exhaustion after spending most of the night talking to Victor Martinez. Once the restaurant had kicked them out, they had walked to the closed coffee shop next door and sat at one of the metal tables outside. Sweating in the evening heat, being devoured by mosquitoes, neither of them had made a move to leave. They had both had horrendous days. They had both studiously avoided any further conversation about them.

Faith had told him about her father, how she missed him, her brother in Germany, her relationship with her mother, and of course Jeremy. Victor had listened so intently, his eyes never leaving hers, his fingers stroking hers in ways that made Faith incapable of thinking about anything other than the feel of his skin, that she had finally given up and stared wordlessly back at him until he started talking about himself.

He had given her the highlights: an early failed marriage, his rise to dean of student services at Georgia Tech. He was the first man in his family to go to college. He was bullying his nieces and nephews to make sure he wasn't the last. He found out she had dropped out of college and started bullying her, as well.

When Faith had finally realized it was three in the morning, that she had to get up for work in four hours, she had finally broken the spell. Victor had taken her hand and kissed her on the cheek, then—very gently—on the mouth. He had walked her to her car, then kissed her again before she'd pulled away.

Even if he never called her again, Faith thought that it was one of the most romantic evenings of her life.

Will came into the office. "Looks like I'm not going to be investigating bingo applications, after all." He slumped into the chair behind his desk. His suit was pressed and his face was shaved, but he looked rumpled somehow. "Did you see the press conference this morning?"

Faith felt the hair on the back of her neck stand up. She'd barely managed a shower, let alone had time to turn on the television. "What?"

"The press conference," he said, as if it was common knowledge. "I thought Amanda pushed it, but it's not like she consults me on—"

"There was a press conference?" Faith realized she had stood up. "Why didn't you tell me?"

"I thought you'd appreciate the sleep."

"Why the hell am I here?" she demanded. "What am I doing—"

"Hold on," Will interrupted. He was still sitting in his chair, a confused look on his bruised face. "What did I do now?"

"What did you do?"

"Whatever it is, I'm sorry. I really am." Will leaned forward. "Let's just talk about this, okay? Please sit down."

His genuine remorse took some of the fight out of her. She sat down. "This is ridiculous."

"Just tell me what you want to do."

"We need to define my position on this case." He still seemed at a loss, so she gave him some options. "Am I still your lackey or school spokesperson or chauffeur or—"

A loud bang came from the office next door, followed by laughter. Phones were ringing. The day shift was starting to straggle in. Will seemed to realize this just as Faith did. He squeezed around his desk and pulled the door closed.

He waited until he was seated again to tell her, "We're in this together."

"Then why aren't you telling me things?"

"I just thought..." He still sounded baffled. "I thought you'd appreciate getting some extra sleep. The press conference was just smoke and mirrors. There was no reason for both of us to have to suffer through it."

Faith could think of all kinds of reasons—a chance to talk to Abigail Campano again, to see the mother and father interacting. The opportunity to find out what the reporters had dug up on their own, or just the common God damn courtesy of being included in the case she had been pouring her life into for the last three days.

Will was looking down at his desk, but Faith had been the mother of a teenage boy long enough to spot guilt when she saw it.

She asked, "What else?" He didn't answer, so she pressed. "I know there's something else, Will. Just go ahead and tell me."

A sense of dread filled his voice. "You're really not going to like it."

Faith waited. She could clearly hear the conversation in the next office—cop talk, somebody bragging about kicking the knees out from under an arrest.

Will said, "I talked to Evan Bernard this morning."

"By yourself?"

"With Amanda."

Faith let that sink in. Was it Amanda who didn't trust her? It would be very like the older woman to make her own decisions and leave Will to clean up the mess. Was Faith mad at the wrong person? On the other hand, if that was the case, if Faith's being left out was coming from Amanda, then why wasn't Will telling her?

She rubbed her eyes, too tired to see through the layers of deceit. "What did he say?"

"In his opinion, we're looking at an illiterate adult, not someone with a learning disability."

Faith found the leap extraordinary. "He got that from three notes?"

"I'm just telling you what he said."

"How can someone get through school without learning how to read and write?"

"It happens," he said, rubbing his jaw.

Faith felt more than snubbed this time. The press conference was one thing, but she had real questions for Evan Bernard, primarily: how could he be so sure from three short sentences that they were dealing with someone who had a learning disability rather than someone who was perfectly normal and trying to cover his tracks?

Will said, "The lab is going to call us when Gordon Chew gets here. He's the fingerprint expert."

"Why didn't you use one of our guys?"

"You only get a few chances to chemically process paper. If there's a fingerprint on one of those notes, Gordon will find it." Will tapped the keyboard on his computer to wake it up. He started reading something, probably his e-mail. "Did you do anything with that vial?"

She was conscious that sound traveled both ways. "I put it in the right hands."

He kept his eyes on his computer, moving the mouse around, clicking. She didn't know if he was pouting or scared to say the wrong thing again. As usual, his topic of choice was the last thing she would have predicted. "I had to have a root canal last year. You're very lucky you're with APD. The GBI's dental plan sucks. I had to pay fifteen hundred bucks out of my own pocket."

Faith made a sympathetic noise, but she was about ready to snatch the keyboard out from under him. "Do you want me to leave you alone so you can play with your computer?"

He had the grace to look guilty. Finally, he sat up in his chair, actually looking at Faith as he talked. "The ransom call from the cell phone came from a tower that services most of Atlanta. The ransom call analysis won't be ready until noon. Charlie still doesn't have anything tangible on the Prius. We're waiting for Paul Campano's DNA to come back to see if it matches Kayla

Alexander. It's been almost three full days since the girl was abducted and it looks like we're going to waste another two hours waiting for people to answer our questions, which, by the way, is only going to lead to more questions."

"You make it sound so easy."

"Yeah, by the way, I'd call your union rep if I were you. The Alexanders are suing the city for mishandling the identification on their daughter."

"Fuck," Faith groaned.

Will tapped his fingers on his desk. "I'm sorry. We're in this together, okay?"

"You mean in the lawsuit?"

He smiled. "Maybe that, too."

Faith couldn't get bogged down in this crap and still do her job. "What's our plan after the fingerprint guy?"

"Amanda wants us to talk to the Copy Right employees to see if they noticed anything suspicious about the construction workers. Then we're supposed to meet her at the Campano house. The kidnapper said he would call at ten-thirty this morning. Hopefully we'll have some new information to go on then, a drop, a new proof of life."

"We've got a solid description of Adam's Chevy Impala on the wire. Every cop in the city will be looking for it."

"Let's just hope it's still in the city."

He sat back in his chair, hands folded across his flat belly. Faith asked him, "Did Amanda tear you a new one?"

"No," he said. "I was surprised. She's very hard to work for."

"I can imagine."

He held up his hand, thumb stretched out at an angle. "See this?" he asked, indicating a faint scar on the webbing. "She shot me with a nail gun four years ago."

"On purpose?"

"That's the question," he said, folding his hands again.

Since this seemed to be turning into a pile-it-on-Amanda party, she told him, "She dated my uncle Kenny when I was a kid."

Will nearly fell out of his chair. "What?"

Faith explained, "My dad's brother. He was a colonel in the Air Force. Amanda dated him for…" She thought about it. Amanda had left Ken right before Jeremy entered high school. "Almost fifteen years."

"I didn't know that."

"Amanda didn't tell you when she put you onto my mother?"

"No, but as far as I know, she never interfered. She just told me to be fair." His voice sounded odd when he answered.

Faith remembered something her mother had told her. At the time, she had found it strange, but now she understood. "My mother didn't talk about you much during the investigation, but one time she told me that she trusted you to do the right thing."

"That's nice," Will said, though she gathered by his expression that he was feeling duped. Faith was beginning to see that this was classic Amanda. She never gave you the entire picture.

She tried to change the subject, talking about his dank office. "The view doesn't really improve in the sunlight."

Will rubbed his jaw again. "No." He was silent for a moment, then said, "I'm sorry I left you out of the phone call. And the press conference. It won't happen again."

She wasn't quite ready to accept his apology, maybe because he kept leaving her out no matter how many times he said he was sorry. "What was Paul's reaction to all this?"

"He was his usual asshole self," Will said. "Trying to control everything."

"What about him?" Faith asked. "Doth he protest too much?"

"Paul's an asshole, but I don't see him doing this kind of thing. He'd have to have an accomplice, a motive."

"I guess we'll know motive well enough when the DNA comes back."

"It's not going to match." He seemed so sure of himself that Faith didn't bother to argue. The obvious culprit in any child abduction case was always the father. Actually, *most* domestic cases ended up pointing a big accusatory finger back at the father, no matter the circumstances. This was Will's case, and if he was so damn sure the man wasn't involved, then there was nothing Faith could do about it.

"I know him," Will said, as if he could sense Faith's skepticism. "All right."

"I'm serious, Faith. Paul didn't do this." He kept pressing the matter. "I know you don't trust my judgment on a lot of things—"

"That's not true."

"Then can I get a word in?"

Faith didn't trust herself to respond. She seemed to be making a habit of sparring with this man, and the end result usually had him feeling perplexed and her feeling like a heel.

Will seemed to realize this, too. "All I am trying to say is that I know this guy. Please trust me. There is no way Paul Campano would be involved in anything that would hurt a kid—especially when it's his own child."

"Okay," Faith agreed. God knew she'd taken more on face value than this. She glanced around the room, feeling a desperate need to change the subject. "I don't mean to pry, but do you mind my asking why you have two bags of home pregnancy kits by your window?"

He actually blushed as he turned around to look at them.

Faith rushed an apology. "I'm sorry. I shouldn't have said—"

"I forgot they were over there."

Faith saw the boxes peeking up from the bags, their happy little logos. If only she'd had access to a kit when she was pregnant with Jeremy. Maybe Faith wouldn't have waited until she was in her third trimester to tell her parents. She put her hand to her neck, wondering where that awful thought had come from. She must have been more exhausted than she realized.

He said, "I think my girlfriend might be pregnant."

His words hung between them, and Faith tried to pin down when exactly their relationship had gone from coolly professional to personal. There was something so kind about him under his awkward manners and social ineptness. Despite her best intentions, Faith realized that she could not hate Will Trent.

She glanced at the myriad kits. There had to be a dozen of them.

"You can't just dip those in the toilet. You have to have a fresh sample."

Will opened his desk drawer and reached his hand all the way to the back. "I've got this," he said, pulling out a test stick. "I found it in the trash. Do you know what this signifies?"

Faith stopped herself before touching the stick, remembering at the last minute that someone had actually urinated on it. She looked at the result panel. There was a single blue line. "I have no idea."

"Yeah," he said. "Anyway, I got all these so I can figure out which brand it is and get the results."

The obvious question hung in the back of her throat—*why don't you just ask her?*—but Faith figured the fact that Angie Polaski hadn't mentioned the test to Will in the first place was proof enough that there was a serious breakdown in communications.

She said, "Let's go through them now."

He was obviously surprised by the suggestion. "No, I couldn't ask you to do that."

"We can't do anything until Bernard calls. Come on."

Will only made a show of resisting. He emptied the bags onto his desk. They started opening the boxes, breaking the plastic seals, finding the test sticks, comparing them to the one on Will's desk calendar. They were nearly to the last one when Will said, "This looks like it."

Faith looked at the plastic-wrapped tester in his hand and compared it to the used one on his desk. "Yep," she agreed.

He unfolded the directions that came with the test, skimming them to find the right section. He glanced up at Faith nervously, then looked back at the directions.

"Let me," she finally said, putting him out of his misery. There was a drawing on the back side. "One line," she said. "That means it's negative."

He sat back in his chair, hands gripping the arms. She couldn't tell if he was relieved or disappointed. "Thank you for helping me with that."

Faith nodded, sticking the directions back in the box.

"Spell-check."

"What?"

"Yesterday, Bernard said that computers make it easier for dyslexics to hide their problem." He shrugged. "It would make sense that someone who was functionally illiterate would do the same thing."

Faith closed her eyes, remembering the threatening notes. "The way the words were jumbled together—they were spelled correctly, right? Is l-e-v a word?" She pointed to his computer. "Type it in."

Will didn't move. "It's a word."

"What does it mean?"

His phone rang. He didn't move to answer it.

Faith had seen him acting strangely, but this took the cake. The phone rang again. "Do you want me to get that?"

He reached over and pressed the speakerphone button. "Will Trent."

"It's Beckey in the lab," a woman with a pronounced Yankee accent said. "Gordon Chew is here."

Will pressed the off button on his computer monitor. He stood up, straightening his jacket. "Let's go."

◆

THE FORENSICS LAB took up the entire second floor of City Hall East. Unlike the rest of the building, which was likely filled with mice and asbestos, the lab was clean and well lit. The air-conditioning actually worked. There were no cracked tiles on the floor or jagged pieces of metal sticking out from the desks. Everything was either white or stainless steel. Faith would've eaten her gun if she'd had to work here day in and day out. Even the windows were clean, missing the great swaths of grime that covered the rest of the building.

At least two dozen people buzzed around the room, all of them wearing white coats, most of them in goggles and surgical gloves as they handled evidence or worked on their computers. There was music playing, something classical that Faith did not recognize. Other than this and the hum of electronics, there was no other noise. She supposed processing blood and combing through carpet fibers didn't call for much conversation.

"Over here," a slim Asian man called across the room. He was sitting on a stool beside one of the lab tables. Several trays were laid out in front of him and a large black briefcase that she was used to seeing lawyers carry was on the floor at his feet. Faith wondered if he'd brought the white lab coat he was wearing or if someone had let him borrow it.

"Gordon," Will said, then introduced Faith.

He offered her his hand. "Nice meeting you, ma'am."

"Likewise," Faith said, thinking she hadn't heard such a lovely, soft drawl since her grandmother had died. She wondered where Gordon had picked it up. He was probably a few years older than Faith, but he had the manners and bearing of a much older man.

Will indicated the notes on the table. Gordon had taken them out of their plastic bags. "What do you think?"

"I'm thinking it's a good thing you called me. This paper is in terrible condition. I'm not going to even try iodine fuming."

"What about DFO?"

"I already put them under the light. It's a mess, man."

"Is there anything special about the brand or the watermark or—"

"Generic as a pair of loafers."

Faith decided that hiding her ignorance was only punishing herself. "I'm not really familiar with chemical processing. Why can't we just dust the paper for prints?"

He smiled, obviously pleased at the question. "I bet you dusted a cigarette butt for prints at the academy, right?" He laughed at her expression. "They've been doing that for as long as I can remember." He leaned back on the stool behind him. "Paper's porous. The natural oil in your fingertips leaves a good, readable print on a hard surface, but when you're dealing with fibers, the oil penetrates and migrates. Dusting it with powder is not going to bring out any latents. You use something like ninhydrin, which reacts with the amino acids in fingerprint residue, and hopefully, you get a pretty little print and we bring home your little girl."

The mood turned decidedly somber as they all considered how important these next few minutes would be.

Will said, "Let's get started."

Gordon took a pair of goggles out of his bag and a pair of green gloves. He told Will and Faith, "Y'all may want to step back. This is pretty toxic stuff." They both did as he advised, but Gordon still handed them paper masks to cover their mouths and noses.

He leaned down and took a small, unmarked metal container out of his bag. He unscrewed the cap and poured some of the contents into one of the pans, careful not to splash. Even through the mask, the fumes hit Faith like a flash of gunpowder. She had never smelled anything so blatantly chemical.

Gordon explained, "Ninhydrin and heptane. I mixed it up last night before I headed down." He capped the metal container. "We used to use Freon, but they outlawed that a few years back." He told Will, "I used the last of my stash two months ago. Hated to see it go."

Gordon used a pair of tweezers to pick up the first sheet of paper. "The ink's going to run a little bit," he warned.

"We already took pictures and made copies," Will told him.

Gordon dropped the paper into the chemical solution. Faith thought it was a lot like the old-fashioned way people used to develop photographs. She watched as he gently agitated the page in the solution. The type print shook, and Faith read the words over and over again as she waited for something to happen.

SHE BE LONGS TOME!!!

Whoever had written that note felt a closeness to Emma Campano. He had seen her, coveted her. Faith looked at the other note.

LEV HER ALONG!!!

Did the kidnapper feel like he needed to protect her from Adam?

"Here we go," Gordon said. She saw stray marks start to develop, forensic proof that the paper had been handled many times by different people. The creases of the folds came up first in a dark orange that quickly turned red. Other stray marks showed smeared thumbprints. A series of swirls came into relief, their color reminiscent of the purple from ditto machines that they used to use when Faith was in school. Thanks to the chemicals, she could see where the paper had been touched over and over again.

Gordon murmured, "That's kind of strange."

Will leaned over, keeping the mask on his face. "I've never seen it turn that dark before."

"Me, neither," Gordon said. "Where'd you find this?"

"A dorm room at Georgia Tech."

"Was it sitting near anything unusual?"

"It was in the pocket of a student. All of them were."

"Was he a chemistry major?"

Faith shrugged. "He worked with adhesives."

Gordon leaned over the pan, staring at the dark print, the distinctive swirls. "This is a left thumbprint. I would say that whoever made it was exposed to some kind of chemical that is reacting to the acetate in my solution."

He reached into his bag and pulled out a magnifying glass. Faith held her breath as she watched him lean over the toxic-smelling pan. He studied all the different fingerprints the chemicals had brought out. "Based on the latents, we've got three different people touching this paper." He looked at the black print again. "I'd say the thumbprint is the only time the third person touched this page." He indicated the position. "It's in the bottom left corner. He was being careful when he handled it."

Will said, "He might have put his thumb there because he was trying not to touch it as he slid it under the door."

"He might very well," Gordon agreed. "I need to dry this, then I can look at the back. Why don't y'all give me a few hours to see what I can come up with? Do you have comparisons of the two people you believe touched this?"

Faith said, "Adam's will be on file. We took Gabe Cohen's to rule him out before we searched Adam's room."

"What about Tommy Albertson's?"

She nodded. Albertson had been an ass about it, but she had managed to get prints off him.

"Well," Gordon began, "get me the comparisons. This is a pretty excellent print, coloring aside. I'll run it through AFIS," he said, referencing the automated fingerprint identification system. "The system's been running slow lately. You know the best way to go about this. Give me the right suspect and I can give you a solid match."

"Will?" A tall woman with spiky blond hair and the requisite white lab coat walked over. "Amanda told me to find you. We got a hit on the sperm from the crime scene."

Will's shock registered on his face. He shook his head, insisting, "No, it can't be the father."

"The father? No, Will, I'm telling you we got a hit from the sex-offender database." She held up a Post-it note.

Faith read the name, hissing, "Jesus, he was right under our nose."

Will seemed just as shocked as she felt. He asked the woman, "Do you have an address?"

Faith told him, "We know where he is."

"His house," Will said. "We need to check his house."

He was right. Faith took out her cell phone and dialed the switchboard. After giving her badge number, she told the operator, "I need ten-twenty-eight on a code forty-four." She read the name from the Post-it note. "Patrick Evander Bernard."

CHAPTER FIFTEEN

WILL SLOWED AT a red light, looking both ways and blowing through the intersection in front of an angry driver.

Amanda's voice was clipped on the phone. "Bernard was picked up in Savannah two years ago for sex with a minor. She was fifteen. He roughed her up pretty badly—bite marks, tearing, bruising. The skin on her palms and knees was ripped open. He pretty much did what he wanted to her."

"Why isn't he in jail?"

"He pleaded it down to reckless endangerment and paid the fine."

Will sped up, passing a truck. "That's a slap on the wrist. Why didn't he go to trial?"

"He met her in a bar. He claimed he took that as proof that she was twenty-one. The prosecutor was scared the jury would equate her sneaking into the bar with asking for trouble."

Will slammed on his brakes, nearly rear-ending a car that was stopped for another red light. "She deserves to be raped for having a fake ID?"

"The parents didn't pursue it. They didn't want their daughter raped again by the court system and the media."

Will could understand their fear. Fewer and fewer rape cases were making it to trial for this very reason. The light changed and he pressed the gas pedal to the floor. "Why was his DNA in the system?"

"It was processed through the rape kit when he was arrested."

"We need to get a copy of his fingerprints to Gordon Chew to match them against the thumbprint on the letter."

"We can't do that."

"Why not?"

"Part of his deal with the district attorney was that his record be expunged if he kept his nose clean for a year."

"But his DNA was still in the sex-offender database."

She mumbled a curse. "That's our fuckup. He should have never ended up in there. He's not a convicted sex offender. Legally, we have no right to use Evan Bernard's DNA or his fingerprints as evidence."

"But if we get a match—"

"Then a judge will throw it out before we even make it to trial."

Will felt the bottom drop out of his case. Unless the teacher was feeling particularly generous—or stupid—they could not get a sample of Evan Bernard's DNA without a court order. A judge would not sign off on the order without probable cause that Bernard had committed a crime. Illegally obtained DNA was not probable cause.

Will stated the obvious. "If we can't use the DNA, we can't link him to Kayla Alexander." He saw the possibilities fall like dominoes. No Kayla, no crime scene. No probable cause, no arrest.

No hope for Emma Campano.

"Faith's waiting outside Bernard's apartment right now. His unit is on the first floor. All the blinds are open. She can see straight into the rooms. There's a garage, but the car is gone. Without the DNA, we can't do anything. She needs legal cause to go inside. I need you to link Bernard to one of these crimes, Will. Get me into that apartment."

Will jerked the steering wheel, swerving the car into the school's parking lot. It felt like a lifetime since he'd been here, though only a day had passed. He thought of Emma Campano again, how a day could be an eternity for her, every second the difference between life and death. Bernard would know that they would come to Emma's school. He would know that they would eventually find out about the arrest, just as he would know that the apartment was the first place they would look. He had to be keeping her somewhere remote—somewhere no one would hear Emma scream.

Two cruisers were parked on the street, away from the school's security cameras. Will jogged toward the front door, directing one team to go around the back of the building and the other to wait at the front. The rent-a-cops on the front steps seemed confused for a moment, but they knew better than to interfere.

Will glanced across the street. The photographers were still there. CNN was doing a live news feed, the reporter's back to the school as she gave absolutely no new information on the case. She would have some information soon enough. This would probably be the scoop of her career.

Will told the security guard, "Get some more of your men around here. Keep the press off school property."

"Yes, sir," the man replied, taking his walkie-talkie out of his pocket.

Will took the steps up to the main building two at a time. He had already debated with Amanda about how to approach this. Emma Campano was in danger, but Evan Bernard could not hurt her while he was at school. Surprise was the only element they had in their favor. The fact that the ransom call was supposed to be made within the next half hour had sealed the deal. If they could catch him on the phone, that would be all the proof they would need.

Will reached out to press the intercom button, but he was already buzzed in. Olivia McFaden waited for him on the other side of the door.

She didn't mince words. "There are two officers with guns in front of my school."

"There are two more in the back," Will informed her, ushering her down the hallway by her arm. He led her into the same conference room they had used the day before. "I'm going to tell you some things and I need you to remain calm."

She jerked her arm away. "I run a high school, Mr. Trent. There's not much you can say that would shock me."

Will did not feel the need to go into the fact that they had found Bernard's sperm inside one of his dead students. Instead, he told the woman, "We have reason to believe that Evan Bernard was having a sexual affair with Kayla Alexander."

Apparently, she could be shocked. She sunk into one of the chairs. "My God." She stood up just as quickly, her mind leaping to the next conclusion. Kayla had been murdered, but Emma was still missing. "He's got students—" She was heading toward the door, but Will stopped her.

"Is there a camera in his room?"

She was still trying to absorb the news, but McFaden snapped out of her surprise quickly enough. "This way," she said, leading him back into the hallway and to the main office. "Colleen," she told the woman behind the desk. "Pull up Mr. Bernard's classroom."

The woman turned to the bank of monitors and tapped some keys. There were six screens in all, each partitioned into smaller images from various cameras around the school. They were all in color, all showing crisp, clear images. Colleen pressed another key and Evan Bernard's classroom filled the middle screen.

There he was in his rumpled jacket and patchy beard, walking up and down the rows of desks, surrounded by teenagers. The class was a small one, maybe a dozen kids in all. They were mostly young girls, their knees clenched together under their desks, pens scribbling nimbly as they recorded Mr. Bernard's every word. No one had their heads down on their desks. They seemed enraptured. Had the fifteen-year-old whom Evan Bernard met in Savannah looked at him the same way? Maybe she did until he raped her.

Will asked, "Is there audio?"

Colleen tapped another key. Sound came out of the speakers,

Evan Bernard discussing the importance of *The Awakening* in American literature.

Will asked, "When is his planning period?"

The principal provided, "Right after lunch, so he gets about an hour and a half between classes."

"Can you give me an exact time frame?"

"Class ends at eleven forty-five. Evan wouldn't have to be back until one-thirty."

Plenty of time, Will thought. Adam's car was parked in the garage at eleven-fifteen. Paul Campano had made the 9-1-1 call at twelve-thirty.

Will asked the secretary, "Do you archive footage?"

"We have everything from every school year since we started recording in 1998," Colleen told him. "What do you need?"

"Two days ago," Will said. "From eleven forty-five until one-thirty."

"Well, that's easy." She kept the image of Bernard on the monitor and pulled up the information on another screen. The woman knew how to work the keyboard and she had obviously figured out what they wanted, because she tracked Evan Bernard's movements as he packed up his briefcase, left his classroom, walked down the hall, exited the building, got into his red Volvo C30 and drove away.

Will tried not to get excited. "When did he return?"

The parking lot was still on the monitor, and she fast-forwarded the camera until Evan Bernard's Volvo showed back up. The car slid into the parking space, stopping on a dime. Bernard got out, glancing around nervously as he adjusted his tie. He ran toward the building. Will thought Colleen was still fast-forwarding, but he saw that the man was, in fact, jogging.

"One thirty-two," McFaden noted from the time stamp. "He was late for class."

The next frame showed Bernard running down the hall. "Back it up," Will said. Something was different, and not just the man's disheveled appearance.

Colleen worked the keys and froze the frame on Evan Bernard

as he jogged down the hall. He was looking right up at the camera. His hair was messed up, his tie skewed.

Will asked, "Can you leave that there and pull up the image of him leaving the first time?"

Colleen went to work, and he stared at the live image of Bernard in his classroom. The teacher was still pacing up and down between the desks, still droning on about literature.

McFaden was still incredulous. "I don't understand how this can happen. Mr. Bernard has been teaching with us for twelve years. There was nothing in his background—"

"You did a check, right?"

"Of course," McFaden told him. "It's state law. All school employees are screened by the police department before we can hire them."

"Oh, my Lord," Colleen whispered. Will saw that she had captured the images of Bernard leaving the school and returning side by side. "He changed his clothes."

The shirts were the same color, but the style looked different. His pants went from black to khaki. Will remembered what Beckey from the lab had told him earlier. Kayla Alexander wasn't the only source of DNA matching Evan Bernard. The seat swatch Charlie had cut out of the Prius had contained traces of Bernard's sperm, too. Of course, none of that got them closer to linking Bernard to Emma Campano. Even if they found a way to get a DNA sample from the teacher, all they could prove was that the teacher had at some point had sex in the Prius with Kayla Alexander.

The telephone on the desk rang. McFaden answered it, then handed the receiver to Will.

Amanda demanded, "Why aren't you answering your phone?"

Will patted his pocket, feeling the pieces of plastic move around.

Amanda didn't wait for his answer. "Did you catch him?"

Will looked at the monitor, Evan Bernard pacing the classroom. "We're waiting until he makes the ransom call."

"He already made it," she told him. "The proof of life was the same tape as yesterday, Will. I told him we had to have a new one or the deal is off."

"Is he going to call back?"

"Four o'clock," she said.

Will checked the digital clock on the wall. Ten thirty-three. "I've been watching Bernard the whole time. He hasn't left the classroom and he hasn't made a call."

"Shit," she hissed. "He's got an accomplice."

✦

WILL KNOCKED ON Evan Bernard's classroom door. The man seemed surprised to find him standing there.

"Agent Trent? Come in."

Will shut the door behind him.

"Actually, leave that open. I've got students coming."

"My partner's keeping them out in the hall."

"I'm glad you're here." Bernard picked up a book off his desk. There were triangles and squares in various colors on the cover. "This is a copy of Emma's reading textbook. I thought maybe you could use it."

"I just wanted to go over a couple of things you said."

"All right." He put the book on the desk, then used his sleeve to wipe the cover, telling Will, "Sorry, I smudged it up a bit."

Will wasn't concerned about fingerprints. "You seemed pretty certain that whoever wrote those notes was illiterate. I'm really not sure what you mean by illiterate, though. I mean, is it like dyslexia? Is that some sort of spectrum diagnosis where somebody can be at one end or the other?"

"Well." He sat on the edge of his desk. "The traditional definition of literacy concerns reading and writing abilities, the ability to use language, to speak in a fluent manner. Then, of course, you could take that out to the next logical step and use it to define a certain level of class or culture." He smiled, enjoying himself. "So, to say someone is illiterate, you would be employing the Latin, 'il,' meaning not or without. Without reading skills, without fluency."

"Without class or culture?" Will asked, gathering from Evan Bernard's cockiness that he had expected the police to turn up on his doorstep. The arrest in Savannah was public record. The man had probably been wondering what was taking them so long.

As if to prove the point, there was a devious lilt to the teacher's tone. "One could say."

"That sounds a little different from the language you used yesterday."

"Yesterday I was in a meeting with my peers."

Will smiled at the dig. He was glad to find the man underestimating him. "What about someone who is functionally illiterate?"

"Strictly going by definition, it is as it sounds. A person who is able to function, or 'pass' if you will, in the real world."

"And you're sure that's the sort of person who wrote those notes?"

"As I said on the phone, I'm not an expert."

"You're an expert in something, aren't you?"

He had the audacity to wink. "Let's just say that I know a little bit about a lot of things."

Will leaned against the closed door, casually crossed his arms. There was a security camera mounted in the corner on the wall opposite. Will knew that he was in the camera's frame, just as he knew that Evan Bernard had signed away his right to privacy when the school had installed the security system. It was to the teacher's benefit at the time, because it meant any spurious allegations of sexual misconduct could be quickly dismissed. On the other hand, it also meant that anything Bernard said or did right now was being recorded on equipment owned by the school, and as such, was completely admissible.

Will said, "I guess you're familiar with your rights. They read them to you when you were arrested in Savannah, right?"

His smile didn't falter. "That was two years ago, Mr. Trent, as I'm sure you know. She was fifteen, she told me she was twenty-one. You're barking up the wrong tree here. This is all just a misunderstanding."

"How's that?"

"I met her in a bar where alcohol is served. I assumed they checked her ID when they let her in."

"If you weren't guilty, why did you plead to reckless endangerment of a minor?"

He held up his finger. "Not a minor. That would be a felony. I was only charged with a misdemeanor."

Will felt a chill from his words. The man was not frightened of being accused, let alone being caught. "Evan, you need to start thinking about what your options are, the best course you can take to make this go easy for you."

Bernard adjusted his glasses, bringing out his teacher voice. "You're wasting your time here, Agent Trent. Now, if you'll excuse me, I've got a class."

"Kayla was a good-looking girl," Will said. "I can see where it'd be hard to resist something like that."

"Please don't insult my intelligence," he said, picking up his briefcase off the floor. He started shoving in papers as he said, "I know my rights. I know I'm being recorded."

"Did you know you were being recorded two days ago when you left the school?"

For the first time, he looked nervous. "I'm allowed to leave campus during my off period."

"Where were you between the hours of eleven forty-five and one-thirty?"

"I drove around," he replied evenly. "It's the first few weeks of school. I had cabin fever. I just needed to get out."

"Get out where?"

"I drove into Virginia Highland," he said, referring to a local neighborhood with coffee shops and restaurants.

"Where did you go?"

"I don't remember."

"Where did you park?"

"I have no idea."

"Should I check for your red Volvo on the traffic cameras at Ponce de Leon and Briarcliff or Ponce and Highland?"

He didn't have an answer for that.

"Or did you cut through Emory? Should I check the traffic cameras there?" Will told him, "You might not have noticed, but the city has cameras at just about every major intersection in town."

"I was just driving around."

Will reached into his jacket pocket and took out a pad of paper and a pen that he had borrowed from the front office. "Write down your route, then I'll go check it out and we can talk this afternoon when school is over."

Bernard reached for the pen, then stopped himself.

Will asked, "Is there a problem? You said this was a misunderstanding, right? Just write out where you were. I'll have one of the patrolmen check it out, then we'll go over your story later."

The teacher took his own pen out of his jacket pocket and started to write. Will could see the nib of his fountain pen moving across the page in quick strokes. Bernard filled the first sheet, then turned to the next, writing more.

"That's enough," Will told him, taking back the tablet. He flipped from one page to the next, then back, before looking up at Bernard. "You teach normal kids, right? Not just the stupid ones."

He nodded, not correcting the gaffe.

Will pretended to read the pages, moving his eyes back and forth. "I just had a question for you, because I do this a lot. I ask people to write things down, and what I've found in the past is that the innocent people are usually so nervous that they forget things. They go back and forth and they scratch things out and they change words around. The guilty people just pick up the pen and start writing, and it's so easy for them because they're just making up shit as they go along."

Bernard put his pen back in his jacket pocket. "That's an interesting observation."

"Evan," Will said. "It's going to go a lot easier for you if we get Emma Campano back to her parents."

"I have no idea what you're talking about. I'm just as outraged as the next person that one of our students has been abducted from her home."

"Do you remember when you first started teaching?" Will asked. "The state did a background check on you, right? You had to go to the police station and give them your Social Security number and your address and then they took your fingerprints. Do you remember that?"

Bernard seemed to realize where this was going. His little game with the pen and wiping down the book had been for naught. "Vaguely."

"What's going to happen when the fingerprints from your card match the ones we found on the threatening letters you slid under Adam Humphrey's door?"

He seemed wholly unconcerned. "I imagine you'll be investigated for fabricating evidence."

"Even if Emma's dead, Evan, if you tell us where she is, a judge will look at that as a positive indication that you tried to do the right thing."

"That's your reality, not mine." He sat back in his chair, the smug look returning to his face.

"Kayla was a troublemaker. Everybody said that. Did she meet you outside of school? It wouldn't have been here, right? It would've been somewhere outside of school."

Bernard shook his head slowly from side to side, as if he felt sorry for Will.

"She's a good-looking girl. I mean, I know, man." Will felt his stomach clench like a fist. "I've been in this school ten minutes and I've already seen some girls..." He shrugged. "Different time, different place, I wouldn't say no."

Bernard took off his wire-rimmed glasses and used the tail of his shirt to clean the lenses. "Not that it's any of my business, but I'd be careful talking like that." He nodded toward the video camera in the corner. "People are watching."

"They were watching two days ago when you came running back to school, too."

He breathed on his glasses, as if there was a spot he needed to get. "I lost track of time. I was late for class."

"Really? I assumed it was because you had to change your pants."

He stopped, his shirttail still in his hand.

"Come stains are hard to wash out, aren't they?" Will smiled. He couldn't use the DNA from the rape kit, but it was perfectly legal for him to lie about finding another source. "Funny thing about come, Evan, it takes more than one washing to get it out."

"You're lying."

Will counted it off for him. "I've got a dead girl with your sperm inside of her and your bite marks on her breast. I've got video showing you changed your pants." Will didn't think about the risk he was taking as he lied. "The same pants we found with your DNA all over them."

"You can't go through my garbage without a search warrant and you have no—"

Will forced himself not to smile, though he ached to tell the man he'd fallen into a trap. "Once the city puts the trash in the truck, I can roll around naked in it if I want."

Bernard shrugged. "Kayla was seventeen. She consented. There's nothing illegal about two adults having sex."

Will chose his words carefully. "This wasn't a recent thing. You've been seeing her for a while."

"Are you asking that because Kayla's birthday was two months ago?" He shook his head, as if he was disappointed that the trap was so obvious. "Our first time having sexual intercourse was two days ago."

"She was a virgin?"

He gave a genuine laugh. "She was the sexual equivalent of McDonald's."

"We found your sperm in Kayla's car."

Again, he seemed unconcerned. "So we had sex in the car."

"Oral? Anal?"

He raised an eyebrow—another trap he saw coming from a mile away. "I watch the news, Mr. Trent. I know that Georgia's laws are very strict where sodomy is concerned."

The arrogant prick thought he had it all wrapped up. "You expect me to believe you just had sex with Kayla Alexander two days ago, but you had nothing to do with her murder?"

"As you said yourself, I had to go home and change my pants. The last time I saw Kayla Alexander, she was alive and heading back to school."

"So you left school, had sex with Kayla Alexander in her car, then came back to school."

"What of it?"

Will could feel his own smile spread across his face. "I've got some more Latin for you, Evan."

Bernard held out his hands in a wide shrug, indicating Will should fire away.

"*In loco parentis,*" Will said. "In place of the parent."

Bernard's hands were still out, but his expression had drastically changed.

"By law, you're Kayla's guardian—her acting parent—during school hours. According to the state, it's illegal to have sex with anyone who is under your supervisory control, no matter what their age is." He gave the same open shrug Bernard had used. "I don't think fucking a minor in her car in the middle of a school day is something a parent is allowed to do." Will added, "Even if it *is* the first time."

Bernard's mouth closed. His nostrils flared. Will could almost see him going over the last two minutes, desperately trying to figure out how he had walked into the trap. The man cleared his throat, but instead of addressing Will, he looked directly into the video camera, saying, "My name is Evan Bernard and I am requesting this interview to be terminated so that I can consult with my lawyer about these spurious allegations."

"Tell me where Emma is, Evan."

"I have nothing to say to you."

"I know you didn't do this by yourself. Tell me who you're working with."

"Mr. Trent, you seem to think you're well versed in the law. I have just asked to speak to my lawyer. This interview is over."

Will walked over to the door and let in the two cops who were standing outside. He told them, "Arrest him."

"For what?"

"Sexual contact"—he turned around, making sure that Bernard was listening—"with a minor."

Will went out into the hallway and leaned against the wall. He could hear the cops reading Evan Bernard his rights, the polite responses the teacher gave in turn, assuring them that he understood everything. The man did not scream or rail against the injustice, he simply seemed to be biding his time, waiting to be processed. It was as if, even as he was being handcuffed, the teacher still thought he held all the power.

If Bernard knew where Emma was being held, he *did* have all the power.

Will sank down onto his heels and put his face in his hands. He wanted Evan Bernard to resist arrest so that he would have to go back into that room and help the cops subdue him. He wanted to grab the man and throw him to the ground. He wanted to beat him the way Kayla Alexander had been beaten.

Instead, he pulled out his cell phone, holding the pieces together so he could make the call.

"Can I go in?" Faith asked, her words rushed. She had been standing outside Bernard's house for the last hour, waiting for Will to give her the word that they had enough evidence for a warrant.

Will thought of the teacher, the smug look on his face, his certainty that he was going to get away with this. "Call the county," he said. "Tell them to pick up Bernard's trash, then go through whatever they put in the truck. I want you to photograph every step you take."

"What am I looking for?"

"A pair of black pants."

"What about his apartment? Can I go in?"

Evan Bernard came out of his classroom, his hands cuffed behind his back, a cop on either side of him. Amanda would be angry at Will for not being the one to escort the prisoner outside, but he wasn't up to smiling for the cameras. The Atlanta Police

Department could have this photo op. Will would be better off spending his time looking for evidence that would convict the bastard.

For his part, Bernard's composure had returned, and he looked down at Will with something like pity. "I hope you find her, Officer. Emma was such a sweet girl."

He kept his head turned, watching Will even as he was being led up the hallway.

Faith asked, "Are you there?"

His hands shook as he struggled not to break the phone into more pieces. "Tear the fucking place apart."

CHAPTER SIXTEEN

FAITH WATCHED IVAN Sambor swing back the metal battering ram and slam it into Evan Bernard's front door. The wooden jamb splintered in a satisfying way, the cheap dead bolt breaking in two as the metal door swung back on its hinges.

She had easily seen inside the apartment from the outside, but Faith walked through the four rooms with her gun drawn, checking the kitchen, the bathroom and the two small bedrooms. Her impression now was the same as when she had first arrived on the scene: Evan Bernard had known they were coming, known that his earlier arrest for sex with a teenage girl would come to light and that the obvious conclusion would be drawn between what happened on the coast and what happened to Kayla Alexander. Bernard had probably stripped the apartment the minute he had gotten home from school that first day.

Faith could smell bleach in every corner of the house. The closet doors had been left open, easily seen from the bedroom windows. There wasn't a speck of dust anywhere—not on the kitchen table, the many bookshelves or, when out of curiosity she decided to check, the blades of the ceiling fans. Even the tops of the doors had been dusted.

Faith holstered her gun and called in Charlie Reed and his

team. She leaned her shoulder against the door outside the second bedroom. The walls were pink. Blue and white clouds were painted on the ceiling. The furniture was cheap, probably secondhand, but it reminded Faith of a bedroom set she had seen in the Sears catalogue when she was a little girl. The small chest of drawers and the four-poster bed were laminated in white Formica with swirly, gold trim outlining the knobs and various other architectural details. Fluffy pink pillows were scattered on the bed. There was framed artwork of Winnie the Pooh with Tigger. It was the sort of room every girl dreamed about in the 1980s.

Outside, she heard Will Trent asking one of the cops where Faith was. He had probably blown through every light on the five-mile stretch between Westfield and Evan Bernard's apartment.

Will's jaw was clenched as he walked down the hallway. He had an air of fury about him, and seeing the girly bedroom did nothing to change his disposition. His throat worked as he took in the pink curtains and lace bedspread. Several seconds passed before he could speak. "Do you think he held her here?"

Faith shook her head. "It's too obvious."

Neither one of them walked into the room. Faith knew there would be no evidence in the white sheets, no telltale strands of hair in the freshly vacuumed carpet. Bernard had kept this showcase for his own benefit. She could imagine him coming into the room, sitting on the bed and living out his sick fantasies.

"It's younger than seventeen," Faith said. "The room, I mean. It's the kind of stuff you'd buy for a ten- or eleven-year-old."

"Did you get the pants?"

"They were in the garbage," she told him. "Do you think we'll get any DNA off them?"

"We'd better," he said. "The second ransom call had the same proof of life from yesterday. Maybe the kidnapper got spooked because he saw us around the school."

"Or she's already dead."

"I can't accept that," Will told her, his voice firm.

Faith chose her words carefully. "Statistically, children taken by strangers are killed within the first three hours of their abduction."

"She wasn't taken by a stranger," Will insisted, and she wondered where he got his certainty. "The kidnapper prerecorded the part about calling back at four. He obviously needed more time. We'll get the new proof of life then."

"You can't be certain of any of that, Will. Look at the facts. Evan Bernard's not talking. We have no idea who his accomplice is. There's not a chance in hell we'll find something here to—"

"I'm not going to have this conversation with you."

So they were back to him being the boss again. Faith bit her lip, trying not to let her sarcasm escalate the situation. He could live in fairyland all he wanted, but Faith was fairly certain that there would not be a happy ending to this story.

Will pressed the point. "I can't believe she's dead, Faith. Emma's a fighter. She's out there somewhere waiting for us to find her."

The passion in his voice was unmistakable, and instead of feeling irritated, she now felt sorry for him.

He said, "I should've gotten more from Bernard. He was so smug, so sure that he was in control. I feel like I played right into his hands."

"You got him to admit to having sex with Kayla."

"He's going to make bail in twenty-four hours. If his lawyer's any good, he'll get the trial postponed until no one remembers who Emma Campano is. Even with the parents pushing for a prosecution, he could end up walking."

"He admitted on tape to having sex with her."

"I hadn't read him his rights. He could argue that I coerced him." Will shook his head, obviously angry with himself. "I screwed it up."

"He knew we were coming to his apartment," Faith said. "This place is immaculate. He didn't clean like this overnight. He prepared the space for us. He's playing some kind of game."

"I should have run a background check on him yesterday."

"There was no reason to," she countered. "We both assumed that the school had checked him out."

"They did," Will reminded her. "Just not recently."

Charlie called from the other room, "Hey, guys."

Faith and Will went into the master bedroom, which had a decidedly more masculine flair. The furniture was heavy, stained a dark charcoal and sitting low to the ground in a sterile, modern way. Over the bed was hanging a huge canvas of a blond-haired, blue-eyed girl. She was obviously young, though not so young that the painting could be deemed child pornography. It was certainly pornographic, though. The girl was naked, her chest thrust out, her legs wide open. There was a sexy twinkle in her eyes, a kittenish pout to her lips. Everything glistened unnaturally.

Charlie was sitting at a desk that was built into an armoire.

"His computer," Charlie said. "Look at this."

Faith saw that the monitor showed a live image of the second bedroom.

Will said, "The camera must be mounted in the Winnie the Pooh poster."

"Christ," Faith whispered. "Are there any files?"

Charlie was clicking through the directory. "I'm not seeing anything," he told them. "We'll have the forensic techs look at this, but it's my guess that an external hard drive was used." He pulled some loose cables out from behind the computer. "These would've recorded sound and video onto the drive. He could completely bypass the computer's hard drive."

"The main computer wouldn't keep any records?"

Charlie shook his head, opening and closing files as he checked for anything incriminating. Faith saw spreadsheets, homework assignments.

She asked, "What about e-mail?"

"There are two addresses on here. One is through the cable company for Internet service. All that's on there is spam—Viagra offers, Nigerian money laundering, that sort of thing. There's no address book, no sent mails, nothing. The other one looks like his school e-mail. I read through everything; they're just correspondences with parents, memos from the principal. Nothing suspicious and nothing personal."

"Could he have kept a new e-mail address on the hard drive?"

"You'd have to ask someone who knows more about computers than me," Charlie said. "Blood and guts I can tell you about. Computers are just a hobby."

Will said, "He wouldn't put a camera in that room unless he was taping himself so he could watch it later. We need to find that hard drive."

"I didn't find anything in Adam's room," Faith reminded him. "His computer was stolen a week before the crime was committed."

"What about Gabe Cohen?"

"Nothing jumped out," Faith told him. "I checked his computer, but like Charlie said, I'm not an expert."

"It'd be a stretch asking to see it again."

She wondered if that was some kind of dig at her for not arresting Gabe Cohen. They were both frustrated and angry. She decided to let the comment pass. "Did you find anything in Bernard's desk at school?"

"Nothing," Will answered. "Maybe the accomplice is keeping the hard drive or a computer for him? Maybe there's a laptop?"

"What about his car?"

"Cleaner than the house," Will said. "Smells like bleach and vinegar."

Charlie stated the obvious. "If you find the video files, that's the smoking gun."

Will said, "I'll get copies of all his phone records, landline and cell."

"This guy is smart," Faith pointed out. "He'd have one of those pay-as-you-go lines. There's no way we can trace them."

"We've already fucked this up twice from making assumptions. Bernard is smart, but he can't think of everything." Will asked, "Charlie, can you check his Internet history?"

Charlie clicked the icon for the Internet browser. A page popped up with a scantily clad teenager doing a split over the words, "Barely Legal." He opened the root directory. "Looks like he emptied the cache, but I can still recover some of the pages." After a few more clicks, he found Bernard's recently viewed pages. The first linked to Westfield Academy's grading program. The next few were retail outlets you would expect a teacher to be interested in—Barnes & Noble, Wal-Mart. Apparently, Bernard had been searching for a copy of *Wuthering Heights*.

"Here we go," Charlie said, pulling up a chat room. Faith leaned in for a closer look, but the site was one intended for teachers who were looking to retire. Another chat room was for West Highland terrier lovers.

Will asked, "What about the first site?"

Charlie went back to Barely Legal. "It's got a disclaimer on the front that says all the girls are of age. As far as the Internet is concerned, as long as they're not obviously underage, like, children, then that's all you need."

Faith looked around the room, feeling a slight sense of disgust as she thought about Evan Bernard sleeping here. She went to the bedside table and opened the drawer from the bottom with her foot. "More porn," she said, not touching the magazines. There was a girl on the front cover who looked about twelve, but the masthead insisted otherwise, proclaiming, *Legal Horny Honeys.*

Will had slipped on a pair of gloves. He pulled out the magazines. All of them had teenage-looking cover girls. All of them implied that the girls were of legal age. "Perfectly legal."

"Detective?" Ivan Sambor's large frame filled the doorway. He held a couple of plastic evidence bags in his meaty hands. Faith saw a large pink vibrator and a set of fur-lined handcuffs, also pink. "Found these in the other room."

Will said, "Tell the lab those have priority."

Ivan nodded, leaving the room.

Faith told Will, "Bernard doesn't have any other properties in his name either in the state of Georgia, the Carolinas, Tennessee or Alabama."

"Let's broaden the search," Will said, though Faith thought that was a shot in the dark. Bernard would not use his real name if he had a silent partner to act as a front.

She said, "I've got a team calling all the storage rental places within a thirty-mile area."

"Check under the names of any family members," Will told her. "We need to know who his friends are. Maybe there's an address book." He glanced around the room, scanning every piece of furniture, every painting on the wall. "The judge limited the scope of our search warrant to evidence tying Kayla Alexander to Bernard. We could argue that we're looking for names of other victims. Even if he's convicted for Kayla, Bernard could be out in two to three with good behavior."

"He'll be a registered sex offender. He'll never teach again."

"That's a small price to pay for kidnapping and murder."

"You're sure he's involved in the other crimes, that it's not just what he said: he had sex with her, she went her way, he went back to school?"

"You saw that bedroom, Faith. He's into young girls."

"All that means is that he is into raping them, not murdering them."

"He learned in Savannah that it's dangerous to leave witnesses."

"Sorry to interrupt," Charlie said, "but maybe you should consider the fact that he was also looking into retiring."

Will seemed puzzled. "How do you know that?"

"The Web site?" Faith asked, wondering how he had forgotten about it so quickly. "Charlie, pull it up again."

Charlie did as she asked, finding the correct Web page. He scrolled through the list of questions and responses. "I'm not sure what screen name he went by. They're all pretty innocuous." He clicked to the next page. "Basically, they're talking about what benefits they retain after retirement, consultancy jobs to help pay the bills—that sort of thing." The screen changed as he selected a new link. "Georgia's teacher retirement program." He leaned closer to the screen to read the details. "All right, this deals with private versus public school teaching. With the state retirement program, you have to have a certain number of years vested to qualify for a pension. Private, you're on your own." He scrolled down, skimming the text. "It says here that they have to go thirty years to get full retirement."

"Maybe he decided he couldn't wait it out," Faith said. "A million dollars would certainly help pave the way toward a comfortable early retirement."

Will told her, "Bernard's only been at Westfield for twelve years. He told us he was teaching in the public school system at one point. Let's find out where he taught before that."

"He would've left in the mid-nineties," Faith said, doing the math in her head. "Maybe there was some impropriety they swept under the rug."

"I know teachers don't make a lot of money, but don't you think it's odd that he's living in this crappy apartment at his age?"

Charlie suggested, "Maybe he's been spending all his spare cash on flights to Thailand to pick up underage girls."

Faith asked, "Do you think we have enough cause to look at his financial records?"

Will shook his head. "We didn't list financial documents in the search warrant."

Charlie cleared his throat. Faith looked at the computer screen. He had pulled up Evan Bernard's accounts at the local credit union. "Let this be a lesson not to store your passwords in your keychains."

Will said, "Check to see if he made any payments to storage facilities."

Charlie moved the mouse around, highlighting each account as he read through the details. "Nothing's popping up. He pays twelve hundred a month for this place. His utilities are about what you'd expect. Groceries, dry cleaners, car payments, a couple of PayPal payments." He read through the rest. "It looks like most of his money goes into his 401-K. The guy's socking it away for retirement."

Faith asked, "What does he bring home every month?"

"Around twenty-three hundred."

Faith stared at the computer screen. She could hear policemen outside the window, laughing about something. Traffic noise from the street filled the air with a low hum. This was the sort of place you rented when you were fresh out of college, not heading toward your fifties and looking to retire. She said, "Evan Bernard's been teaching for how many years and he doesn't own his own house?"

"Could be divorced," Charlie suggested. "An ex-wife could have bled him dry."

"We'll check court records," Will said. "If he's got an ex, maybe she found out what he was doing and left him. If we can corroborate that Kayla was a pattern, we might be able to get a judge to deny bail."

"We already tried the neighbors. Most of them were gone— probably at work. There's a stay-at-home mom in the unit across the garden. She says she's never met Bernard, never seen anything suspicious going on."

"Send a couple of units back around seven tonight. More people should be home by then." Will went to the closet and checked the top shelves. "Maybe he's got a photo album or something."

"We won't find anything he doesn't want us to."

Will kept searching the closet, taking down boxes, checking their contents. "We know he was gone from the school for two hours." He pulled out a stack of yearbooks and dropped them on the bed. There were almost twenty in all, their cheerful covers screaming school spirit. He picked up the top one, which was emblazoned with the Westfield Academy crest, and started thumbing through the pages. "That's not enough time to do the murders, hide Emma and get back to school. The accomplice must have done the heavy lifting. Bernard would have known Emma came from a wealthy family."

"Kayla's parents were well-off. Why not take her, too? Why kill her if she represents money?"

Will closed the yearbook and held it in his hand. "Are we sure Kayla wasn't involved?"

Faith glanced at Charlie, who was still checking out the computer files.

Will didn't seem to mind talking in front of the man. "Kayla Alexander was a nasty piece of work." He dropped the yearbook and picked up the next one. "We haven't found one person who's said otherwise."

"She'd have to be pretty sick to be screwing Bernard in her car while she knew that her best friend was about to be kidnapped." Faith considered something. "Maybe Kayla felt threatened by Emma's affair with Adam."

Will picked up on her train of thought. "Kayla might know that Adam and Emma were parking in the garage. The nosey neighbor told on the girls last year. They had to find somewhere else to park."

"I've been wondering why Kayla parked her white Prius in the driveway of the Campano house when she knew that the last time they were caught skipping, it was because the neighbor saw a car in the driveway."

He stopped searching the pages. "Something's bothered me since I saw the Prius in the parking lot. Everything the killer touched had blood smeared on it: the trunk, the door handles, the steering wheel. Everything except for the duct tape and the rope in the trunk."

"Do you think Kayla brought them for the killer to use?"

"Maybe."

"Hold on," Faith said, trying to process all of this. "If Kayla was involved, why did she get killed?"

"She had a reputation for being nasty."

"You've said all along that the killer must have known her."

His phone started ringing, and he slid it out of his pocket. The thing was pathetic, the pieces held together with Scotch tape. "Hello?"

Faith picked up one of the yearbooks and thumbed through it so she wasn't standing there doing nothing. She glanced up once at Will, trying to read his expression as he listened to the call. Impassive as usual.

"Thank you," he said, then ended the call. "Bernard's finger-prints don't match the thumbprint on the letter."

Faith held the yearbook to her chest. It felt heavy in her hands. "So his accomplice handled the threatening notes."

"Why send the notes? Why show their hand?"

Faith shrugged. "Could be they were trying to scare away Adam so Emma would be alone in the house." She contradicted herself. "In that case, why didn't Kayla just drive Emma to the house? It had to be that they weren't getting along."

Will opened the Westfield yearbook from last year and flipped through the pages. "We need to go back to the beginning. There's a second man out there." He traced his finger across the rows of student photographs. "Bernard's not the kind of guy who gets his hands dirty."

"My friend at Tech said he would probably have news today," Faith told him, hoping she wouldn't have to be more specific about the vial of gray powder she had asked Victor to have tested. Will might have been okay speaking freely around Charlie Reed, but Faith didn't know the man well enough to trust him with her career.

Will said, "Go to Tech. See if there are any results." He found Kayla Alexander's class picture and tore out the page from the yearbook. He handed it to Faith. "While you're there, ask Tommy Albertson if he's ever seen this girl hanging around either Adam or Gabe Cohen. Ask everybody in the dorm if you have to." He flipped to another page and found Bernard's faculty photograph. He tore it out, saying, "Show this one, too."

Faith took the photographs.

Will opened another yearbook, searching for his own copies of the photos. "I'm going to go to the Copy Right and do the same."

Faith looked at the bedside clock. "You said the next ransom call is supposed to come at four?"

Carefully, he tore out the right pages. "The killer is probably with Emma right now, getting the second proof of life."

Faith put the yearbook on the bed. She started to walk away, but stopped, knowing something was different. She fanned out the yearbooks, finding the three that did not belong. They were thicker, their colors not as vibrant. "Why does Bernard have yearbooks from Crim?" Faith asked. The Alonzo A. Crim High School was located in Reynoldstown, a transitional area in east Atlanta. It was probably one of the seedier schools in the system.

Will told her, "At least we know where Bernard taught before he moved to Westfield."

Faith was silent as she thumbed through the pages. She had never been one to believe in fate or spirits or angels sitting on your shoulder, but she had long trusted what she thought of as her cop's instinct. Carefully, she skimmed the index in the back for Evan Bernard's name. She found his photo in the faculty section, but he also sponsored the newspaper staff.

Faith found the appropriate page for the staff photo. The kids were in the usual silly poses. Some of them wearing fedoras that had "press" tags sticking out of them. Some had pencils to their mouths or were eyeballing the camera over folded newspapers. A pretty young blonde stood out, not because she wasn't hamming for the camera, but because she stood very close to a much younger-looking Evan Bernard. The photo was black-and-white, but Faith could imagine the color of her strawberry blond hair, the freckles scattered across her nose.

She told Will, "That's Mary Clark."

◆

ACCORDING TO A very angry Olivia McFaden, within half an hour of Evan Bernard's arrest, Mary Clark had abandoned her classroom. The teacher had simply taken her purse out of the desk, told her students to read the next section in their textbooks, then left the building.

Faith found the woman easily enough. Mary's beat-up Honda Civic was parked outside her family's home on Waddell Street in Grant Park. People took good care of their homes here, but it was nothing like the richer climes of Ansley Park, where professionally manicured lawns and expensive gray-water reclamation tanks made sure the lawns stayed green, flowers kept blooming, all through the summer. Trashcans lined the road, and Faith had to idle the Mini while the garbage truck slowly made its way up the hill, emptying the cans and crawling along to the next house.

Grant Park was a family-friendly neighborhood that managed to be barely affordable while still being in the city limits of Atlanta. Trees arched overhead and fresh paint gleamed in the afternoon sun. The houses were a mixed variety, some shotgun style, some Victorian. All of them had seen a whirlwind of remodeling and renovation during the housing boom, only to find all their paper equity gone when the boom went to a bust.

Still, a handful of houses had been passed by in the race for bigger and better—single-story cottages popped up here and there, neighboring homes looming two and three stories above them. Mary Clark's house was one of these poor cousins. From the outside, Faith guessed the house probably had two bedrooms and one bathroom. Nothing about the house overtly pointed to disrepair, but there was a certain air of neglect to the place.

Faith walked up the stone steps. A large two-toddler stroller of the type used for runners seemed to be taking up permanent space on the front porch. Toys were scattered about. The porch swing looked weathered from its place on the ground. The hardware and chains rusted in a pile beside it. Faith gathered someone had started the weekend project with great intentions but never followed through. The front door was painted a high gloss black, the window curtained on the other side. There was no doorbell. She raised her hand to knock just as the door opened.

A short, bearded man stood in the doorway. He had a small child on either hip, each in various states of oblivious happiness at the prospect of a stranger at the door. "Yes?"

"I'm Detective Faith Mitchell with the—"

"It's okay, Tim," a distant voice called. "Let her in."

Tim didn't seem to want to comply, but he stepped back, letting Faith come into the house. "She's in the kitchen."

"Thank you."

Tim seemed to want to say something more to her—a warning, perhaps?—but he kept his mouth closed as he left the house with the twins. The door clicked shut behind him.

Faith glanced around the room, not knowing whether she was expected to stay here or to find the kitchen. The Clarks had chosen a post-college eclectic style for the living room, mixing brand-new pieces with old. A ratty couch sat in front of an ancient-looking television set. The leather recliner was modern and fashionable, but for faint scratches on the legs that showed signs of a recent visit from a cat. Toys were scattered all over the place; it was as if FAO Schwarz had fired off a bunker-buster from their New York head-quarters.

A quick glance into the open doorway of what must have been the master bedroom showed even more toys. Even at fifteen, Faith had known not to let Jeremy have every room of the house. It was no wonder parents looked exhausted all of the time. There was no space in their homes that belonged completely to them.

"Hello?" Mary called.

Faith followed the voice, walking down a long hallway that led to the back of the house. Mary Clark was standing at the sink, her back to the window. She held a cup of coffee in her hand. Her strawberry blond hair was down around her shoulders. She was wearing jeans and a large, ill-fitting T-shirt that must have belonged to her husband. Her face was blotchy, her eyes red-rimmed.

Faith said, "Do you want to talk about it?"

"Do I have a choice?"

Faith sat down at the table, a 1950s metal and laminate set with matching chairs. The kitchen was cozy, far from modern. The sink was mounted onto a one-piece unit that had been painted a pastel green. All of the cabinets were the original metal. There was no dishwasher, and the stove tilted to the side. Matching pencil marks on either side of the doorway celebrated each growth spurt Mary's twins had experienced.

Mary tossed her coffee into the sink, put the cup on the counter. "Tim said that I should stay out of this."

Faith gave her back her earlier comment. "Do you have a choice?"

They both stared at each other for a moment. Faith knew the way people acted when they had something to hide, just as she knew how to spot the cues that they wanted to talk. Mary Clark showed none of the familiar traits. If Faith had to guess, she would say the woman was ashamed.

Faith clasped her hands in front of her, waiting for the woman to speak.

"I guess I'm fired?"

"You'll have to talk to McFaden about that."

"They don't really fire teachers anymore. They just give them the shittiest classes until they quit or kill themselves."

Faith did not respond.

"I saw them take Evan out of the school in handcuffs."

"He admitted to having sex with Kayla Alexander."

"Did he take Emma?"

"We're building a case against him," Faith told her. "I can't tell you details."

"He was my teacher at Crim thirteen years ago."

"That's a pretty bad neighborhood."

"I was a pretty bad girl." Her sarcasm was loud and clear, but there was pain underneath the boast, and Faith waited her out, figuring the best way to find the truth was to have Mary lead her there.

The woman slowly walked over to the table and pulled out a chair. She sat down with a heavy sigh, and Faith caught a whiff of alcohol on her breath. "Evan was the only bright spot," Mary told her. "He's the reason I wanted to be a teacher."

Faith was not surprised. Mary Clark, with her pretty blond hair, her piercing blue eyes, was exactly Evan Bernard's type. "He molested you?"

"I was sixteen. I knew what I was doing."

Faith wouldn't let her get away with that. "Did you really?"

Tears came into the woman's eyes. She looked around for a tissue, and Faith got up to get her a paper towel off the roll.

"Thank you," she said, blowing her nose.

Faith gave her a few seconds before asking, "What happened?"

"He seduced me," she said. "Or maybe I seduced him. I don't know how it happened."

"Did you have a crush on him?"

"Oh, yeah." She laughed. "Home wasn't exactly nice for me. My father left when I was little. My mother worked two jobs." She tried to smile. "I'm just another one of those stupid women with a father fixation, right?"

"You were sixteen," Faith reminded her. "You weren't a woman."

She wiped her nose. "I was a handful. Smoking, drinking. Skipping school."

Just like Kayla, Faith thought. "Where did he take you?"

"His house. We hung out there all the time. He was cool, you know? The cool teacher who let us drink at his place." She shook her head. "All we had to do was worship him."

"Did you?"

"I did everything he wanted me to do." Mary shot her a searing look. "Everything."

Faith could see how easily Mary had probably played into Bernard's hands. He had given her safe harbor, but he was also the person who could bring it all to an end with one phone call to her parents.

"How long did it last?"

"Too long. Not long enough." She said, "He had this special room. He kept the door locked. No one was allowed in there."

"No one?" Faith asked, because obviously, Mary Clark had seen it.

"It was all done up like a little girl's room. I thought it was so pretty. White furniture, pink walls. It was the kind of room I thought all the rich girls had."

The man certainly was a creature of habit.

"He was sweet at first. We talked about my dad leaving us, how I felt abandoned. He was nice about it. He just listened. But then he wanted to do other things."

Faith thought of the handcuffs, the vibrator they had found in Bernard's special room. "Did he force you?"

"I don't know," Mary admitted. "He's very good at making you think that you want to do something."

"What kinds of things?"

"He hurt me. He…" She went very quiet. Faith gave her space, not pressing the woman, knowing that she was fragile. Slowly, Mary pulled down the collar of the baggy T-shirt. Faith saw the raised crescent of a scar just above her left breast. She had been bitten hard enough to draw blood. Evan Bernard had left his mark.

Faith let out a long breath of air. How close had she come as a kid to being just like Mary Clark? It was the luck of the draw that the older man in her life had been a teenage boy instead of a sadistic pedarest. "Did he handcuff you?"

Mary put her hand over her mouth, only trusting herself to nod.

"Were you ever afraid for your life?"

Mary did not answer, but Faith could see it in the woman's eyes. She had been terrified, trapped. "It was all a game for him," she said. "We would be together one day, and then the next, he would break it off with me. I lived in constant fear that he would finally leave me, and I would be all alone."

"What happened?"

"He quit in the middle of the year," Mary told her. "I didn't see him again until my first day at Westfield. I just stood there like a gawking teenager, like it was thirteen years ago and he was my teacher. I felt all these things for him, things that I shouldn't feel. I know it's sick, but he was the first man I loved." She looked up at Faith, almost begging her to understand. "All the things he did to me, all the humiliation and the pain and the grief…I don't know why I can't break this connection I have with him." She was crying again. "How sick is that, that I still have feelings for the man who raped me?"

Faith looked at her hands, not trusting herself to answer. "Why did Evan leave your school?"

"There was another girl. I don't remember her name. She was hurt really badly—raped, beaten. She said that Evan did it to her."

"He wasn't arrested?"

"She was a troublemaker. Like me. Another kid stood up for him, gave him an alibi. Bernard could always get kids to lie for him, but he still quit anyway. I think he knew they were onto him."

"Did you ever see him again? I mean, after he left school, did he try to get in touch with you?"

"Of course not."

Something in her tone made Faith ask, "Did you try to get in touch with him?"

The tears came back, humiliation marring her pretty features. "Of course I did."

"What happened?"

"He had another girl there," she said. "In *our* room. *My* room." Tears rolled down her cheeks. "I screamed at them, threatened to call the police, said whatever stupid thing I could think of to get him back." She stared at the markings on the doorjamb, the milestones of her children's lives. "I remember it was pouring down raining, and cold—cold like it never gets here. I think it actually snowed that year."

"What did you do?"

"I offered myself to him, whatever he wanted, however he wanted." She nodded her head, as if agreeing with the memory that she had been willing to debase herself in any way for this man. "I told him I would do anything."

"What did he say?"

She looked back at Faith. "He beat me like a dog with his hands and fists. I lay there in the street until the morning."

"Did you go to the hospital?"

"No. I went home."

"Did you ever go back?"

"Once, maybe three or four months later. I was with my new boyfriend. I wanted to park in front of Evan's house. I wanted someone else to fuck me there, like I could pay him back." She chuckled at her naiveté. "Knowing Evan, he would've stood at the window, watching us, jerking himself off."

"He wasn't there?"

"He had moved. I guess he was on to greener pastures, on to our illustrious Westfield Academy."

"And you never spoke to him again—not until you saw him your first day at school?"

"No. I wasn't so stupid that I didn't understand."

"Understand what?"

"Before, he never left bruises where people could see them. That's how I knew it was over. He kicked my face so hard that my cheekbone fractured." She put her hand to her cheek. "You can't tell, can you?"

Faith looked at the woman's pretty face, her perfect skin. "No."

"It's on the inside," she said, stroking her cheek the way she probably soothed her children. "Everything Evan did to me is still on the inside."

✦

WILL WALKED THROUGH the parking lot behind the Copy Right, feeling time start to crush in on him. Evan Bernard would be out of jail this time tomorrow. His accomplice was no closer to being identified. There were no clues to follow up on, no breaks on the horizon. The forensic evidence was a wash. The DNA would take days to process. Amanda was ruthless in her focus. She worked cases to win them, cutting her losses when she felt the odds stacking against her. Unless the four o'clock ransom call revealed something earth-shattering, she would soon start pulling resources, assigning priorities to other cases.

They thought Emma was dead. Will could feel it in the way Faith looked at him, the careful words Amanda chose when she talked about the teenage girl. They had all given up on her—everyone but Will. He could not accept that the girl was gone. He would not accept anything less than bringing a living, breathing child back to Abigail Campano.

He pressed the button beside the door and was buzzed in immediately. As Will walked down the hallway to the Copy Right, he could hear the high-pitched whir of the machines working at full speed. The construction crew on the street added to the cacophony, hammer drills and concrete mixers providing a steady beat. Inside the store, the plate-glass windows facing Peachtree Street were vibrating from the activity.

"Hey, man!" Lionel Petty called. He was sitting behind the front counter, his head bent over a paper plate that contained a very large steak and French fries. Will recognized the logo on the paper sack beside him as that of the Steakery, a fast-food place specializing in large portions of dubiously inexpensive meat.

"You got my phone call!" Petty said, obviously excited. "The construction crew came back this morning. I was shocked, man. Somebody must've screwed up their orders." He looked closely at Will. "Damn, man, you got creamed."

"Yeah," Will said, stupidly touching his bruised nose.

The noise level died down a bit and Petty stood up to check the machines.

Will asked, "The contractors—is it the same crew?"

He stopped at one of the copiers and began loading in reams of paper. "Some of them look familiar. The foreman's been coming in and out of the garage with his big-ass truck. Warren's pissed about it, but there's nothing we can do because we don't technically own the lot."

Will thought about what the manager had told him, how most of their customers never came to the building. "Why does he care?"

"The trash, man—all that litter. It's a matter of respect." He closed the machine and pressed a button. The copier whirred back to life, adding a deep hum to the chorus of spinning wheels and shuffling paper. Loud beeping came from outside as a Bobcat front loader backed into position to move the steel plates off the road.

Petty sat down in front of his meal. "The dust gets dragged all over the carpet. It's so fine that we can't vacuum it up."

"What dust?"

Petty cut into the meat, grease and blood squirting onto the paper plate. "The concrete they use underground."

Will thought of the gray powder. He glanced back at the construction workers. The Bobcat rammed its front shovel into the edge of one of the steel plates, revealing a gaping hole in the road. "What does it look like?"

Petty cupped his hand to his ear. "What?"

Will didn't answer. The hand at Petty's ear held a cheap-looking knife. The handle was wood, the grommets holding it together a faded gold. The blade was jagged but sharp.

Will tried to swallow, his mouth suddenly going dry. The last time he had seen a knife like that, it was lying inches from Adam Humphrey's lifeless hand.

CHAPTER SEVENTEEN

FAITH STOOD OUTSIDE the conference room door in Victor's building. Behind the glass, she could hear the low murmur of male voices. Her mind was elsewhere—back in Evan Bernard's apartment where he kept his pink vibrator and handcuffs in his little-girl bedroom. Were these the same devices he had used on a teenage Mary Clark? What were some of the sadistic things he'd gotten up to with the girl? Mary wasn't telling, but the truth was written all over her face. He had damaged her deeply in ways the other woman could not articulate—would probably never be able to articulate. It made Faith sick just thinking about it, especially when she was certain that Mary was just one of many, many victims the schoolteacher had targeted over the years.

Faith had called the resource officer at Alonzo Crim High School as soon as she'd made her way out of Grant Park. There was no record of the alleged rape that had forced Evan Bernard to leave his position. Mary Clark could not remember the girl's name—or at least she claimed not to. No charges had been filed against Evan Bernard, so the local precinct had no records of an investigation. Of the hundred or so current faculty members, none had been around during the time Mary Clark was being sadistically abused. There were no witnesses, no evidence and no accomplices in sight.

Still, somewhere out there was another person who knew exactly where Emma Campano was. Will seemed to think there was a chance that the girl was still alive, but Faith held no such illusion. If the killer had a living victim, he would have recorded another proof of life for the second call. This was all well planned out. Bernard was the calm one, the one who remained in control. The Campano house told them that the killer, Emma's abductor, was not similarly gifted. Something must have gone horribly wrong.

Faith had ripped open the envelope her gas bill was supposed to be mailed in and used it to store the yearbook photos of Kayla Alexander and Evan Bernard. She opened it now and looked at Evan Bernard's school photo. He was a good-looking man. He could have easily dated women his own age. Without prior knowledge, Faith would have dated him in a heartbeat. A well-educated, articulate teacher who tutored kids with learning disabilities? There had probably been women lined up at his front door. And yet, he had chosen the young girls who didn't know any better.

Just being in the teacher's house this morning had made Faith feel filthy. His barely legal porn and the painting of the young woman on his bedroom wall all pointed to his sick obsession. She was just as furious as Will that he would easily make bail tomorrow. They needed more time to build a case against him, but right now, the only thing they had to go on was a missing hard drive and a fingerprint that did not belong to their only suspect. And still, there was a nagging question in the back of Faith's mind: was Bernard the key to all this, or was he just a disgusting distraction from the real murderer?

Faith could well understand what a forty-five-year-old man wanted with a seventeen-year-old girl, but could not fathom what had attracted Kayla Alexander to Evan Bernard. His hair was going gray. He had deep wrinkles around his mouth and eyes. He wore suit jackets with corduroy patches at the elbows and brown shoes with black pants. Worse, he had all the power in the relationship, and not just because of his job.

By virtue of the fact that Bernard had simply lived longer than Kayla, he was smarter than her. In the twenty-eight years that separated their ages, he'd garnered more life experiences, gotten more relationships under his belt. It must have been so easy for him to seduce the willful child. Bernard was probably the only adult in her life who encouraged Kayla's bad behavior. He would have made her feel special, as if he was the one person who understood her. All he would have wanted in return was her life.

· At the age of fourteen, Faith had been similarly tricked by a boy who was only three years her senior. He had compromised her in so many ways by holding the threat over her head that if she stopped seeing him, he would tell her parents all the things she had done with him. Faith had just dug herself deeper and deeper, skipping school, breaking curfew, being at his beck and call. And then she had gotten pregnant and he had tossed her aside like a piece of garbage.

The conference room door opened as the meeting adjourned. Men in suits poured out, blinking in the sunlight coming through the windows. Victor seemed surprised to find Faith waiting for him. There was an awkward moment where she reached out to shake his hand just as he went in to kiss her cheek. She laughed nervously, thinking she couldn't adjust to who she was supposed to be right now.

"I'm here for my job," she told him by way of an explanation.

He held out his hand, motioning for her to walk with him. "I got a message that you called earlier. I was hoping it was for a date, but I reached out to Chuck Wilson anyway."

Wilson was the scientist who was analyzing the gray powder Charlie Reed had found. "Does he have anything?"

"I'm sorry, but I haven't heard back from him yet. I made him promise he'd get to it today." He smiled. "We could go to lunch and check with him afterward."

"Sooner would be better. Is there a way to call him?"

"Of course."

They went down a small stairway. She told him, "I need to talk to one of your students, too."

"Which one?"

Faith played with the envelope in her hand, the pictures of Kayla and Bernard. "Tommy Albertson."

"You're in luck," Victor said, glancing at his watch. "He's been waiting for me in my office for the last hour."

"Is he in trouble?"

"That's what the meeting was about." Victor took her arm and led her down the hallway. He lowered his voice. "We've just gotten approval to begin the process of expelling him."

The parent side of Faith experienced a mild form of panic at the thought. "What did he do?"

"A series of extremely stupid pranks," Victor told her. "One of which resulted in destruction of school property."

"What property?"

"He backed up the toilets on his hall last night. We think he used socks."

"Socks?" Faith asked. "Why would he do that?"

"I've given up asking myself why young boys do anything," Victor commented. "My only regret is that I won't be the one who gets to tell him he's out of here."

"Why not?"

"He gets an opportunity to face the expulsion committee and explain his case. I'm a tad concerned because there are some kindred spirits on the panel. It's made up of Tech graduates, most of whom participated in their fair share of idiocy while they were on campus, and most of whom went on to excel in their chosen careers."

Victor reached in front of her and opened the door marked "Dean of Student Relations." His name was in gold letters under the title, and Faith felt a shocking thrill at the sight of it. Her brief bouts of dating were usually with men whose titles generally tended toward the more generic: plumber, mechanic, cop, cop, cop.

"Marty," Victor said to the woman behind the desk. "This is Faith Mitchell." He smiled at Faith. "Faith, this is Marty. She's worked with me for almost twelve years."

The women exchanged pleasantries, but there was a definite understanding between them that they were sizing each other up.

Victor put on his official voice as he told Faith, "Detective Mitchell, Mr. Albertson is a nineteen-year-old adult, so you don't need my permission to talk to him. You're more than welcome to use my office."

"Thank you." Faith tucked the envelope under her arm and walked to another door with Victor's name on it.

Her first thought as she entered the office was that it smelled like Victor's aftershave and looked as masculine and handsome as he was. The space was large with a bank of windows that looked down on the expressway. His desk was glass on a chrome base. The chairs were low slung but comfortable looking. The couch in the corner was sophisticated, black leather, only marred by the teenage lump sitting on it.

"What are you doing here?" Tommy Albertson wanted to know.

"I'm here to help you with your grief counseling. Apparently, you've been so distraught about what's happened in your dorm over the last few days that you've been acting out."

The large lightbulb over his head flickered before finally turning on. "Yeah," he agreed. "I'm pretty worried about Gabe."

"Do you know if he has a gun?"

"I already answered that question," he reminded her. "No, I don't know if he had a gun. I didn't know he was depressed. I never met that girl—either of them. I just kept my head down, you know? Kept out of everybody's business."

"Is that why you're in Dean Martinez's office when you should be in class?"

"All just a big mix-up," he told her, his shoulders going up in a shrug.

She sat down in one of the chairs across from the couch. "You're in a lot of trouble here, Tommy."

"I'll be fine," he assured her. "My dad's on his way here to straighten everything out."

"There's not a lot to straighten, considering you destroyed school property."

He shrugged again. "I'll pay for it."

"You will? Or your dad will?"

Again, he shrugged. "What does it matter? He'll make a donation or buy a couple of football uniforms and it'll all be over." He added, "Plus, you know, it's like you said—I was acting out." He grinned. "I'm really torn up about Adam, and then I find out my buddy's depressed and leaving school? Man, too much."

Faith clenched her jaw, trying not to let him know he had gotten to her. She opened the envelope and showed him Evan Bernard's photo. "Have you ever seen this man?"

The boy shrugged.

"Tommy, look at the photo."

He finally sat up on the couch and looked at the picture of Evan Bernard.

Faith asked, "Have you ever seen him?"

Albertson glanced up at her, then back at the photo. "Maybe. I don't know."

She had never in her life wanted so desperately to slap the truth out of anyone. "Which one is it?"

"I said I don't know."

She kept the picture out. "I need you to really look at this, Tommy. It's important. Does this man look familiar to you?"

He sighed, exasperated. "I guess. Was he on TV or something?"

"No. You would have seen him around campus. Maybe Adam or Gabe was with him?"

Albertson took the photograph from her and held it up, studying the face. "I don't know where I've seen him, but he looks familiar."

"Can you think about it some more?"

"Sure." He gave her the photo and slumped back on the couch.

Faith could not hide her irritation. "*Now*, Tommy. Can you think about it now?"

"I am," he insisted. "I told you, he looks familiar, but I don't know where I've seen him. He kind of reminds me of Han Solo. Maybe that's where I recognize him."

Faith slotted the picture back into the envelope, thinking she looked like Harrison Ford more than Evan Bernard did. "How about her?"

Albertson didn't have to be asked twice to look at Kayla Alexander. "Wow, she's fucking hot." He narrowed his eyes. "She's the chick who died, right?"

Faith knew that Alexander's photo had been all over television for the last three days.

He frowned, handing back the photo. "Man, that's sick, getting wood for a dead girl." When Faith did not take back the picture, he dropped it on the table, a sour expression on his mouth.

"You never saw her before?" Faith asked, tucking the photo back into the envelope.

He shook his head.

"Thanks a lot, Tommy. You've been a real big help." She stood up to leave.

"I can call you if I remember anything." He was smiling in a way that he obviously thought was charming. "Maybe give me your home number?"

Faith bit her lip so that she wouldn't say anything back. His lack of compassion was galling. She wanted to remind him that Emma Campano was still missing—possibly dead—that a boy who was his age and in his school, someone who had slept less than ten feet from him, had been brutally murdered and that a killer was still at large. Instead, she got up and walked across the room, making herself pull the door to gently so as not to give him the satisfaction.

She kept her hand on the closed door, willing herself to calm down. Victor and his secretary were watching her expectantly. She wanted to rail against the kid, to curse him for being such a heartless bastard, but she did not. It was a bit early in their relationship for Victor to see her bitchy side.

"So?" He stood with his hands in his pockets, his usual smile on his face. "Was he useful?"

"As much as a bag of hair," she told him. An idea occurred to her. "Did you search his room?"

"What for?"

Faith had thought it inconsequential at the time, but now she said, "For the pot I found in his sock drawer when I was searching Gabe Cohen's things last night."

Victor's smile widened. "Marty, if you could have campus security check into that?"

"Certainly." The secretary picked up the phone, giving Faith a look of approval.

Victor told Faith, "We have a strict policy on drugs. Automatic expulsion."

"I think that might be the best news I've heard all day."

"Here's some more: Chuck Wilson called back. He says he's got a pretty good guess on what your substance is. He's across the street at the Varsity if you want to go over and find him."

Faith felt a flash of heat in her face. She had put the stolen evidence in the back of her mind, treating it as an intangible thing, but now there was no turning away from what she had done.

"Faith?"

"Great." She made herself smile.

He opened his office door. "Are you sure you can't grab a quick bite? I know that fast food isn't very romantic..."

If Victor wasn't ready to see her bitchy side, he certainly didn't need to watch her wolfing down a chili steak sideways with a PC. "I appreciate the invitation, but I've got to meet my partner on this case."

"How's it going?" he asked, leading her to the building lobby and outside. "Any luck?"

"Some," she admitted, but wasn't more specific than that. Evan Bernard's arrest did not feel like an accomplishment when they still had no idea where Emma Campano was.

"It must be hard for you," he said, squinting in the sun as they walked past the football stadium. Large brick buildings were opposite; more student housing.

"The not knowing is hard," she admitted. "I keep thinking about the girl, what it must feel like for her parents."

He pressed his hand to the small of her back, indicating a one-way street on the right. Faith took the turn, and he continued talking. "I've dealt with a lot of students' problems over the years, but nothing like this. The whole campus feels tense. I can't imagine what it's like at the girls' school. We've lost students before, but never to violence."

Faith was quiet, listening to the soothing sound of his voice, enjoying the sensation of his touch through her thin cotton blouse.

"This way," Victor said, indicating where the sidewalk narrowed. A tall iron railing cut into the sidewalk, the ground sloping downward.

Faith stopped. They were about two blocks from the North Avenue bridge that crossed I-75 and led to the Varsity. "What's this?"

"You've never used the tunnel before?" Victor asked. She shook her head and he explained, "It's a shortcut under the interstate. I wouldn't use it in the middle of the night, but it's perfectly safe now." He took her hand as if to assure her—as if she didn't have a gun on her hip and the ability to use it.

He continued playing the part of tour guide as they walked. "The Varsity was founded by a Tech student by the name of Frank Gordy. He opened it mainly to service the school, but that's changed quite a bit over the years. We try not to let our students know Gordy dropped out of school in 1925 to start the restaurant. Between Steve Jobs and Bill Gates, it's hard enough to convince technology majors that there's actually a reason to complete your degree."

"You know I can't say anything," Faith commented. She'd told him last night that she had dropped out of college a year from graduating. Jeremy had inherited her love of math, and seeing him get his degree was more than enough.

Victor reminded, "Tech has a wonderful adult enrollment program."

"I'll keep that in mind," she answered, humoring him. You

didn't need trigonometry to arrest a vagrant for public intoxication.

They were inside the tunnel, but Victor did not move his hand from her back. Above, Faith could hear the rumble of traffic passing over their heads. She wondered how many Tech engineers had worked on the highway project, and whether or not the city planners had known about the secret passageway. The tunnel was large, about twelve feet wide and at least twenty yards long. The ceiling was low, and though Faith wasn't normally the type, she felt a bit claustrophobic.

Victor continued, "I'm sure you know that the Varsity is the largest drive-in fast-food restaurant in the world. It covers two city blocks. This tunnel comes out on the north side of the building at Third Street."

"I don't remember this part of the tour when Jeremy visited the campus."

"It's a well-kept secret. You should see this place during football games. It's wall to wall."

Faith felt herself sweating, even though it was cooler underground. Her heart started pounding for no reason and no matter how far they walked, the stairs lining the tunnel exit seemed to get farther away.

"Hey." He sounded concerned. "You okay?"

She nodded her head, feeling silly. "I just—" She realized she was clutching the envelope and slipped out the pictures to make sure she hadn't creased them. When she looked up at Victor, she felt her panic from a few moments before start to return. His face was hard, angry.

She asked, "What is it?"

He glared at her, his fury almost tangible. "What are you doing with pictures of Evan Bernard?"

"How do you—"

He quickly closed the space between them, grabbing her right arm. His grip was tight. He was left-handed. Why hadn't she noticed that before?

"Victor—" she breathed, panic taking hold.

"Tell me what you know," he demanded. "Tell me right now."

Faith felt her right arm go numb where Victor was grabbing her. "What are you talking about?" she asked, her heart beating hard enough to hurt.

He pressed, "Was this some kind of sting operation?"

"To catch you doing what?"

"I have no connection to that man. You tell them that."

"You're hurting me."

Victor let go of her. He looked down at her bare arm, the mark he had made. "I'm sorry," he said, walking back to his side of the tunnel. He ran his fingers through his hair, pacing nervously. "I don't know Evan Bernard. I had no idea what he was doing. I never saw him with students, I never even saw him on campus."

She rubbed her arm, trying to get the feeling back. "Victor, what the hell are you talking about?"

Victor put his hands in his pockets, rocked back on his heels. "Just tell me, Faith. Does this mean anything to you, or are you investigating me?"

"For what? What did you do?"

"I didn't *do* anything. That's what I'm trying to tell you." He shook his head. "I really liked you, and this was all some kind of game, wasn't it?"

"Game?" she demanded. "I've spent the last three days trying to find the sick fuck who killed two people and abducted another to do God knows what to her. You think this is some sort of game?"

"Faith—"

"No," she snapped. "You don't get to sound like the reasonable one here. Tell me exactly what's going on, Victor, starting with your connection to Evan Bernard."

"He's been a part-time tutor for over twenty years. Our students aren't exactly well versed in liberal arts. He helped them with their course work."

"Was Adam Humphrey one of his students?"

"No, we fired Bernard last year. He taught remedial classes during summer term. We found out he was having an affair with a student. Several students. He's suing us—he's suing me—for wrongful termination."

"Why you personally?"

"Because the program fell under student services. Bernard's suing anyone who was remotely connected with the tutoring program. He lost his state pension, his benefits, his retirement."

"It's illegal for him to have sex with students."

"Not unless you catch him red-handed," he countered in disgust. "None of the girls would testify against him."

"Then how did you find out?"

"One of them came forward. He was pretty rough with her. There was some kind of fight and she got hurt. She didn't come to us until a few weeks later. I tried to get her to go to the police, but she wouldn't. Her word against his, right? She was scared of being paraded in front of the media. She was scared of being ostracized by the campus." His lips went into a thin line. "It's disgusting enough that it happened, but for him to sue us..."

"Why isn't this public knowledge?"

"Because he wants money, not headlines, and the university sure as hell isn't going to call up CNN and give them the scoop. It's only about the money, Faith. That's all it ever boils down to." He wiped his mouth with the back of his hand.

"He teaches at a high school. Did you know that?"

"The lawyers told us not to contact them. He could sue us for slander."

"It's not slander if you're telling the truth."

"That's a high-minded attitude when you're not looking at fifty thousand dollars in legal bills to defend yourself against a bastard you've never even met." He crossed his arms over his chest. "I'm sorry, Faith. I saw the photos and I thought they sent you to get me."

"It's not a criminal case."

"I know that," he said. "I'm just so..." He shook his head, leaving her to fill in the blanks. "I'm paranoid. I worked damn hard to get where I am and I don't want to lose my job and my house because of some asshole who can't keep his dick in his pocket." He shook his head again. "I'm sorry. I shouldn't use that kind of language. I shouldn't have grabbed you, either. I'm under a tremendous amount of stress. That's not an excuse. I know that."

"Why didn't you tell me about this before? We spent the night together talking about everything *but* this."

"For the same reason you didn't talk about your case. It was nice to just talk to a human being about normal stuff. I've been dealing with this lawsuit all summer. I just wanted somebody who sees me as Victor the nice guy, not the administrator who's being sued because students got poached on his watch."

Faith wrapped her arms around her waist, frustration building to the boiling point. Emma Campano had been abducted by a madman. How many more people had been standing idly by while the girl was being brutalized, her friends were being killed? "You have no idea what you've done." He tried to respond and she shook her head. "This man could be connected to my case, Victor. He was sleeping with one of the girls who died. His sperm was found inside her body."

His mouth opened in shock. "What are you saying?"

"That Evan Bernard is a suspect in our case."

"He kidnapped that girl? He killed..." Victor seemed truly horrified by the prospect.

She was so angry that she felt tears come into her eyes. "We don't know, but if you'd shared this information with me two days ago, you might have spared another girl from—"

Footsteps echoed in the tunnel. Faith shielded her eyes from the harsh lights and made out a round figure making its way toward them. As the man got closer, she could see that he was wearing shorts, a T-shirt and a white lab coat that was stained with catsup.

"Chuck," Victor said, his voice strained as he tried to get back his composure. He reached toward Faith, but she shrugged him off. He still managed introductions. "This is Faith Mitchell. We were just coming to find you."

By way of greeting, Chuck said, "Shockrete."

Faith asked, "Sorry?"

"Your gray powder is Shockrete. It's a high-density concrete that's reinforced with titanium fibers."

"What's it used for?"

"Retaining walls, wine cellars, skateboard parks, swimming pools." He glanced around. "Tunnels."

"Like this one?"

"This baby's old," he said, patting the low ceiling. "Besides, I found granite in the mix."

"Like Stone Mountain?" she asked, referencing a mountain that was several miles outside the city.

"That particular granite is known for its clusters of tourmaline, which aren't common to other granites. I'm no igneous petrologist, but my guess is that it's our trusty three-hundred-million-year-old Atlanta bedrock."

She tried to put him back on point. "So it came from a tunnel in the city?"

"I'd say a construction site."

"What kind?"

"Any kind, really. Shockrete's sprayed on the walls, the ceiling, to hold back soil."

"Would it be used in water main construction, fixing lines under the road?"

"Almost exclusively. As a matter of fact—"

There was more, but Faith was running too fast to hear him.

CHAPTER EIGHTEEN

WILL REPEATED HIS question. "What does the concrete powder look like?"

"Like you'd expect," Petty answered, indicating the glass door Will had just walked through.

He could see it now. Light gray footprints across the blue carpet. Will glanced around the room, the furiously working copiers, the empty storefront. Anyone who had been in the Copy Right or the parking lot could have tracked through the concrete dust and deposited it anywhere, but only one of them was holding a knife that matched the one used to kill Kayla Alexander and Adam Humphrey.

He asked Petty, "Are you the only one here?"

The man nodded, chewing another bite of steak. "Warren should be back soon. He's out making a delivery."

"He has a van?"

"Nah, it's just down the street. We walk over the deliveries sometimes. It kind of breaks the monotony."

Outside, the jackhammer kicked in, the vibrations so hard that Will could feel the floor shaking under his feet.

Will raised his voice, asking, "Do you ever make deliveries?"

He shrugged. "Sometimes."

"What?" Will asked, though he had heard the man well enough. "I can't hear you over the jackhammer."

"I said sometimes."

Will shook his head, pretending he still couldn't hear. This wasn't going to be like Evan Bernard. Will would not leave this building without a suspect in handcuffs and a solid case to back the arrest. Petty had the knife, he had the opportunity and he certainly had the motive—what better way to end his illustrious career at the Copy Right than to retire with a million dollars cold hard cash in his pocket? Having Emma Campano in the process would be icing on the cake.

Was that enough, though? Was this pathetic pothead the kind of man who could beat a girl to death and take another away for his own pleasure? Faith had said she'd be the ruler of the world if she could spot a killer from a hundred paces. Was Lionel Petty someone who hid murder in his heart, or was he just caught up in something bad—the wrong place at the wrong time?

Either way, Will wanted to get Petty away from the exit and in an enclosed space where he could talk to him. He especially wanted him to put down the knife.

He told the man, "I still can't hear you."

Petty cupped his hands to his mouth, making a joke of it. "Sometimes I make deliveries!"

Will knew the office was in back of the room. He guessed that all the paperwork would be kept there. He yelled to Petty, "I need to see who you deliver to."

Petty nodded, dropping the knife and standing up. He started to leave, then changed his mind. Will reached around to his paddle holster as Petty's fingers moved toward the knife, but the man only scooped up a handful of French fries. He ate them as he led Will to the back of the store. At the door to the office, he pulled out a ring of keys.

Will asked, "Does Warren always leave those with you?"

"Never, man." He jammed a key into the lock, pushed open the door and sat down in front of the desk. The noise was somewhat buffered in the small room, and Petty spoke in a normal tone. "Warren forgot his keys last night. I don't know what's up with him. He keeps forgetting things." He opened a desk drawer and started to riffle the files. "It's hilarious, because he really hates to fuck up."

Will stood in the doorway, feeling the breeze of the air-conditioning freeze the sweat on his back, gluing his shirt and vest together. He leaned into the door frame, reaching his hand around to his back, finding his gun snugly tucked into the paddle holster.

Petty mumbled to himself as he searched the files. "Sorry, man, Warren has his own system for filing things."

"Take your time," Will said. He looked at the CDs lining the walls, the way the colored jewel cases were stacked together in their own particular order. It reminded him of his own CD collection at home, the way he identified certain albums not by their words, but by their colors, their recording logos, their artwork.

Will felt a prickling sensation work its way up his spine. "What about the customer files on the shelves? Does Warren have a system for those, too?"

"The CDs?" Petty laughed. "Shit, man, I can't even begin to tell you how he's got those filed. I'm not even allowed to *touch* them."

"But Warren knows where everything is, right?"

"He can find it with his eyes closed."

Will doubted that. Warren would need to see the colors, the patterns, before he could find the disc he needed. "Were you working here the day Emma was abducted?"

"I was off, man. Total headache."

"Is Warren left-handed?"

Petty held up his hand in response. Will couldn't tell which one it was; discerning between left and right was something his brain could not easily manage.

"Here we go," Petty said, pulling out a file. "Ignore the typos. Warren's such a freaktard. He's, like, incapable of spelling anything, but he won't admit it."

"What do you mean?" Will asked, though he already knew the answer. Warren color-coded the CDs, relying on visual cues to help him find the right file. The evidence had been staring Will in the face the first time he'd come into the manager's office to look at the security tape. Warren used the color-coding system for the same reason as Will: he could not read.

Petty said, "Warren's all right most of the time, but the dude won't admit he's wrong about anything. It's like working in the fucking White House around here."

"I meant the typos. You said he can't spell. What do you mean?"

Petty shrugged, handing him a sheet of paper. "Like that, man. I mean, it's like he's in kindergarten, right?"

Will glanced down at the sheet. His stomach roiled. He couldn't see anything but lines.

"Wait till you see this." Petty opened another drawer, and between the hanging files, Will saw several knives like the one Petty had been gripping.

"Where did you get those?"

Petty leaned down, stretching his hand to the back of the drawer. "Uh, the cafeteria down the street. Are you going to report us?"

"Warren steals them, too?"

"We both do, man. The Steakery only gives you those cheap-ass plastic knives." He sat up, holding a book in his lap. "I'll take 'em back, dude. I know it's stealing."

Will motioned toward the book. "Let me have that."

Petty handed it over. "Pathetic, man. He's always acting like he's perfect, right, that he's some kind of mental genius, and then he sneaks in with this? Classic Warren. What a loser."

Will stared at the front cover. He couldn't read the title, but he instantly recognized the multicolored triangles and squares. Evan Bernard had shown him a similar book this morning. It was the same kind that Emma Campano used.

"Open it up," Petty said. " 'See spot run.' 'See Jill wet her pants.' I mean, it's, like, a book for retarded one-year-olds. Cracks me up, man."

Will didn't open the book. "Where did he get this?"

Petty shrugged, leaning back in the chair. "I go through his stuff sometimes when I get bored. I found it shoved in the back of the drawer about a week, two weeks ago." He didn't seem ashamed of the habit, but he offered another piece of information to redeem himself. "Warren's got these weekly reports that he's supposed to send to corporate. I go through his computer and make it look less like a moron did it."

"He doesn't use spell-check?"

"Dude, spell-check is not Warren's friend."

There was no computer on his desk. "Where's his computer?"

"He used to keep it here, but lately he's been carrying it with him in his briefcase." He pumped his fist up and down suggestively. "Probably trolling porn on the wireless we pick up from the coffee shop."

"What kind of computer is it?"

"Mac. Pretty sweet."

"Does he have a car?"

"He hoofs it."

"He lives close by?"

"Not far. He takes MARTA." Petty finally got suspicious. "Why are you asking all these questions about Warren, man?"

Will thumbed through the book. The pages fell open to the center where someone had used a plastic laminated card to mark the page. Will looked at the card, saw Adam Humphrey's picture.

There was a buzzing sound. Petty turned around in the chair to squint up at the security cameras. He pressed a button on the desk, saying, "Speak of the devil."

Will watched the monitor as Warren Grier opened the glass door out in the parking deck.

"Stay here," he told Petty. "Lock the door and call 9-1-1. Tell them that an officer needs immediate assistance." Petty sat frozen in his chair, and Will told him, "I'm not fooling around, Lionel. Do it."

Will pulled the door closed behind him. The jackhammer had stopped, but the copiers were still running, the clack of papers humming in his ears. Will was at the counter by the time Warren made his way to the front. The man was wearing his blue Copy Right shirt and carrying a beat-up brown briefcase in his hand.

He was understandably alarmed to see Will standing behind the counter. Warren asked, "Where's Petty?"

"Bathroom," Will told him. Warren was on the other side of the counter, just a few feet away. Will could have reached out and grabbed him by the collar, yanked him over the counter without missing a beat. "I told him I'd catch the phones for him."

Warren glanced down at Petty's lunch, the knife. "Is everything okay?"

"I'm here to show you guys some photos." Will reached into his jacket pocket and pulled out the yearbook pages, hoping the fact that his heart was about to beat out of his chest was not as evident as it felt. He fanned out the photos so that Kayla was in front, half of Evan Bernard's face obscured behind her. "Do you mind taking a look at these for me?"

Slowly, Warren put his briefcase on the floor. He stared at the pictures a good while before he took them. "I've seen this girl on the news," he said, his tone of voice a few octaves higher than normal. "She's the one who was stabbed, right?"

"Beaten," Will corrected, leaning down on the counter so he could get closer to Warren. "Someone beat her to death with his fists."

There was a slight tremble to the young man's hand, a nervousness that Will shared. The photo of Bernard was still visible, and Warren moved his fingers to cover it with Kayla's image. "I thought she was stabbed."

"No," Will said. "The boy was stabbed — just once in the chest. His lung collapsed."

"The mother didn't kill him?"

"No," Will lied. "He died from the knife wound. We got the coroner's report this morning." He added, "It's sad, really. I think he just got in the way. I think whoever killed him was just trying to keep him away from Emma."

Warren kept staring at the photo of Kayla Alexander.

"Kayla wasn't raped," Will told him, trying to imagine Warren

Grier in a fury, straddling Kayla Alexander, plunging the knife into her chest over and over again. Adam Humphrey would have been next, a single stab wound to the chest. And then Emma...what had he done to Emma?

Will said, "We don't think the killer is that kind of person."

"You don't?"

"No," Will said. "We think whoever killed Kayla just got angry. Maybe she said something to him, goaded him into it. She wasn't a very nice person."

"I...uh..." He still stared at the photo. "I could guess that from looking at her."

"She could be very cruel."

He nodded.

"The other man," Will began, fanning out the pictures so that Evan Bernard was fully visible. "We've arrested him for raping Kayla."

Warren did not respond.

"His sperm was inside her. He must have had sex with her right before she went to see Emma Campano."

Warren kept his eyes on the photos.

"We just want her back, Warren. We just want to return Emma to her family."

He licked his lips, but said nothing.

"Her mother looks just like her. Have you seen her picture on the news?"

Warren nodded again.

"Abigail," Will provided. "In the pictures they're showing, she's beautiful, don't you think? Just like Emma."

His shoulders went up slowly in a shrug.

"She doesn't look like that now, though." Will felt the tension between them almost as if another person was standing there. "She can't sleep. She can't eat. She cries all the time. When she realized that Emma was missing, she had to be sedated. We had to call in a doctor to help her."

Warren spoke so quietly that Will had to strain to hear. "What about Kayla? Is her mom upset?"

"Yeah," Will said. "Not as much, though. She understood that her daughter was not a very nice person. I think she's relieved."

"What about the guy's parents?"

"They're from Oregon. They flew down last night to collect his body."

"Did they take it back?"

"Yes," Will lied. "They took him back home to bury him."

Warren surprised him. "I didn't have parents."

Will forced a smile, conscious that there was a twitch to his lip. "Everybody has parents."

"Mine left me," Warren said. "I don't have anybody."

"Everybody has somebody," Will said.

Without warning, Warren dropped to the floor. Will leaned over the counter, trying to stop him, but he wasn't fast enough. Warren was on his back, flat to the ground. He held a short-nosed revolver in his hands. The muzzle was a few inches from Will's face.

"Don't do this," Will said.

"Hands where I can see them," Warren ordered, wriggling to stand. "I've never used a gun before, but I don't think it matters when you're this close."

Slowly, Will straightened up, keeping his hands in the air. "Tell me what happened, Warren."

"You're never going to find her."

"Did you kill her?"

"I love her," Warren said, taking a step back, keeping the gun trained on Will's chest. "That's what you don't understand. I took her because I love her."

"Evan just wanted the money, didn't he? He pushed you to take Emma so he could cash in. You never wanted to do it. It was all his idea."

Warren did not answer. He took another step toward the hall that led to the parking garage.

"Emma wasn't his type, right? He likes girls like Kayla, the ones who fight back."

Warren kept inching toward the exit.

Will's words came out in a rush. "I grew up in care, too,

Warren. I know what it's like on visiting days. Sitting there, waiting for someone to pick you. It's not about having a place to live, it's about having someone there who looks at you and really sees you and wants you to belong to them. I know you felt like that when you saw Emma, that you wanted to—"

Warren put his finger to his lips, the way you would quiet a child. He took another step, then another, and he was gone.

Will vaulted the counter. As he reached the hallway, he saw Warren shouldering open the back door. He pursued the man, bursting through the exit, rounding into the parking lot in time to see Warren slam into a bright red Mini.

Will jogged toward the car as Faith got out. Warren was obviously dazed, but adrenaline kicked in as he realized Will was closing in. He stepped on the bumper and jumped clear of the car, making a break for the street.

"It's him!" Will screamed at Faith, bolting over the Mini. He ran out into the street, furiously searching for any sign of Warren. He spotted the man almost a block down the road and gave chase, his arms pumping, his legs screaming.

The afternoon heat was intense, nearly suffocating him as he ran after the younger man. Will gulped hot air and exhaust into his lungs. Sweat poured into his eyes. Will saw a red blur in his periphery and realized that Faith was in her car, driving against traffic. The Mini bumped furiously up and down as it careened over metal plates in the road.

Warren saw Faith, too. He veered off the main road, going down one of the side streets that led into Ansley Park. The younger man was fast, but Will's stride was twice his. He managed to close the gap between them as he took the turn down the side road. Even when Warren ran into the woods, Will was able to make up time. He had always been a marathoner, not a sprinter. Long distances were his passion, endurance the only thing he could offer to any competition.

Warren was obviously the opposite. As he maneuvered through the thick woods, he started to lag, and the space between the two men got shorter and shorter. The man kept looking over his shoulder, his mouth gaping open as he gasped for breath. Will was inches from him, close enough to reach out and grab the collar of his shirt. Warren knew this, could obviously feel the heat on the back of his neck. He did the only thing he could. He stopped short and Will was going so fast that he practically flipped over Warren's head as they both slammed into the ground.

Dirt and leaves kicked up as each man scrambled to stand. Will tried to roll over, but his foot was caught in something. He jerked his leg, furiously trying to free himself. Warren seized the advantage, straddling him, pointing the gun at Will's face and pulling the trigger.

Nothing happened.

He pulled the trigger again.

"Hold it!" Faith screamed. She had somehow gotten in front of them. Her body blocked out the sunlight, her hands casting a shadow across Will's face. Her gun was trained squarely between Warren's eyes. "Drop it, motherfucker, or I will blow your brains back to Peachtree."

Warren stared up at her. Will could not see the man's eyes, but he knew what Warren was looking at. Faith was tall and blond and pretty. She could be Emma or Kayla or even Abigail Campano. The sun was behind her. Maybe it gave Warren the impression that an angel was standing over him. Maybe you did what you were told when there was a gun in your face.

Warren dropped his weapon. It hit Will's chest, then fell onto the ground.

Will put his hand on the revolver as he rolled out from under the man. His leg came free from the vines with a gentle pull. He realized he had stopped breathing. He felt light-headed and slightly ill.

"You have the right to remain silent," Faith said, her handcuffs clicking around Warren's wrist. "You have the right to an attorney."

Will sat up, the dizziness taking over for a few seconds. He held the gun in his hands. Smith & Wesson classic model 36, 1⅞" with a blue case. The serial number was gone. Duct tape covered the grip to keep fingerprints from transferring. The weapon had been professionally prepped.

He guessed that Adam had bought a gun, after all.

Will opened the cylinder and turned it upside down. The revolver was designed to hold five rounds. Three bullets fell into the palm of his hand. Will stared at the shiny brass, smelling the scent of powder mixed with oil.

If Warren had pulled the trigger one more time, Will would be dead right now.

CHAPTER NINETEEN

FAITH WAS STRUCK by how normal she found
Warren Grier. He was average looking, the sort of
young man you wouldn't think twice about letting
into your house to fix your toilet or check for a gas leak.
Considering what had happened to Kayla Alexander and
Adam Humphrey, what had most likely been done to
Emma Campano, Faith had expected a monster, or at the very least
an arrogant sociopath like Evan Bernard.

Instead, she found Warren Grier almost pitiable. His body was
thin and wiry. He couldn't make eye contact with her. Sitting in the
chair across from her in the interrogation room, his shoulders
hunched, his hands clasped low between his knees, he reminded
her more of Jeremy that time he'd gotten caught stealing candy
from the store than a cold-blooded killer.

She cleared her throat and he glanced up at her, shy, as if they
were in high school and she was the cheerleader who was nice to
him when her friends were not looking. He seemed almost grateful
to be sitting across from her. Had she not seen him with her own
eyes less than an hour ago pointing a gun in Will Trent's face, Faith
would have laughed at the prospect of this introspective, awkward
man being capable of such a thing.

Faith had only drawn her gun twice in her career. It was not a

thing a police officer did lightly. You did not pull your weapon unless you were ready to use it, and there were a finite number of circumstances that justified that happening. Standing there in the
woods, looking down at Warren Grier, watching his finger pull
back on the trigger, she had been fully prepared to pull back her
own finger.

But it would have been too late. Faith had been following procedure. She could have safely told any review panel that she was
doing the job as she had been trained to do: you give a warning
first, then you shoot. Faith knew now that she would never again
give that warning. Warren had already pulled the trigger twice by
the time she got there. The only thing that had kept him from
pulling it a third time, sending the firing pin into the back of a bullet, the bullet through the back of Will's brain, was . . . what?

She felt a rush of heat just thinking about the close call. Faith
had to remind herself that the irrational side of Warren Grier was
the one that they needed to keep in mind at all times. Evan Bernard
was the cool and collected one. Warren was the reactionary, the
person who was capable of a frenzied murder. He had abducted
Emma Campano. He had stabbed Adam Humphrey. He had
beaten Kayla Alexander to death.

Faith realized that over the last twelve hours, she had allowed
herself to think that Emma Campano was probably dead. Now she
found herself coming to terms with the possibility that Emma was
still alive, and that the only way to find her was through the killer
sitting on the other side of the table.

She hoped to God that Will was up to the challenge.

Warren said, "The construction guys say that the water main
should be fixed soon. That'll be nice to have the street clear, finally."

Faith turned slightly in her chair, facing away from him. There
was a camera on a tripod at the head of the table, their every movement being recorded. She thought about Evan Bernard's little-girl
room and wondered if Warren Grier had sat in front of the computer next door, watching him. They hadn't found a hard drive in

the man's apartment. They hadn't found a laptop computer or any-thing remotely incriminating.

"They sure were busy this afternoon," he said. "It was very noisy."

She felt her pity seep away, her disgust take hold.

According to Lionel Petty, Warren spent a lot of time in his of-fice with the door closed. Had he watched Emma and Adam in the parking lot on the security monitor? Is that when he'd first spotted Emma? How did Kayla fit into all of this? Where did Evan Bernard come in?

Faith had been processing Warren through the system, watch-ing him get photographed and fingerprinted and searched. Will had told her about Warren's dingy apartment on Ashby Street down-town. It was a one-room affair with a toilet down the hall, the sort of place you moved into when you just got out of jail. Warren's landlady was shocked to hear that her quiet tenant of ten years had been arrested. He never went out except for work, she had told Will. He never had friends around.

So where was he keeping Emma Campano?

As if he could read her mind, Warren said, "You won't find her."

Faith did not respond, did not try to read any sense of hope in his words. Warren had tried several times to engage her in conver-sation. She had taken the bait the first few times, but quickly learned that he was playing her. He wanted to talk about the weather, the news story about the drought—anything to engage her in meaningless conversation. Faith had learned a long time ago that you never gave suspects what they wanted. It put the relation-ship on the wrong foot if they thought that they were the ones in control.

There was a knock at the door, then Will came into the room. He had several neon-colored file folders in his hand. He nodded at Faith as he checked the camera, making sure everything was work-ing properly.

Warren said, "I'm sorry I tried to kill you."

Will smiled at him. "I'm glad you didn't succeed."

It showed remarkable restraint, and Faith was again struck by how very little Will Trent acted like a cop. He straightened his vest, making sure his tie was tightly tucked in, as he sat down beside Faith. The man looked more like an accountant who was about to start an audit than a cop.

Will told Warren, "Your fingerprint matches the note that was slipped under Adam Humphrey's door last week."

Warren nodded his head once. He stayed hunched over the table, his hands between his knees. His chest was pressed into the metal top the way babies do when they're trying to stand.

Will asked, "Did you try to warn Adam away?"

Warren gave a single nod again.

"May I tell you what I think happened?"

He seemed to be waiting for just that.

"I think that you planned this out well ahead of time. Evan Bernard needed money to pursue his legal case against Georgia Tech. He lost his pension, his retirement benefits, everything," Will told Faith. "We found out that he sold his house last summer to pay his legal bills." He shook his head, indicating they had checked the house and found nothing.

Faith wondered what other information he had unearthed while she had been sitting on Warren. She glanced at the colored file folders, and Will gave her an uncharacteristic wink.

Warren asked, "Did you get adopted out?"

Faith didn't understand the question, but Will obviously did.

"No," he answered. "I left when I was eighteen."

Warren smiled, a kindred spirit. "Me, too."

"Did you meet Bernard when you got fostered out? Did he teach at your school?"

Warren's face was placid.

"I think that Evan Bernard introduced you to Kayla Alexander. He needed Kayla to open the front door for you, to make sure that Emma was at home. Maybe she was supposed to keep Adam calm while you took her away." Warren did not confirm anything. "Was Kayla the one who told Emma to start parking in the garage?"

Warren said, "Kayla told Emma to park there last year so her parents wouldn't find out they were skipping."

"Let's go back three days ago, the day of the crime. Did you use the path in the woods behind the Copy Right to walk to the Campanos?"

"Yes."

"Did you have the knife and the gloves with you?"

"Yes."

"So you went there intending to kill somebody."

He hesitated, then shrugged in answer.

Will thumbed through the files in his hand and opened the green one. "We found this in your desk at the copy center." He showed Faith the photograph before sliding it toward Warren. The picture showed Emma Campano walking with Adam Humphrey. The two teenagers had their arms around each other. Emma's head was tilted back as she laughed.

Will said, "You liked watching her."

Warren did not respond, but then Will hadn't really asked a question.

"Did you think that Adam wasn't good enough for her?"

He remained silent.

"You knew Emma was special. Who told you she had a reading problem like you?"

"I don't have a reading problem." His tone was defensive, a radical change from the conversational manner he had adopted before.

Will opened another folder, this one blue, and showed Faith an official-looking form. "This is an evaluation from a clinical psychologist who interviewed Warren when he was released from the state's care." Will put the sheet of paper down on the table, turning it toward Warren. Faith saw that there were colored dots on the page. Will put his finger on the blue one. " 'Antisocial,' " he read, moving down to the red dot. " 'Sociopathic tendencies.' " He moved his finger down to the next dot, then the next, calling out, " 'Anger control issues.' 'Poor aptitude.' 'Poor reading skills.' Do you see this, Warren? Do you see what they said about you?" He paused, though obviously he didn't expect an answer. Will tucked the form back into the folder, and the tone of the interview suddenly changed when he said, "Well, I guess it doesn't matter if you can see it, because it clearly says that you can't read it."

Pain flashed in the other man's eyes as if he had been betrayed.

Will kept chipping away, his tone soft, as if he could be both the good and the bad cop rolled into one. "Is that why you dropped out of school when you were sixteen?"

Warren shook his head.

"I guess school wasn't that fun since they stuck you with the stupid kids." For Faith's benefit, Will explained, "Warren was put into special education classes when he was fifteen, even though his IQ tested within the normal range."

Warren looked down at the table, his eyes still glistening.

Will said, "It's kind of sad when the short bus pulls up in front of the orphanage."

Warren cleared his throat, struggling to speak. "You're never going to find her."

"And you're never going to see her again."

"I have her up here," he insisted, pressing his finger to his temple. "I have her with me all the time."

"I know she's alive," Will said, sounding so certain of himself that Faith almost believed him. "You wouldn't kill her, Warren. She's special to you."

"She loves me."

"She's terrified of you."

He shook his head. "She understands why I had to do it. I had to save her."

"What does she understand?"

"That I'm protecting her."

"Protecting her from Bernard?"

He shook his head, biting his lip, refusing to give up the teacher.

Will opened a red file folder and took out yet another sheet of paper, which he slid Warren's way. " 'It is my opinion that Warren

Grier has an undiagnosed reading and written language disability. This, combined with his average IQ and antisocial behavior—' "

Warren whispered, "She's going to die, and it's all going to be on you."

"I'm not the one who took her from her family. I'm not the one who killed her best friend."

"Kayla wasn't her friend," Warren said. "She hated her. She couldn't stand her."

"Why?"

"Kayla made fun of her all the time," Warren said. "She said she was stupid because she had to have special help after school."

"Was Kayla mean to you, too?"

He shrugged, but the answer to that question was lying dead down in the morgue right now.

"Tell me what happened that day, Warren. Did Kayla let you into the house?"

"She was just supposed to let me into the house and shut up, but she wouldn't stop. She was pissed about Adam, that he was upstairs having sex with Emma. She kept going on and on about how stupid Emma is, and how she doesn't deserve to have a boyfriend. She said Emma is stupid like me."

"Did Kayla start yelling?"

"When I hit her." Warren amended, "Not hard, though. Only to get her to shut up."

"Then what happened?"

"She ran up the stairs. She kept screaming. I told her to stop, but she wouldn't. She was supposed to help with Adam. I was supposed to hold the knife to her neck so he wouldn't try anything, but she just went crazy. I had to hit her."

"Did you stab Kayla?"

"I don't know. I don't remember. I just felt someone grab my hand, and it was him, it was Adam. I didn't mean to hurt him. I just stood up, and the knife went into his chest. I didn't want to hurt him. I tried to help him. I tried to warn him to go away."

"Where was Emma when all of this was happening?"

"I heard her crying. She was in the closet in one of the rooms. She had . . ." His voice caught. "The room was so nice, you know? It had a big TV, and a fireplace, and all these clothes and shoes and everything. She had everything."

"Did you hit her?"

"I wouldn't hurt her."

"But she was unconscious when you carried her down the stairs."

"We went outside. I don't know what was wrong with her. I carried her. I put her in the trunk, then I went to the parking garage like I was supposed to."

"Like Bernard told you to?"

He looked back at the table again, and Faith wondered what kind of hold Evan Bernard had over the young man. For all appearances, Bernard preferred girls. Was there another side to his depravity that they had yet to find out about?

Will asked, "Where did you take her, Warren? Where did you take Emma?"

"Somewhere safe," he said. "Somewhere we could be together."

"You don't love her, Warren. You don't kidnap somebody if you love them. *They* come to *you*. *They* choose *you*. Not the other way around."

"It wasn't like that. She said she loved me."

"After you took her?"

"Yeah." He had a grin on his face, as if the news still surprised and astounded him. "She really fell in love with me."

"You really think that?" Will asked. "You really think you belong in her world?"

"She loves me. She told me."

Will leaned closer. "Guys like you and me, we don't know what it means to be in a family. We don't see how deep that bond is, we never feel how much parents love their children. You broke that bond, Warren. You took Emma away from her parents just like you were taken away from yours."

Warren still shook his head, but with sadness more than certainty.

"What was that like for you, being in her room, seeing the good kind of life she had when you had nothing?" His voice was low, confidential. "It all felt wrong, didn't it? I was there, man. I felt it, too. We don't belong around normal people like that. They can't take our nightmares. They don't understand why we hate Christmas and birthdays and summer vacations because every holiday reminds us of all the time we spent alone."

"No." Warren shook his head, vehement. "I'm not alone now. I have her."

"What do you picture for yourself, Warren? Some kind of domestic scene where you come home from work and Emma's cooking you dinner? She'll kiss you on the forehead and you'll drink some wine and talk about your day. Maybe after, she'll wash the plates and you'll dry?"

Warren shrugged, but Faith could tell that was exactly the sort of life the man envisioned.

"I saw your booking photos when they arrested you downstairs. I know what cigarette burns look like."

He whispered a quiet, "Fuck you."

"Did you show your burns to Emma? Did she get sick the same way you do every time you see them?"

"It's not like that."

"She had to feel the scars, Warren. I know you took your clothes off. I know you wanted to feel her skin against yours."

"No."

"I don't know which is worse, the pain or the smell. First, it's like little needles digging into you—a million at a time just burning and stinging. And then the smell hits you. It's like barbecue, isn't it? You smell it in the summer all over the city, that raw flesh burning in the flames."

"I told you, we love each other."

Will's tone was almost playful, as if he was giving the windup for a joke. "You ever feel your skin in the shower sometimes, Warren? You're soaping up and your hand goes to your ribs and you feel the little holes that were burned into your flesh?"

"That doesn't happen."

"They're like little suction cups when they're wet, right? You put your finger in them and you feel yourself get trapped all over again."

He shook his head.

"Did you beg for it to be over, screaming like a pussy because it hurt so bad? You told them you'd do anything, right? Anything to make the pain stop."

"Nobody hurt me like that."

Will's tone got harder, his words came faster. "You feel those scars and it makes you so angry. You want to take it out on some-one—maybe Emma with her perfect life and her rich daddy and her beautiful mother who has to have a doctor come knock her out because she can't bear the thought of being without her precious little girl."

"Stop it."

Will slammed his hand against the table. They all jumped. "She doesn't belong to you, Warren! Tell me where she is!"

Warren's jaw clenched as he glared at the table in front of him.

Spit flew from Will's mouth as he moved even closer. "I know you. I know how your mind works. You didn't take Emma because you love her, you took her because you wanted to make her scream."

Slowly, Warren looked up, facing Will. His anger was barely controlled, his lips trembling like a rabid dog's. "Yeah," he said, his voice a hoarse whisper. "She screamed." His face was as controlled as his tone. "She screamed until I shut her up."

Will sat back in his chair. There was a clock on the wall. Faith listened to it slowly ticking away the time. She looked at the cinder-block wall in front of her rather than give Warren the satisfaction of her curiosity or Will the intensity of her concern.

She had worked with cops who could stand in the pouring rain and swear on a stack of Bibles that the sun was shining. Many times, she had sat in this very interrogation room and listened to Leo Donnelly, a man with no children and four divorces, rhap-sodize about his love of God and his precious twin baby girls in or-der to lure a suspect into a confession. Faith herself had at times fabricated an invisible husband, a doting grandmother, an absent father, in order to get suspects to talk. All cops knew how to spin a yarn.

Only, this time, she was certain that Will Trent was not lying.

Will put his hand on the stack of folders. "We found your adoption records."

Warren shook his head. "Those are sealed."

"They are unless you commit a felony," Will said, and Faith studied him, knowing that this was a lie, trying to figure out what cues he gave when he was not telling the truth. His face was just as impassive as before, and she ended up turning her attention back to Warren so that she did not drive herself mad.

Will said, "Your mother is still alive, Warren."

"You're lying."

"She's been looking for you."

For the first time since Will had entered the room, Warren glanced at Faith, as if he could engage her maternal instinct. "That's not fair."

Will said, "All this time, she's been looking for you."

He opened the last folder. There was a sheet of paper inside. He turned the page around and slid it toward Warren. From where Faith sat, she could see that he had copied a memo about appropriate attire for on-duty, undercover officers. The city's seal at the top had been duplicated so many times that the rising phoenix looked like a blob.

Will asked, "Don't you want to see your mother, Warren?"

His eyes filled with tears.

"There she is," Will said, tapping the paper. "She lives less than ten miles from where you work."

Warren started rocking back and forth, his tears wetting the page.

"What kind of son is she going to find in you?"

"A good one," the young man insisted.

"You think what you've done is good? You think she's going to want to be around the man who kept a young girl from her family?" Will pressed a little harder. "You're doing the same thing to

Emma's parents that was done to your mom. You think she's going to be able to love you after finding out that you knew how to get Emma back to her family, but you wouldn't do it?"

"She's safe," he said. "I just wanted to keep her safe."

"Tell me where she is. Her mother misses her so much."

He shook his head. "No," he answered. "You're never going to find her. She's going to be with me forever. There's nothing that can come between us now."

"Stop the bullshit, Warren. You didn't want Emma. You wanted her *life*."

Warren looked at the file folders in front of Will as if he expected something even worse to be pulled out, some information even more damaging to be thrown into his face.

Will tried again. "Tell us where she is, and I'll tell you your mother's address."

Warren's eyes did not stray from the files, but he started whispering something so quietly that Faith could not make out what he was saying.

"I'll go get her myself. I'll drive her over to see you."

Warren kept whispering, his mouth moving in an unintelligible mantra.

Will said, "Speak up, Warren. Just tell us where she is so we can give her back to her parents who love her."

Faith finally understood his words. "Blue, red, purple, green. Blue, red, purple, green."

"Warren—"

His voice got louder. "Blue, red, purple, green." He stood up, screaming, "Blue, red, purple, green!" He started waving his hands, his tone rising to the top of his voice. "Blue! Red! Purple! Green!" He ran toward the door, trying the knob. Faith was closest to him, so she tried to pull him away. Warren's elbow caught her in the mouth and she fell back against the table.

"Blue! Red! Purple! Green!" he screamed, running full on into the concrete wall. Will went after him, wrapping his arms around the man. Warren kicked, screaming, "No! Let me go! Let me go!"

"Warren!" Will let go of him, keeping his hands out wide in case he needed to grab him again.

Warren stood in the middle of the room. Blood dripped down his face where he had slammed his head into the wall. He lunged toward Will, swinging his fists wildly.

The door flew open and two cops rushed in to help. Warren tried to run out the door, but they wrestled him to the floor, where he wriggled frantically, jerking his hands away from them as they tried to cuff him, screaming all the while. His foot kicked up, catching one of the officers in the face.

The Taser came out. Thirty thousand volts screamed through his body. Almost immediately, Warren went limp on the floor.

Will sat back on his heels, his breath coming in pants. He leaned over Warren, hand on his chest. "Please," he begged. "Just tell me. Tell me where she is."

Warren's lips moved. Will leaned down to listen to him. Something passed between the two men. Will nodded once, very much like the curt affirmations Warren had given them earlier. He sat up slowly, hands in his lap, telling the cops, "Take him away."

The officers scooped up Warren like a bag of potatoes, dragging him toward the door. They would take him to his cell and let him sleep off the shock.

Faith looked at Will, trying to understand. "What did he say to you?"

He pointed to his file folders on the table, leaning over as if he was still too breathless to speak. Faith looked at the files. They were in the wrong order, but she could see it now: blue, red, purple, green.

Warren had been yelling out the colors of the folders.

✦

THE HOMICIDE SQUAD room had not improved during Faith's three-day absence. Robertson's jockstrap still dangled from the top drawer of his desk. A blow-up doll marked as "evidence" during the last birthday party sat on top of the filing cabinet, her mouth still opened in a suggestive O even as the air slowly drained out of her once curvaceous body. Leo Donnelly's desk was cleared but for a famous old photograph of Farrah Fawcett that he had obviously cut out of a magazine. Over the years, the margins of the photo had been embellished with graffiti and artwork that was more suitable for a middle school boys' bathroom.

Adding to the overall masculine effect, the shift was changing, an event Faith always likened to a football locker room during halftime. The noise was deafening, the smells alarming. Someone had turned on the television that hung from the ceiling. Someone else was trying to find a station on the ancient radio. A burrito heated in the microwave, the odor of burned cheese wafting through the air. Baritone bellows filled the room as detectives tromped in and out, turning over cases, giving each other the business about whose dick was bigger, who would solve a case first, who was turning over a dog of an investigation that would never be solved. In short, the whole room was filling with testosterone the way a cloth diaper filled with shit.

Faith glanced at the television set as she recognized Amanda's voice saying, "... *proud to announce that an arrest has been made in the Campano kidnapping.*"

Someone yelled, "Thanks to APD, you cunt."

There were more words tossed Amanda's way—bitch, snatch, whatever base and degrading terms other cops could conjure to denigrate a woman who would have them all pissing in their pants if she got them alone in a room for more than five minutes.

The handful of detectives closest to Faith's desk gave her curious glances—not because she was working the case, but because of the language. Faith shrugged, looking back at the television set, watching Amanda expertly handle the reporters. She could still feel their eyes on her, though.

This sort of testing took place almost on a daily basis. If Faith told them to shut up, she was a ballbuster who couldn't take a joke. If she ignored it, they took her silence for tacit approval. It didn't stop there. If she spurned their sexual advances, she was a lesbian. If she dated any of them, she would be labeled a whore. Faith couldn't win either way, and striking back in similar terms took up too much of her time. The pouting, the passive-aggressive whining—Faith had already raised one child, and she wasn't ready to take on twenty more.

And yet, she had always loved working here, loved feeling like she was part of a brotherhood. This was why Will Trent did not act or talk like a cop. He didn't sit in a squad room. He didn't bullshit over beers with Charlie Reed and Hamish Patel. He was certainly part of a team, but working with him was like working in a bubble. There was never the hum of people in the background, the jostling of egos and assignments. His was a more focused way of doing the job, but it was so different from what Faith was used to that, now that she was back among her fellow detectives, she felt like she no longer belonged. She had to admit that for all Will's faults, at least he listened to what she had to say. It was nice to have a discussion with a colleague who didn't ask "What're you, on the rag?" every time she disagreed with him.

Faith looked back at the television. Amanda was nodding as a reporter asked about Westfield Academy, the arrest of Evan Bernard. She looked absolutely radiant, and Faith had to admit she was in her element on camera. The reporters were eating out of the palm of her hand. "Mr. Bernard is certainly a person of interest."

"You interested in this?" one of the detectives yelled. Faith did not have to glance over to know the man was probably cupping his genitals.

Amanda answered another question. "The suspect is a twenty-eight-year-old man with a storied past."

Off camera, a reporter asked, "Why aren't you releasing his name?"

"The arraignment in the morning will make it part of the public record," she said, sidestepping the obvious, which was that they were keeping Warren's name out of the press as long as they could in order to keep some helpful do-gooder from offering him legal advice. The fact that Lionel Petty had already submitted an I-Report to CNN.com of him and Warren Grier standing beside one of the copy machines at work would soon work against them.

Another reporter was obviously thinking the same thing as Faith. "What about the missing girl? Any leads on her whereabouts?"

"We believe it's only a matter of time before Emma Campano is found."

Faith noted that the woman did not say whether the girl would be found dead or alive. She felt a sudden pang of envy for Amanda and her position. Like Faith's mother, Amanda had worked her way to the top. If Faith had to put up with a little misogyny now and then, she could not imagine what it was like for her mother's generation.

Amanda had started in the secretarial pool, just like Evelyn Mitchell, back when the women officers had to wear below-the-knee wool skirts as they fetched coffee and typed up requisitions. Amanda had clawed her way to the top, only to have a bunch of idiots with primordial ooze dripping out of their noses heckle her as she broke one of the biggest cases the city had seen since Wayne Williams was spotted tossing a body into the Chattahoochee.

And where was Faith after all those years of progress and women's lib? She was still in the equivalent of the secretarial pool, she supposed. To be fair, she had volunteered for the task of cataloguing all the evidence Will had taken from Warren Grier's tiny abode. That was before she'd seen the piles of boxes they had taken from the boardinghouse and stacked around her desk. There were at least six of them, all filled to the top with papers. Warren was a pack rat, the kind of man who couldn't throw out a receipt or a movie ticket. He still had pay stubs from the copy center that went back almost ten years.

Faith touched her jaw, bruised and tender from where Warren's elbow had caught her. She had found an ancient Lean Cuisine in the back of the freezer in the break room. The bag was hard as a rock, but it felt good on her mouth. She hated getting hit. Not that anyone particularly enjoyed it, but Faith had learned a long time ago that puking was her natural response to pain. Holding a bag of frozen spaghetti and meatballs was not helping matters. A small price to pay considering what Emma Campano had probably gone through.

Will was escorting Warren Grier to the holding cells. There was only one question he had yet to get answered: Where was Emma? Even if the girl was still alive, time was running out. Faith thought about the conditions in which she might be kept: locked up in a room somewhere or, worse, shoved in the trunk of a car. Today, the temperature had hit one hundred before noon. The heat was unrelenting, even at night. Did Emma have water? Did she have food? How long before her supplies ran out? Death by dehydration took a week to ten days, but that was without a head wound and the broiling heat. Were they going to spend the next two weeks counting off the hours until Emma Campano could no longer draw breath?

"Hey, Mitchell. How's it working with that rat?" Robertson asked. He was sitting at his desk, leaning so far back in his chair that it looked like it might break.

"Fine," she told him, wondering why no one was giving Will credit for letting the Atlanta police duckwalk Evan Bernard out of Westfield Academy in front of the rolling cameras.

Robertson wagged his finger at her. "Be careful around that fucker. Never trust a Statey."

"Gotcha. Thanks."

"Fucking GBI. Taking our case, making it look like they did all the heavy lifting." There were noises of agreement from around the room.

What selective memory they all seemed to have. Faith would've probably been joining in if she hadn't been there that first day, watching Will connect the dots that had been in front of them all along.

Robertson seemed to be waiting for her to say something else, maybe take a jibe at Will or make a nasty comment about the GBI, but Faith was at a loss. A week ago, the words would have rushed out like beer from a tap. Now, the well had run dry.

Faith turned back to the work in front of her, trying to block out the noises of the squad room. She didn't have the strength at the moment to start going through the boxes from Warren's apartment, so she concentrated on her computer screen. Will had used a digital camera to take pictures of Warren Grier's living quarters, and she scrolled through the series of shots, which showed basically the same small room from six different angles.

Every mundane detail of Warren's existence had been captured, from his toiletries to his sock drawer. There were boxes and boxes of papers under his bed, overflowing with school report cards and official-looking forms from his time in the foster care system. There was a close-up of a manual for a Mac laptop computer, a phone number scribbled on the front. Faith tilted her head, wondering why Will had turned the camera upside down.

She picked up her cell phone and dialed the number, sticking her finger in her other ear to block out the noise. The phone rang once, twice, then a local theater picked up and started giving movie times for the next shows. No news flash there. The six billion ticket stubs sitting in a box at Faith's feet revealed his passion for the silver screen.

Faith went back to the pictures, trying to divine a clue that might lead to the missing girl. All she saw was the sad one-room apartment where Warren had lived all of his adult life. There were no photographs of family, no calendars with dates marked for dinners with friends. From all appearances, he had no friends, no one he could turn to.

That was no kind of excuse, though. By his own admission, Will had grown up under similar circumstances. He had lived in state care until he was eighteen. He'd become a cop—and a damn good one. His social skills left something to be desired, but there was something underneath all his awkwardness that was oddly endearing.

Or maybe it was something her mother had told her ages ago: the easiest way for a man to get into your heart was if you imagined what he was like as a child.

Faith clicked through the photos again, trying to see if anything stood out. She ran through the usual suspects: a garage, a storage facility, an old family cabin in the woods. None of these seemed to be likely hiding places that Warren could use. He had no car, no extra belongings to store, no family to speak of.

Something had to break. There had to be a path back to Emma Campano that was not yet illuminated. Evan Bernard was going to make bail in less than twelve hours. He would be back on the street, free to do what he wanted until his trial date for having sex with Kayla Alexander. Unless they found something to link him to the crimes at the Campano house, he was looking at nothing more than a slap on the wrist, probably three years in jail, then he would get his life back.

And then what would he do? There were too many other ways for a man with an interest in girls to find victims. Church. SAT tutoring. Youth groups. Evan Bernard would probably move out of state. Maybe he would fail to register as a sex offender in his new town. He might live near a swimming pool or a high school or even a day care center. Warren Grier was not going to flip. Whatever hold Bernard had on the young man was unbreakable. The only thing Faith and Will had done was make Bernard's life from here on out more difficult. They had found absolutely nothing to keep him locked up for the rest of his miserable existence, and nothing that brought them closer to finding Emma Campano.

And then there was the fact that Faith knew how these guys tended to work. Bernard had raped the girl in Savannah, but that couldn't have been his first time, and Kayla would not be his last. Was there another girl out there that he was grooming for his sick fantasies? Was there another teenager who was going to have her life turned upside down by the sick bastard?

Faith put down the frozen bag, working her jaw to make sure no permanent damage had been done. She put her hand to her face and, unbidden, the memory of Victor stroking her cheek came back to her. He had called three times on her cell phone, each message progressively more apologetic. In the end, he had resorted to blatant flattery, which, being honest, had done a good deal to help crack her resolve. Faith wondered if there was ever going to be a time when she understood any of the men in her life.

Will Trent was certainly an enigma. The way he had spoken to Warren in the interrogation room had been so intimate that Faith found herself unable to look him in the eye. Had all of that really happened to Will? Was he the damaged product of the state adoption program, just like Warren Grier?

What Will had said about the cigarette burns had felt so real. Under the jacket and the vest and the dress shirt, was he hiding similar scars? Faith had been in central booking when they took the photographs of Warren's damaged torso. As a police officer, she had seen many cigarette burns on many victims as well as suspects. They were unsurprising at this point, the kind of thing you expected alongside the tattoos and the track marks. People did not generally choose a life of crime for the adventure. They were junkies and criminals for a reason, and the reason usually could be found in their early home life.

Was Will just a really good liar? When he talked about what it felt like to touch the burn marks, was he speaking from experience, or making a calculated guess? Three days had passed since she'd first met the man and she knew as much about him now as she had on that very first day. And she still did not understand how he worked the job. Warren had tried to kill him, but instead of sticking the younger man in with pedophiles and rapists, Will had walked him down to the cells to make sure he got one to himself. And then there was Evan Bernard. Any cop worth his salt knew that the best way to sweat out someone like that arrogant prick was to stick him in with the nastiest motherfuckers on the cell block, yet Will had basically given him a pass, sticking him in with the shemales.

Faith figured it was too late in the day to guess his strategy — and besides, it wasn't as if he ever consulted her on anything. He kept all the details of the case locked up in his head and maybe, if Faith was lucky, he let some of it out when the mood struck him. He worked like no other cop she had ever met. There wasn't even a murder board in his office — a chronological listing of what happened when, who did what, the suspects and the victims pictured side by side so that clues could be tracked, leads could be followed.

There was no way he could keep it all in his head. Maybe he kept it all on his precious tape recorder. Either way, if something happened to Will, there would be no logical point for the next lead investigator to pick up on. It was such a blatant disregard for procedure that Faith was shocked Amanda allowed it to happen.

Analyzing Amanda and Will's relationship was just wasting time. Faith went back to the computer, her hand resting on the mouse. The screen flickered up, showing a photograph of Warren Grier's bookshelf. Faith hadn't put it together before, but she found it pretty odd that a man who could not read would have books in his home.

She squinted her eyes at the titles, then thought better of it, giving her eyes a break and clicking the button to zoom in on the photo. There were several graphic novels, which made sense, and what looked like manuals for various pieces of office equipment. The spines were all sectioned together by color rather than title. The books on the bottom shelf were taller, the words blurred from being out of the camera lens's center frame. Faith guessed from their size that they were art books—the expensive type that you put on your coffee table for show.

Faith zoomed in closer on the bottom shelf, but still could not make out any of the titles. Something was familiar about the thick gray spines of three of the books. She put her chin in her hand, wincing at the pain from her bruised jaw. Why did the spines look so familiar?

She opened one of the boxes from Warren's apartment, looking to see if any of the books had been packed. They all seemed to contain papers and receipts from over the last ten years. Faith skimmed through the stacks, wondering why in the hell Will had taken all of this crap from the scene. Was it really necessary for them to know that Warren had paid a hundred ten dollars to Vision Quest for an eye exam six years ago?

More important, why would Will waste Faith's time asking her to go through stuff that was basically trash? She felt her irritation building as she skimmed page after page of useless documentation. Faith could understand why Warren would keep all of this—he would have no way of knowing whether or not it would be important one day, but why would Will want it catalogued into evidence? He didn't strike her as a needle-in-a-haystack kind of person, and with Bernard and Warren behind bars, there were certainly better uses to make of her time.

Slowly, Faith sat up in her chair, holding the dated bill in her hands but not really looking at it. Her mind flashed on different scenes from the last few days: Will reaching for the directory at the dorm even though the sign clearly said it was broken. The way she had found him at the school yesterday morning, his head bent over the newspaper as he touched his finger to each word on the page. Even at Evan Bernard's house today, he had thumbed through every page of the yearbooks rather than simply turning to the index and looking up the man's name, as Faith had done when she'd found the photograph of Mary Clark.

Two days ago, after Evan Bernard's insightful diagnosis that the abductor was functionally illiterate, Faith had had but one question: How can someone get through school without learning how to read and write?

"It happens," Will had told her. He had sounded so certain. Was that because it had happened to him?

Faith shook her head, though she was only arguing with herself. It didn't make sense. You had to have an advanced degree to get into the GBI. They didn't let just anybody in. Barring that, every government agency functioned on mounds and mounds of paperwork. There were reports to fill out, requisitions to be filed, casebooks to be submitted. Had Faith ever seen Will fill out anything? She thought about his computer setup, the fact that he had a microphone. Why would he need a microphone for his computer? Did he dictate his reports?

Faith rubbed her fingers into her eyes, wondering if lack of sleep was making her see things that weren't there. This simply was not possible. She had worked with the man almost every hour of the day since this whole thing started. Faith was not so stupid that she missed something that glaringly obvious. For his part, Will was too smart to be bad at anything so basic.

She looked back at her computer screen, concentrating on the books Warren had stacked along the bottom shelf. Questions about Will still pulled at her thoughts. Could he read the titles? Could he even read the threatening notes that had been slid under Adam Humphrey's door? What else had he missed?

Faith blinked, finally realizing why the three books on the bottom shelf looked so familiar. Here she had been questioning Will's abilities when an important piece of evidence practically glowed right in front of her.

She pulled out her spiral-bound notebook, looking for the phone number she had scribbled down at the school this morning. Tim Clark answered the phone on the third ring.

"Is Mary there?"

Again, he seemed reluctant to let his wife speak to the police. "She's taking a nap."

She was probably exactly where Faith had left her, staring into the backyard, wondering how she was going to cope with her memories. "I need to speak to her. It's very important."

He sighed, letting her know he wasn't happy. Minutes later, Mary came onto the line. Faith felt bad for thinking her husband was lying. The woman sounded as if she'd just been woken from a very deep sleep.

"I'm sorry for disturbing you."

"Doesn't matter," the woman said, her words slurring. Faith didn't feel so bad when she realized Mary Clark had obviously been drinking.

"I know you don't remember the name of the girl Evan was accused of raping back at Crim," Faith began. "But remember you said he had an alibi?"

"What?"

"Back at Crim," Faith repeated, wanting to reach through the phone and shake her. "Remember you said that Evan left the school because of a rape allegation?"

"They couldn't prove anything." Mary gave a harsh laugh. "He always gets away with it."

"Right," Faith coaxed, staring at her computer screen, the

familiar gray spines of the Alonzo Crim High School yearbooks on Warren Grier's bookshelf. "But that time, you said he got away with it because there was a student who served as an alibi."

"Yeah," Mary conceded. "Warren Grier." She almost spit out the words. "He said they were together after school for some tutoring or something."

Faith had to be sure. "Mary, are you telling me that Warren Grier gave Evan Bernard an alibi for a crime thirteen years ago?"

"Yeah," she repeated. "Pathetic, right? That little retard was even farther up Evan's ass than I was."

CHAPTER TWENTY

WILL REACHED FOR a paper cup but found the dispenser empty. He peered into the long cylinder mounted to the water cooler, making sure there wasn't a cup stuck in the tube.

"I got more in the back," Billy Peterson offered. He was an older cop who had been in charge of the cells for as long as anyone could remember.

"Thanks." Will stood with his hands in his pockets, afraid the tremble would come back and give him away. He felt a familiar coldness building inside of him, the same coldness he had developed when he was a child. Watch what's happening, but keep yourself removed from the fear, the pain. Don't let them know they've gotten to you, because all that will do is inspire them to get more creative.

Will never talked about the things that had happened to him—not even with Angie. She had seen some of it go down, but Will had managed to keep most of his dark secrets stored tightly in his mind. Until now. The things he had told Warren Grier, the awful secrets he had shared with him, were thoughts that had been building up inside Will for a long time. Instead of feeling catharsis, he felt exposed, vulnerable. He felt like a fraud. And a heel. There was no telling what was going through Warren's mind right now as he sat alone in his tiny cell. He was probably wishing he had pulled that trigger a third time.

For just a split second, Will found himself not blaming the man. He couldn't block out the Warren from the interrogation room, the sadness in his posture, the guarded way he looked up at Will as if he expected to be kicked in the face at any moment. Will had to remind himself of what Warren had done, the people whose lives he had ruined—and still might be ruining even as he was in custody.

The cell Will had put Warren in was not much larger than the room that the killer called home—a hovel compared to Emma Campano's palatial bedroom with its professionally designed throw pillows and giant television. Will had been struck by the sense of loneliness he'd felt as he went through the younger man's meager belongings. The neatly stacked CDs and DVDs, the carefully arranged sock drawer and color-coded hanging clothes, all reminded Will of a life he could have just as easily lived himself. The heady sense of freedom he'd felt at eighteen, out in the world on his own for the first time, had quickly been replaced by panic. The state did not exactly teach you to fend for yourself. You learned from a very young age to accept whatever they gave you and not ask for more. It was through sheer luck that Will had ended up working for the state. With his problems, he did not know what other job he was qualified to do.

Warren must have been in a similar position. According to his personnel record at the Copy Right, Warren Grier had worked there since dropping out of high school. Over the last twelve years, he had been promoted to the position of manager. Still, he only made around sixteen thousand dollars a year. He could've afforded a nicer place than the one-room dive on Ashby Street, but living below his means must have given Warren some sense of safety. Besides, it wasn't as if he could fill out an application to get a nicer apartment. If he lost the Copy Right position, how would he go about looking for a new job? How could he fill out an employment application? How could he bear the humiliation of telling a stranger that he could barely read?

Without his job, Warren couldn't pay his rent, couldn't buy food, clothes. There was no family to fall back on, and as far as the state was concerned, their responsibility had ended when Warren had turned eighteen. He was completely and totally on his own.

The Copy Right had been the only thing standing between Warren Grier and homelessness. Will felt his own stomach clench in a sense of shared fear. If not for having Angie Polaski in his life, how close to Warren Grier's meager existence would Will be?

"Here you go," Billy said, handing Will a cup.

"Thanks," Will managed, heading toward the water cooler. Many years ago, Amanda had kindly volunteered Will for a Taser demonstration. Memories of the pain had receded quickly, but Will could still recall that for hours afterward, he'd suffered from a seemingly unquenchable thirst.

Will filled the cup and stood at the gate to the cells, waiting to be buzzed back through. Inside the lockup, he kept his eyes straight forward, aware of the stares he was getting through the narrow panes of steel-enforced glass in the cell doors. Evan Bernard was on this wing, at the opposite end of Warren's cell. Billy had put him in with the transgendered women, the ones who still had their male equipment. News had already leaked out that Evan Bernard liked raping young girls. The tranny cell was the only place they could think of where Bernard would not get a big dose of his own medicine.

Will opened the narrow slot in Warren's cell door. He put the cup on the flat metal. The cup was not taken.

"Warren?" Will looked through the glass, seeing the tip of Warren's white, jail-issued slipper. The man was obviously sitting with his back to the door. Will crouched down, putting his mouth close to the metal slot. The opening was little more than twelve inches wide by three inches high, just enough to slide a meal tray through.

Will said, "I know you're feeling alone right now, but think about Emma. She's probably feeling alone, too." He paused. "She's probably wondering where you are."

There was no response.

"Think about how lonely she is without you," Will tried. "No one is there to talk to her or let her know that you're okay." His thigh started to cramp, so he knelt on one knee. "Warren, you don't have to tell me where she is. Just tell me that she's okay. That's all I want to know right now."

Still there was no response. Will tried not to think about Emma Campano, how terrified she would be as time slowly passed and no one came for her. How merciful it would have been if Warren had just killed her that first day, sparing her the agony of uncertainty.

"Warren—"

Will felt something wet on his knee. He looked down just as the slight odor of ammonia wafted into his nostrils.

"Warren?" Will looked through the slot again; the white slipper was tilted to the side, unmoving. He saw the bed was stripped. "No," Will whispered. He jammed his arm through the open slot, feeling for Warren. His hand found the man's sweaty hair, felt his cold, clammy skin. "Billy!" Will screamed. "Open the door!"

The guard took his time coming to the gate. "What is it?"

Will's fingers grazed Warren's eyes, his open mouth. "Call an ambulance!"

"Shit," Billy cursed, flinging open the gate. He slammed his fist into a red button on the wall as he jogged toward the cell. The master key was on his belt. He slid it into the lock and jerked open the door to Warren's cell. The hinge squeaked from the weight of the door. One end of the bedsheet was looped around the knob, the other end wrapped tightly around Warren Grier's neck.

Will dropped to the floor, starting CPR. Billy got on his radio, calling out codes, ordering an ambulance. By the time more help arrived, Will was sweating, his hands cramping from pressing into Warren's chest. "Don't do this," he begged. "Come on, Warren. Don't do this."

"Will," Billy said, his hand resting on Will's shoulder. "Come on. It's over."

Will wanted to pull away, to keep going, but his body would not respond. For the second time that evening, he sat back on his knees and looked down at Warren Grier. The younger man's last words still echoed in his ears. "Colors," Warren had said. He had figured out Will's filing system, the way he used the colors to indicate what was inside the folders. "You use colors just like me." Warren Grier had finally found a kindred spirit. Ten minutes later, he had killed himself.

Another hand went around Will's arm. Faith helped him stand. He hadn't realized she was there, hadn't seen the circle of cops that had formed around him.

"Come on," she said, keeping her hand on his arm as she walked with him up the hallway. There were catcalls, the kind of remarks you expected men behind bars to make when a pretty woman walked by. Will ignored them, fighting the urge to slump against Faith, to do something foolish like reach out to her.

Faith sat him down at Billy's desk. She knelt in front of him, raised her hand to his cheek. "You had no way of knowing he'd do that."

Will felt the coolness of her palm against his face. He put his hand over hers, then gently pulled it away. "I'm not much good at taking comfort, Faith."

She nodded her understanding, but he could read the pity in her eyes.

"I shouldn't have lied to him," Will said. "The stuff about the cigarette burns."

Faith sat back, looking up at him. He could not tell whether she believed him or was simply humoring him. "You did what you had to do."

"I pushed him too hard."

"He put that sheet around his own neck." She reminded him, "He also pulled the trigger, Will. You would be dead now if those chambers had been full. He may have been more pathetic than Evan Bernard, but he was just as cold and calculating."

"Warren was doing what he was programmed to do. Everything he had in his life—everything—was a struggle. No one gave him anything." Will felt his jaw clench. "Bernard's educated, well liked, he has a good job, friends, family. He had a choice."

"Everyone has a choice. Even Warren."

She would never understand because she had never been completely alone in the world. He told her, "I know Emma's alive somewhere, Faith."

"It's been a long time, Will. Too long."

"I don't care what you say," he told her. "She's alive. Warren wouldn't have killed her. He wanted things from her, things he was in the process of taking. You heard how he talked in the interview. You know he was keeping her alive."

Faith did not respond, though he could see the answer in her eyes: she was just as certain Emma Campano was dead as Will was that the girl was alive.

Instead of arguing with him, she changed the subject. "I just talked to Mary Clark." She walked him through the discovery of the yearbooks in the photographs Will had taken of Warren's apartment, the phone call to the teacher wherein Mary Clark confirmed that Warren had given Bernard an alibi all those years ago. As Faith spoke, Will could finally see everything coming into focus. Bernard would have been the only anchor in Warren's life. There was nothing the young man would not have done for his mentor.

Faith told him the other things the teacher had said. "Bernard let them come to his house and drink, smoke, do whatever they wanted. Then, when he was finished using them, he tossed them away."

"He probably tutored Warren," Will guessed. "He would've been the only adult in his life who tried to help him instead of treating him like there was something wrong with him." Warren would have lain in front of an oncoming train if Bernard told him to. The young man's refusal to implicate the teacher suddenly made sense.

"This shows a pattern with the girls," Faith told him. "Bernard will get more time in prison if Mary tells a jury what happened to her."

Will did not believe for a second that Mary Clark finally had the strength to confront her abuser. "I want him to die," he mumbled. "All those girls he raped—he might as well have killed them. Who was Mary Clark going to be before Evan Bernard got hold of her? What kind of life was she going to have? All that went out the door the minute he set his sights on her. That girl Mary was going to be is dead, Faith. How many other girls did he kill like that? And now Kayla and Adam and God knows what Emma's going through." He stopped, swallowing back his emotions. "I want to be there when they put the needle in his arm. I want to jam it in myself."

Faith was so taken aback by his vehemence that, for a few seconds, she could not trust herself to speak. "We can look for other witnesses," she finally told him. "There have to be other girls. Tie it in with the allegations at Georgia Tech and he could get thirty, forty years."

Will shook his head. "Bernard killed Adam and Kayla, Faith. I know he didn't do it with his own hands, but he knew what Warren was capable of. He knew that he had complete and total control over him, that he could pull the trigger and Warren would shoot." Will thought about Warren, how desperately he must have wanted to fit in. Sitting around Bernard's house with the other kids, drinking beer and talking about all the losers who were still at school, must have been the closest he ever came to being part of a family.

Faith said, "The room in his house thirteen years ago was just like the one we found in Bernard's apartment. He's been doing this for years, Will. As soon as his picture goes out on the news, we're going to have—"

"Where?" Will interrupted. "Did Mary say where the house was?"

"I thought you checked his last residence?"

"I did." Will felt the final piece click into place. "Bernard's background check showed another house. He bought it fifteen years ago and sold it three years later. I didn't think anything about it, but—"

Faith took out her cell phone, dialed in a number. "Mary knows where the house is."

FAITH DROVE, FOLLOWING the Atlanta police cruiser down North Avenue. The lights were on, but the siren was silent. Will was silent, too. He kept thinking about Warren Grier, the soft give to his chest as Will tried to press the life back into his heart. What had compelled the man to wrap the sheet around his neck, to take his own life? Was he afraid that he would not be able to hold out much longer, that Will would push him so hard that he would end up betraying Evan Bernard? Or was it just a means to an end, Warren's desperate, grand plan to make sure that he spent the rest of his life with Emma Campano?

The cruiser bumped along construction sites in front of the Coca-Cola building, streetlights illuminating the road. Faith slowed so that the bottom of her car would not be ripped apart.

She said, "I don't want to find the body."

Will looked at her profile, the way the blue lights flashed against her pale skin. He understood what she meant: she wanted Emma Campano to be found, she just didn't want to be the one who discovered her. "She's going to be alive," Will insisted. He could not think otherwise — especially after Warren. "Emma is going to be alive, and she's going to tell us that Evan Bernard did this, that he put Warren up to everything."

Faith kept her own counsel, staring at the road ahead, probably thinking that Will was a fool.

Houses started to appear on the side of the road, dilapidated Victorians and cottages that had been boarded up long ago. Ahead, the cruiser's lights cut off as they approached Evan Bernard's old address. There were no streetlights here. The moon was covered in clouds. At almost midnight, the only source of light came from the automobile headlights.

"Look," Faith said, pointing to the car Adam Humphrey had purchased from a departing grad student. The blue Chevy Impala was one car among many rusted-out heaps parked along a desolate stretch of North Avenue. There had been a priority alert out for two days to locate the vehicle. No one had reported seeing it. Had the car been sitting here the whole time, Emma Campano rotting in the trunk? Or had Warren left her alive to let nature run its course? Even at this time of night, the heat was unbearable. Inside the car would have been twenty to thirty degrees hotter. Her brain would have literally fried in the heat.

Will and Faith got out of the Mini. He shined his Maglite on the houses and vacant lots that lined the street as they walked toward the car. Most of the homes had been torn down, but three had survived. They were utilitarian, wood-frame structures that had probably been thrown up after the Second World War to accommodate Atlanta's population explosion.

Bernard's house was at the end, the street numbers still nailed to the front door. The windows and doors were boarded over. Hurricane fencing had been erected to keep out vagrants, but that hadn't stopped them from digging under in several places. Various drug paraphernalia on the sidewalk and littering the street indicated that some hadn't even bothered to do that.

One of the cops from the cruiser was checking the interior of the Impala. His partner stood beside the car, a crowbar in his hand. Will took the bar and wedged it into the trunk. Without pause, he popped the lock, the metal lid creaking open. They all gagged from the smell of feces and blood.

The trunk was empty.

"The house," Faith said, shining her flashlight back at the looming structure. It was two stories tall, the roof sagging in the middle. "There could be junkies in there. There are needles all over the place."

Wordlessly, Will walked toward the house. He dropped down, wriggling under the fence, pulling himself up on the other side. He did not stop to help Faith as he headed up the broken concrete walk to the house. The front door was nailed shut. Will thought one of the boards over the window looked loose. He pulled it free with his hands. His flashlight showed the dust on the sill had been rubbed away. Someone had been here before him.

He hesitated. Faith was right. This could be a crack house. Dealers and junkies could be conducting business inside. They could be armed, high or both. Either way, they would not exactly welcome the police into their shooting den.

One of the porch boards squeaked. Faith stood behind him, her flashlight shining on the ground.

He kept his voice low. "You don't have to do this."

Faith ignored him as she slid in between the rotted boards.

Will checked on the other cops, making sure they were guarding the front and the rear of the house, before going in after her. Inside, Faith had her gun drawn, the flashlight tucked up beside the muzzle, the same way every cop had been trained to do. The house felt claustrophobic, with its low ceilings and trash piled into the corners. There were more needles than he could count, clumps of tinfoil and a few spoons—all the signs that the space was an active shooting den.

Faith pointed down, meaning she would search this level. Will drew his gun and went toward the stairs.

He tested his foot on each tread, hoping he would not step on rotted wood and end up in the basement. There was a tingling at the base of his spine. He reached the top of the stairs, keeping his flashlight aimed low. There was a sliver of moonlight coming through the boarded windows, just enough to see by. Will turned off the light and gently placed it on the floor. He stood there, listening for sounds of life. All he heard was Faith walking downstairs, the house groaning as the heat soaked into the wood.

Will smelled pot, chemicals. They could be in a meth lab. There could be a junkie hiding behind one of the doors, waiting to stick Will with a needle. He stepped forward, his foot crunching broken glass. There were four bedrooms upstairs with one bathroom between them. The door at the end of the hall was closed. All the other doors had been taken off their hinges, probably stolen for scrap. In the bathroom, the fixtures were gone, the copper pipe pulled out of the wall. Holes had been punched into the ceiling. The plaster walls were broken along the light switches where someone had checked for copper wire in the wall. It was aluminum,

Will saw, the kind that he had ripped out of his own house because building codes had outlawed its use many years ago.

Faith whispered, "Will?" She was making her way up the stairs. He waited until she was with him, then indicated the closed door at the end of the hallway.

Will stopped in front of the only door. He tried the knob, but it was locked. He indicated that Faith should step back, then lifted his foot and kicked open the door. Will knelt, pointing his gun blindly into the room. Faith's flashlight cut through the dark like a knife, searching corners, the open closet.

The room was empty.

They both holstered their weapons.

"It's just like the other one." Faith shone her flashlight over the faded pink walls, the dirty white trim. There was a bare double mattress on the floor, dark stains flowering at the center. A tripod with a camera was mounted in front of it.

Will took the flashlight and checked the slot for the memory stick. "It's empty."

"We should call Charlie," Faith said, probably thinking about the evidence that needed to be collected, the DNA on the mattress.

"He knows better than to leave traces of himself," Will said. He could not get Evan Bernard's smug face out of his mind. The man was so certain that he wouldn't get caught. He was right. At the moment, all they could charge Bernard with was having sex with Kayla Alexander. Will did not know what the statute of limitations was for Mary Clark, nor was he certain that the woman would testify against a man whom she still considered in many ways to have been her first lover.

There was a scraping noise. Will turned around to see what Faith was doing, but she was standing completely still in the middle of the room. He heard the scrape again, and, this time, he realized it was coming from the ceiling.

Faith mouthed, *Junkie?*

Will skimmed the low ceiling with his flashlight, checking every corner of the room. Like the rest of the house, the plaster had been busted out around the light switch. Will saw a dark stain around the hole, what might be a footprint. There was a hole above his head, insulation and Sheetrock hanging down in pieces.

"Emma?" He almost choked on the girl's name, afraid to say the word, to give himself hope. "Emma Campano?" He slammed his hand into the ceiling. "It's the police, Emma."

There was more scraping, the distinctive sound of rats.

"Emma?" Will reached up, tearing chunks of Sheetrock down from the low ceiling. His hands did not work fast enough, so he used the flashlight to make the opening larger. "Emma, it's the police." He dug his foot into the hole in the wall, propelling himself up into the attic.

Will stopped, halfway in the attic, his foot firmly supported by the lath in the wall. Hot air enveloped him, so intense that his lungs hurt from breathing it. The girl lay in a heap up against the eaves. Her skin was covered in a fine, white powder from the Sheetrock. Her eyes were open, her lips together. A large rat was inches from her hand, his retinas flashing like mirrors in the beam of the flashlight. Will pulled himself the rest of the way into the attic. Rats scrambled everywhere. One darted across the girl's arm. He saw scratch marks where the animals had dug into her skin.

"No," Will whispered, crawling on his hands and knees across the supports. Blood congealed on her abdomen and thighs. Welts strangled her neck. Will swung the flashlight at a greedy rat, his heart aching at the sight of the girl. How could he tell Paul that this was how he had found his daughter? There was no smell of decay, no flies burrowing into her flesh. How could any of them go on knowing that only a few hours had separated the girl from life and death?

"Will?" Faith asked, though he could tell from her tone of voice that she knew what he had found.

"I'm sorry," Will told the girl. He could not stand her blank, lifeless stare. He had not believed once during the investigation that she was dead—even when evidence had stacked up to the contrary. He had insisted that there was no way she was gone, and now, all he could think was that his hubris had made the truth that much more unbearable.

Will reached over to close her eyes, pressing his fingers into the lids, gently lowering them. "I'm sorry," he repeated, knowing that would never be enough.

Emma's eyes popped back open. She blinked, focusing on Will. She was alive.

CHAPTER TWENTY-ONE

FAITH STOOD IN Emma Campano's hospital room, watching Abigail with her daughter. The room was dark, the only light coming from the machines that were hooked up to the girl. Fluids, antibiotics, various mixtures of chemicals designed to make her well again. Nothing could heal her spirit, though. No medical device could revive her soul.

While Faith was pregnant, she had secretly decided that the baby in her womb was a little girl. Blond hair and blue eyes, dimples in her cheeks. Faith would buy her matching pink outfits and braid ribbons into her hair while her daughter talked about school crushes and boy bands and secret wishes.

Jeremy had pretty quickly shattered that dream. Her son's feelings ran toward uncomplicated matters involving football and action heroes. His musical tastes were deplorable and hardly worth talking about. His wishes were hardly secret: toys, video games and—to Faith's horror—the slutty little redhead who lived down the street.

The past few days, Faith had let her mind go to that dark place every parent visits at one time or another: what would I do if the phone rang, the police knocked on the door, and some stranger told me that my child was dead? That was the terror that lurked in every mother's heart, that gruesome fear. It was like knocking on wood or making the sign of the cross—letting the thought come into your mind served as a talisman against the thing actually happening.

Watching Emma sleep, Faith realized there were worse things than getting that phone call. You could get your child back, but her identity—her essence—could be gone. The horrors Emma experienced were written on her body: the bruises, the scratches, the bite marks. Warren had taken his time with the girl, living out every sick fantasy that he could conjure. He had given her neither food nor water. Emma had been forced to defecate and urinate in the same room in which she slept. Her hands and feet had been tied. Repeatedly, she had been strangled to the point of passing out, then resuscitated. The girl had screamed so much that her voice was nothing more than a raw whisper.

Faith could not help herself. Her pity did not lie with the child, but with the mother. She thought about what Will had said earlier, how Evan Bernard had by all rights killed Mary Clark. There were two Emma Campanos now—the one before Warren, and the one after. That little girl Abigail had nursed and played peekaboo with, the pretty child she had taken to school in the mornings and dropped off at movie theaters and malls on the weekends, was gone. All that was left was the shell of her girl, an empty vessel that would be filled with the thoughts of a stranger.

Abigail was obviously thinking of these things. She could barely touch the girl, seemed to have to force herself to hold Emma's hand. Faith herself could not even meet the mother's eyes. How could you mourn the death of your child when she was still alive?

Abigail spoke softly. "She's awake."

Slowly, Faith walked over. They had tried to question the girl on the way to the hospital, firing questions at her one after the other. Emma had lain on the gurney, her eyes staring blankly at the ambulance ceiling, her answers coming out in monosyllabic bites. She had gotten progressively agitated until she was cowering against the rails, the impact of her ordeal slowly sinking in. She had become so hysterical that they had sedated her so that she would not hurt herself. Her reaction was strikingly similar to her mother's.

"Hi, honey," Faith began. "Do you remember me?"

The girl nodded. Her eyelids were heavy, though the medication had long worn off. The clock on the heart monitor read 6:33 a.m. Light peeked out around the edges of the metal blinds over the window. The sun had risen unnoticed as she slept.

They had figured out quickly that it was the men who set her off. The male paramedics touching and prodding, even Will trying to hold her hand, had made her panic like a trapped animal. Emma could not stand the sight of any of them, could not tolerate the male doctors. Even her own father upset the girl so much that he became physically ill.

Faith asked Emma, "You sure you want to do this?"

She nodded.

"I need to ask you some questions," Faith told her. "Do you think you can talk to me?"

She nodded again, wincing at the pain when she moved.

Abigail's fingertips touched her daughter's arm. "If it's too much—"

"I want to," Emma insisted, her voice strained, like a person much older than her few years.

"Tell me what you remember," Faith urged, knowing that the girl had probably been doing everything she could to forget.

"It was Kayla," she said, her tone certain. "We heard her screaming. Adam went out in the hall, and I saw the man stab him."

"Warren?"

She nodded.

Abigail reached for the glass of water beside the bed. "Drink something, honey."

"No," she refused. "I need to say."

Faith was surprised at her courage, but then she remembered that twice now, Emma Campano had been written off for dead and twice the girl had fought back. "Tell me what happened."

"Adam told me to hide in the closet." She paused, some of her resolve breaking. "The next thing I remember, I was in the room, and the man was on top of me."

Faith asked, "Did he say anything to you?"

"He said that he loved me." She glanced quickly at her mother. "I told him that I did, too. He was nicer when I did."

"That was smart," Faith told her. "You did what you needed to do to keep him from getting angry."

"Are you sure..." The girl squeezed her eyes shut. The heart monitor beeped. Cold air came out of the vent over the bed. "You're sure he's dead?"

"Yes," Faith told her, putting all the certainty she could in her voice. "I saw him myself. He died last night."

She kept her eyes tightly closed.

"Are you sure that no one else came?" Faith asked. This had been the first question put to the girl, and she was just as unequivocal in her answer then as she was now.

"No."

Faith could not let it go. She had to be sure. "Warren didn't talk about anyone he was working with? No one came into the room with you?"

Her eyes were still closed. Faith thought that she had fallen asleep, but the girl's head moved slowly from side to side. "No one," she said. "I was completely alone."

Abigail reached out, but pulled back her hand, not knowing where she could touch her daughter, which spots would cause comfort or pain. She admitted as much, saying, "I don't know what to do."

Faith took the woman's hand and wrapped it around her daughter's. "You already lost her once. It's up to you to make sure you don't lose her again."

✦

FAITH COULD SEE Will and Amanda standing at the end of the hallway outside Emma's room. Both of them looked up at her expectantly. She shook her head, letting them know that Evan Bernard was still in the clear.

Amanda took out her phone and Will said something to stop her. Faith could not hear his voice and, frankly, she did not care. She went back to the row of plastic chairs lining the hallway and sat down with a groan. Her exhaustion was so deep that she felt dizzy. Sleep was all she needed, just a few minutes and then she could go with Will to scour Warren Grier's apartment again. They would turn the man's office upside down at the Copy Right, interview everyone who had ever known him or come into contact with him. Mary Clark had remembered Warren and Bernard together. There was bound to be someone else out there who knew even more than she did.

Faith's head jerked up as she caught herself dozing. Her phone was ringing. She took it out of her pocket, checking the caller ID. It was Victor again. He was nothing if not persistent.

"You gonna get that?" Will asked.

Faith looked up at him. He looked as tired as she felt. "He'll call back." She tucked the phone back into her pocket. "What was that about?"

He slumped into the chair beside her, his long legs blocking the hallway. "The prosecutor says the judge won't deny bail." He rubbed his eyes. "Bernard's going to be out on the streets before noon."

"Did yelling at Amanda help?"

"It's easier to blame her for all the evil things that happen in the world." He put his face in his hands, exhaustion slowing down every move. "What did I miss on this, Faith? How can we keep him locked up?"

Faith thought about what was behind the door across the hall. Warren was dead, but there was still someone out there who should be punished for the crime. They had to make a case against Bernard. Will was right—he had to be punished.

She asked, "What did Amanda say?"

"She's moving on. Emma is back, we've got one dead prisoner and a lawsuit from the Alexanders to deal with. This case has basically been downgraded because we have a living victim." He shook his head. "What kind of job is this where a dead seventeen-year-old is more important than a living one?"

"My boss hasn't taken me off this yet," Faith told him. "I'll work with you as long as they let me."

"Well, that's the other thing."

Faith could hear the trepidation in his voice and it shot a cold chill through her. "Did Amanda find out about the gray powder?"

He looked at her, confused. "Oh," he said, understanding. "No, worse than that. Amanda is going to ask you to be my partner."

Faith was so tired that she was certain she had heard wrong. "Your partner?"

"I understand if you don't want to do it."

"It's not that," she said, still not sure she'd heard correctly. "Your partner?" she repeated. "Amanda's been keeping me off every important event in this case," Faith said, thinking the missed press conference was just the icing on the cake. "Why would she want me on her team?"

Will had the grace to look guilty. "That was actually me keeping you out of the loop," he admitted. "But not on purpose. Honest."

She was too tired to manage anything but an exasperated, "Will."

"I'm sorry," he said, holding out his hands in an open shrug. "But, listen, it's best you know what you'd be getting into."

"This is the last thing I expected," Faith admitted. She was still unable to wrap her head around the offer.

"I told you about the crappy dental." He held up his hand, showed her the scar from the nail gun. "And keep in mind that Amanda doesn't take prisoners."

Faith rubbed her face. She let the enormity of the situation sink in. "I keep hearing those clicks in my ear from Warren dry-firing on you." She paused, not trusting herself to speak. "He could have killed you." She added, "And I would have killed him."

Will tried for levity. "You seemed pretty cool to me." His voice went up in a falsetto as he mimicked, " 'Drop it, motherfucker!' "

She felt her cheeks redden. "I guess my inner Police Woman came out."

"Pepper Anderson was a sergeant. You're a detective."

"And *you* are pathetic for knowing that."

He smiled, rubbing his jaw. "Yeah, you're probably right." He waited a few seconds before saying, "I mean it, Faith. I won't take it personally if you say no."

She cut to the heart of the matter. "I don't know if I can do this kind of job every day. At least with the murder squad, we know where to look."

"Boyfriend, husband, lover," Will said, a familiar refrain. "I'm not going to lie. It takes the life out of you."

She thought of Victor Martinez, his many phone calls. Jeremy was finally out of the house. She had met a man who might possibly be interested in her despite the fact that she was painfully ill-prepared for an adult relationship. She'd finally managed to get some grudging respect around the homicide squad, even if their highest compliment so far was, "You're not that stupid for a blonde."

Did Faith want to invite more complications into her life? Shouldn't she just coast through on her detective's shield, then work private security like every other retired cop she knew?

Will glanced up and down the hallway. "Did Paul just disappear?" he asked, and she realized it was a question meant to put them back on more comfortable footing.

Faith was glad for the familiar ground. "I haven't seen him."

"Typical," he remarked.

Faith turned in her chair to look at Will. His nose was still bruised, a sliver of blue tracing beneath his right eye. "Did you really grow up in foster care?"

He didn't register the question. His face stayed blank.

"I'm sorry," she apologized, just as he answered, "Yes."

Will leaned forward, his elbows on his knees. Faith waited for him to say something, but he seemed to be doing the same thing with her.

She blurted out, "Moms I'd like to fuck."

"What?"

"That first day with Jeremy. You asked me what a MILF is. It stands for 'Moms I'd Like to Fuck.' "

He narrowed his eyes, probably trying to put it into context. He must have remembered, because he said, "Ouch."

"Yeah," Faith agreed.

Will clasped his hands together. He twisted around his watch and checked the time. Instead of making a comment, pulling some small talk out of the air, he simply stared at the floor. She saw that his shoes were scuffed, the hem of his pants caked with dirt from climbing under the fence to the North Avenue house.

"What did Warren say to you?" she asked. "I know that he said something. I saw the way your face changed."

Will kept staring at the floor. She thought he was not going to answer, but he did. "Colors."

Faith did not believe him any more now than she had before. "He told you the colors on the file folders?"

"It's a trick," he answered. "Remember what Bernard said, about how dyslexics are good at hiding their problem from other people?" He looked back at her. "The colors tell you what's inside the folders."

With all that had happened in the last few hours, Faith had almost forgotten her earlier revelation about Will's inability to read. She thought about the psych evaluation Will had shoved in Warren's face, the way he had pressed his finger to each differently colored dot as he called out the findings. Will had never looked at the words. He had let the colors guide him.

"What about the last sheet?" she asked. "Warren was functionally illiterate. He had *some* ability to read. Why couldn't he see that it was a dress-code memo?"

Will kept his eyes trained at the wall opposite. "When you get upset, it's harder to see the words. They move around. They blur."

So Faith wasn't crazy, after all. Will did have some sort of reading problem. She thought about the way he always patted his pockets, looking for his glasses, when there was something to read. He hadn't noticed the rural route address on Adam Humphrey's license or read the Web page on Bernard's computer that talked about teacher retirement. Still, she had to admit if you stacked him up against Leo Donnelly or any other man in the homicide division, he came out the better cop.

She asked, "What other tricks would Warren use?"

"A digital recorder. Voice recognition software. Spell-check."

Faith wondered if she could have been any more blind. She was supposed to be a detective and she had missed all of the obvious signs right under her nose. "Is that why Warren fixated on the colors?" she asked. "Did he see the different colors on your file folders and figure out you—"

"Colors," Will interrupted. "He said the colors." A big, sloppy grin spread across his face. "That's what Warren was trying to tell me."

"What?"

He stood up, excitement replacing exhaustion. "We need to go to the copy center."

CHAPTER TWENTY-TWO

WILL WALKED DOWN through the cells, not looking at the crime-scene tape covering the open doorway where Warren Grier had hanged himself. He could feel the cold stares of the prisoners follow him to the end of the hall. There were the usual sounds of jail: men talking trash, other men weeping.

Evan Bernard was in one of the larger holding cells. Men who raped young girls were always targeted by other prisoners. The ones who were attached to sensational cases could pretty much kiss their lives good-bye. The transgendered cell was the only safe place for a man like Bernard. The women were usually arrested for crimes of circumstance: stealing food, public vagrancy. Most of them were too feminine to get construction work and too masculine to turn tricks. Like Evan Bernard, they would have been torn apart in the general population.

The teacher had his hands hanging outside the bars, his elbows on the supports. The cell was a large one, at least fifteen feet wide. Beds were stacked three high across the space. As he walked up, Will noticed that the women were all huddled around a single bunk, as if they, too, could not stand the sight of Evan Bernard.

Will had a sheet folded up under his arm. The material was

thick prison issue, bleached and starched to within an inch of its life. When he propped it up between the bars, it stayed that way.

Bernard made a point of looking at the sheet. "Poor kid. The girls are crazy upset."

Will glanced into the cell. The girls looked ready to rip him apart.

Bernard said, "I'm not talking to you without my lawyer present."

"I don't want you to talk," Will said. "I want you to listen."

He shrugged. "Nothing else to pass the time."

"Do you know how he did it? How he strangled himself?"

"I assumed he was the victim of some sort of police brutality."

Will smiled. "Do you want to know or not?"

Bernard raised his eyebrow, as if to say, *Go on*.

Will took down the sheet, unfolding it. He explained as he worked. "It's hard to figure out, right? It doesn't make sense that you can asphyxiate yourself just sitting on the floor." He looped the sheet through his hand, wrapping the material around his arm.

"What you do is, you tie one end around the doorknob, and then you loop it around your neck like this." Will jerked the sheet tight, his skin pressing out between the folds. "You kneel down with your head close to the knob, and then you start breathing really fast and really hard until you hyperventilate."

Bernard smiled, as if he finally understood.

"And then, just before you pass out, you kick your legs out from underneath yourself." Will pulled the sheet away. "And then you wait."

"It wouldn't take long," Bernard said.

"No, just a few minutes."

"Is that why you came down here, Mr. Trent, to tell me this tragic tale?"

"I came down here to tell you that you were right about something."

"You'll have to narrow that down for me. I've been right about so many things."

Will looped the sheet through the bars, letting the material hang down either side. "You told me that dyslexics were good at developing tricks so that they can blend in with everybody else. True?"

"True."

"It got me to thinking about Warren, because that day he went to Emma Campano's house, there were lots of things for him to remember." Will listed them out. "What time Kayla was going to let him into the house. Where Emma's room was. How many pairs of gloves to bring. Where to transfer her from one car to the other."

Bernard shook his head. "This is fascinating, Mr. Trent, but what on earth does it have to do with me?"

"Well," Will began, digging in his jacket pocket for his digital recorder. "Since Warren couldn't write down lists, he made recordings."

Bernard shook his head again. He wouldn't have recognized the recorder because it belonged to Will. "Warren used his cell phone to make recordings," Will explained. "He transferred them to compact discs that he kept filed along with customer artwork at the copy store."

Bernard seemed less sure of himself.

"Blue, red, purple, green," Will repeated. "That was the sequence he used for his discs." He clicked on the player. Evan Bernard's voice was easily distinguishable. *"No, Warren, the rope and tape will be in the trunk. Kayla will give you the keys."*

Warren mumbled, *"I know, I know."*

On the tape, Bernard was obviously agitated. *"No, you don't know. You need to listen to what I'm saying. If you do this right, none of us will get caught."*

A girl's voice they had verified was Kayla Alexander's, said, *"You want me to write it down for you, Warren? You want me to make a list?"*

Will clicked off the recorder. "You can hear the rest in court."

"I'm going free in an hour," Bernard said. "My lawyer told me—"

"Your lawyer doesn't know about the DVDs." Charlie Reed

had been wrong about the cables in back of Bernard's home computer. They had been attached to a recordable DVD drive.

Will told the man, "We have at least a dozen videos showing you in your special room, Evan. My partner is at Westfield Academy with Olivia McFaden right now. We made stills from the videos—pictures that show the girls' faces right alongside yours. So far, they've identified six students from the school." Will asked, "How many more do you think we'll find? How many women do you think are going to come forward?"

"I want my lawyer. Now."

"Oh, he's coming. He seemed really eager to talk to you when I told him about the new charges." Will put his hand on the sheet, pushing it into the cell. "Here you go, Evan. I don't want you to ever think that I didn't leave you enough rope to hang yourself with."

◆

BETTY WAS ON the couch when Will came home, which meant that Angie wasn't there. He took off his jacket and loosened his tie as he adjusted the thermostat. He had been in the house less than a minute and he was already annoyed. Angie knew he liked to keep the air on for Betty. She tended to get nasty heat rashes in the summer.

The answering machine was flashing. There was one message. Will pressed the button and heard Paul Campano's voice come out of the speaker.

"Hey, Will," he said, and that was enough. Will stopped the tape, not wanting to know what the rest of the message said. He didn't want to hear Paul humbled or grateful. The man had said his name instead of calling him Trash. That was all that Will had ever wanted to hear.

He scooped the dog off the couch and took her to the kitchen, where he was surprised to find her water bowl was filled. He examined Betty's bug-eyed face, as if he could tell whether or not she had stopped drinking just by looking at her. He was fairly certain Angie hadn't bothered to fill up the bowl during the day. Betty licked Will's face and he gave her a pet before putting her down on the floor. He scooped some kibble in her food bowl, then tossed her a piece of her favorite cheese, before going into the bedroom.

It was like an oven in the back of the house. He stripped out of his vest, shirt and pants as he walked to the bed, tossing them all on a chair. Will wasn't sure what time it was, but he was so tired that it didn't make a difference. The fact that Angie never made the bed actually seemed like a good thing as he slid between the sheets.

Unbidden, a long, heavy sigh came out of his chest as he closed his eyes. He put his hands on his chest, then he put them down at his sides. He rolled over. He kicked the sheets off. Finally, he ended up on his back again, staring up at the ceiling.

The phone rang, piercing the solitude. Will debated whether or not to answer. He checked the clock. It was ten in the morning. There was no one in the world right now that he wanted to talk to. Amanda wasn't about to pat him on the back, the press would not know how to get his phone number and Angie was off doing her own thing—whatever that was.

He picked it up before the machine clicked on.

"Hi," Faith said. "Are you busy?"

"Just lying around in my underwear." There was no response. "Hello?"

"Yes." She said the word like a statement, and he realized that yet again he'd blurted out the wrong thing. He was about to apologize when she said, "I told Amanda I'm taking the job."

Several responses came to mind, but Will weighed them out, not trusting himself not to say something stupid. "Good," he managed, more like a croak.

"It's because we caught him." Bernard, she meant. "If we hadn't, I probably would've been fine going back to my little desk in the murder squad and biding my time until retirement."

"You've never struck me as the type of cop who works on a time clock."

"It was a really easy habit to fall into when I was partnered with Leo," she admitted. "Maybe it'll be different with you."

He laughed. "I can honestly say that I've never had a woman look at being stuck with me as a positive thing."

She laughed, too. "At least I can help you with your reports."

Will felt his smile drop. They had not discussed Faith's obvious realization that there were second-graders in her neighborhood who could read better than Will. He said, "I don't need help, Faith. Really." To cut some of the tension, he added, "But, thank you."

"All right," she agreed, but the strain was still there.

He tried to think of something else to say—a joke, a bad pun about his illiteracy. Nothing came except the glaring reminder that there was a reason he did not tell people about his problem. Will did not need help with anything. He could pull his own weight, and had for years.

He asked, "When do you start?"

"It's complicated," she said. "I've got a provisional certificate until I finish my degree, but, basically, I'll be in your office first thing a week from Monday."

"My office?" Will asked, getting a sinking sensation. He knew how Amanda worked. She had come down to his office a year ago and noted that, if Will kept his knees up around his ears, another desk could easily be wedged into the space. "That'll be great," he said, trying to keep things upbeat.

"I've been thinking a lot about Kayla."

He could tell as much from her tone of voice. "You mean the lawsuit?"

"No. Her motivation." Faith was silent again, but this time she seemed to be gathering her thoughts. "Nobody liked Kayla except Emma. Her parents were shitty. The whole school hated her."

"From all reports, she was reviled for a reason."

"But Bernard's such a manipulative bastard, it's hard to tell whether or not she was in it for the thrill or because he told her to do it."

Will did not want to accept that it was possible for a seventeen-year-old girl to be so sadistic. The only thing he knew for certain was that with Warren dead and Bernard pointing his finger at everyone but himself, they would never really know the truth. "I doubt even Kayla knew the difference."

"Mary Clark *still* doesn't know."

He considered the poor woman, the damage that had been done to her psyche. On the surface, Mary was living a good life: well educated, married with children, teaching at an upscale school. And yet, all of that meant nothing because of something tragic that had happened to her over a decade ago. It was the same way he had thought of Emma early on in this case: everything she survived would make her want to die every day for the rest of her life. If the GBI and the Atlanta police and every other police force in America really cared about stopping crime, they would take all the money they poured into prisons and the courts and homeland security and spend every nickel on protecting children from the bastards who preyed on them. Will could pretty much guarantee the investment would pay off in saved lives.

"I should go," Faith told him. "I'm having lunch with Victor Martinez in two hours and I'm still wearing the same clothes he saw me in last time."

"The guy from Tech?"

"We'll see how long it takes for me to screw it up."

"I can give you some pointers."

"I think I manage that sort of thing well enough on my own." She made noises about going, and he stopped her. "Faith?"

"Yes?"

Will struggled to make a grand statement, to welcome her into his life, to find a way to make it clear that he was going to do whatever it took to keep things running smoothly. "I'll see you in a week."

"All right."

Will hung up the phone, and a million better things to say came to mind, starting with telling her that he was glad she had made the decision and ending with him begging her to forgive any and all future monkey business. He lay in bed, eyes on the ceiling, and ran through their phone conversation. Will realized that he knew exactly when she had decided to take the job. They were at the copy center, listening to Evan Bernard, Kayla Alexander and Warren

Grier planning the abduction of Emma Campano. Both of them were punch-drunk with exhaustion, and their foolish grins must have alarmed Charlie Reed, though the man had held his tongue.

She was right about one thing: as bad as the last few days had been, catching Evan Bernard made it all worthwhile. They had brought Emma Campano home. Warren Grier had meted out his own punishment, but there had been value in what he'd left behind. Kayla Alexander had gotten justice, too, no matter what her involvement had been in the crime. There was a certain satisfaction in those resolutions, a certain reassurance that what you did out on the streets actually mattered.

Yet, Will wondered if Faith knew that her father had an out-of-state bank account with over twenty thousand dollars in it. Will was two weeks into the Evelyn Mitchell case before he thought to check for accounts under her dead husband's name. The savings account was at least twenty years old and the balance had fluctuated over the years but never dropped below five thousand dollars. The last withdrawal had been three years earlier, so it was hard to track where exactly the money had been spent. Evelyn Mitchell was a cop. She would know better than to keep receipts. As a matter of fact, if Will hadn't found the account, he would have assumed from the way she lived her life that she was clean. She had a small mortgage, modest savings and a six-year-old Mercedes she had bought used.

It must have been expensive raising your child's child. Doctor appointments, field trips, schoolbooks. Jeremy wouldn't have had insurance. Will doubted fifteen-year-old Faith's policy covered childbirth. Maybe that's where the money had gone. Maybe she had figured there was nothing wrong with using drug dealers' money to take care of her family.

There were tax issues, of course, but Will did not work for the IRS. He worked for the GBI, and it was his job to present the evidence to the lawyers and let them decide what case they were going to bring. Will had been mildly surprised when he heard that Evelyn Mitchell was being forcibly retired instead of prosecuted. He had been on the job long enough to know that the higher up you were, the less likely you were to swing, but the bank account was the proverbial slam dunk. Now he knew why the woman had escaped with her pension. Amanda must have pulled some pretty long strings to keep her almost-sister-in-law out of prison.

The front door slammed. "Willy?"

He was silent for just a moment, feeling the painful sting of his solitude being interrupted. "In here."

Angie narrowed her eyes when she found him lying in bed. "You're not watching porn, are you?"

Considering Evan Bernard's sex tapes, it would be many hours before he could think about porn again. "Where were you?"

"I went to see Leo Donnelly in the hospital."

"You hate him."

"He's a cop. Cops go to see cops when they're in the hospital."

Will would never understand that code, the secret language that came with wearing a uniform.

Angie said, "I heard you got your guy."

"Did you hear my prisoner killed himself while he was in my custody?"

"It wasn't your fault." Automatic, the cop's gesundheit of absolution.

"He was one of us," Will told her, not wanting to say Warren Grier's name aloud, to make him a living person again. "He was in and out of foster homes all his life. He finally left at eighteen. He was all alone."

Angie's eyes softened for just a moment. "Were you with him when he died?"

Will nodded. He had to believe that he had been there for Warren, even as the man took his last breath.

She said, "Then he wasn't alone, was he?"

Will rolled over on his side so that he could look at her. She was wearing shorts and a white blouse that was so thin it showed the black bra she was wearing underneath. Leo Donnelly must have loved that. He was probably telling half the squad room about it right now.

Will said, "I know you know you're not pregnant."

"I know you know."

There was nothing much more that he could say on the topic.

She asked, "Do you want a sandwich?"

"You let the mayonnaise go bad."

She gave a sly smile. "I bought a new jar at the store."

Will felt himself smiling back. It was, he thought, the nicest thing she had done for him in a really long while.

She started to leave, then stopped. "I'm glad you solved your case, Will. No one else would've gotten that girl back alive."

"I'm not so sure about that," he admitted. "You know a lot of this stuff is just chance."

"Be sure to tell that to your asshole teacher."

Evan Bernard. Was the reading teacher's impending prosecution the product of chance, or was that all down to Will's insight? Eventually, whoever was leading the investigation would have checked all of the CDs in Warren's office. Evan Bernard might have been in the wind by then, but they would have found the evidence.

She said, "Maybe if you're good, we can buff the coffee table again."

"Maybe the chair. My knees are hurting."

"I'm not going to marry an old man."

He didn't say the obvious, which was that she wasn't going to marry anybody. Angie hadn't put her house on the market, she wore her engagement ring only when it suited her and as long as Will had known her, the only commitment she had ever stuck to was one to never stick to commitments. The only promise she had ever kept was that she kept popping back up in his life no matter how many times she told him she was not going to.

She had bought him mayonnaise, though. There was some kind of love in the gesture.

Angie leaned over the bed and gave him an uncharacteristic kiss on the forehead. "I'll let you know when your sandwich is ready."

Will fell onto his back and stared up at the ceiling. He tried to remember what it felt like to be alone. As far back as he could remember, there had never been that sense of complete isolation you got when there was no one else out there in the world who even knew your name. Angie had always been a phone call away. Even when she was seeing other men, she would drop everything to come to Will's side. Not that he had ever asked her to, but he knew that she would, just as he knew that he would do the same for her.

Did having Angie in his life mean that Will would never be as alone as Warren Grier? He thought about the scene he had described to the younger man during the interrogation, the picture Will had painted of domestic bliss: Warren would come home to find Emma cooking dinner for him. They would share a bottle of wine and talk about their day. Emma would wash the dishes. Warren would dry. Describing the scenario had been so easy for Will because he knew in his heart that Warren's dreams would closely parallel his own.

Until recently, Will's house had looked like Warren's tiny room on Ashby Street—everything neat, everything in its place. Now Angie's stuff was strewn about, the imprint of her daily existence firmly melding into Will's. Was that a bad thing? Was the inconvenience, the disruption, the price that human beings paid for companionship? Will had told Warren that guys like them didn't know how to be in normal relationships. Maybe Will had landed himself right in the middle of one without having the capacity to recognize the signs.

Clicking announced Betty's entrance in the bedroom as her toenails struck the wood floor. It was as if the dog had been waiting for Angie to leave. She jumped onto the bed and looked at him expectantly. Will covered himself with the sheet, thinking it was mildly inappropriate to be undressed in front of the dog. Betty seemed to have her own issues. He saw what looked like potting soil on her snout.

Will closed his eyes, listening to the creaks and groans of the old house, the compressor kicking in as the air conditioner whirred to life. Betty crawled onto his chest and took three turns before settling down. She had a little wheeze when she breathed. Maybe her hay fever was back. Will would have to take her to the doctor for some antihistamine tomorrow.

He heard Angie cursing in the kitchen. There was the sound of a knife hitting the floor, probably covered in mayonnaise. He could picture her wiping it up with her foot, tracking it across the tile. Betty would probably find the spots and lick the greasy residue. Will wondered if dogs could get food poisoning and decided the risk was too great.

Carefully, he scooped Betty off his chest, then put on his pants and went to help Angie in the kitchen.

EPILOGUE

THE ANSLEY PARK house sat vacant. The furniture had been auctioned. The walls and floors had been stripped. Special cleaning crews had erased the blood, the scenes of crime. Yet everything was still exactly the same in Abigail Campano's head. Sometimes she would be in the kitchen of their new house or walking up the staircase and remember Adam Humphrey's face, the dark red of his eyes as she squeezed the life out of him.

Despite—or maybe because of—the objection of their lawyers, Abby had written his parents a letter. She had told them what Emma had said about their boy, how he was kind and good and gentle. She had apologized. She had freely admitted her guilt. She offered them everything she had and was fully prepared to give it. Abigail had herself been a lawyer and she knew full well what she was doing. Two weeks later, a note had arrived in the mailbox among the various detritus strangers send strangers in times of catastrophe. There was no return address, but the postmark showed a rural town in Oregon. Two short sentences were on the card inside: *Thank you for your letter. We pray that we all find the strength to carry on.*

It seemed like such a trite statement, the sort of thing Jay

Gatsby would say, or the parting line at the end of an old black-and-white war movie: *Carry on, old sport! Carry on to freedom!*

Two months later, life continued around them, but there was still the underlying threat of menace, as if they all expected it to be taken away from them. And how much they had to lose! The new house in Druid Hills was spectacular, even larger than the Ansley one. There were eight bedrooms and nine bathrooms. There was an office, a gym, a sauna, a wine cellar, a screening room, a keeping room, a mudroom. The carriage house offered two full baths and two more bedrooms. Walking around the apartment over the garage, Abigail had wryly commented that should tragedy ever befall their family again, at least she and Paul would have more space to get away from each other.

He did not laugh at her observation.

She bought furniture, ordered bed linens, spent so much money online that the credit card companies called to make sure her identity had not been stolen. Everyone else seemed to be getting back to normal, or what Abigail thought of as the "new normal." Beatrice was back in Italy. Hoyt had returned to his mistress. His wife was safely ensconced in the Puerto Rico house. Abigail was certain there was another mistress in there somewhere. Her father had been talking an awful lot about London lately.

Even the press had finally moved on. *People* magazine and the television producers had dropped out early on when it was made clear that the Campano family had no desire to share their story with the world. There were the requisite self-proclaimed friends who came out of the woodwork to talk about Emma, and the ex-friends who talked about Abigail and Paul. Worse were the tabloids. They stood on the other side of the gate at the end of the driveway, screaming at anyone who left the house. "Hey, killer!" they would say, spotting Abigail. "Killer, how does it feel to know you murdered someone?"

Abigail would keep her face neutral, her back to the vultures as much as she could, then go into the house and collapse in tears. They called her cold one day, then praised her as a savage mother bear protecting her cubs the next. They asked her what she thought of Evan Bernard, the man who had brought all of this misery to their door.

Every time Bernard opened his mouth, a news team was there, reporting live from the jail where he was being kept. If coverage started to die down, he made statements, gave surprise jailhouse interviews and presented exclusive documents from his troubled past. Then the analysts would have their field day, expert after expert dissecting every nuance of Bernard's life: where he had gone wrong, how many kids he had helped during his career. Women came forward, so many young women. They all insisted that despite the tape, despite the video evidence, he was innocent. The Evan Bernard they knew was a kind man, a gentle man. Abigail itched to be alone with the bastard, to wrap her hands around his kind and gentle neck and watch the pathetic life drain from his beady black eyes.

Listening to it all was maddening, and Abigail and Paul had gotten into the habit of turning off the news, skipping the talk shows, because they could not contribute anymore to Bernard's celebrity. They had been doing this anyway whenever Emma walked into the room. The truth was that it had made Abigail feel dirty, as if she were reading her daughter's diary behind her back. Paul had even canceled his subscription to the morning paper. Dispatch had failed to get the notice. There were so many wet bags of newsprint clumped at the end of the driveway that the woman from the neighborhood association had left a letter in their mailbox.

I regret your misfortunes, but Druid Hills is an historical district, and as such, there are rules.

"*An* historical district," Abigail had mimicked, thinking the woman had an historic stick up her ass. She had written a furious letter in response, full of condescension and vitriol. "Do you know what it's like to know an animal raped your child?" she had demanded. "Do you think I give a rat's ass about your fucking rules?"

The screed had turned into a journal of sorts, page after page filled with all the horrible things that Abigail had kept choked in the back of her throat. She hadn't even bothered to read it before tearing it to shreds and burning it in the fireplace.

"Bit warm for a fire," Paul had said.

"I'm cold," she had told him, and that was that.

It wasn't until recently that they could even *go* to the mailbox without having a reporter document their every step. Even the last, desperate tabloids had moved on when, a few weeks ago, a pregnant woman in Arizona had gone missing and her husband had started to look awfully suspicious. Abigail had secretly watched the television down in the gym, studying pictures of the twenty-six-year-old brunette, thinking, jealously, that Emma was much prettier than the mother-to-be. Then the woman had shown up dead in a vacant lot and she had felt petty and small.

With the reporters gone, they were all alone. There was nothing in their lives to complain about but each other, and that was patently forbidden. Emma had only left the house once a week since they had moved here. Paul literally brought the rest of the world to her doorstep. She was homeschooled. Her yoga instructor came to the house. The hairdresser paid a monthly visit. Occasionally, a girl would show up to do her nails. Kayla Alexander and Adam Humphrey had been Emma's only close friends, so there were no other teenagers knocking on her door. The only person Paul could not bribe to come see her was her therapist. The woman's office was less than a mile up the road and Paul drove Emma there every Thursday, sitting outside the door, ready to rush in if she called for him.

Father and daughter were closer than ever now, and Abigail was hard-pressed to think of reasons why he should not give Emma everything she wanted. The irony was that she wanted so little now. She didn't ask for clothes or money or new gadgets. She just wanted her father by her side.

Paul had started working five days a week rather than his usual six. He ate breakfast with them every morning and supper every evening. There were no business trips or late-night dinners. He had turned into the perfect husband and father, but at what cost? He was not the same anymore. Sometimes Abigail would find him alone in his office or sitting in front of the muted television. The look on his face was painful to see. It was, she knew, the exact look she must have during unguarded moments.

And then there was Emma. Often, Abigail would stand in the open doorway of her daughter's room just to watch her sleep. This was her angel of old. Her face was smooth, the worry lines on her forehead erased. Her mouth was not tense, her eyes not filled with darkness. Then there were times Abigail went into the room and Emma was already awake. She would be sitting in the window seat, staring blankly out the window. She was there in the house, sitting not less than ten feet from where Abigail stood, but it felt as if somehow time had fractured, and Emma was no longer in her room but a million miles away.

For years, Abigail had worried that her daughter would turn out exactly like her mother. Now she worried that she would not turn out at all.

How could this have happened to them? How could they survive? Paul wouldn't argue about it anymore. He got up and went to work. He drove Emma to her appointment. He made phone calls that kept their lives moving. They had sex more frequently, but it seemed utilitarian more than anything else. When she noticed there was a pattern, that Paul seemed to be interested in her exclusively on Wednesday and Saturday nights, she felt relieved rather than insulted. She wrote X's in her calendar, marking out the days. It was something to plan for, something that she knew would happen.

Abigail found herself looking for more patterns in her life, more things she could rely on. Because of therapy, Emma was crankier on Thursdays, so Abigail started making pancakes for breakfast. On Fridays, she seemed sad, so movie night was instituted. Tuesdays were the worst. All the bad things had happened on a Tuesday. None of them talked much those days. The house was quiet. The stereo in Emma's room was not turned on. The television was kept low. The dog no longer barked. The phone seldom rang.

This was the new normal, then—the little tricks they all learned to cope with what had happened to them. Abigail supposed it wasn't so far removed from how things were before. She met with decorators, she spent money on things for their new home. Paul still had his secrets, though this time there was no other woman involved. Emma was still lying to them about where she went during the day, even though she never left the house. "I'm fine," she would say, even though just seconds before she had been a million miles away. They would believe her, because the truth hurt more than the lie.

So Abigail went about the process of going about her life. The days were getting shorter now, and she knew that they could not go on like this forever. Eventually, things would have to change, but for now, this new status quo was the only thing that was keeping them all going. She supposed in the end that Adam Humphrey's parents were right.

Sometimes, all you could do was pray for the strength to carry on.

ACKNOWLEDGMENTS

Kate Miciak, Kate Elton and Victoria Sanders were their usual intrepid selves while I was working on this novel, and I would like to thank all three ladies for their continued support. Add to that list Irwyn Applebaum, Nita Taublib, Betsy Hulsebosch, Barb Burg, Sharon Propson, Susan Corcoran, Cynthia Lasky, Carolyn Schwartz, Paolo Pepe, Kelly Chian and all of the other champs at Bantam. I feel very fortunate to be working with a group of people who are so dedicated to books.

I feel very lucky to have my friends around me—you know who you are. DT, my hero, I am humbled by your kindness. FM, your pithy observations are a constant source of humor. DM, how far we've come together thanks to your gentle heart. And as for you, Mo Hayder, don't pretend you don't try to freak me out just as much. I am not the one who clogged up a sewer with a pair of amputated hands.

At any rate—

My daddy brought me chocolate cake one night while I was hard at work on this book, thus confirming my view that he is the best father in the world. As for DA...all the love from my lips...

ABOUT THE AUTHOR

KARIN SLAUGHTER is the *New York Times* and internationally bestselling author of *Beyond Reach, Triptych, Faithless, A Faint Cold Fear,* which was named an International Book-of-the-Month Club selection, *Indelible, Kisscut,* and *Blindsighted;* she contributed to and edited *Like a Charm.* She is a native of Georgia, where she currently lives and is working on her next novel.